FUGITIVES FROM EARTH

BRAD WHEELER

ISBN: 978-1466475274

Printed in the United States of America

Composition done in Scrivener for Windows:

http://www.literatureandlatte.com/

Front cover font: "Space and Astronomy" by J0hnnie

Back cover font: "Neuton" by Brian M Zick

Image by Pat Rawlings, April 1988, for NASA's Johnson Space Center

Kindle edition also available.

For Leah

Acknowledgements

No novel, even one produced without an agent or traditional publisher, is wholly the work of just one person, and I want to thank everyone who pitched in to make this book happen.

Thanks first to my family, for their patience and support. Double thanks to my wife, Leah, without whom I never would've made it through the first draft.

For editorial and marketing support, I owe a great deal to the members of the Northwest Independent Writers Association, particularly Mike Chinakos, Adam Copeland, Andy Bunch, and Pam Bainbridge-Cowan. Marketing sucks and I would've only sold copies to family without their help. Special thanks to Pam and Mike for spotting a bazillion errors and making this second edition happen.

Thanks to my alpha readers, James Barratt and Thomas Baily, for putting up with my uneven prose and utter non-ending, and providing much-needed advice and encouragement.

I wrote a big chunk of this novel at Case Study Coffee in Portland, the best writer's hangout I know of. Thanks for the awesome work environment. Additional thanks to Mary Robinette Kowal and Shanna Germain for the company there as I struggled.

And this probably goes without saying, but any and all mistakes or errors in this book are mine and mine alone.

PART I: THE MOON

Chapter 1

The elevator ride from Rosetta Lovelace's office to Ronaldo Chen's took exactly 34 seconds from the time that the doors closed. In recent months, she'd been making it so often that she'd developed an instinct for the precise second that the doors would open again, and in the moments before she straightened her cuffs and brushed some lint off of her collar. Chen liked people presentable; to him, one's physical appearance reflected one's dependability and reliability.

The elevator doors opened directly onto Chen's office. He had no secretary; his expert systems regulated access to the office twenty-four hours a day. Besides, having an anteroom would've spoiled the effect.

Walking into the office was like walking out of the Belt Group, Limited headquarters in Portland, Oregon State, Northern Pacific Coalition, and walking into the parlor of some gilded age captain of industry. Just like those industrialists, Chen was intimately interested in the markets for rare metals, but nobody from the early twentieth century could've even guessed where Chen's company mined its ores.

"Rosetta! Good morning." Chen, as usual, had the energy of man eighty years younger. He was standing next to a percolator of coffee on top of the suite's bar, a piece designed with the same art deco flourishes as the rest of the room. Even the percolator itself was sculpted and carved into elaborate geometric shapes. "Have some coffee," he said, gesturing to a steaming cup on the table.

Rosetta walked over, heels clicking on the marble floor, and took the offered cup. As she took a sip of the excellent-smelling brew, Chen watched her critically. He was a very slight man of vaguely multi-ethnic complexion, his skin a few shades lighter than Rosetta's dark brown. Despite celebrating his one hundredth birthday just weeks before, he was still sprightly and animated; anyone who took him for the simple old man his appearance might suggest got what he deserved.

"Excellent coffee, Mr. Chen. And good morning to you too."

"Yes, a lovely, isn't it. So lovely that I was seriously disturbed that it had to be spoiled by such bad news."

"Oh?" Rosetta took another sip of coffee and stared out the suite's enormous gallery windows. The sun had risen over the horizon half an hour ago from the perspective of this room, though it was not yet dawn for anyone living at ground level. There were certain privileges of rank.

Chen had wandered over to his desk and called up a file on his computer. With a gesture, he increased the size of the display by three times, enough for her to see it across the room.

"I'm not sure if you can read this from over there," he said, "so I'll do it." He cleared his throat dramatically. "'It is the opinion of the analysis section that the *Atlas* Project cannot be recovered without significant expenditure of assets, in addition to the deployment of numerous and capable individuals to recover the ship in question.'" He turned toward Rosetta, ran a hand through his thin hair, and awaited her reaction.

She sighed. He was waiting for her to tell him that she'd been trying to make this point for weeks. Rosetta finally admitted that she couldn't quite resist. "Mr. Chen, you're well aware that this has been the opinion of my analysts for some time now."

"Yes, I know." He waved her off and wandered over to the sun-facing window before continuing. "Maybe I've been an idealist, Rosetta. Don't get me wrong—the reason that I made you special attaché to my office is because you're not afraid to give me bad news. The fact is, though, sometimes I'm not even capable of hearing it."

He turned back to her. "So. The *Atlas* is lost. Three billion in research, construction, and marketing, and all we have to show for it are some advertisements and some unhappy stockholders."

"Let's not be fatalistic, Mr. Chen." She said, holding her hands up. "There may still be some chance for recovery, although I won't lie—we're looking at millions in personnel expenses just to take the chance. I think you'll agree, though, that it would be entirely worthwhile."

"You're damned right. With those advanced extraction techniques, the mobile refinery systems, we're a full decade ahead of the competition. A few more of those ships, and those fellows at Asteroid Dynamics or United Aerospace won't stand a chance in the metals market. Your department's budget won't be a problem, even if I have to pay my own money. Get me that ship back, Rosetta. Follow any lead you can and take any steps you have to. I'll be in a meeting tomorrow with the UNASCA folks—I want you to sit in. Get me any information you can by that point, and we'll see if we can't maybe get some more subsidies.

"Oh, and take a cup of coffee with you when you go."

Chen returned to his desk, sat down, and reduced his monitor to normal size, swinging the holographic image back to face him. It was plainly a dismissal.

Rosetta drank her coffee in three large gulps, wishing she had time to sufficiently admire the high quality of the beverage, and returned to the elevator. 34 seconds later, she was back on her floor.

As she walked through rows and rows of cubicles, past conference rooms full of marketers, accountants, and psychologists working out Belt Group's latest marketing campaigns, Rosetta set her mind in order. She'd been waiting for Chen to finally agree with her findings for weeks now, and now that she had finally been released to act, there was no time to be lost.

Rosetta's office was clean and Spartan, just the opposite of Chen's lavish suite hundreds of meters above. It was also much smaller, but that suited her. The usual mass of messages had piled up even in the duration of her short meeting: production reports from Belt Group's asteroid miners, warnings of labor troubles on Jupiter, press releases about decreased production from Belt Group's helium-3 extractors in the atmosphere. Compared to the *Atlas*, this was of little consequence.

Well, perhaps *some* consequence. Despite some of Chen's more dire predictions, Belt Group, Ltd was sufficiently diversified that the loss of the *Atlas* wouldn't kill them. They had plenty of other ships in the belt, Trojans, and elsewhere, both wholly owned and contracted. That was to say nothing of their helium-3 extraction plants on Jupiter. Provided the labor troubles there fizzled out, their Jupiter operations alone could keep them afloat for quarters. Belt Group provided for nearly a quarter of Earth's energy needs, and that wasn't going to change overnight.

She'd just filed the last of her messages under "later" when she heard a rapping knock on her door frame.

"Problem, boss?" Forrester said, leaning back against the doorjamb, raising an eyebrow expectantly. He was, as always, the very image of self-confidence in his immaculately pressed suit and a body that had received at least as much attention. His boyishly good looks and easy charm belied a steely mind and equally firm hand. Sometimes he seemed almost attractive to Rosetta, but she had only to think of some of the things he'd done on her orders and that stirring died away.

"As a matter of fact, there isn't." Rosetta smiled and pointing toward the pile of familiar looking documents on his monitor. "I have some good news for once. The muzzle's off. Mr. Chen wants the ship back, now that some 'independent analysis' has shown that she's not going to come back on her own. He wants the ship yesterday, and no expense will be spared. I trust we understand each other?"

"We understand each other perfectly," Forrester said, flashing her a perfect smile. "I'll get my best people on it right away. We're keeping this one quiet, right? Nothing big yet?"

Good for him for asking. Forrester's extreme willingness to undertake investigation, manipulation, and outright violence for Belt Group was useful, even admirable. He knew just how to put the pressure on just so to get whatever he wanted, and he always wanted what Belt Group wanted. He usually operated through a stable of agents and thugs, to be sure, but he knew how to keep the strings on his puppets short.

"Will that be a problem?" Rosetta asked.

"Not at all, but it will limit the number of people I'd consider 'my best.'" He made a dismissive gesture. "Don't even worry about it. As it happens, I've just uncovered some leads that might make all of this pretty easy."

Rosetta straightened in her chair. "I'd hoped so. Do tell."

"I shall." He walked over to her desk and swung the screen around. As he moved, the air swirled around Rosetta and she could smell the understated—and expensive—fragrance that always followed Forrester around. It was not unpleasant.

Forrester swung the screen back around. The document on top was a list of mining ships, a fairly random assortment, and their probable itineraries. "We've received reports that the *Atlas* may have deviated from her assigned course sooner than expected, which would also change the number of other ships that might've been the last to see her. I've got solid leads on a few of them now. Don't worry about this at all, Rosetta—now that I have the funds, we'll blow this thing wide open."

Rosetta nodded. "If you pull this off, I swear to you we'll both get to name our price."

"Boss," Forrester said, flashing her another pearly-white smile, "I was hoping you'd say that."

Joanna Newton and Thomas Gabriel rode the Brighton monorail in silence. Gabriel, as always, gave off an air of perfect calm and intense calculation at the same moment. For her part, Joanna stared out the monorail tram's tiny windows at the lunar landscape sliding along below them. The long lunar day was nearing its end, and the lunar rocks cast long, jagged shadows over the silvery landscape.

Abruptly, another shadow, smooth-edged, flashed over the ground outside the car, disappearing off the other side. Joanna looked up to see a small spacecraft briefly eclipse the sun before disappearing entirely as the star's brilliance polarized the tram's upper windows.

"That'll be them, I expect," Gabriel said, sounding bored.

"Probably. Listen, Gabriel," Joanna said, quietly even though the monorail was empty but for the two of them, "I wish you'd tell me why you wanted to meet these people in person so quickly. I'm perfectly capable of handling your appointments."

"Joanna, dear girl, these people have very important business and I would hate to keep them waiting."

Joanna had plenty of suspicions about the type of business that Gabriel liked to perform in addition to his official duties. Being a colonial administrator under the United Nations Space Colonization Administration, especially for a large colony like Brighton, ought to keep one man plenty busy to avoid any need for side jobs.

Then again, Gabriel had never shown any particular appreciation for his job, save for the possibilities that it provided him. This didn't make Joanna any more comfortable being alone on the monorail with him. They had only set out for the landing pad a few moments before and she was already fantasizing about being back at home.

The tram glided silently to a stop near one of the farthest landing pads. A triangular Shuttle Delta was just settling on the pad, one of the type that landed at Brighton by the dozens every day. The ship was painted in sun-faded, dust-pocked blue, with the name *Fisher King* stenciled near the cockpit blister. By the time the tram had stopped completely, a tracked caterpillar had already attached itself to the ship's airlock, and Joanna could see several people transfer over to it. Detaching itself, it started for the monorail dock, and Joanna felt herself tensing up all over.

She was promising herself an hour-long sonic massage just as the shuttle pulled up to the dock and disgorged its three passengers. Gabriel stood to greet them, and Joanna felt compelled to rise, stand behind him, and try to hide how desperately she wanted to be somewhere else.

"You must be Captain Montgomery," Gabriel said, extending a hand to the tall, sandy-haired man who led the trio. "I'm Thomas Gabriel, UNASCA administrator. A pleasure."

The captain took Gabriel's hand graciously, and Joanna could see him flinch as Gabriel applied one of his famously intense handshakes. "Call me Stephen," he said, extracting himself from Gabriel's grip. "This is my second in command, Eileen Cromwell," he said, to a very tall, very thin woman with close-cropped dark hair and an equally dark expression. "And this is my engineer, Benjamin Riley." Riley appeared even less comfortable than the woman, and he was far shorter and rounder.

"You had a good flight, I presume?" Gabriel asked once they'd been seated and the monorail started back for the city. "A good landing?"

"Our flight's lasted three years, Administrator Gabriel," Captain Montgomery started.

"Tom, please." Gabriel flashed a disarming smile.

"All right, Tom. Like I said, our flight's lasted three years, and most of them were just fine."

"A good haul?"

Montgomery shrugged modestly, but his expression was guarded. "It was decent."

Gabriel smiled, chuckled. "Why the guarded tone, Captain Montgomery? I'm almost detecting a certain element of...distrust?" He chuckled again, glancing at Joanna as if to suggest that the whole thing were just a little joke, like they were at a dinner party. Joanna felt like rolling her eyes, but instead just turned to look out the window.

Long shadows stretched across the gray landscape below them. The sun was right on the horizon, foretelling the long lunar night that was just a few days away. There was no twilight on the Moon; mere minutes separated the blinding radiance of the sun from the dark, starry night. Joanna preferred the night, it seemed quieter, more peaceful. The wash of stars overhead—when she was somewhere dark enough to see them—reminded her of camping when she was little.

After a moment, she heard Montgomery's answering chuckle, albeit one with somewhat less self-assurance than Gabriel's. It was hard to beat Gabriel for self-assurance; Joanna had long since given up. "All right, Tom, I'll be honest. I've heard certain rumors about you, and not all of them are flattering."

"What he means," said Eileen Cromwell, the tall woman, "is that a lot of people think you're scum." Was she trying to get a rise out of Gabriel? Provoke a reaction? It wasn't going to work.

"Ms. Cromwell, rumors fly faster than the speed of light, but they don't carry as much information. I am an administrator of the largest colony in the Solar System, fully authorized by the United Nations Space Colonization Authority." He glanced at Joanna as if seeking her confirmation, and she nodded, suddenly clear on why he'd brought her along on these ridiculous negotiations: legitimacy. Joanna knew how harmless she looked; no thug or criminal would ever bring her along for something under-the-table.

"We understand that, Tom," Montgomery said, flashing a brief and disapproving look at Cromwell. "The only rumor that concerns me is the one that says you pay fairly and honestly for reputable information."

Cromwell leaned forward and added, "What he means is that we have some information that we heard you might pay us handsomely for." She rolled her eyes and leaned back. "So let's cut to the end of this little dance."

The other man, Riley, hid a smile. Stephen

shrugged. "The lady tells it right."

"And so do you, Stephen. I always pay well. Shall we?"

A shadow fell over the monorail as the bulk of Brighton Tower cut off the sun. Ahead, Joanna could see the yawning doors of the depot at the Tower's base open and ready to receive them. Joanna spent so much time inside the tower and so little outside that it was easy to forget how huge the building was. It might've been tiny if placed in any major terrestrial city, but the Tower's dozen stories and flying buttresses were still an impressive sight. It utterly dominated the flat, dark landscape of the Mare Serenitatis and the scattering of landing pads around the monorail line. It was a crowning achievement of human engineering, and Joanna always felt a tingle of indefinable pride whenever she laid eyes on it.

It was all the more impressive for what lay beneath: a sprawling underground city, 50,000 people strong and growing rapidly. Aside from the lack of windows and the lower gravity, one might almost think it was on Earth, so extensive were its amenities. People responded to that; tourism was a major source of income for Brighton, and tourism was exploding. It was almost cheap to get to the Moon now, from Earth.

The tower's architecture was dominated by the planetary-orbit logo of the United Nations Space Colonization Authority, positioned so that anyone riding the monorail would be unable to miss it. Brighton was everything that UNASCA wanted its colonies to be: large and clean but bustling and ever expanding. More than anything, UNASCA wanted everyone to know that they were in charge. If the news stories and blogs were to be believed, they could use all the positive PR they could get; every day there was more bad news from Jupiter.

Of course, on Brighton, it was all an illusion. Joanna glanced at Gabriel out of the corner of her eye, saw him chuckling at some small joke Benjamin Riley had made. Gabriel was in control on Brighton, no matter what UNASCA believed. She wondered if it was like that on all the colonies.

They pulled into the depot airlock, and the tram stopped while the pressure was equalized. As the far doors opened and the tram moved into the multi-story industrial space of the Depot, Gabriel was blathering. "I could never make my living out in the belt like you folks do. Certainly I can understand the desire for independence, the allure of a hard day's labor, but I confess that I'm perhaps too dependent on my luxuries."

"Belt mining isn't a life for everyone, that's for sure." Captain Montgomery gestured broadly at the monorail station. "This all certainly has its own appeal."

"It's very, very appealing," Eileen said dismissively. "Now, can we please get down to business?" Her voice had a plaintive edge to it. Joanna glanced back in time to see Stephen set his jaw. It appeared to be an old argument that Eileen was playing out rote.

"Just a moment—my office is a few levels up."

The monorail door opened almost immediately onto the main elevator cluster, a series of thick columns rising out of the mass of crates and containers that filled the Depot's mostly open space. A few Brighton citizens were already in the elevator that arrived; Gabriel made sure to greet each of them by name as they rode up. The people loved Gabriel, that was for sure. He was attentive to their needs, at least so long as they didn't look too closely at his, and he could play to a crowd with the best of them.

By the time they reached the uppermost part of Brighton Tower, it was just the five of them. Joanna spilled out of the elevator with the rest, hastening to open the door for the party as Gabriel continued to regale them with trivia and anecdotes about life on Brighton, his personal history, and similar things.

As she was blocking the door sensor, she happened to meet Eileen's eye. She was the last of the party to enter Gabriel's office, and she seemed to be walking slower and more cautiously than her male companions. As she met Joanna's gaze, her expression mutated from the dark glower she'd been wearing into something more calculating.

At last they were inside the office. Joanna, ignored now by Gabriel and the rest of the party, slipped in after them and let the door close. She idly wondered if Gabriel would let her just take the rest of the day off, but she decided she didn't want to be gone if she was needed—Gabriel took very poorly to those who made him look bad in front of his "business acquaintances." With a heavy sigh, she looked at the clock—still four hours until quitting time.

"Now, as the young lady said, on to business. Drinks?" Gabriel walked to the sideboard while the *Mary Ellen*'s crew sat in a conversation circle to the side of Gabriel's massive desk. It was just a quartet of wire chairs, nothing special, but that was the point: Gabriel always used it when he wanted to appear on the same level as whoever he was speaking to. Hard to do that behind the lunar-steel edifice that was his desk.

When the libations had been dispensed, Gabriel handed out glasses and took his own place in the circle. "Now, I have heard of the so-called disappearance of the *Atlas*. You won't see it on the news or in the blogs of course, but I've heard of it."

"Cutting right to the chase," Montgomery said approvingly. "I admit I'm a little surprised that you've heard something, though. It seems very hush-hush. When I talked to Gordon Chan on *Celestia* he wasn't sure you would be aware."

Gabriel chuckled. "Chan is a very conservative man. I'm sure he was trying not to get your hopes up." Of course Gabriel had heard something, Joanna scoffed to herself. A pin could hardly drop in the Solar System without the man picking up on it. He was like an octopus, arms everywhere. She was starting to get a tight feeling in her gut. Gabriel was a cunning negotiator, and far more ruthless than most people gave him credit for. He was playing the friendly act straight here; Joanna was just waiting for him to drop the hammer.

Joanna watched the liquid slowly fall back into the glass, trying to determine if he was buttering up, or getting buttered. The latter, probably. Gabriel was a cool character and Joanna could tell that Cromwell and Riley were already getting nervous dealing with him. No, Riley was getting nervous. Cromwell was getting more and more annoyed.

"And," Gabriel continued, "not only have I heard this information, but I do happen to know an approximate value for it. It's not easy to unload, of course. Belt Group won't even admit that they lost the ship, let alone pay money for information on it. You couldn't just turn this over to any information broker on the Deep Space Network."

"Truly?" Stephen leaned forward.

"Truly. You need face to face contact. UNASCA's information office is the best in the Solar System; they'd find out the moment you put your information on the DSN." Gabriel leaned forward and loudly placed his glass on the table. "I'm prepared to write down some initial figures. Take your time and think it over; I'm not too worried about losing out to another buyer at this stage of the game."

Gabriel drew out a dataslate, made a few quick marks with a stylus, and handed it to Captain Montgomery. The latter's eyes widened noticeably as he took in the figure, and it took him a moment to get his tongue back. Joanna couldn't see the number from here, but for a man who commanded a fifty million dollar ship to blink at it, it must've been a lot.

Joanna felt her stomach leap into her throat. Gabriel didn't part with large sums lightly, and he had not driven a hard bargain here.

"This is...very generous, Mr. Gabriel."

"Tom, please."

"Well, Tom. I'm not sure what to say."

"No need to say anything now, as I said. Take it back to your hotel and think it over."

"Well, I hadn't planned to stay long on Brighton. My ship is at *Luna 1* unloading its cargo; I should really return to the rest of my crew."

"They'll be fine for 24 hours," Gabriel said, gesturing dismissively. "How about a suite at the Hotel Brighton for the three of you? My treat."

"Stephen, we have responsibilities..." Cromwell said quietly, but he barged right ahead, leaving her to fume at his back.

"That would be great, Tom."

"Wonderful." He pressed a button on his desk, and the door opened. "My lovely assistant will guide you down there." Abruptly, Joanna realized he was talking about her and straightened, throwing up a smile that she didn't really feel. Unlike Gabriel, she hadn't made an art of it.

"Enjoy!" Gabriel smiled wide. One of *those* smiles.

They stayed quiet until the elevator doors closed. As the girl Joanna pressed the button for the lower concourse and the tone had sounded, Eileen slugged Stephen in the arm.

"You ass. What were you thinking?"

"I don't know, Eileen," Stephen said in an odd tone, tipping his head toward Joanna. "What was I thinking?"

Eileen glanced at the girl. She seemed to grow a half meter taller outside of Gabriel's presence. It spoke volumes to his character, but it didn't mean that she wouldn't report everything to him later. Assuming that he didn't have the whole place wired regardless. Eileen tamped down her frustrations and stared straight ahead.

"Nothing, Stephen. Nothing at all." There was no more talking until the doors opened again.

Then, they stepped out into the concourse, and complaining was far from Eileen's mind.

The *Mary Ellen*'s route typically took her from Earth out to the belt via Mars, Ceres, Vesta, or the *Robert Hunt*, whichever outpost was most convenient for their mining grounds. The typical trip took three years, give or take, with maybe half the time spent mining with a full crew of geologists and miners, and half the time spent running cargo back to an outpost with just a skeleton crew.

They didn't make it back to Earth very often, and the last time they'd been here, they hadn't seen any reason to make it to Brighton. What a difference the last six years had made.

The place was *crowded.* Not just cramped like some outer system research station, but bustling like an old world market, with people of every description moving along the concourse or shopping at the kiosks or forming informal little conversation circles. There might've been a half-dozen other places off Earth that Eileen would've described as *crowded.*

And this was just one level. Eileen could see down through an artfully-shaped hole in the floor down to the next concourse level, and beyond that through another hole into a third level. They were all as busy as the first. It was a shock after being so close with so few people for so long. Magnificent as it was, Eileen wasn't sure how long she could tolerate it.

"Wow." Stephen's expression, however simple, encapsulated what they were all feeling.

"Our permanent population just reached 45,000," Joanna said, as if reading their minds. It couldn't have been hard. "We usually have a transient population of five to ten thousand at any given time." She gave a little smile; she didn't make eye contact.

"That's very impressive," Eileen said. "I was twenty years old before I saw this many people in one place, and that was on Earth."

"Administrator Gabriel tries very hard to make this a welcoming place for everyone," Joanna said, her tone growing slightly cold. "The UNASCA tourism policies help a lot."

"I can see why the government DSN sites always mention Brighton as if it's such a big thing," Ben said, rubbing his hands together expectantly. "So, where's the hotel?"

The Hotel Brighton was on the first concourse level, and in retrospect it would've been impossible to miss even without Joanna's guidance. It was designed to evoke the art deco sensibilities of Old New York with lines and starbursts everywhere; everything was smooth and rounded.

Joanna checked them into their rooms, gave them a couple of standard tourist brochures along with the codes for their rooms, and fairly fled. Eileen decided that must've been her fault, since now that the shock of the city was wearing off, her frustrations were building back up and it must've been obvious to anyone that looked at her.

They decided to grab some food, and as Eileen sat she just couldn't contain herself anymore.

"Damn it, Stephen, you're being reckless with that scum," she hissed.

"I think I'm with Eileen on this one, chief," Ben said, glancing over the menu.

"That's enough, guys. Of course he's scum. I know it, you know it, that assistant of his knows it. If he wasn't scum, we wouldn't be talking to him."

"Wonderful," Eileen muttered, leaning back in her chair and taking a look around the lounge.

The Hotel Brighton was by far the most opulent hotel in Brighton, or so the advertising on the local DSN suggested. High ratings, but lots of noise complaints—it was a common tourist destination for Earth's newlyweds. There was a lot of glass and wood, which Eileen couldn't help but run her hands over. In space, she had seen many things, but wood was not one of them. To get it anywhere but Earth in buildable quantities was tremendously expensive. Here, though: it was real.

"You want to say something, Eileen? I don't think that everyone heard you."

"Stephen, I think I've been plain enough, okay? I don't see how this extra money is worth the risk of dealing with these criminal types. Greed doesn't become you."

Stephen jerked as if struck. Eileen could see Ben gritting his teeth.

"What? It doesn't. This is out of character for you and I just don't buy that money has everything to do with it."

"Greed," Stephen said, plainly biting his tongue, "has *nothing* to do with it. It's the same thing out in the belt: I see a big score, I go for it. I don't risk anyone's life unnecessarily, and we all come away happy and wealthy. Nothing different here. Let's order, for heaven's sake."

Eileen could feel her frustration start to mutate into concern. There was something eating at him, something that had been in the back of his mind since at least Mars.

"I don't buy that."

Stephen rolled his eyes. "Fine. Maybe I just don't care for the idea of handing it over to UNASCA, just for the pride of being a good citizen. Gabriel may be scum, but that kind of scum has its uses. UNASCA, I would argue, doesn't. Not anymore."

"I don't know, you heard about Titan, the infiltration of their recycling systems, the governor's idea of martial law..." Ben said, opening his menu with a smile.

"Okay, maybe they have a few uses. But not "twenty percent of gross profits-worth of uses Maybe I want to keep all of what I make for once. I'd expect you," he said, pointing at Eileen with his still-closed menu, "of all people to appreciate that."

Eileen snorted and opened her own menu. Stephen continued at a whisper, with a conspiratorial look around. "We'll be okay. We'll just do a quick back-and-forth tomorrow morning, I'll settle for a lowball offer, and we'll be on our way back to Earth. Two month's leave for sunny beaches, forests, maybe some rainfall..."

"Flatlander," Eileen said, smiling.

"I have my human weaknesses, excuse me. Seeing some blue after two years of black, gray, a little white...heavenly." Ben nodded emphatically as Eileen shook her head.

The waiter bounced over to take their order and the meal continued with substantially better humor. Eileen was more than happy not to think about their earlier argument, and when thoughts of this *Atlas* information entered her mind at all she plowed them over by trying to enjoy her food, or enjoying watching her fellow diners.

Eileen hadn't spent much time on the moon, and compared to a native or long-term resident, she was an awkward, shambling thing, bouncing around like she was unfamiliar with her own feet. There was no way that she could ever hope to match the graceful bounds of a native during her day- or week-long visits, but compared to the flatlander visitors arriving for the hotel's dinner hour, she might have been a dancer. Each step ended with a head bonking against the room's high ceiling or with a crash into a table or some other ornamentation, and each of these missteps were accompanied by the tittering laughter of the stumbler's companions.

She was already missing the solitude of space travel and was not looking forward to Earth. Well, if Stephen was right, at least she'd have some extra money to spend there. Maybe his idea wasn't the worst.

"Well, what did you think, Joanna?" Gabriel asked as she delivered his evening mail. She had very much hoped to be allowed to call it a day after delivering his new business partners to the Brighton Hotel, but Gabriel had summoned her back and she'd occupied herself as best she could with busy-work. The evening mail was generally the last task of her day, and she was already thinking of the massage booth that awaited her down on Concourse Thirteen, across from her tiny apartment.

So deep was she in thought that his question startled her more than it ought to have. "I'm sorry, what? About what?"

"About the crew of the *Mary Ellen*, naturally. You've seen them more than I at this point. What do you think about them?" He was leaning back in his chair, fingers steepled, one eyebrow cocked critically in her direction.

"Um," she stalled, trying to decide what he wanted her to say. She couldn't figure it out so she decided on non-committal. "I think that they were nice people. They didn't say much while I arranged for their room."

"Hmm? Pity. They didn't ask about me?"

"No. Well, they...no." Joanna immediately regretted inadvertently extending the conversation, and resolved to answer only when absolutely necessary in the future. When dealing with Gabriel, this wasn't hard usually. The man loved to talk.

"And he didn't happen to let slip anything about this data he's selling?" Joanna shook her head, and he nodded. "Well, he knew even more than he was letting on. He's an amateur, Joanna. Not used to operating on the fuzzy side of...hmm." He trailed off for a moment, moving his lips silently, and Joanna waited patiently for him to remember to dismiss her.

He stared out at the lunar surface for some time before nodding firmly and grinning at Joanna. "Did you finish those certification documents, my dear Joanna? You know how UNASCA so loves its paperwork, and I'd hate to disappoint them."

"Yes, sir. I filed the last of them this morning, but Vice-Secretary Yamagachi said that he'd have to delay the inspection for a few days. I guess they're running a little short on inspectors? He sent over some waiver forms that he'll need when the inspectors arrive."

"That's our government, Ms. Newton. Short on people, long on paperwork." He gave Joanna a sidelong glance. "I tell you what. I'll take care of the waiver forms; go ahead and call it a day. In fact, go ahead and take tomorrow off too; I've got a meeting with the Lunar Development Commission at Tranquility Park tomorrow and I'll be out of the city all day."

"Oh. Thank you, sir." Joanna blinked. Something about his tone of voice seemed a little odd, and suddenly she couldn't wait to be out of the office.

"My pleasure. You do good work, Joanna. I reward competent subordinates."

Trying to stifle a smile of surprise, she nodded, turned and made it halfway to the door before he called to her, "Oh, one more thing. Just so I don't have to bother checking myself, what rooms did they get at the hotel?"

"Um, one-thirteen and one-fourteen, sir."

"Good. Thank you." He dismissed her with the slightest wave of his hand, and she fled gratefully from the room as Gabriel continued sitting, fingers steepled, and mouth moving without a sound.

Chapter 2

Eileen watched the dark wine fall slowly into her glass. Stephen was putting on quite the show of pouring, and she chuckled as he lifted the bottle higher and higher in the air, guiding the flow with a practiced eye.

"Bravo," she said, smiling, as he tilted the bottle back up and put it on their hotel room's sideboard.

He gave a little bow and picked up his own glass, settling on the bed next to her. "Well, here's to another successful voyage and a little extra spending money for our vacation."

"Cheers," Eileen said, raising her glass with him. The wine wasn't great; radiation did unpleasant things to even the best vintages. But it still burned nicely all the way down, and a few sips warmed her body and relaxed her mind. They drank in silence for a few minutes, neither wanting to disturb their rare moments of quiet and privacy.

After a few moments, Eileen broke the silence. "Sorry for attacking you earlier. I don't actually think you're greedy." She swished her wine pensively.

"Well, thanks for saying so. And don't get me wrong, I'm glad you feel comfortable speaking up."

She chuckled. "It'd be pretty disingenuous of me to be otherwise, considering." She gestured to the single queen bed and chuckled, but the laugh faded in a moment. "I know that UNASCA isn't the most popular thing right now, but I sure hope you're not taking a risk, even a small one, just to stick it to them."

Stephen snorted, an indelicate sound but still endearing. "No, I'm not just trying to stick it to UNASCA. Not entirely, anyway. But you know how much they take off the top. I just like the idea of getting a full return on my labor, like I said. It's entirely a financial consideration, but maybe with a side-dish of rebellion."

Eileen rolled her eyes feelingly. "Fine, fine. I just want to get it over with."

"You and me both. Hang on."

He grabbed his handset off the table and sauntered into the bathroom, whistling. Eileen took a few more sips of wine, letting her mind wander, until she realized that he'd been in there for quite awhile. Eileen wasn't sure, but it also sounded like he was talking to someone in there. Awkward.

He finally emerged to find her staring at him, eyebrow raised, lips curled. "What? I really had to go."

"Sure you did," Eileen winked. "Sure you did."

"I did." He walked over to the sideboard, his gait awkward in the low gravity, and started fiddling with his overnight kit.

"Then who were you talking to in there? Another girlfriend?"

"No. No!" Stephen said with mock seriousness. He palmed something from his kit and stuffed it into a zippered pocket before landing heavily beside Eileen again, putting his arm around her. "No. It's not. It's, um, sports scores. You know that *Trespasser* is down to only four contestants, and they haven't even released the gliders yet? Fun stuff. But very secret." The bed looked to be little more than a hammock, but in the light lunar gravity they were far more comfortable than they appeared.

Eileen chuckled and pushed him away. He always got a bit amorous when he'd been drinking. "You don't trust me with your secrets, eh? What about our relationship?." As he fell on the bed she scrabbled after his pocket, grasping the zipper before he shoved her back, the two of them giggling and squabbling like children.

"Okay, okay, get off, get off!" Stephen said, flailing madly at her. Eileen shrieked, trying to avoid him spilling her drink, and reflexively bounced right of the bed. As she slowly fell to the ground, she managed to throw her drink to the side and keep it from splashing all over her. As it painted the far wall, she desperately tried to suck in air. Damn, laughing felt good.

"Okay, I'll tell you what it is. It's the *Atlas* data, okay? Big secret." He put his fingers to his lips in a shushing motion. Eileen made a zippering motion over her mouth and waited for him to continue.

"On this little cube," he said, patting his pocket with exaggerated care as the laughing died down, "is the last known course, heading, speed, velocity, direction, orientation, rotation, and disposition of Belt Group, Limited's fancy new mining ship *Atlas*. Plus, some choice footage of that sweet load they pulled right out from under our noses. Also, it has that encrypted databurst we intercepted; I figure Gabriel can do whatever the hell he wants with that."

The two of them sighed in unison, thinking of that load. Spectrograph showed strong platinum lines after a chance meteor impact, and the *Mary Ellen* had abandoned their own extractors to lay claim to the asteroid as soon as possible. Sadly, that brand new bastard with its heavy engines and advance scout ships had hit the asteroid just a few days before they could, despite taking risks with their engines.

Of course, even if they had grabbed it, UNASCA's contract with the *Mary Ellen* would've taken forty percent right off the top for "high value materials." Maybe it was just as well.

"Anyway, I had Crazyhorse scrub all traces of the data from the *Mary Ellen*'s computer. See, contrary to what you might think, I'm not a sucker. I know how people like Gabriel work. I'm not taking anything for granted."

"You think he might try something?"

"I don't know," Stephen said, finally, a slight note of sobriety creeping into his voice. "Maybe it's not worth it. Maybe we should head back up home tonight, ditch these hotel rooms, and make for Earth right away. Maybe it's not worth it."

"No, no, no," Eileen said, fumbling around for her glass, which kept scooting away from her in gentle arcs as her fingers slipped off its wine-slick surface. "You've got to do it now. We're committed. This Gabriel would probably have us all murdered if we tried to flee now. If only there was some sort of regional government authority that we could appeal to, in order to remain safe." Eileen put a finger to her chin in exaggerated caution, and Stephen laughed hard, his sobriety evaporating.

"I guess we might as well go through with it. We're no worse off if he decides to be a cheat, right? UNASCA would probably just confis-uh, steal this data if they knew we had it. Might as well see if we can sucker a few cents out of Mr. Gabriel. Here's to Gabriel, in fact, and his pennies." Stephen raised his glass and drained the last of the purple liquid as Eileen pretended to do the same with her empty glass, a single drop slowly falling from the glass's rim onto her tongue.

Eileen woke up suddenly. A quick glance at the clock glowing faintly against the wall showed that it had only been a few hours after she'd finally crashed against her bunk and fell into the kind of uninterrupted, unperturbed sleep that she was only capable of when half-intoxicated.

Nature was calling, and by the time she'd finished in the bathroom she discovered that she was no longer tired. There was no day/night cycle in Brighton just as there was none on the *Mary Ellen*, but whenever she underwent changes in gravity her sleeping cycle always took a little while to adjust. She wasn't looking forward to the sort of change that Earth's gravity would bring.

As she pulled her jumpsuit from the room's laundry and stepped into it, her mind was occupied with thoughts of

Earth. She'd only spent a few months on Earth her entire life and frankly couldn't see what the big deal was. Sure, there were some great sights and the fresh air most definitely had an intoxicating effect, but that all wore off after a week or two and then it was just a crowded, dirty place—and always too cold or too warm—where she really had no idea how to behave. Definitely no idea why everyone was looking forward to it so much.

She stumbled out into the hall, wiping sleep from her eyes, following the signs for the lobby and the early-morning breakfast that her room computer told her should already be out. That was, she supposed, one thing about shipboard life that couldn't compare to Earth, or really any large colony—the variety of food.

As she shoveled a plate full of eggs and bacon—real bacon, not the compressed protein that passed for it aboard ship—into her mouth in the lobby, she realized that she wasn't really looking forward to Earth, but she was looking forward to her morning meeting even less.

At length, Ben joined her, as did Stephen. All of them looked a little bleary, but it was comforting to Eileen that she wasn't alone in having her sleep disrupted by gravity, even as light as it was.

"You know, I'm looking forward to seeing Mom and Dad, but I kind of hope that Alicia won't be there," Ben muttered. "She'll have her master's degree by now, and did I tell you? Her husband got elected to some NORPAC council or other. Agricultural Commission, that's what it is."

"Just show them that picture you took of that lightning storm last time we were at Jupiter," Eileen said, pushing her plate out of the way. Seeing the dark side of

Jupiter illuminated by bursts of lightning traveling several Earth diameters was a powerful sight. No photograph would ever do it justice.

"Yeah, or that picture of Eileen you took after she swapped out those fuel cells last month," Stephen said, grinning. "I don't think that space suit ever forgave you."

Eileen allowed herself a tight smile as the other two chittered like old women. "Let me just state, for the record," she said, holding up one finger, "that you should blame Melissa and not me. After all, if she doesn't bother to consul the drug interaction database before prescribing…"

"Small consolation to your suit," Ben said. "You still owe us what, a hundred dollars worth of disinfectant, and you never bothered to replace that rancid old jumpsuit."

"Why would I, when it has such fond memories attached to it?" Eileen smiled sardonically. "Maybe you should just tell her that your trip was 'fine.'"

"Heh. I usually do." Ben chewed for a moment, swallowed, and asked, "So, what are you going to do, Eileen?"

"Um, well," she said thoughtfully, "I guess I'm not really sure. See some sights, I guess. I don't exactly have a lot of family to visit, or a childhood home to see, or anything like that. Maybe I'll go for a hike if I can get a guide on short notice."

"A guide? Are you planning on hiking through the Amazon or something?" Ben snorted, putting down another rasher of bacon.

"Hey," Eileen snapped, a little more harshly than she intended. "Not all of us grew up among trees and blue skies, okay? I don't want to get eaten by a bear or poisoned by mushrooms or something like that. This isn't going to be a homecoming for me, remember. This is just another stretch away from home."

Ben chewed on his lip for a moment before quietly saying, "Sorry."

Eileen rubbed a temple. "No, it's all right. I'm just anxious about this little deal with Mr. Gabriel, is all. I'm sure I'll have a fine time on Earth; I just want to get back to Ceres at some point. See the folks, you know? I'm sure we'll make it on the next trip."

The conversation hit a lull for a moment before Stephen pulled his handset out of his pocket, glanced at it, and replaced it. "Should be another hour or so before the administration office opens, and I still need to get our customs paperwork figured out. Should probably call the cooperative, too, maybe see some sights. You guys want to come along?"

Ben said he would, but Eileen demurred. "I'm not feeling much like walking today. I'll meet you at the base of Brighton Tower in one hour, okay?"

They said their goodbyes and Stephen and Ben walked toward the elaborate lobby and out onto the concourse. Meanwhile, Eileen signaled a waiter.

There were few things less enjoyable to Joanna than going into work on a day off. This wasn't to say that she loved coming in when she had to, of course. Just her luck, she'd been distracted enough at work yesterday that she'd walked out of the office and left her handset sitting in her desk. Sure, she could've watched movies and sent emails from the workstation in her apartment, but she loved spending the day doing nothing but loafing in bed, and her workstation wasn't quite up to meeting her there.

Gabriel was supposed to be at Tranquility Park, and his office should've been empty. Regardless, it was an hour before the office even opened and a good hour and fifteen minutes before he could've been counted on to show up, but he was there. Joanna had stepped off the elevator into the lobby anteroom, just a few paces from her desk, and stopped suddenly when she heard loud laughter from inside the office. She froze.

The office and the lobby were actually two hermetically sealed compartments within the tower, and it took a loud voice to penetrate that isolation. There was no way that she could've imagined it.

Well, no matter; without her to point them out, Gabriel probably wouldn't even notice someone standing in the lobby. A few quick strides and she was at her desk, her fingerprint opening the drawer. She'd just picked up her handset and was dropping it in a pocket when the door into Gabriel's office opened.

Gabriel was speaking, barely able to force his words out past his incessant chuckles. "And of course their room is bugged. The hotel knows which side its bread is oiled on."

His companion, following Gabriel out of the office, was likewise snorting with unfriendly laughter. He was a swarthy man dressed in workout clothes: sweats and running shoes designed for the Moon. He walked with the assurance of a long-time Moon-dweller, same as Gabriel, a walk that Joanna herself hadn't quite mastered. "So this is all aboveboard, then?" He sounded surprised."

"Absolutely; it's a UNASCA imperative. It's a little

confidential, but a certain group will pay very, very well to get that data returned."

"Very good, very good," said the other man. They pressed the button for the elevator, still not noticing Joanna, and the door opened immediately since Joanna had just taken it. They stepped in, wiping tears off their faces, but just before the door shut, Joanna heard Gabriel ask, "Tell me, did you find anything on their ship?"

They could only be talking about Captain Montgomery and the others. Joanna realized that she shouldn't be surprised that Gabriel wasn't planning on making an honest deal, and she further realized that she shouldn't feel bad for the Captain and his crew. It sounded like he knew what he was getting into. Maybe they even had a plan for dealing with it.

But history suggested that it wouldn't work. Gabriel always got what he wanted in Brighton, right up to his position as administrator. If he couldn't steal this information he wanted, or if the price to buy it was too high...

Suddenly, she realized who the man was. Razcjek was his name, and he'd just been in the news when she first arrived on Brighton, someone had been caught getting privileged access to the personal files of several young women around the city. He'd been caught, had a mug shot that ended up in the paper, but nothing had ever come of it. Now she knew why.

Joanna was starting to very much regret coming in on her day off.

She sat down at the wire chair in front of her desk, the spot normally reserved for visitors, and rubbed her forehead. Not yet mid-morning, and she already had a headache coming on, and that seemed unlikely to be the worst thing about her day.

There was no point in getting involved in Gabriel's games. So far, she'd stayed a healthy distance from the scheming in Brighton, and so far it had worked out for her. This time, though...she felt a pang of conscience. Despite trying to assure herself about the miners' preparedness for a betrayal, she knew that it wouldn't be enough. Never was.

And unlike most of the people Gabriel tried to con, these people weren't criminals. They'd actually seemed pretty nice; they'd thanked her quite politely for her help. Joanna sighed, trying to massage the throb out of her temples. Unfortunately, she knew what the right thing to do was, and if she deliberately did the wrong thing, well...how did that make her any different than Gabriel himself?

Her decision made, she hit the elevator button and took the car as it came. This wasn't a call to make from either the office or her personal handset.

About fifteen minutes before they needed to leave for the Tower, Stephen and Ben returned to the lobby.

"We were getting some strange looks on the concourse," Stephen explained sheepishly, "when I suddenly remembered that I hadn't showered after last night."

Ben added, "So we were doing our best to remember all that happened to raise such an odor, and couldn't." He made a big show of smelling Eileen. "You better join us. I mean, take a shower too." He winked at her, elbowed Stephen, and the two of them started back toward their room, Eileen following. Obviously they'd decided to prematurely take the edge off the negotiations; they were acting like children.

Her handset went off. She glanced at the source address, saw it was local but unfamiliar. Frowning, she answered the call.

"Yeah?"

"Stephen Montgomery?" The voice was female, soft and somehow familiar.

"No, it's Eileen Cromwell, his second in command. You're calling for the *Mary Ellen*'s compliance officer?"

"I guess—this is the address your ship has on file with the port authority. I'm Joanna Newton, assistant to Thomas Gabriel? We met yesterday and I showed you to your hotel."

"Oh, right. We just need to shower and we'll be right up to meet with your boss."

The line was quiet for just a moment. When she finally spoke, the words tumbled out in a hurried cascade. "No, that's not why I'm calling. This might sound ridiculous, but I think that you might be in trouble. See, you know that Gabriel has this reputation, but maybe you're not entirely prepared to deal with it."

Eileen stopped, letting the two men walk ahead. Ducking into a small alcove in the rear of the Hotel Brighton lobby, she said, quietly and calmly, "Care to explain?"

"I just saw him in his office with this local data thief. He didn't want me in the office today, but I had to come back for my handset and I overheard him. He never wants me in the office if he's doing anything, um, illegal. Besides, I heard them talking about bugging your hotel room, and doing something with your ship. Ms. Cromwell..."

"Call me Eileen."

"Eileen, I think that you might be in some danger."

"If he's so dangerous, why would UNASCA even keep him around?" There was something borderline unreal about this situation.

"Maybe he serves their purposes? I have no idea." Joanna's voice was low and fast, as though she were afraid of her conversation being interrupted at any moment. "I just wanted to warn you. There's not much else I can do. Um, would you let me know if everything is okay later?" There was a certain unspoken aspect to that request, but Eileen didn't have the time to dwell on it.

"Sure thing."

"Thanks. Um, good luck." With that, the call ended.

What a strange call. More than likely, Gabriel truly was as scummy as he appeared, and he was trying to put one over on them. Good thing that Stephen had gone to the trouble of securing all the data to his person—once again his instincts had paid off and he'd get to take all the credit for them not getting swindled. Eileen chuckled, feeling some of the adrenaline rush of the phone call wear off.

She caught up with Stephen and Ben halfway up the stairs. "Strange call. Apparently Gabriel's secretary caught him with someone she called a 'data thief.'"

"Oh, that rascal," Stephen chuckled. "Good luck to him. He probably just realized he might actually have to pay up on his first offer."

"All the same," Eileen said, "be careful what you say in the rooms. Sounds like Gabriel had them bugged."

"Is that so," Ben said, and they all started back up the stairs. They still talked, continuing the conversation they'd been having when Eileen had interrupted, but she found them walking a little more slowly, looking around a little bit more, and maintaining a little bit more alertness.

As Ben shut his door, and Stephen fumbled with the thumb pad on his, Eileen smiled at him.

"Hey handsome," she said.

"Hey smelly," he replied, winking.

"Let's get this whole deal over with."

"Okay," he said, nodding exaggeratedly and smiling.

Blushing just a little bit, not sure why she felt compelled to say anything, she just nodded again and turned to her own room. She was trying to examine exactly how she was feeling, other than "strange," when she detected some movement in the darkened space.

Eileen paused for just a moment before turning on the lights, and she had just that briefest moment to turn her body before the shape rushed at her.

It hit her with a leaping bound. In the Moon's one-sixth gravity, she flew back out the door like in a bad movie, hitting the opposite wall in the hallway before tumbling to the floor. The shape emerged into the hallway light, resolving into a man in dark clothes and a perfectly black facemask.

"Stephen!" She shouted, trying to get to her feet. She pushed up hard against the ground, bouncing her body into the air, as the man made for the stairwell that she'd only recently come up.

She was no good in lunar gravity, and if he hadn't fouled himself against a clot of tourists making their way into the same door he was trying to make his way out of, she would've lost him right then. And she was not going to lose him.

Stephen's door swung open, he looked at her concernedly, and then followed her path of flight—for she was trying her best to run after the man who plainly had a great deal more experience dealing with lunar gravity than she—and instantly sussed the situation.

"Go!" He shouted after her, but she was gone.

Running on the Moon was hard. Actually, proper running was impossible, and Eileen was still struggling to find cadence with the shallow skipping that fast movement required. The door was an automatic hatch-type mechanism that she was barely able to keep it from slamming in her face.

Hauling it open and staring down the stairwell, she could see the man several flights below, taking each flight at a bound. There was no way that she could catch him even if she wasn't off balance. On the other hand, the gravity here was minimal, right?

The stairwell was square, and with the stairs running around the outside there was a small empty space that ran all the way to the bottom of the shaft at the lobby, ten flights below. It was just large enough to admit a thin human.

Fortunately, Eileen was very thin. She didn't even think, just vaulted over the railing and started to fall.

Slowly, very slowly, she picked up speed. The man was probably five flights below her, and with his long bounds he wasn't going downward as fast as she was. He realized it, too, and with a moment's hesitation, threw open the door on his level and bounded through it.

Eileen grabbed the railing on that level as she passed it. Even with one-sixth gravity she was moving quickly enough that the jolt as she stopped wrenched her arms painfully, but she ignored it, climbing over the railing and propelling herself through the door as it closed.

The hotel was a giant L shape, with stairwells at both ends, and he was plainly headed toward the other one in hopes of outrunning her. On level ground, unfortunately, he was right—he'd mastered a gliding skip that looked incredibly awkward but propelled him far more quickly than Eileen's stumbling gait.

It was pissing her off. To be robbed by the man paying her hotel bill and out maneuvered by a man who had probably spent half her time in space was making her blood boil. Every stumble or brush against the ceiling had her seeing red, and she finally gave up, planted her feet against the ground, and dove forward.

This was one area where she'd had plenty of practice—she'd been jumping and diving in low gravity since before she could walk, and she wasn't letting a two-bit Moon thief show her up.

She almost missed him. In fact, she hit the ground before her hand brushed the heel of his shoes. That touch was enough to throw of his one stride, and Eileen felt a thrill of triumph as he hit the wall and pushed against it to recover.

He didn't make it. Eileen, grinning savagely now that the chase had turned her way, now that she felt properly predator again, jumped off the ground once more and hit him square in his center of mass. Ever so slowly he fell, Eileen's added mass visibly slamming him hard into the ground.

He let out a huff of air. Eileen shouted, "Gabriel sent you, huh? Did he think that you two could get away without paying, huh?"

She raised a fist to punch him, not caring about what it might do to her hand, but this guy was no idiot. While she was ever so slightly outbalanced, he shoved hard against her, and in the lunar gravity she was light enough for him to push aside. She ducked reflexively as he aimed a kick at her face, and by the time she recovered he had too, hitting the entrance to the second stairwell hard and throwing himself through it.

Eileen felt a snarl rise up in her throat. She leapt through the hatch before it could close behind him, poised to leap, and nearly got her head blown off.

She saw the snub-nosed pistol an instant before he fired, and she blindly threw herself to the side, landing awkwardly, her ears ringing in the instant after the loud report. She knew that if he wanted to kill her she was already dead, but it seemed that he was more interested in escape.

She could feel her fear rise, crash headlong into her anger, and sink again. She didn't think, she just ran after him, taking the landings one at a time, not sure how she would get past the pistol when she reached him but certain that it wouldn't stop her from removing his fucking head.

He burst through the lobby-level doors, out of the stairwell. She followed directly behind him, ready to dodge the next pistol shot, but he wasn't paying attention to her. He was paying attention to Stephen and Ben who, either not seeing the weapon or not caring, were bounding awkwardly forward toward the hotel's main doors, ready to cut him off and cut him down.

Eileen wanted to shout at them, to warn them, to tell them to let her handle the man. She could take him, they couldn't. But before she could do it, the man saw that they were going to reach the lobby doors before he did, and took matters into his own hands.

Eileen could see the pistol now: a snub-nosed model for shipboard personal defense. Small magazine, low penetration, but more than enough killing power for an unarmored human at close range. He emptied the magazine in the general direction of Stephen and Ben, scattering them and startling a scream from the clerk behind the concierge's desk.

Then, he was through the doors and in their level's main concourse. Eileen was braced to follow him, looking forward to catching up with him now that he was unarmed, when she happened to glance over toward Stephen and Ben, checking if they were all right.

That was when she saw Stephen in a slowly expanding pool of bright red.

Eileen didn't remember running over to him. The next thing she realized, she was at his side, marveling at the quantity of blood, the soaked front of his shirt, his ragged breathing. Ben was calling for help, demanding that someone call the ambulance. Eileen couldn't find her voice.

"Eileen," Stephen managed to choke out, and she started.

"Stephen, hang on," she said, keeping the quaver out of her voice as she quickly tore off her undershirt, pressing it against the wound on his chest, knowing that it wouldn't be enough. "You'll be okay. The medics will be here soon."

"Eileen," he said, wheezing. "Eileen, don't let...Gabriel..." It all seemed so unreal, like she was watching someone else treat him, like she was in a dream or a memory of a past that had never been.

"Stephen, stay quiet, please. Help's on the way." She pressed the shirt against the wound, felt the hot sticky blood pump in time with his heart. It wasn't stopping.

"Eileen, don't let this...be the end. Gotta...stay the course."

As she pressed the shirt down with all of her might, trying through sheer will to stop the blood gushing from him, the corner of his mouth turned up in a tiny, but distinct smile. And then he died.

Chapter 3

The main offices of the United Nations Space Colonization Authority were just a short flight from the Belt Group building. Rosetta had spent hours the previous day trying to organize her files, get Forrester's agent's intel all sorted together (and properly redacted, of course), and decide what Belt Group's official position was going to be regarding the *Atlas* scenario.

Chen was riding with her in the Belt Group ship as they swooped low over the blue waters of the Willamette River, following it downstream to the Oregon City neighborhood. He sat pensively in his seat, his brow furrowed and his mouth turned down. He looked like Rosetta felt.

In a city known for its mile-high skyscrapers, the UNASCA building was somewhat out of place. Flying through the skyline, you could circle for hours trying to find it amid the tree-covered microarcologies and business complexes of the Portland metro area. Only by following the river was it obvious, and even then the simple glass and steel structure, devoid of greenery, seemed a throwback to a less advanced time.

The UNASCA building snarled air traffic for two kilometers in all directions with its busy pads. As they circled, waiting for a landing pad to open up, Rosetta asked, "How much longer are we going to put up with this?"

The corner of Chen's mouth twitched. "Do you mean the short notice before important meetings or the terrible traffic?"

"I meant UNASCA in general."

"Ah," Chen nodded sagely. "I see."

"Well, you can be as sardonic as you like," Rosetta said, "but sooner or later we're going to have to make a break with them. A public break. I'm not telling you something you don't know."

"Rosetta, I know how much you dislike these meetings, but please...patience. Our timetable is moving quickly already. Any faster and we risk the whole thing coming undone."

"Yes, sir." He was right, of course, but meeting with UNASCA always put Rosetta in a bad mood, and when she was in a bad mood she got reckless.

"Tell me, what news of the Free Jovians?"

The old man was just making conversation. He had to already know. Either that, or he was testing her, and she disliked being prodded. "No news beyond the last dispatches, sir. Production is down on all helium-3 extractors, and spontaneous demonstrations have broken out in Foundation Home on Europa over the last couple of weeks."

"No, not spontaneous. It's Solomon Gracelove." Chen's voice carried a thoughtful edge; the chiding tone had disappeared. He stared out the window, his face dappled with reflections from the river and the skyscrapers that straddled it. "He's biding his time, Rosetta, just as we are. This is what they don't teach you in school, what they can't teach you, but industrialists have known it since Carnegie and Rockefeller. Neither of us can be entirely sure of the other, so neither of us is willing to take the first move. So, we tolerate UNASCA for now, we accept their help with the *Atlas*, and we wait for the tipping point to come. Mark my words, it will be soon."

Rosetta tried to match his thoughtful tone. "So, if dealing with UNASCA all buddy-buddy is our backup plan, what's theirs? What's Gracelove's?"

"That," Chen said as the car jerked and they started their descent, "is why I have you."

And that, Rosetta thought, is why I have Forrester. The man had heard rumors, of course, but nothing concrete. Still, he'd produce results eventually. He always did.

When they had finally landed on the rooftop pad, they were escorted into the depths of the UNASCA building by a functionary. The walls were painted to match the carpet, all in the UNASCA livery of red and gold. Impressionistic sculptures of planetary orbits, comet collisions, and enormous spiral galaxies lined the hallway, each bathed in the soft glow of indirect lighting. The building might have been small, but it was a living testament to the enormous wealth and power of its organization. No wonder that it was the only portion of the old United Nations to have survived.

There was an enormous conference room at the end of this hallway, with richly paneled French doors leading into it; these automatically opened at their approach. The simple conference room—aside from its table, chairs, refreshment cart—had a stunning view of the lazily flowing Willamette, which ran directly under this room several hundred feet below.

As Rosetta and Chen took their seats around the table, Rosetta took a moment to quietly survey those already present. There was Yessenia Pruitt, deputy administrator of UNASCA. Her presence was a bit of a surprise—normally a routine meeting like this, even with a man like Ronaldo Chen, would be handled slightly farther down the food chain.

Yessenia was in good spirits, but her companion distinctly was not. Rosetta had met many times with Israel Moen, the UNASCA head of corporate relations. All of Belt Group's substantial contracts with various governments were arbitrated through his office, and UNASCA was the largest buyer of Belt Group's refined goods.

Moen was a dour-looking older man, one with a tendency to stare upward when he was speaking, as if the person he was conversing with was a foot or two taller than they were. He started talking when they were seated, before the steward had taken their coffee orders.

"I understand that you're willing to come forward with some news regarding the *Atlas*, Rosetta? Oh, good morning to you, of course. We're pleased that we're finally having this meeting."

Chen looked sourly at Moen but didn't say anything. Rosetta cleared her throat, refusing to be put on the defensive at the beginning of the meeting.

"Mr. Moen, as you know Belt Group always makes the highest effort to stay compliant with all UNASCA regulations, including those related to missing or lost vessels. So, when I tell you that we do have news of the *Atlas* that might fall under this category, you have to understand that it was only recently determined."

Moen smirked and looked like he was about to make a smartass reply, but Pruitt's even, grandmotherly voice cut him off. "Ms. Lovelace, Rosetta, neither you nor Belt Group are on trial here. We're working together on this case," she said, glancing significantly at Moen, "and we're interested in whatever you have to say."

"Thank you, Yessenia."

"Please continue."

"Very well." Rosetta steepled her fingers on the hardwood table. "As Mr. Moen has apparently already heard, we have not received regular communications from the *Atlas* in several months. She was last sighted by independent sources in the belt, engaged in normal extraction and refining operations, but we believe that she has moved toward the outer system. We don't know why we've lost contact, and we don't, just yet, have a plan for regaining it."

Moen looked like he was biting his tongue. "So you feel that this vessel qualifies as 'lost'?"

"I believe that it qualifies as 'missing.' We don't know why she abandoned her normal plan of operations, and we don't know what her goals in the outer system are, but we have no reason to believe that she's been destroyed." She glanced at Chen, realizing that she wanted his permission to say what she'd been planning to say. He nodded minutely.

Rosetta turned back to the UNASCA representatives, particularly Moen. "We believe that the ship may have been stolen."

Yessenia wore an expression of polite concern, while Moen appeared to be barely holding back an expression of humorous disbelief. For a moment, neither said anything.

It was the latter who finally got control of himself. "I'm not sure if I follow you. How does one 'steal' a vessel displacing hundreds of thousands of tons way out in the middle of the Solar System?"

"That's quite simple, Mr. Moen. We think that her captain, Constance Kelley, and some of the senior officers may have been bought out, possibly by rival corporations, possibly by other, unknown agents. They may have delivered the *Atlas* to another party in the outer system."

Moen shook his head. "I can't believe this. There hasn't been a case of shipjacking in space in a century. How would they have maintained control without a steady ground uplink?"

"The *Atlas* was designed to operate with minimal ground support. With minimal support of any kind, in fact."

"What about supplies then? Water? Food?"

Rosetta smiled patiently, but she could feel her annoyance starting to build. "Mr. Moen, this line of questioning is entirely beside the point—water is common in the outer system, and the *Atlas* is designed to be self-sufficient food-wise for many years. That technology wasn't cheap, Mr. Moen; that's why we want the ship back."

Moen appeared to be ready to argue further, but Yessenia cut him off. "You're quite right, Rosetta, this is beside the point. Of course we would appreciate the opportunity to review your data, but whether the *Atlas* was stolen, lost, or has merely fallen out of communication, UNASCA will cooperate with Belt Group to achieve a satisfactory resolution to this situation."

Rosetta spread her hands. "Naturally, the only resolution that we would consider satisfactory would be the recovery of the *Atlas* and her crew intact."

"Naturally."

At this moment, Chen spoke for the first time since the initial pleasantries of their arrival. "So what can UNASCA offer us?"

Yessenia smiled at him. She leaned forward, elbows on the table, fingers steepled. "Well, we're willing to accept a Belt Group liaison to work with our analysis people. We're also willing to put out the notice—quietly, mind—that we'd appreciate data related to the past or current condition of the *Atlas*. We can also probably spare a few ships and telescopes for search duty."

"That's very generous of you, Mrs. Pruitt," Rosetta said, a little surprised at her openness. UNASCA generally operated as a walled garden, allowing visitors the ability to interact with them in certain, pre-approved (some might say ritual) ways. Once they wanted to get a little deeper into the system, to see how it worked, they were politely but firmly rebuffed. Except, of course, for right now. For some reason.

"It's all we can do," Yessenia said modestly. Rosetta noted that Moen was doing an unsuccessful job of hiding his disapproval. "After all, let's be honest. Space travel is nearing something of a second renaissance.

"Now that most of the big capital investments have been finished for decades, the people of Earth have finally resolved themselves to the idea that space travel isn't just for the rare, well-paid few. We have new émigrés daily applying for jobs in the outer system. New propulsion techniques like those on the *Atlas* are an important part of that question. Ditto its advanced refining techniques; if we make Venus and Ceres less important to the Solar System's economy, then we can accelerate the exploitation of outer system resources.

"So, you can see what we think of the *Atlas*. She's just as important to our goals as to yours. Therefore, we want her back nearly as much as you do. It's simplicity itself."

Rosetta stroked her chin. This had obviously been thought out well in advance; UNASCA's intelligence operations were as good as might be expected for such a ubiquitous operation.

"In that case," she said, "we gladly accept whatever help UNASCA has to offer. We do have one particular favor to ask, however. There is a strong chance that one of the last ships to see the *Atlas* may still be hoarding data that would help us track her down."

"Really?" Yessenia cocked an eyebrow.

"Really. Some of our agents report that someone in Brighton has been making inquiries Earthside for the unloading of some unusual data. Data involving a missing ship." Rosetta's tongue worked the inside of her mouth for a few moments. Yessenia might not like this part. "We have reason to believe that this 'someone' is Thomas Gabriel, Brighton's administrator."

Yessenia and Moen exchanged wry glances at this news. So they were in on the joke.

"Yes, Mr. Gabriel is certainly a unique character." Yessenia said.

"If it's true that he's been involved, then that seals the case. He must be removed," Moen said with an air of finality. Rosetta blinked at this. His office had already issued a recall for Gabriel, delivered by Forrester's agent. Was Yessenia being kept out of the loop? Forrester was going to get a huge kick out of that.

"We're glad you think so. If we could have some documentation in that regard from your office, our agent is already on-site." Rosetta inclined her chin to Moen, curious to see how he would react, but he simply nodded. Pity.

"We're trying to backtrack the chain of incidence here. Only a fool sells information over the DSN, so they're probably trying for a handoff, which means the ship is probably in lunar orbit," Rosetta said. "We would like your permission to board and detain any vessel that we can definitively connect to the data."

"Well," Yessenia said, cutting off Moen again. "Bring it up to us first. We have to watch our public relations, especially at a time like this." She shrugged. "They'll have to put in somewhere, and we are everywhere. We'll catch them on the far side if nothing else."

"Certainly."

There was a moment of silence as the conversation

dropped off.

"Well, if there's nothing else, I'm sure that we can finish the rest of this virtually." Yessenia said, standing. "Your liaison can start over here whenever they're ready. We're all in this together, as I said."

"You've been most kind," Chen said, quietly.

Yessenia nodded with a polite smile, and they were escorted from the room by the functionary who had led them in.

When they were back in the car, ascending through the forest of skyscrapers, Chen said, as if to himself, "I wonder who could best keep an eye on UNASCA."

Rosetta turned to him. "I was planning on sending Forrester, head of my analysis section. He has certain skills..."

"I'm fully aware of Robert Forrester's skill set, Rosetta. I don't entirely approve, but I can't deny that he gets things done. Make it happen."
He scratched at the thinning hair on his head. "Yessenia's a nice person, and usually sincere. Even so, I suspect that there's something strange going on over at UNASCA. We'll have to tread carefully on this one. I don't want to be caught holding the short end of this stick."

Rosetta couldn't help but agree. Not that there was much that could be done at this point. She turned back to the window, watching the river float lazily underneath them as they turned back toward city center.

Joanna heard about the murder the next morning. She'd told her room computer to list off some headlines while she was putting together a quick breakfast, and had nearly dropped her toast on the floor when it had said, "Murder at Hotel Brighton."

"Go back and give me an abstract," she found herself saying, praying that she'd misheard, that it was somebody else.

It wasn't. "The captain of belt mining ship *Mary Ellen*, staying at the famous Hotel Brighton, met his abrupt end early yesterday morning. Witnesses reported a scuffle in the upper floors that spilled out into the lobby, and as the captain was attempting to bar the alleged murderer's exit, he was shot several times with an illegal weapon."

The report went on to provide some background on the ship and the man. Belt miners, ready to unload a shipment of valuable ores in Earth orbit, stopped at the moon for R&R, and similar factoids. The article implied that the entire thing was the result of random violence, and ended by advising people to report if they saw a man matching the description of the killer. Joanna felt oddly detached; the situation was so unreal.

"What about Eileen Cromwell? Is she mentioned in this report or any other one about the same event?" She asked the computer.

"That name turned up no correlated results."

A cover-up? Maybe they just hadn't been present. Didn't matter; it all meant the same thing, something so ridiculous that she could barely make herself think it: Thomas Gabriel had tried to steal the data, just like she'd suspected, and just as she'd feared, the miners hadn't been ready for it.

He had killed a man! And if he even suspected that Joanna knew a thing about it, what was to stop him from killing her?

Joanna reflected darkly that she'd gone from happily, if reluctantly, getting ready for work to sheer terror in the space of five minutes. She felt somehow silly being afraid for her life, like anyone would want to kill her for anything. But she'd been way too closely involved with Eileen and Gabriel. It honestly seemed like there might be something to her fear.

But, well, Gabriel couldn't just hire someone to go murder her. As far as she knew, he kind of liked her, in a perfunctory sort of way. At least, she hoped so. And, she hadn't even really thought him capable of killing *one* person. What's to say that he wouldn't do it again?

Joanna was afraid, but it was all so unreal that routine took over, and she headed in to work. Even so she didn't even leave for her shift until the time she should have been arriving.

She sat down at her desk quietly, hoping that Gabriel wouldn't notice her late arrival. As soon as Joanna turned on her computer, though, she could see that Gabriel wasn't even in. Maybe she had blown everything a little out of proportion, and now that she was in the familiar space of the lobby, her earlier fear seemed just a little childish. People's lives were only threatened that way in videos and books.

Joanna worked diligently on her reports and scheduling throughout the morning, often times losing herself completely in her work, or in the calming music playing through the shotgun speaker that only someone in her chair could hear. The entire situation grew a little more distant, a little more unreal, as time went on. For that,

Joanna was profoundly thankful.

Halfway through the uneventful day, a tone sounded on Joanna's desk, telling her that someone had selected her office from the tower's elevator cluster and was on their way up. She straightened her blouse and dusted her lapels as the elevator doors opened, admitting...admitting a very singular looking woman.

She was dark-skinned, with close-cropped dark hair, and muscles. There were no muscles like that on the Moon; on a world where maintaining anything like a reasonable body mass could be a challenge, to see someone with rippling abdominals or well-defined biceps was to see an offworlder.

And Joanna could barely stop looking at her. She strode toward the desk using the skip-hops of the lunar natives, but doing it in such a way that imparting something of a dancer's grace to the normally awkward steps. A sudden thought crossed her mind—what would Gabriel have to do with a person this competent?

"Excuse me," the woman said in an unadorned alto.

Joanna abruptly realized that she'd been staring and stammered, "Yes, yes, I'm sorry. This is Thomas Gabriel's office, how can I help you?"

"My name is Bronwyn Calleo. I represent Belt Group, Limited, and I will see Mr. Gabriel at once." She had the voice of a woman who gave commands easily and expected obedience. Joanna felt the pit of her stomach tighten as she was forced to not obey.

"I'm sorry, he's not in right now. In his office, I mean. Um, can I make an appointment? The earliest opening is, um," she said, scrambling for that screen.

"No, I do not wish to make an appointment. You will let me into his office, and I will wait for him there."

"I can't..."

"You can. And you will." The woman leaned forward and planted a venous, well-defined hand on the edge of Joanna's desk. She could feel a tickling as a drop of sweat ran down her back, and she was honestly scared. Bronwyn's voice and expression were even, but the threat was in her body language.

"I, um, suppose..."

"Good."

Joanna stood up to let the woman into Gabriel's office feeling as though she could be knocked over with a feather. It wasn't until after she had taken a step that she abruptly realized that his office was probably locked. She didn't have a key.

She felt like crying as she turned back to the stranger, who was calmly regarding her much as a lion might regard a sickly gazelle. "Listen, I'm sorry, but I don't have a key. His office is locked, and he doesn't let anyone, doesn't let me in. I don't know how to open the door without his permission, but maybe if you want to wait, you could just wait for him out here?" She was babbling, but couldn't stop herself.

The woman seemed to have pity on her and relaxed her intense posture a bit. It seemed like the temperature of the room dropped ten degrees in that instant. "Very well; I will return later. Please do not mention to anyone that I was looking for him."

With that, she walked back to the door with that same dancer's grace, got in the elevator, and left. It was some minutes before Joanna trusted herself to go back to her desk, sit down, and sob into her hands.

The last day had been nothing but a blur to Eileen. It was as if only moments before she'd been pulled, blank minded, from Stephen's corpse as the doctors placed their emergency gear on his body. They'd pumped in blood and stabilizers, catheterized his heart, tried tissue lattice reconstruction, but none of it had worked. He was just as dead now as he had ever been.

Ben hadn't complained when Eileen had refused to meet with Gabriel, or when she'd brusquely filed a flight plan back to the *Mary Ellen.* He hadn't even complained when it'd taken her three times as long to perform the orbit sync maneuvers because she was so damned angry.

And now, in these familiar surroundings made alien by his death, she felt angry, sad, and empty all at the same time. Like a zombie, she walked around the habitation ring, or floated through the crew areas, not thinking, not caring, as dead to the world as Stephen himself. The rest of the crew was there, each mourning in their own way, but she felt entirely alone.

It had been in this very ship that Stephen had first hired her. Nearly a decade they'd lived and worked together, but only in the last year had their relationship become...less professional. Oh, hells. How much time had they lost being coy? And now, just as their relationship had turned from amorous to loving, he was gone, and she was alone. At least there was a small comfort in the familiarity of that feeling.

The entire crew was assembled in one of the common areas of the hab ring, a section of the torus with large, empty modules for relaxation, either alone or in company. Now, they were all together but felt alone anyway. She was there with Ben, sullen faced, Melissa, her face red from crying, and Almika, the newest member of the crew nonetheless moved to a profound funk.

As she spun Stephen's datacube in her fingers, Eileen ran through the situation in her head for the millionth time. She did all she could, right? The man was too fast, too strong...but maybe, if she hadn't slowed him down, Stephen wouldn't have been able to catch up.

"Aw, shit." she buried her head in her arms. It was such a stupid thing to die for.

The rest of the crew looked at her with mild interest. Their own, equally powerful emotions had sapped all of their strength

"What is it?" Ben asked, rubbing his face with a hand.

"It's bullshit," she said, feeling a little more fire creep into her voice. With relish, she let it out. "We just got chased oft the Moon by some sac-less creep hiding behind a hired gun after he killed one of our...friends," she said, choking over the last word. Even that sadness, Eileen was pleased to note, dissolved under the tiding of rising anger. "And here we are, moping."

"What are you thinking?" He asked, the weariness growing a little more profound in his voice.

"Something! Not nothing. I don't know," she said, feeling herself deflate. After a moment of sinking back into her chair, though, she stood again and started anxiously pacing the room, watching the monitors showing a variety of entertainment beamed from the Earth to the Moon.

They'd been muted, but even the visuals were bothering her. At her command, Crazyhorse turned them all off.

"Eileen, UNASCA can't just let people be murdered on their colonies. They'll look into it and they'll find the guy. There aren't many places for a killer to go on Brighton." Melissa spoke, her voice sounding dry and cracked.

"Sure there is: right to the top of the tower. You didn't see Mr. Thomas Gabriel, emperor potentate of Brighton. He was so slimy you could smell it. Stephen thought—we thought he was harmless. Not so much." She dropped the datacube on the table. "If that man thought Stephen's life was worth *this*, then he deserves the worst I can do to him."

"Eileen," Melissa repeated, the weariness in her voice matching Ben's, "I doubt that UNASCA, even worthless as it is nowadays, would appoint a murderer or friend of murderers to high office. That's ridiculous."

"I'll agree that he wasn't trustworthy, or at least didn't look it, but I also have a hard time believing that he could have someone killed like that." He sighed. "Listen, Eileen, I know how you're feeling. I was there too. It could've been any one of us. It's natural to feel a little bit of survivor's guilt, but you just have to remind yourself-"

Eileen cut him off by kicking over a low table. "Damn it, Benjamin! This isn't just about guilt. It's about justice, and you know full well that UNASCA wouldn't know justice if I mailed them a book on it!" She emphasized her expression by kicking over another table and a chair. In the near-Earth gravity of the *Mary Ellen*'s hab ring, they hit the ground with a satisfying impact. "It's like Solomon Gracelove says: we need to take justice into our own hands."

"Eileen," Almika said quietly, "he's talking about workers."

In a low, dangerous voice, Eileen replied, "I'm talking about something a little more immediate."

They were quiet for a few moments. Eileen resumed her pacing, glowering, while the others sat and watched. She could feel the energy, the rage building up and she yearned with desperate need to unleash it on someone or something.

Finally she couldn't contain it any longer. "I shouldn't be up here. I'm going back down." Eileen slammed a fist against the wall and moved toward the door as if it brooked no discussion.

"Wait, back down there? For what?" Ben said, standing.

Eileen turned back and flashed him an ugly look. "I'm going to go back down there, I'm going to go to that Gabriel's office, and I'm going to confront him. I'm going to ask him if he tried to rob us, and I'll look deep into his eyes, and I will know if he tries to lie to me. If he does, he's dead. If he admits it, he's dead. If not..." she trailed off for a moment. "If not," she continued after a pause, "I'll know."

They were all quiet, but Eileen could see each of them working out in their own mind how to talk her out of it. Ben was the only one brave enough to say something, but she'd shoot him right down and have none of it.

"Eileen," he said at last, looking very tired.

"Ben, I'm going. You can come, or you can stay."

"Eileen, let me finish, damn it. I was going to say that you're the captain of this ship now. There's more to your life than just avenging yourself or Stephen. You have to think of your responsibilities. Our cooperative-"

"Res-responsibilities? Are you joking? He just got killed, Ben. He's not coming back. This is my damned responsibility, to Stephen! I'm going back down there, and the cooperative be damned."

With that, she turned and stalked out of the room. Twenty minutes later, having talked to nobody else, she undocked the *Mary Ellen*'s short-range shuttle, pulled gently away from the ship and the massive station that she was docked to, and deorbited. She left the datacube behind.

Chapter 4

Gabriel immediately wished that he hadn't sent Joanna away. Not that he derived tremendous comfort from her presence, but he figured if someone came for him he could pin anything on her, and she didn't have the spine to put up a fight.

And someone was coming for him, there was no doubt about that. Ever since that idiot from the lower concourse he'd hired had pulled a pistol—a military snubnose, of all the things, the fool—there was no question of it. The only uncertainty at this point was who they would represent.

They might be UNASCA, finally unwilling to turn a blind eye to his excesses. Unlikely; if the news was to be believed at all, they couldn't afford the scandal, something that had worked tremendously to his advantage. It might be Belt Group, Inc.; if they thought that he had some information on their missing ship. That was more likely, but there wasn't a lot they could do to him. They had almost no interests on Luna, whereas there was little he was not interested in.

But that didn't reassure him. The rumors that had already reached him, from his contacts on Luna 1 and Tranquility Park, that someone had been seen asking after him. Someone who exuded confidence. Damn it.

He had to get out of his office, maybe on a business trip to one of the smaller colonies. The administrator of the Farside Observatory had suggested multiple times that he join their poker table, maybe it was time to join them.

No, that was ridiculous. He was safest here, where he had the greatest support base, where he could call in favors. Besides, nobody intimidated Thomas Gabriel, administrator of UNASCA's largest colony, in his own domain? If they thought they could do it, they were welcome to try.

Several hours passed. He was never in his office this late, but whoever it was, they were close and they'd look first for him here. Let them come, he figured. They weren't going to see him run to some bolt-hole, like a coward. He'd done nothing wrong. At least, nothing they could prove.

And yet, they hadn't come, and he was getting ready to leave for the day regardless; certain people would be asking after him in much more mundane fashion down at the Triple Nickel. Just as he was leaving, he heard the tone from Joanna's desk indicating that someone was coming up the elevator.

He didn't have time to resume his position of power behind his desk, so he just leaned back against the hatch leading into his office, and waited. Setting his face into an implacable mask was a familiar thing for him, and he had it in place in moments.

The elevator door opened, revealing a woman of very distinctive appearance and poise. His first instinct was to give her the head to toe, accumulating data for his complex sexual preference algorithm. Dark skin, tight clothing, and substantial muscle mass, sharp-looking but not unattractive face—she'd be perfect, if she didn't look like she could've killed him at will. He felt the internal edifice of his composure crack ever so slightly. Hopefully it didn't show.

She glided off the elevator in a practiced stride, graceful as an animal. "Thomas Gabriel, UNASCA administrator."

"I am. Might I ask your name?"

"I am Bronwyn Calleo of Belt Group, Limited." The elevator door closed and Bronwyn leaned back casually against it, mirroring his pose but exuding supreme confidence and control.

He was more than willing to rise to that game. "So, Bronwyn, you've come for me specifically? The conventional method is to make an appointment with my secretary during normal business hours. I'm a very busy man."

"So I have heard. In this case, I needed you alone."

"Well, as it happens I was just leaving for the day. If you're willing to conduct business, I have some openings tomorrow-"

She cut him off. "Don't play games with me, Mr. Gabriel. You have made some poor decisions. I have been dispatched to retrieve certain data that you have been attempting to sell Earthside."

"I do deal in information for some interested parties. There's nothing illegal about-"

She cut him off again. "Three days ago, you indicated to Mr. Howard Liang of Hong Kong that you were in possession of data related to the Belt Group ship *Atlas*. I will take that information now, as well as your assurance that you will give it to nobody else."

Gabriel blinked. He'd expected someone to be after him about the murder, or some of his other extracurricular activities. Gabriel knew that he'd broken the law any number of times; he reveled in it. No reason to hate himself for it. But for that information? It was just a ship, surely Belt Group didn't have reason to pursue him like this.

"I was trying to sell it to UNASCA, of course. All above-board."

"You are a UNASCA employee. You should have turned the data over at once, but no matter. You will do so, now, to me."

He then realized where the real problem was going to lie, here. He didn't even have the data—his talk to Liang was just a negotiating ploy. Sure, the data would've gotten to UNASCA eventually, and Gabriel would've made a tidy profit. He colored that a win. Except, of course, that they had failed to find anything on Montgomery's ship, and Razcjek had killed a man. Stupid, stupid.

So, in a novel decision, he decided to tell the truth. "I'm sorry, Bronwyn, but I don't have the data."

She raised one eyebrow and her entire body language changed. What had been a casual expression of supreme control abruptly shifted to one of extreme hostility. The internal struts of Gabriel's self-confidence, under repair from Bronwyn's first appearance, cracked a little bit again. Through sheer force of will, he prevented it from showing.

"Is that so?" When Gabriel just nodded, she continued, "I am not certain I believe you."

"I'm sorry to hear that, Bronwyn, but it's the truth. Now, if you'll excuse me, it's Friday, I've had a long day today, and I would very much like to enjoy my weekend." He pushed himself off the wall, took two gliding steps toward the elevator, and reached for the button.

He didn't see Bronwyn move. The next thing he knew, his right arm was numb and he was being bodily lifted and flung through the air. He hit the wall about where he had been leaning, managing to catch himself before he settled to the floor.

"What the-" Bronwyn was on top of him. A sharp, painful blow to his side ended his attempts to stand up, and as he lay on the floor Bronwyn turned him on his back with one booted foot, and planted her heel on his neck.

Gabriel's mind was still trying to reconstruct the painful events of the past few seconds when Bronwyn spoke, her voice even and calm, "You may or may not have the data that I am after. However, I cannot risk that you might be lying, so we are going to have a lengthy conversation. You will tell me everyone who might be in possession of that data, or has spent large amounts of time with those who might have it.

"If you are very lucky, then at the end of this conversation, you can begin your weekend. If not, then you should know that I have been authorized by UNASCA to remove you from your position."

Gabriel could do nothing but choke his approval.

He burned with shame, and he knew that he couldn't let her get away with this.

Joanna couldn't sleep. In her dreams the mystery woman hadn't left calmly, hadn't accepted her explanation for why Joanna couldn't let her into Gabriel's office. Instead, she'd grown angry, violent, had attacked Joanna and hurt her badly. She would awake, tangled in the sheets, covered in a cold sweat, and be thankful the dream was over. Yet when she went back to sleep it would be just the same, except that she would suffer some humiliation instead of dying. It was a terrible night.

They reminded her of the strange dreams that she'd had in zero gravity on the way to the Moon, or when she'd first moved into the apartment but before she'd grown used to the lower gravity. It affected the psyche in subtle ways, and seeing those effects crop up again just reinforced the idea that Joanna had never really gotten used to the Moon. In many ways it was just as alien to her as it had been the day that she'd moved in. When she sent out her resume, she was sending it to companies on Earth, and ideally ones in NORPAC.

But that was for tomorrow. Today, Joanna just wanted to relax and people watch, as she sometimes did on the Grand Promenade. It was the level immediately beneath the lunar surface and Brighton Tower, one of the first underground areas to be built. Originally it had been a home for astronauts and the people who maintained the digging robots that were carving additional tunnels, but for decades it had been renovated into a sort of miniature Vegas, full of neon and laser glamour. It was also the first place that tourists to the Moon would go, and even though she'd never grow used to the Moon, at least Joanna could feel good that she was more used to it than these people.

Joanna purchased a coffee from a stall in the concourse and took a seat on a bench over Lover's Leap, staring down the massive tunnel ringed with additional concourses. There weren't many people compared to her home in Juneau, but watching them try to move more than made up for it. For a brief moment, she was completely content with her decision to try to head home.

"Excuse me, miss?" Joanna turned, and frowned as she noticed the Brighton Security guard standing there. He was just in his patrol jumpsuit, electrolaser and prod in his holsters, but something about his posture worried Joanna.

"Yes, officer?"

"Joanna Newton?"

"Um, yes..." For the first time, Joanna noticed that the guard was not alone—others were creating a little barrier pushing the small but appreciative crowd that had gathered. What was going on?

"Come with us, please." The officer stepped back to allow her to stand.

She left her coffee on the bench, growing more concerned. She hadn't broken any laws, there had to be something else.

Gabriel. There was no question. Something had happened to him, something involving that woman, and now she was getting caught in the fallout. That bastard. She should never have kept silent about her suspicions, and now she would pay for it. Could she have been more naive?

The Brighton concourses were dotted with small

security booths, and they brought Joanna inside one of them. She had never been in one before, and she had barely seen the inside of this one before she was seated on a small electric cart with two officers. The cart sped through the concourse, its emergency lights flashing, until it reached a vehicle lift, which it took down. And down. And down.

They were on the bottom-most level. There was little construction down here yet, just a large series of partitions that were under construction and the massive lunar steel structural supports. The floor and ceiling were plain stone, and she could see in several directions for hundreds of meters into the poorly-lit space.

There was no reason for them to bring her down here; the main security building was in the tower. Down here, there was...nothing. It was deeply unsettling, but when Joanna asked one of her guards, he just sighed and told her to be quiet. She'd find out.

They drove past piles of raw materials, construction robots, and various bits of heavy machinery to the far corner of the level, one that had been somewhat further built up. There were several established buildings here, and the walls looked solid, reaching from floor to ceiling. A door in the wall bore the security office's symbol; she was escorted through this, through an office whose furniture was still secured to pallets, and into a very new-smelling conference room.

Inside this conference room was a low table, one chair, and Bronwyn Calleo. The woman stood with sinuous grace, like a cat, and Joanna felt a very animal fear at the back of her mind.

"Wait," was all Joanna had time to say before the

security officers shut the door. She heard a lock engage behind them.

"Do not be alarmed. I've spoken with Mr. Gabriel, and he indicated you as a possible party of interest in my mission."

It was a few moments before Joanna found her voice, and she was pleased she could speak with nary a quaver. "What mission? Who *are* you?"

"It's come to my attention that you may have some data of extremely significant interest to Belt Group, Limited. I need you turn it over at once, and make certain arrangements to prevent you from speaking of it to any other party." Bronwyn's pose was confident but casual, and her voice was even, almost bored, as if she was repeating a common set of phrases by rote.

"But, I don't have any data! I'm not even sure what you're talking about." But she knew that wasn't entirely true. She didn't have any data, of course, but she did know what Bronwyn was talking about—it had to be about Gabriel and Montgomery's deal, and his murder.

Oh hell. Gabriel had tried to frame her.

In the same instant that she started desperately hoping it was untrue, Bronwyn said, "Mr. Gabriel has named you a person of interest, and has provided certain evidence that you spent significant time with other parties of interest. I cannot risk that you know more than you have already revealed." Her voice was still even, though a harder edge was creeping into it.

"Wait, what do you mean? I don't know anything! I'm a free citizen and a UNASCA employee!"

"Belt Group has reached an agreement with

UNASCA. I am sorry, but we have been empowered to place you under indefinite arrest." Of course they had that power—she was being interviewed in a security office, and UNASCA had always been accused of abusing its position as sole colonial authority with things like indefinite arrest for suspected troublemakers.

But she hadn't thought it would ever happen to her. Joanna Elaine Newton, a criminal.

Just like Dad.

She wanted to cry but she forced the tears back and forced some clarity into her voice.

"On what charge?"

"Industrial espionage."

"I want to speak to a lawyer," Joanna said, not expecting her request to be granted.

She was right. "That cannot be permitted. As of this moment, you are under complete interdict. No outside communication is permitted." She elevated her chin, and an officer who must have been waiting for that signal walked into the room.

"Ma'am?" Joanna at least drew some satisfaction from the fact that he didn't sound happy to be taking orders from Bronwyn.

"Please secure her in one of the new cells. You will receive further instructions from Mr. Gabriel's office presently."

"Ma'am." Then to Joanna. "Come on. Please don't make this difficult."

She didn't. And a few moments later, she was in a jail cell so new that the prefab steel walls were spotless and unscuffed. There was a cot with a flat pillow and a single blanket. It had all happened so fast she felt like she was lagging behind her own body.

Oh hell. What would her mother think, or her grandmother? Another relative in prison for a thoughtless white-collar crime. She was innocent, but she doubted that anyone would give her the benefit of the doubt. Not after her father loudly proclaimed his innocence while his employees' retirement funds bottomed out.

She felt like she was sinking into an abyss. The anger, the loneliness that she'd felt standing on the other side of those walls reflected back on her a hundred times. When the tears came, Joanna let them.

Eileen didn't kill herself on her way back to the Moon. It took her an extra few orbits to line up her re-entry, and she lost patience with herself calculating burn times, but a few hours later she was landing at Brighton, and a few minutes later she was riding the elevator up the Brighton Tower.

She had taken the precaution of arming herself. Brighton security was second to none if you arrived with the passenger flights, but woefully inadequate to the task of screening the private craft that were continually landing. What inspections there were much more focused on catching illegal cargos than illegal weapons, and Eileen had no cargo.

Getting through customs was similarly simple. Her weapon would show up on a standard scan, but it was simple to stash it in a cleaning cart on its way through the express lane and recover it after she'd passed through the scanner. As she retrieved the weapon, Eileen wondered idly how much money had been spent on the security that she had just bypassed without a care.

There were weapon scanners periodically throughout the concourses and the tower, but they were optimized to find explosives and, ridiculously, UNASCA privacy law required them to be plainly labeled. They would probably be more intense near Gabriel's office, but once she was there, she wouldn't care who knew that she had a weapon.

After all, she planned on making it pretty obvious.

The elevator opened up into the lobby of Gabriel's office. It was empty—this late after hours, there was no receptionist, and that girl Joanna was home asleep, if she was lucky. Eileen wasn't sure if Gabriel was going to be in his office, although if he wasn't she had absolutely no objection to waiting there for him.

She glided forward as silently as possible, taking light steps to keep her float time down, and pressed the button to open the door.

The pressure door accordioned open, and Eileen was momentarily elated to see Gabriel at his desk. He looked shitty. Good for him.

But he wasn't alone: there was a tall, dark skinned, muscular woman with him, and she looked like trouble.

So Eileen pointed the gun at her first when they both looked up. "All right, you two."

Gabriel was sitting at his desk looking as sweaty as usual, the top few buttons on his work shirt opened. He looked terrible. The woman who was standing over him straightened and said nothing.

"Oh, wonderful," Gabriel said breathlessly. He

looked somewhere between panic and resignation.

"Yeah, that's right. Sorry your friend isn't going to do you much good."

"You are Eileen Cromwell?" the woman asked, her voice even and confident. She was awfully calm for someone having a gun pointed at her face; it was unsettling.

"That's me," Eileen said, waving the gun slightly to reassure all present that she was still carrying it. "You want to start something?"

"My name is Bronwyn Calleo, and I am an agent of Belt Group, Limited. Eileen Cromwell, I must insist that you turn over all data related to the *Atlas* Project to me at once. Furthermore, you will submit to a binding contract that will place you in protective isolation for a period of no greater than twelve months." Her voice was maddeningly even.

"Sorry, babe," Eileen said, "you don't get to make the rules now. Where'd you dig this piece of work up, Tom?"

"I have recently made the same request of Mr. Gabriel. He has been most cooperative. To be specific, he indicated your recently deceased captain and several members of your crew. You were among them."

"Well, isn't that nice. Looks like things have been working out just great for you, Gabriel." Eileen laughed, and it was a scary sound. "I don't give a damn. I have just one question for you, and then we can put an end to this ridiculous charade. Did you hire the man who killed Stephen Montgomery?"

He looked terrified, a far cry from the man of impeccable dignity that he presented when they had first met. "Oh, listen, ah, Eileen..."

"Just tell me," Eileen said, a little afraid of how disturbed her voice sounded. Her vision was narrowing on Gabriel, and she felt what might have been the first stirrings of madness.

"Well, I did. No, wait," he shouted, because she was straightening her arm to shoot. "Don't do it! It was an accident. I did hire a man to steal the data, but I didn't know he'd be armed, and I sure didn't expect anyone to get killed."

He was almost weeping; it was a pathetic display. One she intended to put an end to shortly. Stephen had parents, siblings, and friends, and he was gone now. Gabriel was a pathetic specimen of humanity who left only sadness in his wake. Killing in his name was as easy as squeezing the trigger. So she did.

As she tightened her grip on the trigger, she caught a glimpse of movement, saw Bronwyn take a flying leap over the table. She was turning her arm to point the gun at her instead, but in the briefest of instants before Bronwyn hit, she knew that it wasn't going to be fast enough.

There was a loud discharge as the gun fired. Bronwyn hit Eileen like a meteor, bearing her hard to the ground and knocking the wind out of her lungs with a loud gasp. The gun clattered away as Eileen tried to scramble to her feet; Bronwyn hit what must've been a nerve cluster because Eileen's entire body spasmed, then started tingling like she'd slammed her elbow.

Bronwyn was standing over her, and she was powerless; it took all of her effort just to breathe.

"Now, Eileen Cromwell, we shall discuss the recovery of your crew and the data."

Chapter 5

Joanna felt like she was losing her mind. She'd had her cry, tried to sleep, and now had been staring at the utterly featureless steel walls of her prison cell for, what, hours now? She could occasionally hear someone moving in the next room, or possibly above her, but no matter how many times she called, nobody responded.

It was amazing how your priorities changed after a few hours in prison. She'd cried for ages, worrying about what her parents would think, how she'd manage to get back to Earth, even stupid things like getting the stuff from her apartment after she'd been released. It had all seemed so overwhelming. Now, after hours behind bars, her priorities had more to do with getting something, anything to happen.

"Excuse me?" She called for the dozenth time, getting no response. She was contemplating just screaming—she had a good screaming voice; the other girls in high school had always admired its piercing quality.

Would it go through a quarter-inch of Lunar steel? Probably. She was willing to find out.

She was charging her lungs for the scream of her life when she heard a scuffle. It sounded like someone was throwing furniture around in the next room, most likely a construction crew getting things set up for the office's actual opening. Maybe they'd be sympathetic to her screaming. Time to charge up a good one, then.

Joanna was taking a deep breath when the door to the cell block slammed open, and a woman was shoved against the wall just next to it. Joanna couldn't see much through the cell's tiny window, but there was something a little familiar about the woman. Someone else who had worked for Gabriel, maybe? The thought of him systematically selling out his entire staff to save his own skin got her blood boiling.

"Go to hell," the woman shouted, only to receive a sharp cuff to the face as another couple of security officers piled into the room after her. The force turned the woman halfway around, so that Joanna could see her face.

"Eileen Cromwell?" Joanna said, rising from the cot.

Sure enough, it was. She looked surprised.

"Wha?" was all she got out before her expression changed to one of extreme pain as the guards brought a prod down on the back of her neck.

They opened up one of the cells across from Joanna, tossed Eileen's pliant body inside, and slammed the door shut.

The cell block was designed for prisoners to be retained on a strictly short-term basis. The cells were partitioned with sheets of steel, with tiny mesh windows in the doors and ventilation ducts on the ceiling. The halogen lights, always at daylight-brightness, seemed to leach what little color the room had.

"Eileen?" Joanna said, her face up against the mesh. "Sorry."

All she got back was a groan.

"What are you doing here, though? I thought that nobody could find you after your captain's death." A sudden wave of sadness coursed through Joanna's body at the thought of what she'd been unable to prevent. "I am so sorry that I couldn't have stopped it. I knew that Gabriel was trying something, and...I should've done more. I'm sorry, Eileen."

Eileen reached up to her cot, and with a sound of extreme exertion, levered her body onto its elastic surface, face raised toward Joanna. "It's okay. Your warning looks like it's gotten you into enough trouble."

"Yeah. I don't know what I'm doing here, to be honest, but I don't think it has anything to do with that." A sudden thought crossed Joanna's mind. "Wait, what are YOU doing here? If you'd been under suspicion of something they should've held you in one of the conventional cells."

"I guess that someone was just a little too...interested for that to be a possibility."

"Gabriel?"

"Yeah. In his defense, I did try to kill him. His pet bitch caught me, though. Damn, was she fast."

Joanna cocked her head. "Wait, you're talking about that dark-skinned woman with all the muscles, right?"

"Right the first time." Eileen groaned again.

"She doesn't work for Gabriel. I thought that she was going to kill him. She came looking for him yesterday when he was out, and I thought she was going to kill *me*."

"It looked like she had him by the short ones. My own bad luck for catching him when she was there." Eileen finally spared a glance around the room. "So why here, I wonder? Maybe whoever that woman works for wants to keep this on the quiet. That'd figure, seeing as you got arrested on no charges."

"Oh, they had charges. 'Industrial espionage.' Whatever that means."

"It means that I owe you an apology, I think." Eileen sat up gingerly, and with another sound of extreme exertion managed to get herself to a sitting position. She stayed there, taking deep, deliberate breaths, back against the wall. "Thank goodness for that one sixth gravity." She turned her head to Joanna. "I think that you got taken because Gabriel or that Bronwyn woman thinks that you have the data that Stephen was trying to sell."

"But you didn't tell me anything! Brighton's surveillance cameras should've proved that."

"Doesn't look like she wanted to take chances."

"What was that data, by the way? Why is everyone so interested in it?"

"Why people are so interested in it, I have no idea. We just happened to see Belt Group's new flagship working the belt. They snagged a huge score right under our noses, too. We watched them tear apart an asteroid full of enough platinum for me to retire, refined the stuff on-site with their fancy on-board smelters, and then they took off toward

Jupiter with tons of precious metals. That was, let's see, almost nine months ago.

"So Stephen gets back to Earth, and hears from a few friends of his that there's serious interest in that data. Nobody knows why, but some feelers are out saying that the data is worth something to the right people—UNASCA, Belt Group, who knows. The one who was willing to pay the most was, you guessed it, Gabriel."

"Why would Belt Group want to pay for data on their own ship?"

"Good question. Maybe someone got greedy. Like I said, that was a once-in-a-lifetime haul." Eileen shifted on her bed. "Now, if you don't mind, I'm going to get some sleep. I feel like someone hit me with a sack of bricks."

Joanna was far too wound up to sleep, but Eileen collapsed and Joanna could hear her breathing softly a few moments later. At least there was someone else here in the same boat, and Eileen seemed much more confident. Maybe she was just as helpless and in the dark, but she seemed much more comfortable there. Joanna had been spending so much time thinking of trivial things, but odds are that she wasn't even close to in as much trouble as the *Mary Ellen*'s crew.

There wasn't much else that Joanna could do but try to fall asleep. She pulled the cot's thin blanket over her still-clothed body, laid her head on the hard, uncomfortable pillow, and tried to sleep.

To her surprise, she managed to doze off, but her sleep was fitful and interrupted by frightening waking dreams. It was almost a blessing when the door to the cell block was thrown open and a security officer ran the tip of his prod over the mess of her cell door, making a tap-tap-tap sound loud enough to be heard in orbit.

"All right, rise and shine. Moving day."

Joanna was up in a flash. "We're being released?"

"Sorry babe, but no. Transfer to higher security up in the tower."

"Who-" Joanna started, but the guard cut her off huffily.

"I don't have time to explain. Come on, get a move on. You too, Raven," he said gesturing to Eileen's dark haired head where it was buried in her pillow.

It took him several minutes to wrangle them—Eileen in particular—into position and shove them out the door. The rest of the office was still packed away much as it had been when Joanna had arrived some hours before, and they were loaded on a very similar looking vehicle.

Their ride up the elevator into the tower wasn't long, but Joanna was surprised at exactly how sensation-starved she'd been. It was almost so overwhelming to be out that thoughts of escape hadn't even occurred to her. And if they'd occurred to Eileen, well, her groaning and head-holding suggested that she wasn't feeling up to it.

They emerged from the elevator on one of the lower levels of Brighton Tower. There, they got off the cart and were marched through a side corridor to a much more complete-looking security office. They were tossed into a conference room that looked as though it had seen much better days, and left there.

The clock on the wall showed that Joanna had been in her other cell for about twelve hours. It had felt like ten times that long.

"You okay?" She whispered to Eileen. There was no obvious surveillance in this room, but there were few parts of Brighton—of the Moon in general—that were not under continual audio and video monitoring. They were watching the two of them, Joanna would've bet.

"I'll survive, probably," Eileen said, lifting herself onto a chair and laying her head on the table.

"What do you think is going on?" Joanna found herself eager to talk, about anything. Being in prison had been bad enough, but this waiting was much, much worse. Eileen responded with a non-committal sound, and Joanna found herself pacing the room, full of so much pent-up energy that she wanted to scream.

At length, the door opened again, and it was that woman! Bronwyn Calleo looked ten times as deadly as when she'd confronted Joanna in her office; her face was still calm and inscrutable, but there was a slight tinge of anger that sent shivers of terror right down Joanna's spine.

"Eileen Cromwell and Joanna Newton. I am afraid that plans have changed. You will need to accompany us to a designated UNASCA facility for a formal inquest."

"Um," Eileen said, raising her head, "on what charges? Industrial espionage?"

"That is correct."

"UNASCA doesn't have authority on Earth."

"We are not going to Earth, Eileen Cromwell. You should know that anything you say can be recorded and used against you in court."

"I must've missed that part of my license packet," Eileen said wryly. She didn't seem intimidated by Bronwyn in the slightest in spite of the increasing vexation that the large woman was showing her. Joanna was jealous. "So, let me guess. This means that you couldn't get a hold of my crew, so we get the squeeze all by ourselves."

Bronwyn twitched. It was subtle, but on a face as immobile as hers she might as well have screamed in frustration. "Plans have changed. You will wait here until a ship is prepared for us, and then we will depart for Earth. Be advised that as of your initial arrest, you have been bound by law and as such, your surveillance waivers, if any, have been nullified."

"Yeah. Whatever. Listen," Eileen said, jerking a thumb back toward Joanna, "would it help if I said that she's completely innocent? She's probably more innocent in general than anyone in UNASCA, so maybe she could just stay here if I go peacefully with you?"

"That decision is not mine to make," Bronwyn said. "You both will accompany me as planned."

"Mmm." Eileen laid her head back on the table. "Let me know when it's time to go."

Bronwyn nodded curtly and made to glide out of the room, but Joanna called, "Wait! Don't UNASCA rights allow us access to legal representation? When do I get to see my lawyer?"

"I..." Bronwyn paused for just a moment. "I cannot answer that question."

With that, she was gone, ignoring Joanna's furrowed brow.

"The more things change, the more things stay the same." Eileen smirked. "Bad luck for us both."

"But I'm innocent. We're innocent!"

"'Then we have nothing to fear,' right?" Eileen's

smirk grew even deeper. "Joanna, you seem like a sweet girl, but are you seriously naive enough to fall back on that hope?"

That shut down the conversation for good for a few moments. Then, after a few minutes, Eileen said, quietly, "Joanna, could you knock on that door and ask for some analgesics for me? This headache just won't go away."

"Sure, Eileen. Sorry again for distracting you before."

"No, it's not from that blow," she sighed. "It's been with me since, well, you know."

"Yeah," Joanna muttered, circling the table and trying the door. The red light on the panel indicated that it was locked, and sure enough, it was. She pressed the call button on the inside several times, got no response, and hammered on the door a few more times. She got no response until she saw the shadow of a security officer gliding by, and he took pity on her and opened the door.

"What?" he snapped, his dark face contorted in anger.

"Sorry to bother you," Joanna said, trying not to let her voice crack, "but my friend really isn't feeling good. Could you spare some analgesics and a glass of water."

"All right, fine," he muttered, shutting the door. A few moments later he returned with a glass and a couple of pills. He sat them on the table, giving Eileen a critical look before turning to leave.

In one smooth motion that utterly belied the pain she claimed to be in, Eileen grabbed the guard's electrolaser, shoved it into his back, and fired in drive-stun mode. The man twitched once and fell slowly to the floor. Eileen caught him as he did and laid him down out of view of the door.

Her back to the now unlocked door, Joanna stared, transfixed at the sight.

"What?" Eileen said as she went through the man's pockets. "I'll be damned if I'm going to have my rights trampled on. Either way, what they're doing to you and I is unjust and I'm damned pissed off about it." She tossed the man's weapon to Joanna, who caught it as if she was afraid that it was going to explode.

"What? You know how those work, right?" Eileen was moving to the door. She wasn't graceful or even competent in her movements; she'd obviously not spent a lot of time on the Moon.

Joanna stared at the weapon in her hands. It felt like it weighed a million kilos, and she couldn't tear her eyes away from it. Eileen was trying to escape from prison. Some part of her mind objected strenuously in legal terms, but the bigger part of her mind was just terrified.

"Hey, you with me? We need to get the hell out of here. My ship should still be on landing pad 22L, if they haven't moved it. As long as the *Mary Ellen* is still in orbit, we should be able to reach her before they even know that anything is wrong. If not, well, we can always make it to Earth with the shuttle alone."

"But, but," Joanna pointed to the unconscious guard. Things were happening too fast. She felt like she needed to sit down, or throw up, or both.

"Come on," Eileen said, impatiently. "You can either stay to get recaptured, or you can come with me and we can work out the rest later."

Without waiting for any other response, she left. Joanna hesitated for a moment, thought of those hours alone in the jail cell, and reluctantly followed.

The security office where they'd been stuffed was only a very small precinct office. There was another conference room like the one they'd been locked into, a door to a small cell block, and a few officers, the warden and motor pool managers. They weren't prepared for much of an escape attempt, much less Eileen bursting through the prison block door, already blasting away.

The electrolaser fired what looked like a solid, perfectly linear bolt of lightning, making a sound like thunder. When it hit the desk officer in the front office, he crumpled without a sound just as the guard in the conference room had. Likewise with the officer emerging from the corner office.

That left just the two of them standing in a silent, ozone smelling office. After a few seconds, even that was gone.

"My good heavens," Joanna muttered, fist in her mouth as she surveyed the damage. "What the hell am I doing?"

"Taking this. Come on, let's go!" Eileen tossed her another stunner, and then she left the office with perfect casualness, as though she had just been a guest rather than a prisoner.

It was only after following Eileen out the door that Joanna realized that she'd crossed an invisible boundary. Not a physical one, that was obvious enough, but an emotional one. She was no longer unjustly imprisoned, but she had now indisputably broken the law, one that she could not claim ignorance of.

It was terrifying, and it was driven home a few moments later as Eileen hammered the elevator controls. The smooth voice of a virtual intelligence blared out from hidden speakers, his voice seeming to fill the entire space of the tower.

"Attention residents of Brighton Colony. This is a general security alert. Two prisoners have escaped the custody of Brighton Security. They are known to be armed and dangerous. If you see them, please alert Security immediately. Do not attempt to apprehend them yourself." Meanwhile, the displays that lined the corridors of the Tower, and certainly those that lined the concourses below as well, had replaced their normal advertising content with pictures and text descriptions of Eileen and Joanna.

"I...I don't think I can do this, Eileen," Joanna said, dropping her electrolaser and backing away from the elevator. "This is getting to be way too much."

"What? It's too late to back out now. You want to get locked up without trial in a prison out in the middle of nowhere? Are you crazy?"

"But I'm a criminal! I don't want to be a criminal! I just want to live a normal life watching after a desk. That's all that I ever wanted. This type of excitement is so incredibly far beyond anything that I ever-"

Eileen cut her off by grabbing her shoulders and giving them a hard shake. "Hey! Cut it out. You can stay if you want, but if you want to come with me, you need to decide now. Hmmm," Eileen turned toward the elevators. The displays indicated that the cars were all stopped at the Tower's ground level, which meant that security had locked them down.

"Quick," Eileen said, whirling back. "Is there another way down? Stairs?"

Mute, Joanna pointed toward a door a few steps on down the corridor that bore the label "Maintenance access only."

There was a cry from behind them. Two security guards were running down the corridor toward them, pulling their electrolasers as they went.

It was like a large animal was bearing down on her. Reasonably she might have stayed there, surrendered, and everything might have turned out okay. But when there were several large men gliding down the hall, using the low gravity to give them superhuman bounds, drawing weapons, it all got a little more confused.

Joanna turned and followed Eileen toward the maintenance access.

Gabriel took another strong pull from his bottle. Bronwyn had been very careful, very controlling, but she hadn't restricted his access to alcohol. Maybe she figured that it would make him more pliant and controllable. She was probably right, but that didn't stop him from taking advantage.

Bronwyn returned to the office after taking a call in the outer lobby. Funny that just a day or so ago—had it only been a day?—Joanna would be out there right now taking appointments and running interference. That had been a good life. Perhaps it would come back once Bronwyn finally realized that he had nothing to show her.

"Your tickets have been processed. You will be

returning to Earth tonight at 2000 hours."

Gabriel blinked. "What? Returning to Earth? What the hell for?"

"You have been formally recalled." She tossed a computer slate down on his desk. His mailbox was open, and the top unread message read, in official UNASCA header, "Notice of Recall."

Wonderful.

Gabriel blinked. "Do I at least have time to pack up my things?"

"They will be sent for."

Even better. He looked forward to hearing about what the people who were to pack his things up found.

He was just starting to deliberate on the wisdom of protesting the order when the alarm sounded. It took Gabriel a moment to identify it, since he'd never heard it in action before: security alert. General lockdown.

Bronwyn listened to the alert without moving, then turned angrily to Gabriel. It was marvelous what that woman could do with just a raise of an eyebrow, the slight change of the angle of her mouth. "Your doing, I presume?" she said.

"I had absolutely nothing to do with it," Gabriel said, inclining his head. He still had a bit of dignity left, and he was going to ride it as far as he could. "You've been with me this entire time. I've scarcely had the chance to use the restroom, what with your supervision."

Bronwyn huffed a bit at that, but didn't rise to the bait. Pity. "Very well. Your timetable has been accelerated. Please remain here until I return for you." She took one gliding step before turning back for dramatic effect. "Be advised that your recall notice has attached to it a writ of pursuit, authorizing licensed individuals to track down and apprehend you by force should you fail to abide strictly by the terms of your contract. Be further advised that I am so licensed."

With that, she was gone. And he was stuck.

Gabriel toyed with the idea of going on the run anyway, just to irk that stone-faced woman, but he decided against it. Too undignified. But he just couldn't resist trying something out on her.

Bronwyn hadn't cut command access from his console yet. Rather, she'd ordered it cut, but the technician had owed Gabriel a favor, one he'd cashed in with an significant glance.

Sitting up gingerly, feeling like the local gravity was six times Earth instead of one sixth, Gabriel typed the override password into his console. With that access restored, it was trivial to call up the colony directory and patch himself into Kurita, head of Brighton security.

"It's been a hell of a long time since I've heard from you," Kurita said, sounding surprised.

"What? I've been out of commission all of two days."

"Yeah, out of commission," Kurita said, making a drinking gesture.

"I'm serious. I find myself in dire straits. Some representative from Belt Group slash UNASCA is putting the squeeze on me. It's intolerable. And now I find out that I'm being recalled."

"So can I have your office?"

"Damn it, this is serious." Gabriel hit the table with

his fist. "I'm sending you a picture of this woman. I want you to do what you can to make her uncomfortable. All in the name of the lockdown, of course." He tapped a few commands, transmitting the picture that his office surveillance system had discretely captured.

"Received. Hmm. Not your usual type."

"To say the least, but circumstances have changed. And you're welcome to the office. I daresay I won't be needing it in the very near future."

"I do. And if this is the last we talk, then thank you. I've greatly enjoyed our professional relationship."

"Agreed. Goodbye." Kurita leaned forward and the image disappeared. Pity they'd never be able to go drinking together again. The man had such tremendous taste in women and liquor. He only hoped that he'd get a chance to find out what security would try to pull against Bronwyn.

Ah well. Nothing he could do about any of that now. Another strong pull on the drink bottle helped put his mind at ease.

Joanna floated down the stairs with Eileen. She could hear security slam through the maintenance doors above them, one of the officers gruffly issuing orders to his men.

"Eileen!" Joanna whispered harshly. Her heart was beating incredibly fast, even though the gliding jumps weren't very taxing in the low gravity.

"I heard them." Eileen was only a flight ahead of her. They were just a few stories up from the surface, but they were tall stories and they didn't have much of a lead on the security officers.

"Eileen," Joanna repeated.

"What?" Eileen took a corner sharply, bounding down the next flight of stairs.

"How are we going to reach the monorail?" Joanna landed right behind her, looking up through the wire stairs to see the first of the security force just two levels above. "It's going to be locked down. And that's saying nothing about getting to your ship."

"We'll figure something out, I'm sure."

That didn't do much to reassure Joanna. When the two of them burst out of the maintenance door at the lower level, Joanna's heart sank even further.

They'd emerged in the crowded monorail depot and cargo transfer lock that made up the entirety of Brighton Tower's ground level. It wasn't that heavily traveled, since there was nothing to see or do there, and the monorail was only used by ship crews and tourists. However, a cargo ship must've just landed, because at the moment there was a much larger than average number of cargo managers, crate busters, and maintenance personnel operating the power lifters and skiffs necessary to move the cargo about.

They had perhaps a second to catch their breath. "There!" was all Eileen had a chance to shout, and without even seeing what she was pointing at, Joanna followed. The situation was all so unreal, she felt like she was on autopilot.

However, it soon became clear what Eileen was referring to. A large enclosed cargo hauler, loaded down with containers, was powered up in the middle of the cavernous space. Joanna knew that these models were secured against vacuum, but it wasn't considered reliable for industrial work. Most of the crew ended up using their space suits anyway.

"Stop them!" shouted the security officers, slamming through the door behind them. Joanna risked a look back and saw that they were close. Very close.

They both had their electrolasers out, bringing them into firing position.

"Joanna," Eileen said, coming to a stop.

"What?"

"Run!" She knelt and fired.

Eileen's first shot went wide, but the second hit a guard dead on, and he crumpled like a sack of meat. The other guard, however, had taken the time to aim his shot. He was not firing from the hip.

Joanna felt herself freeze as Eileen was hit. The blow was glancing as Eileen tried to roll out of the way at the last minute, but with a stunner it didn't matter. She still collapsed like a sack of rocks.

And then it was just Joanna and the last security officer. He slowed down his running glide, looking much more confident. Joanna felt her gaze flick over the scene, trying to find some inspiration, something that she could do. She felt helpless—without Eileen here, she was far, far beyond her own abilities and experience.

The guard was radioing in his report as he gestured at Joanna with his weapon. Stand over there, he was saying, next to the crawler. Joanna couldn't tell what he was saying, so dense with jargon it was, but she understood that command well enough.

He walked over to Eileen, weapon still trained on Joanna, and kicked her unconscious body. He just hauled back and laid into her. Joanna winced as the blow connected, winced for Eileen who was unable to do so. This might be far beyond her own experience, but there were some things that she just knew were wrong.

There was a commotion at the far end of the depot. Joanna couldn't make it out clearly, but-

It was Bronwyn. In her massiveness, she was obvious from across the depot, making giant, graceful strides toward their position. That must've been who the officer was reporting in to—she certainly seemed to have Brighton security by the throat.

This time it was different, though. Rather than the annoyed but respectful tones that security had used with her in the past, this officer half-turned toward her and shouted, gruffly, "All right, hold there. We've got these two well in hand."

"Pardon, officer, but UNASCA has granted me extradition privileges for these prisoners. I require-"

"Hold up there, blondie." The guard said, turning to attempt to face Bronwyn and Joanna at the same time. "Directives have changed. Word is from Mr. Kurita that we're supposed to take these two into local custody and *under local jurisdiction*. And that's what I'm going to do."

"Don't be foolish," Bronwyn said. "You already demonstrated your incompetence in that regard." She took a large step toward Joanna.

"I said hold it right there! Don't take another damned step." The guard's weapon was now pointed at Bronwyn, whose normal, implacable look was visibly melting into annoyance, and in turn transmuting into anger.

"Officer, do not force me to take drastic steps. I require..."

Joanna could see the officer weigh the options in his head before firing. He'd made the wrong decision, though. That left Joanna to make hers.

Bronwyn saw the same thing. With a single practiced move, she lunged forward and struck the man's wrist in some particular way that sent his weapon flying. As the man stared in open mouthed awe at his now empty weapon hand, she struck again—one, two, three blows with a closed fist and the man was on the ground.

Bronwyn relaxed for a moment, taking in the scene with some pride. "I would say that you've made the wrong decision. So has Gabriel, I would gamble. As for you, Joanna Newton," she said, turning.

She didn't finish her sentence. Joanna had seen what had happened to the guard and was frankly terrified of it happening to her. So she'd lunged for Eileen's weapon while Bronwyn was dispatching the guard, and in the moment that Bronwyn turned for her, she fired.

Bronwyn had unbelievable reflexes. Even as Joanna was pulling the trigger and the realization of what was going on sank in, she bent over backwards and threw her body to the side, and Joanna missed. In horror, she fired again, and this time the Moon's lighter gravity betrayed Bronwyn: she'd kicked off with such power that she was left floating, unable to affect her course. Joanna tagged her out of the air.

She collapsed just as all the others had. Joanna stood, transfixed, among the scattered, unconscious bodies. The workers were starting to close in, equally in awe. Joanna could hear them discussing whether they should alert security or try to take her in themselves. It seemed that none of them were eager to be the first to try; they'd certainly get blasted.

Joanna had never been muscular, and after a few months on the Moon her strength had degraded even more, despite UNASCA-mandated exercise. But adrenaline gave her strength, and she grabbed the back of Eileen's jumpsuit and hauled her toward the waiting cargo vehicle, one hand still pointing the stunner at the assembling crowd.

There were calls of, "Just put the weapon down, hon.," and "Come on, it's okay," but Joanna didn't listen, and she didn't stop hauling Eileen until they were inside the cargo hauler.

The crawler—little more than a sealed, bulbous cabin mounted on a treaded flatbed with a crane—wasn't going to be as simple to operate as Joanna had expected. There were few controls that she could easily identify, and there was no obvious way to turn the thing on. There was a throttle, and a steering wheel, and a bunch of blank displays that could've been anything from radios to sensors. Making sure that Eileen wasn't going to fall out of the passenger seat, Joanna ran panicked hands over the lifeless buttons and levers.

Outside, the first guard that Eileen had blasted was twitching. Several of the workers scrambled over to him and tried to help him up—Joanna could see as much between frantic glances over the controls. She poured over the list of different displays on the multifunction units, hoping that one of them would relate to starting the damned thing and steering it. Why couldn't they be as simple as the cars at home?

Joanna was starting to panic. As she glanced up at the crowd, she saw that now the second guard was getting to his feet, his expression angry, and several of the workers, no doubt much, much more familiar with the vehicle than her, were rooting about for tools. If they found some way of disabling the crawler, she was a goner.

Well, if she couldn't get the crawler going, maybe she could do so for Eileen.

"Come on, Eileen! I need some help here!" She shouted. In the confined space of the crawler's control bubble, her voice seemed unnaturally loud. Eileen wasn't moving, and there were people approaching the crawler with power tools and great caution.

Quickly, Joanna unlocked the driver's door, leaned out, and fired the stunner wildly at the approaching workers. The aim that had tagged Bronwyn was gone; rather, she was just firing at anything that moved. She didn't hit anyone, but they scattered and fell back.

She locked the door again, and checked Eileen. This time, the woman jerked when prodded, but all the shouting Joanna could manage didn't elicit any other response.

Fine, so it was up to her. "Come on, baby. Please work for me just this once. Just give me something!" She pounded a fist on the console in frustration, then glanced out the curved window to check on the situation in the bay.

What she saw nearly drove her into a panic. Bronwyn was already getting up; she must've had an iron constitution.

Near tears, Joanna started hammering on knobs and throwing any switch she thought might have some chance of starting the vehicle or getting it to move.

At last she got lucky—pressing an orange button caused a whirr of activity somewhere in the crawler's innards, and the thing came to life.

It was like a tank. Now that it was started, the controls were easy enough to figure out—one lever was the throttle for the right side, and one lever for the left. They could be locked together to move straight ahead. There were some other levers that seemed to control a lifting arm on the crawler's top that she ignored.

She wasn't sure how she was going to get out the sealed cargo lock of the depot, but at least she was moving now, and Bronwyn couldn't do anything to her while she was randomly, haphazardly swinging thousands of kilograms of heavy machinery around.

Joanna kind of liked it.

There was a groan from the seat next to her, and Joanna looked down to see Eileen stirring. She felt tension drain from her limbs in relief as the other woman sat up with bleary eyes.

"Are we still on the Moon? It feels like there's ten gravities, not a sixth of one."

Joanna laughed, nearly giddy. She wasn't sure whether it was fear or continuing relief that drove the laughter. "I have no idea what to do, Eileen. I've never done this before. I don't even like action movies!"

"Ah, okay. Hang on. We need to switch seats." When they had done so, Eileen took the controls with more assurance. "Joanna, check out that number above the airlock, and dial it into the radio. That should open the thing, if they haven't locked it down."

Joanna keyed in the numbers as Eileen had indicated. For one horrible moment, nothing happened, and they were still headed toward the opening at top crawler speed. Worse, Bronwyn was nowhere in sight.

Then the door lurched once and started rolling up. The heavy panes of vacuum resistant material crawled up out of their way, and the vehicle came to a stop inside the cargo airlock. Another couple of clicks and the door closed.

They were now alone inside the airlock with no way to open the other side.

"Second frequency, hurry!" Eileen said, pointing urgently to the numbers. Joanna keyed this in just the same, but the only result was warning flashers inside the lock blinking yellow.

"That means that there's a failsafe fault," Eileen said, frowning. "There's someone or something in the airlock that the computer thinks won't survive vacuum exposure."

"Bronwyn," Joanna said quietly.

"Yeah. I could override it if I knew their system better, but as it stands now I wouldn't lay odds on it." Eileen steeled herself. "We're going to have to punch through the outer door. This thing isn't fast, but it's heavy, and mass is going to do the trick."

"Won't that kill her?"

"The only thing that could be worse would be her surviving. Now hang on, I don't want to kill us."

Joanna kept a careful eye out as Eileen put the crawler in reverse, pointing the rear toward the outer door. That was when they saw her: Bronwyn was standing directly in front of them, wearing nothing but her station clothes, and looking as angry as Joanna had ever seen her. Even now, in the crawler's sealed cabin, Joanna could barely stand to make eye contact.

"You ready?" Eileen asked, gritting her teeth.

"Yeah, yeah," Joanna said, doing likewise. "Go for it."

There was a strange sensation. The rear MFD showed them trundling toward the doors with ever increasing speed, and directly in front of them Joanna could see Bronwyn taking long, graceful strides toward the airlock's emergency shelter. Not that it would do her much good if the outer door was breached.

In the seconds, or microseconds before the crawler hit the door with thousands of kilograms of mass, Joanna had just a moment to reflect on how improbable this entire situation was. She had only been in her bed thirty-six hours before, and now she was on the run from the law, risking her life, and for what? This dark haired girl that she knew so little about? It sure as hell wasn't for Gabriel's sake, she reflected darkly.

And that was all that she had time to reflect on. The crawler hit the door with teeth-jarring force. Joanna was thrown forward in her seat as things happened in slow motion.

The crawler stopped just as quickly and just as incompletely as it would've on Earth, but the gravity was so much less that it bounced high in the hair, a meter or more, since it hit off of its center of gravity and the cab was levered upward.

Joanna was just cognizant that her back was pointing downward at a forty five degree angle, and then they fell back down, slowly at first but with increasing speed.

When they hit again, Joanna's restraints automatically tightened, keeping her from flying out of her seat. As it was, they were knocked around the cabin hard, and a few loose instruments that the crawler's actual operator had not secured went bouncing around.

Then, all was quiet for a moment, except for a persistent and nagging hiss. First Joanna thought it was all in her head, just a side effect of her near-concussion, but then she heard Eileen swear, and the curse carried just enough fear in its anger and frustration that Joanna was able to make a guess as to what the sound meant.

"We have a leak, don't we."

Eileen just nodded.

"Then what are we going to do?" Fear causes increased respiratory activity, which taxes a strained life support system, she remembered hearing in the boring safety briefing that had been a part of her first day on Brighton. But how long did they have? How taxed were their supplies anyway?

"I think," Eileen said, her voice tense, "that we need to hurry."

Chapter 6

Ben pulled himself through the hatch into the *Mary Ellen*'s bridge and floated over to his station. Actually, Melissa noted, he didn't take up his station, he took up the commander's station, the one that had been Stephen's—she felt a sharp, wrenching blast of grief, forced it back down—and was now technically Eileen's.

Of course, Eileen wasn't here to claim it. She wasn't anywhere, as far as Melissa could see. She and Crazyhorse had been monitoring the public DSN feeds coming up from Brighton and hadn't yet found word one about Eileen. Either she was keeping quiet, which seemed unlikely, or her actions had been suppressed, which seemed far-fetched. Still, it was possible; information control was one of UNASCA's few strong suits.

At least they knew she wasn't dead. That sort of information was always the hardest to suppress. Melissa hoped.

"Still nothing?" Ben asked, his hands tracing the

shape of the command console. He didn't look at her.

"Still nothing," Melissa confirmed, her tone equally soft.

Ben was quiet for a moment, staring at his hands as he caressed one control after another, his mind obviously elsewhere. Then, "She has fifteen minutes. Then you'll ask for permission to undock, and we can finally get this worthless trip over with."

"Ben, she's the captain," Melissa reminded him gently.

"We have responsibilities," Ben snapped, flicking between screens until he brought up the orbit information display, "to people besides the captain. We've got to unload this cargo, got to get paid. If Eileen's okay, she can buy a ticket to Earth on a public transport."

"Ben, I don't think it would kill us to stay for just a *few* hours longer."

"Damn it," Ben said, finally whirling to face her. "We need to move on. Eileen can't hold this entire ship hostage with her stupid revenge fantasies. What do you think Stephen would say about that?" He nearly choked on those last words, and averted his eyes. When he spoke again, his voice was softer. "There's more to this ship than just Eileen."

Melissa fought down another surge of sadness, this time tempered with a dose of anger. When she trusted herself not to say something she'd regret, she spoke slowly but firmly. "Ben. We can afford to give her a couple of hours. You aren't captain. I can make Crazyhorse override anything you try to do."

Ben jerked as if shot. "You're joking."

"Try me." Her knuckles were aching from their death grip on the edge of her console.

They held each other's gaze for a long moment. Melissa was sure that he was going to put her promise to the test, but Crazyhorse spoke up and in so doing, prevented possible bloodshed.

"Excuse me, but I have information from the surface that you might find interesting."

"What?" Ben barked, not taking his eyes off Melissa.

"An all-points bulletin was just issued for two prisoners who have staged a break from a Brighton Security holding cell. No names are provided, but the description of one of the prisoners matches Eileen precisely." Crazyhorse's calm, even voice drained some of the tension out of the room.

Some, but not all. "Who's the other prisoner?" Ben asked, *still* not breaking his stare.

"As I said, no names were provided, but here is the official description: 'female, 1.6 meters, 25 to 30 standard years old, brown hair, blue eyes, light skin.'"

It didn't sound familiar to Melissa, but Ben frowned, his gaze drifting off her. "That's, um...Joanna. Joanna Newton. Assistant to the administrator; she escorted us to our hotel the other day. She and Eileen seemed to hit it off."

"That doesn't make any sense; if she's the administrator's assistant, what would she be doing in prison?" Melissa turned to her console, instructed Crazyhorse to start a search correlating this story with any others he could find.

"You didn't meet Thomas Gabriel. It would not surprise me at all to hear that something weird is going down." He paused, absently rubbing his nose. "Well, it doesn't matter. If Eileen's in trouble, we can't just leave. Damn it all," he cursed, turning back to his console.

"So," Melissa drew out the word, "what are we going to do?"

Ben sighed. "Stand by to undock. Crazyhorse, plot us a geosynchronous orbit as close to Brighton as possible, and contact UNASCA control for authorization."

"Understood," the computer replied, and Melissa saw the orbital dynamics take shape on her console.

"Putting us in a good position? You're not going to launch a rescue, are you?"

"Hell no," Ben scoffed. "But we can't just abandon her. If she manages to extract herself—and I wouldn't put anything past Eileen if she's in one of her moods—then I want to be ready to receive her."

"Sir, I'm obligated to inform you that harboring a prisoner is a serious violation of the UNASCA criminal code."

"You have to search your libraries long for that info, Crazyhorse?" Ben snapped.

"As I said, I'm obligated to inform you, not to stop you." Crazyhorse was not offended.

"Good. Melissa, let Almika know we're undocking in five."

Eileen threw the crawler into gear and they took off across the lunar landscape at what Joanna considered a distinctly unimpressive speed. The crawler's treads kicked up dust behind them in a perfect parabola.

"I don't want to distract you," Joanna said, swallowing hard, "but is this as fast as this thing goes?"

"I guess so," Eileen said, wincing as they hit a rock, lurching the vehicle up hard. "I think we damaged the engine or transmission or something when that door shut on us."

"And, um, how much air do we have left?" Joanna wasn't sure she wanted to hear the answer.

Eileen glanced significantly at a small analog dial mounted on the dashboard, then turned her attention back to the sharp gray expanse of the lunar landscape. The dial's needle was still well within the green zone, but it was moving visibly toward the red. And the green zone was not very big. And the hissing noise had not grown any quieter.

"I'm going to see if I can find the leak," Joanna said, unfastening her restraints and turning around in her seat.

"Good luck," Eileen muttered, not turning her attention away from the landscape.

The hiss seemed to be coming from the back part of the cabin. Joanna stuck her head behind the seats, turning her head back and forth, trying to triangulate the sound. It was definitely toward the floor.

"So, where are we going, exactly?" She asked, crawling as far as she could toward the cabin's rear, bracing herself as the crawler lurched over another rock.

"My ship is on pad nineteen," Eileen said. "I'll open the airlock remotely and we can get in that way."

Something in the tone of her voice...

"But Eileen, we don't have any space suits. How are we going to get aboard?"

Eileen didn't respond. Joanna glanced up, saw her jaw clenched, eyes staring fixedly out the front of the cabin, and decided that pressing for more information wasn't worth it. It was exactly as bad as she had feared.

But that was in the future. It wouldn't matter if they ran out of air first. With deliberate effort, she forced it out of her mind and returned to trying to find the leak. She felt around the floor with a hand, hoping to feel a hint of airflow that might point toward a cracked or ruptured part. The slightest breeze seemed to be pulling toward the driver's side, and she stretched her hand that direction.

She found it, after a fashion. A complex-looking set of conduits filled the cabin behind the two seats, most of them bolted to the frame of the crawler. The air was leaking somewhere deep in those conduits, too deep for her to reach. And now that she was close, the hiss was unsettlingly loud.

"I found it, but I can't reach it," Joanna said, trying to get her head closer. Maybe there was some way...

But there wasn't. She could only find a general area, not a specific leak. No way to patch it, then.

She sat up with a sigh, hands anxiously kneading the seat's fabric. Brighton Tower still dominated the landscape behind them, receding ever-so-slowly. Joanna jerked, leaned forward, squinting.

Moving lights at the base of the tower. She couldn't quite make out what was going on, but whatever they were, dust was getting kicked up in irregular patterns.

Oh, hell.

"Eileen, they're chasing us!" Joanna turned forward, scrambling for her restraints.

"Oh, good," Eileen said, grinning slightly.

"What? Are you serious?"

"Sure I'm serious," Eileen said, whirling the crawler around so that a hulking Shuttle Alpha laden with Orbital Dynamics cargo pods interrupted line of sight with their pursuers. "It means that at the very least, they want us alive. It's not like they'd bother trying to shoot us if they wanted us dead. They could just wait for us to run out of air."

"Unless they've figured out what you're planning!"

Eileen glanced in the rear view display, her grin vanishing. "Oh. Right."

"So what are you going to do?" Joanna tried not to let her voice rise too high.

"Um." Eileen jerked the controls again, driving the crawler under the wing of a massive lander from TTM24, LLC. Joanna glanced at it wistfully as they passed; it was the same ship that she'd been on when she first landed on the Moon. If someone had joked that she'd be passing it as she ran for her life a few months later, she would've found the idea hilarious. In retrospect, it didn't seem that funny.

"I think they're gaining on us," Joanna said, glancing at the rear view. In fact, that was a dramatic understatement; the Security trikes were much faster than this heavy cargo crawler. They were just passing the Shuttle Alpha and gaining rapidly on the TTM24 ship.

"You don't say." Eileen gritted her teeth. Joanna looked anxiously between her and the rear view, and felt her heart sink. There wasn't going to be any escape. Nothing Eileen or Joanna could do would make their vehicle move any faster. They were outpaced, outnumbered, outgunned even. They were going to get caught.

"There's my ship," Eileen said, her voice betraying just the slightest hint of strain. "Pity."

They had just passed another Shuttle Alpha on pad seventeen, and Joanna could see the triangular form of a Shuttle Delta resting on the next pad. She recognized the livery; it was the same ship she'd greeted with Gabriel a few days or a million years before. The name *Fisher King* was painted in dust-scarred yellow along the ship's side.

Joanna caught movement out of the corner of her eye, and saw that one of the trikes had caught up to them. They were insubstantial vehicles, just a life-support bubble in a three-wheeled frame. They half-drove, half-flew in the light lunar gravity, moving easily three times faster than their crawler.

"On our right, Eileen!"

Eileen glanced over, frowned, *jerked* the controls that direction. The crawler almost overbalanced; in the lower gravity with so little cargo, the indelicate maneuver was almost too much for them. Joanna could see the Security driver jerk in surprise, running over a rock in the process. The light trike flew a dozen meters into the air, landing with gentle slowness some distance ahead.

Just as Joanna was recovering from that first maneuver, she saw a flash of color to the left. She managed to suppress most of a shriek as one of the trikes steered toward them. Eileen cursed, jerked away, nearly over-corrected, bringing the crawler's treads most of the way off the dusty ground.

The Security man got overconfident, crowded into them. Wearing a manic grin, Eileen jerked the controls again *toward him.*

The crawler might've been light without any cargo, but the trikes were far lighter. Joanna saw the trike's driver staring at them in horror as the bulk of the crawler slammed into his light vehicle. A horrible crunch, felt more than heard, reverberated through Joanna's seat and suddenly the trike fell behind them. The structure supporting its front wheels looked twisted and strange as the Security vehicle spun around to an awkward halt.

"Okay," Eileen panted. She reached for the radio panel, tapping keys as fast as she could. They'd almost arrived at pad nineteen, Joanna saw, trying to catch her own breath. The other trike was circling back around, but it was anyone's game now. Her chest felt constricted, and she was breathing hard.

In sudden realization, she stared in horror at the air pressure meter. The needle had buried itself well in the red zone. There was maybe one needle diameter between its current reading and "zero."

"Joanna, listen to me carefully," Eileen said, her voice clipped and precise. "We're going to have to go outside, okay?"

"Okay." Joanna was barely listening. She watched with growing horror as the intact trike, fully recovered, steered a beeline toward them.

"I need you to hyperventilate to get as much oxygen as possible. When I tell you, you need to exhale as fully as you can, okay? Exhale, or you're dead. You understand?"

"Okay," Joanna said again, eyes fixed on the hypnotic sight of the trike gunning for them.

"Breathe, damn it!"

Joanna jerked, started taking deep breaths as they

crawler ground to a stop. They were right up against the head-level airlock on the Shuttle Delta's nose, the cone splayed wide like the maw of some metal beast.

"Okay, exhale. Exhale!"

Joanna forced air out of her lungs, wrenching her diaphragm to empty her chest. Then, without warning, Eileen popped the emergency seals.

The air pressure remaining inside the crawler blew the hatch clear off. She felt a sharp pain in her ears and the cabin was instantly filled with white vapor that persisted an infinitesimal moment before behind sucked clear out the open hatch.

Joanna felt her chest heave as the last dregs of air were sucked out of her lungs. Daggers of cold plunged into her flesh, cutting clear to bone as she watched Eileen jump out of the crawler in perfect silence. She felt the saliva on her tongue bubble and boil, watched in horror as bruises spread over her exposed flesh.

As she stumbled out after Eileen, a lesson from her emergency training jumped to the forefront of her mind. In vacuum, a human has at most ten seconds of useful consciousness. How many seconds had it been?

Removed from the shade inside the crawler and exposed to the full force of the Sun, her skin burned as though afire. Joanna took two steps toward the open airlock, her lungs aching, black spots forming in front of her eyes. She tripped at the airlock's threshold, reached out a hand to grab the burning hot airlock ladder, falling to her knees in the dust.

How many seconds left? Her mind felt fuzzy. The black spots were expanding, crowding out her vision. Her muscles aching, she wrenched herself up into the airlock, groping with blind desperation for handholds. Was Eileen in there? Where were the controls?

Joanna was so tired. Would someone work the controls? Was she supposed to? Even as she considered this, she felt her mind drift back to Earth, to the forested hills around her home. So different from the stark, black-and-white lunar landscape.

Some time later, she fell asleep.

Chapter 7

The trip back to the *Mary Ellen* was hellish. Eileen's skin was covered with a blotchy red network of ruptured capillaries, and she could feel sunburn blisters swelling even under her clothing. And Joanna was even worse off; she'd suffered more from hypoxia and had spent most of the trip semi-conscious with an oxygen mask around her face. Eileen felt like she could've slept for days, but that wasn't in the cards. She had to fly.

Fortunately, Brighton Security was reluctant to force entry into the Shuttle Delta, which gave Eileen enough time to run an abbreviated startup sequence. Even though a single fault might mean their death, there wasn't time to check every system. Risking her life a second time in as many minutes wasn't as quite as hard as the first time, and in a few moments, she had the engines online.

A hard burst from the hover engines sent the hardsuited Security men scrambling away, leaving *Fisher King* hovering a dozen meters over the lunar surface while Eileen worked through the agony in her skull and plotted an escape course. She muttered a quick thanks that the *Mary Ellen* was in an easily accessible orbit.

By the time they'd docked, Eileen was exhausted, in pain all over, and feeling bad for Joanna, who had seemed to take everything even worse. Doing her best to avoid Joanna's blistered skin, Eileen helped her through the airlock and into the *Mary Ellen*, where the rest of the crew was waiting in nervous anxiety, nearly bouncing in the zero gravity.

To his credit, Ben had waited until they'd reached the rotating habitation rings and the medical bay before asking any questions, and once they *had* arrived, he listened patiently while Eileen explained what had happened. She gave as thorough a recounting of the story as she could, trying to ignore the looks of increasing horror on the faces of the rest of the crew, trying to ignore the discomfort of increased gravity.

"You know that wherever we put into port, UNASCA's going to take us into custody? We can't go back to Earth, unless you want to get stuck there." Ben said, leaning against the autodoc cabinet and folding his arms.

Eileen re-read the autodoc's instructions and broke off the cap of a red combi-pen, jabbed the needle into her thigh. "Yes, Ben. I know." Her head pounded, her entire body ached from vacuum exposure, and she was starving. Ben was lucky that she didn't stab him in the eye with her needle.

"But there are still places we can go, right?" Eileen took another of the red pens, winced as she injected it.

"I was looking forward to spending some time on

Earth, not on Titania," Ben snapped. "I hear that Uranus is cold this time of year."

Eileen grabbed a pouch of triexetine anti-radiation meds and slammed the cabinet door shut. "You think I wanted it to be this way? If you were so obsessed with your vacation, you should've just left the two of us behind. Two corpsicles might only be a minor inconvenience."

Ben worked his mouth like he was going to come back with something really biting, but he visibly restrained himself. "Fine, Eileen. Sorry. To you too, Joanna. But seriously...this ship can't take a long haul into the outer system. And neither can her crew."

"There are places we can go in the inner system, Ben. You're probably not going to be crazy about them, but they're there."

"And what about me?" Joanna asked, taking Eileen's offer of another triexetine pouch. The color of her skin was already starting to normalize after the injection.

"We've put you in a ton of danger, and we're not going anywhere safer. There's got to be some way to return you to Earth. UNASCA can't touch you there." Even as she said it, Eileen realized it wasn't realistic.

"We try to approach Earth," Ben said, his vigor having died down a little bit, "UNASCA will try an intercept. And even if they don't, they'll repossess the ship and arrest us if we ever leave the surface again. You think you could handle that?"

Eileen pursed her lips. He was right—UNASCA couldn't risk that the *Mary Ellen* would do something stupid. Of course, if they thought that she would do something stupid they'd just blow her out of the sky. So it was a damned fine line to walk. And Ben was right—there was no way she could handle permanent exile to Earth. She could barely handle her occasional visits.

"So Earth is out of the question. Fine." Eileen tapped a few more instructions into the autodoc. "Ditto the belt; can't lay low with the kind of traffic they get out there. Jupiter might be an option—I'm sure that we could get some Free Jovian sympathizers to hide us—but like you said, I don't think this ship can take a trip to the outer system."

There was a chorus of reluctant agreement from those present. It was an open secret that the population of Jupiter's various moons was no longer, in the strictest sense, under UNASCA control. It seemed like every few days while they were out in the belt that they got unauthorized transmissions from rebel groups. They'd show up one day, issue a manifesto, and then they'd read in the news that the group was raided and dissolved by UNASCA agents. And right next to that story would be news of another new group taking credit for some new sabotage. It didn't take a scholar to figure out what was going on.

"We can only handle a trip to an inner system destination. I can only think of one place where we might have a reliable ally." She raised an eyebrow at the other three. While they were working it through, she gave Joanna a few more instructions from the machine and dug into the medicine cabinet again.

Ben and Melissa exchanged incredulous glances. "You're not serious," Melissa said, grinning despite herself.

"There's no way she's serious," Ben said, not grinning.

"I'm entirely serious," Eileen said, grinning widest of all. "Venus." She closed the cabinet with gentle finality, her grin not fading as she swallowed a dose of epinephrine. "Ben, do you still have my data cube?"

The man pulled it out of his pocket, regarded it hesitantly, and handed it off to Eileen. "As promised. What do you plan to do with it? I don't think Gabriel's buying any longer."

"Well, we've decided to go to Venus. I've got some ideas for us there." Eileen put the cube in her jumpsuit pocket, zipped it closed. She'd rather lose a limb than that data, after Stephen's...loss. She felt a fresh wave of grief rise up, threatening to choke her, but she slammed an iron gate down in her heart. Not now.

"Hold on just a damned second," Ben said. "I think 'decided' is a touch too strong a word."

"Is 'captain' too strong a word for you too, Ben? I'm in charge of this ship now that Stephen's no longer with us." She hadn't meant to say it in quite that way. She pressed the lump of grief that rose into her throat back down behind the gate.

"I know what the situation is," he snapped back, "but I think that in this situation we deserve to at least make our opinions known."

"And what's your opinion, Ben?" Eileen was standing now, hands planted on hips, staring him down, daring him to try to usurp her authority. Stephen would never have stood for it—no captain could stand any defiance in space, where the slightest disobedience at a crucial moment could be fatal. Space was dangerous, even after two centuries of manned spaceflight.

Ben stared at her with a knowing frown. Melissa and Almika just looked uncomfortable, and Joanna was staring in something approaching horror.

"I just don't like the idea," he finally said. "But what else do you want me to suggest? Mercury?"

"Actually," Melissa pointed out, "I should've mentioned this earlier, but there is still the delta-v question."

"Oh, right," Eileen said, deflating a little bit.

"Wait, what do you mean?" Joanna asked. "You mean the amount of velocity you can change, right?"

"Right. Since we were just planning on heading to Earth, we didn't take on any fuel at *Luna 1*. On a full fuel load the *Mary Ellen* could hit just about anywhere in the Solar System if we were willing to spend enough time. On our current load, our options are a little more limited."

"Could we make Venus?" Eileen asked.

"Probably. Crazyhorse?"

The computer's voice filtered through the wall speakers. "We could complete a direct transfer to Venus within ten weeks with our remaining hydrogen propellant, allowing for a generous safety margin."

"So there you have it," Eileen said. "Venus. That's also one of the few places where we could refuel without drawing UNASCA scrutiny."

She pushed off the cabinet and strode out of the room. There was no point in delaying any further; she needed to get to the bridge and set a course before her nerve gave out. When Eileen wasn't talking, it was all too easy to remember how far out on a limb they were going.

UNASCA's daily presence in their lives tended to be nothing but forms that needed filling out, a heavy tax that needed paying, a contract that needed approval, a delay before starting on a voyage. It was easy to forget that the money they took in was used to support a massive range of services that could be directed against them in moments. Everything from gunships to spies to hackers could target them directly, and the UNASCA warrant for their arrest would exert its own kind of pressure.

Ben followed, looking unhappy. Melissa, on the other hand, looked almost liberated. Almika and Joanna still looked confused. "Maybe I'm missing something," Joanna said, "but isn't Venus pretty much the last place we would want to go if we wanted to avoid UNASCA?"

"I'm a little curious on that point as well," Almika added.

"Well, kids," Melissa grinned with thin menace, "that's because you haven't been on this ship long enough. And by long enough, I mean for about, what, five years?"

"A little over," Ben corrected her, swinging his legs onto the ladder leading to the *Mary Ellen*'s central, zero-gravity sections.

"A little over five years ago. We did a little favor for a fellow named Tarn Stefanovic. He's kind of the smuggler king of the Solar System. You think that UNASCA's having problems with Jupiter because that's in the news, but really, UNASCA has way less control over Venus than they think. It's all in the hands of the manufacturing conglomerates, and all them have an interest in keeping Tarn and his friends quiet." As she spoke, Melissa kept glancing at Ben, grinning at his increasing discomfort.

"Why?" Joanna asked, floating out from the ladder into the central gear staging area. It was large and empty; the mining gear and racks that would normally fill the space had been offloaded at Ceres.

"Because Tarn allows them to break UNASCA's monopoly on trade, in addition to operating more conventional smuggling like drugs and porn. He's a decent guy, though, assuming you're nice to him. And we did him a major solid five-ish years ago. I know that Stephen kept up with him ever since, but I don't know if I'd trust him this far." Melissa stared pointedly at Eileen before pushing after her, toward the bridge.

"He'll serve," Eileen said over her shoulder. "Remember the encrypted message we intercepted, from the *Atlas*? That's got to be one of the last messages anyone ever received from them. Tarn will have the resources to crack it *and* the resources to keep us hidden. And, we can reach him. I don't see another option."

When they reached the bridge, the crew scattered to their usual stations. Almika reported in from the rear engineering modules. Joanna, for her part, hovered uncertainly in the entrance, "So are you coming with us?"

Joanna finished chewing her mouthful and said, even quieter, "Eileen, I'm scared. I've been following you because everything else seemed like a worse choice. This is so far outside my experience...I just feel adrift." She sighed. "I shouldn't have followed you out of that prison cell."

Eileen nodded slowly. "If it's any consolation, Bronwyn would've had you shipped to Neptune and worked you over until she was sure that you didn't know anything, or until there was nothing left to interrogate. You get me?"

"Maybe. But it'll hardly matter if I end up way across the Solar System anyway. And even worse, my family will think that I'm a criminal."

"I'm sure that Stefanovic will have resources to get a message to them."

Joanna scoffed. "Are you joking? Escaping prison, running away from Earth—it'll look terrible. Getting a message from a known smugger won't help." She still hovered at the bridge hatch, as if crossing the threshold were some irrevocable thing. "And even if it wasn't so obvious, they'd assume the worst."

"Of you? Why?"

"My father...well, I left Earth for reasons other than wanting to explore," she said quietly. "It's private."

"I don't mean to interrupt," Ben said, not making eye contact with either of them, "but if you're dedicated to this crazy idea, captain, we should get going *now*."

Eileen let out a long breath. Joanna wasn't the only one on the verge of something irrevocable. "Right. Joanna, if you want off on *Luna 1*, this is your last chance. We need to move."

Her mouth set in grim line, Joanna wordlessly pushed herself toward one of the auxiliary terminals in the rear of the bridge and strapped herself in. Eileen met her eyes for just a moment and nodded. "All right. Make the ship ready for departure. Crazyhorse, plot me a minimum-time course for Venus."

As she shifted in her seat, Eileen could feel Stephen's datacube in her pocket. *Slam*, went the iron gate; her grief welled up behind it, surging, unable to break through. Not yet, not until he was avenged. If not on Gabriel, then on UNASCA, Belt Group, on the whole system if necessary. His death would be the first spark of a grand conflagration; Eileen promised that she would burn everything and everyone that had in any way contributed to his death until, at long last, they could both rest in peace.

The executive conference room filled the second floor of Belt Group's Portland headquarters, just below Chen's penthouse. With just Rosetta and Forrester present, the space seemed cavernous and bare, despite the elegant and substantial rococo decor, the wings of observer galleries, and the massive stone conference table. Windows on all sides were dark, with the occasional flash of aerodyne or dirigible running lights.

Rosetta and Forrester had fled up here for a desperately-needed change of scenery. There was altogether too much work to do, all if it far more important than mere sleep. Caffeine would have to suffice.

"Next crisis?" Rosetta's head lay on the dark, cool stone of the cable, nestled among dataslates and hardcopies related to a half-dozen of the company's operations. She wondered if the VP of marketing, or the chief of human resources had these sorts of piles. Maybe she was in the wrong job.

"The *Atlas*," Forrester said, stretching audibly. "You'll like this; we've got something new today."

"Oh?" Rosetta peeked up at him, watched him reset the three massive screens hovering over the table. She briefly scanned the headlines, frowned, sat upright. "Administrator Thomas Gabriel and the prison break from hell, eh?"

"Well, we have official word that Gabriel's in UNASCA custody now, but informal reports suggest that he doesn't actually know anything." Forrester leveled an indecipherable gaze her direction. "I tried to get my agents in to question him, but they were refused. Refused by *UNASCA*. What do you suppose that means?"

"I suppose it means that our 'partners' in this enterprise have their own agenda. Color me surprised."

"You want my people to force the issue?" Was that a note of hope in Forrester's voice?

Rosetta considered it for a moment. "No. I'll let Chen know; we'll try to put a little top-down pressure on them via Yessenia and Moen."

Forrester laughed. "You know that the orders came direct from that little rat's office. Yessenia Pruitt might be on the level, but if Moen meant half the things he said in that meeting of yours, I'll hang up my spurs."

Trying to massage away the headache she felt brewing behind her temples, Rosetta rested her head in her hands. "I think your instincts are probably correct. What of the prisoners?"

"They made it into orbit, rendezvoused with a ship, the *Mary Ellen*. She's a mining vessel out of Ceres, and—get this—she was working the belt not far from where we lost contact with the *Atlas*. Her captain was the one trying to sell data related to her to Administrator Gabriel, on Brighton, although based on what UNASCA is saying, we now believe that he died without being able to offload it."

Rosetta pursed her lips, absently pushing a dataslate around with an index finger. "So...someone on that ship still has data related to the *Atlas*."

"It would stand to reason." Forrester shrugged.

"Robert, I want that ship, and I want that data.

Chen's breathing right down my neck about this. He wants the *Atlas* situation put to bed." Rosetta drummed her fingers, thinking about that morning's meeting with her boss. Chen very rarely got angry, but at times Rosetta felt that he was too easily frustrated. This had been one of those times.

One of UNASCA's hidden specialties was information control. They had near-complete influence over the Deep Space Network of satellites and orbital transmitters that allowed the internet to propagate, throughout the Solar System. When they said that they hadn't picked up any data on the *Atlas*, Rosetta had little choice but to believe them. Certainly the fact that Belt Group stock hadn't plummeted was a sign that they were correct."

"I understand." Forrester nodded.

"It may very well be that the *only* extant information on the *Atlas* is in the hands of someone on that ship. Do you understand me?"

"I understand," Forrester repeated, hesitant. "Don't take this the wrong way, but...how sure are you that they actually *have* the data they claim to have? This recovery operation is getting expensive and frankly, I think we're relying too much on UNASCA."

"Tell me, Robert. How many other solid leads to you have?" Rosetta raised an eyebrow. "Hmm?"

Forrester shifted in his seat. "Not many."

"Exactly. And until you do have one, this is where our resources are going."

"Very well," Forrester sighed and handed a dataslate to Rosetta. The screen showed a few specs of that ship, the

Mary Ellen, and a projected heliocentric orbital track.

Rosetta studied it for a moment, frowning. Then, "They're going to Venus?"

"UNASCA's got them on telescope right now."

"Why fly straight into the lion's den?" Rosetta muttered, thinking aloud. It didn't take very long. "Oh. You know what it is?" She leaned back in her chair and regarded Forrester. "They're hoping to take refuge with some smuggler kingpin, hide out right under our noses. That's the only thing that makes sense; UNASCA's presence on Venus is too strong for it to be anything else."

Forrester shrugged. "The smugglers certainly do have UNASCA wrapped around their fingers. Fortunately, we're not without assets there. I'll dispatch another team to intercept them when they arrive."

"Liaise with UNASCA assets if you can, Robert. I want to keep this on the level if at all possible. But," she emphasized the point with a finger to Forrester's chest. "But, I want *us* to get access to that data. When and if we release it to UNASCA is my responsibility and Chen's. Tell your agents: *do not* let UNASCA get their mitts on the data or the people. You with me?"

Forrester hid a smirk behind his hand. "You sure we're all friends here? You sure you don't just want to go to war against UNASCA now?"

"Oh, come off it. We're partners, but that doesn't mean it has to be an equal partnership. You and I both know it's never been that way before. This time, though, we have a possible advantage and I want to keep it that way. So, let me ask again: You with me?"

"I'm with you," Forrester said. He rapped his

knuckles on the table and stood. "I think that's the bulk of it for now, but there are a few other, minor issues we should take a look at."

"Go for it," Rosetta said, leaning back and staring out the window. She felt that headache coming on again, and the more she thought about this *Atlas*, the worse it got.

When they launched the *Atlas*, they had been on a tipping point. Belt Group was poised on the brink of ascendancy, with only their obsolete contracts to UNASCA and a few press releases between them and the lion's share of the belt mining market.

Now everything seemed to be oscillating more the other direction. Chen had made it clear: the loss of the *Atlas* would not only trigger a panic among the investors, but a severe loss of face before UNASCA and their competitors. There would be no renegotiation of the unequal contracts, there would be no cornering of the market. They would just be another player scrambling for a piece of the pie, carrying a load of dead weight from the failed *Atlas* project.

Rosetta sighed again, barely listening to Forrester's talk of labor disruptions on their Jupiter helium plants and supply disruptions on Venus and Mars. If they didn't catch these fugitives and recover their data on Venus, or if that data didn't lead to the recovery of the *Atlas,* then she should just update her resume and not bother coming in to work the next day.

She was depressing herself, and her headache was surging again. She tried to focus on Forrester's reports. It was impossible, though, to ignore all her worries. She had ten weeks to arrange a response. If Forrester's men failed, if *she* failed, then all would be for naught.

PART II: VENUS

Chapter 8

"It's bright," Joanna said, floating in the Mary Ellen's observation lounge, staring the waxing crescent of Venus directly before them. It was in fact behind the *Mary Ellen*—a small pressure variance in the ship's engines had called a halt to their deceleration, and they could see Melissa in her spacesuit working on some exterior component.

"Yeah, the Sun's energy is almost twice as powerful here as it is on Earth." Eileen was floating next to her, braced against the small compartment's wall. "If it makes you feel any better, you're not missing anything—the top cloud layer is a uniform white, pretty much."

"Too bad; it looks so pretty in the pictures."

"Those pictures are designed for ignorant tourists like you," Eileen said, giving Joanna a playful shove.

Joanna stuck her tongue out and turned back toward the crescent. "Like I said, too bad. Still, it is sort of pretty like it is." She looked a little closer to the window. "What are those specks around it? Not the stars."

"Nope. You're looking at light reflecting off some of the orbital factories, or maybe the solar collectors. Or it might be a ship making a deorbit burn, although I doubt it; they'd be dangerously close to the incoming traffic lane."

"Right, because of the power of their engines."

"Exactly. I'd rather not get bathed in microwaves and gamma rays right now."

Joanna chuckled, eyes never leaving the window. Even though their situation was marginally less desperate than before, it seemed to Eileen that Joanna had at least come to accept it. Or she had come to ignore it; there was something about being in the black between planets that allowed one to forget about life. Even though nine weeks had passed, they were so conducive to a sort of unattached emotional state that they seemed to be mere days. It was a singular phenomenon that Eileen had never grown used to in her entire life.

It helped that they'd kept her busy. UNASCA could open as many academies as it liked, but the best spacers were the ones given just enough classroom training to survive, and then taught the important skills in space. Eileen and Melissa had been drilling Joanna on everything from basic maintenance tasks to astrophysics. Nine weeks wasn't long enough to learn much, but Joanna was smart, and she'd picked up a lot."

"I was just thinking. Why should they allow us to dock in orbit?" Joanna said, jerking Eileen out of her own unattached state.

"Oh. Well, we need to give Tarn a call pretty soon here, before we enter a parking orbit. We'll have a pretty serious inclination to most of the facilities and spacedocks, so we don't technically have to talk to control yet."

"Oh, fun. Sounds like it'll be a great conversation."

"Enough of that." Eileen pushed herself through the observation lounge hatch, through the corridor that connected it to the axial habitation modules, and through the payload office into the control center. Only Ben was present, with Melissa out on the exterior hull. Almika was supporting her from the rear machine shop. Joanna popped into the control center behind her, and took up the rear monitoring station.

Eileen slipped into the copilot's chair and called up the orbital display on her primary screen. It showed a straight line moving from their ship, making a slight arc around Venus, and then heading deeper into the system and impacting the Sun some months in the future. Once they engines were back online, they'd round it out for a picture-perfect orbital insertion.

Before that was done, though, there was a call to make. "Ben, I'm going to call Tarn. You might want to jack in. Ditto Joanna," she said, turning her head to look at the rear station, "but best not to say anything. I want to play our cards close to our chest, here."

Ben gave her a thumbs up moments later, and Joanna did the same, smiling and making a lips-zipping gesture.

Eileen typed in the frequency that she'd found in Stephen's private files. Her mind tried to drift toward the memories of opening those files; her chest started to clench in grief. No, not now. Not yet. She slammed an iron gate over her emotions while she still could. Joanna wasn't the only person Eileen had kept busy over the trip. There were things she didn't want to think about either.

The commlink connected at long last, and Eileen cleared her throat. "This is *Mary Ellen* to Aunt Anna. How's the weather around Venus?"

For a moment, there was nothing, then a heavy male voice, distorted by distance and encryption, replied, "Who the hell is this?"

"This is Eileen Cromwell in command of the *Mary Ellen.* Is Tarn Stefanovic still resident at this address?"

"One moment." There was a click as the radio was disconnected, and then nothing. Eileen's display was ticking up the value of the thrust needed to put them in the proper orbit. At length that number would cross the "total delta-v remaining' value and they'd be hosed, but Eileen didn't anticipate any problems on that score.

The radio clicked back on. The voice that answered was still male, but deeper and more mellow. "Stefanovic here. This is the *Mary Ellen*?"

"Eileen Cromwell, captain."

"Eileen? I heard about Stephen. My condolences—he didn't deserve that sort of death."

No, he hadn't. Eileen felt the iron gate rattle, but it held. It was becoming a ritual. "Thanks, Tarn. I have a favor to ask."

"I know what you're going to ask, Eileen, and I can't say yes. You're way too hot right now. What's more, we have it on pretty good authority that you're being pursued, to say nothing of what the UNASCA forces here will do to you."

The message that they were under general arrest had arrived just as they'd cut their engines after making full thrust for Venus. That meant that not only was Belt Group and UNASCA on her tail, but that they'd have to deal with all the security officers of any colony that they visited. Ben hadn't been happy, given that they were headed to one of the most important ones.

Ben rolled his eyes, but Eileen ignored him. "Is that nervousness I hear in your voice, Tarn? Is the smuggler king of Venus quaking at the thought of UNASCA intervention?"

Stefanovic didn't sound amused. "Not nervousness, just patient consideration. For instance, I'm considering the fact that we could just turn you in right now. There's a reward, you know."

"Don't be like that, Tarn. We don't have many other choices."

"Pity. Then I guess you're shit out of luck. Sorry I can't help."

"Wait just a damned second," Ben burst in. "Tarn, this is Ben Riley. You want to know why UNASCA and Belt Group are after us? I bet the bulletin doesn't say why we're wanted." Eileen's eyes widened, she made a cut-off gesture at Ben. He cheerfully ignored it.

Stefanovic chuckled, a deep throaty sound. "It says you broke out of prison in Brighton and violated UNASCA orders to heave to."

"And why do you think we were in prison?"

"The bulletin wasn't specific," Tarn said after a moment.

"Tarn, it's because of some data we're carrying," Eileen broke in. As long as they were throwing the truth out on the broadcast, she wanted to have control of the conversation. "You've heard of the *Atlas*, right? Belt Group's new refinery ship?"

"Everyone's heard of the *Atlas*."

"Have you heard about its disappearance, then?"

This time, the pause dragged on. Eileen glanced at the communications panel to check that the carrier signal was still coming in. Finally, Stefanovic, affecting a weary tone, muttered, "I guess you'd better get over here. I can't promise anything, you understand, but you can rest assured that most likely, I won't turn you right in."

Eileen felt a wave of relief cascade through her entire body. "Thank you, Tarn. We'll make it worth your while; the *Ellen* is still carrying some high grade ore from 117364 Euphrates. And it's the good stuff, too: iridium, rubidium, various calcites, even some organics from the surface. It's yours if you put us up for a few weeks, maybe put the *Ellen* through one of your chop shops to help us make our next port of call."

There was another dramatic sigh over the radio circuit. This one was Tarn's. "Eileen, it's not going to 'blow over.' You've been hearing the rumors from Jupiter, right? UNASCA's cracking down in a big way."

"Tarn..."

"Just get over here before I changed my mind."

Eileen paused. She glanced over at Ben, who looked as though he wanted to throttle someone, but nodded his assent nonetheless. Joanna looked concerned but shrugged in her direction. She turned back to the radio. "All right. Where do you want us to dock?"

"Give me a few minutes to arrange some things. Unless I can't do that, you'll be docking at *Presidium*, a small refit shop. The owner owes me big and he's in deep enough with UNASCA that he can't turn you in without hurting himself. Just get permission from Venus control under the name '*Julia Constant*.' I'll forward you the registration information."

"Done," Ben said, tapping a few commands into his console.

"I had better not regret this," Tarn said, as though to no one in particular, and with a click, the carrier signal cut off. For a moment, the *Mary Ellen*'s bridge was silent except for the whirring of the air conditioning.

"That was close." Ben slid his headset down around his neck and stretched.

"I didn't think he was going to go for it," Joanna said, letting a nervous chuckle escape before clamping her jaw down on it.

"You two of little faith. Tarn's a big softie. He and Stephen got on well together. Tarn'll give us a fair listen for his sake, if nothing else." Memories bubbled up, but she pushed them back down. Later, she promised herself. Later when she could do him justice.

"Well, I was right," Joanna said, still smiling. "It was an interesting conversation."

Eileen grinned tightly. "To say the least. As soon as Melissa's back inside we'll make ready to burn for our assigned orbit. *Presidium*, here we come."

Presidium resolved from a speck into a structure, then into a massive bulk. It was small by the standards of the largest shipyards, those capable to constructing a dozen ships the Mary Ellen's size or larger, but it was still big enough to dwarf the Ellen herself.

The main part of the station was a massive open ended cylinder, one large enough to admit two ships the *Mary Ellen*'s size. This was surrounded by supply modules, truss sections enclosing bays of spare parts of all sizes, and also some cargo modules and bits of loose superstructure. Radiators projected into space wherever there was enough structure to shadow them from the sun.

Bolted to this, almost as an afterthought, was the collection of modules that formed the stations habitable area. There were four rotating rings for artificial gravity, plus a large number of microgravity modules. According to *Presidium*'s DSN site, it boasted a crew of almost fifty, plus accommodations for the crews whose ships were being worked on.

Joanna watched with impatience as the ship engaged in docking maneuvers. In space, she had discovered, nothing happened fast, and this operation was no exception. It was easy to see why: the massive *Mary Ellen* and the even more massive *Presidium* could hardly move on a whim, and even the slightest accidental love tap could spell disaster. Watching the ponderous giants move toward a delicate kiss made her a little nervous.

"Twenty meters to contact. Forward one quarter. Left point five. Up zero. Rotation right on x-ray," Melissa called from the pilot's seat. She was scanning an immense number of readouts at the same time, flicking her eyes between them with a practiced air.

"You are nineteen meters to contact. Bay has been depressurized and waiting for contact. Crews standing by," replied the station controller, his voice piped throughout the control room. Joanna could see space-suited figures grappled to the massive struts now surrounding the *Mary Ellen* as she backed into dock.

The next few meters passed without event as Melissa and the station controller called out to each other, confirming each other's measurements. There were five meters left when Eileen radioed her directly. "Joanna, I want to you to come with Ben and I to see Tarn."

"What? Why?" she whispered, afraid of distracting Melissa as she multi-tasked with an easy confidence that Joanna envied.

"Honestly? Because you're sweet and innocent and I think he'll be nicer to us when you're there."

"Um. Thanks." Joanna decided to be happy that she wasn't considered a hardened criminal by *everybody* yet. Her arrest warrant wasn't something she wanted to acknowledge even to herself. "I'll head over just as soon as the docking is complete."

"Two meters. Forward one sixteenth. Neutral, neutral. On the x-ray," Melissa said. She wasn't even sweating.

"We have you on the x-ray. Rotation neutral." Melissa counted down the last meter by centimeters. "Eight hundred. Looking good. Nine hundred, on the ball."

There was the slightest of bumps. It wouldn't have woken Joanna up out of a light nap. "Contact," said station control. "We have hard seal."

"Contact confirmed, seal confirmed. Engines baffles on. RCS to safe."

"Gantries closing. Restrict your EM radiation."

In her external camera display, Joanna could see the *Presidium*'s massive superstructure arms jerk to life and start closing inward around the *Mary Ellen*. They could've enclosed a ship twice the diameter of the *Ellen*, but since that wasn't necessary they were choking down.

Joanna floated through the payload office, the tunnel to the observation lounge, and the rear machine shop to the *Ellen*'s main axial passage. This was sealed off during normal flight operations to save air and power since it just led to the ship's water and fuel stores, but it also led to the *Ellen*'s forward dock, where the *Fisher King* was docked.

Joanna floated through the forward dock into the tiny cabin, suppressing a shudder as she remembered the *last* time she'd boarded the Shuttle Delta, on the Moon. It wasn't a pleasant memory.

Ben and Eileen were already there, working through some preflight launch steps that Joanna could barely follow. They greeted her and got right back to work.

The shuttle was docked in a sealed compartment at the front of the *Mary Ellen*, behind her meteor screen. This compartment held the majority of the tools that the Ellen would use for her mining trade, most of which Joanna couldn't even identify; there were a number of large drill-like devices, and several containers marked with symbols for high explosives and radiation.

"I think we're ready. You'd better hold onto your seat," Eileen said to her, smiling. The forward end of the docking bay actuated outward from the bay before splitting into quarters and pulling away, leaving the bay open to space.

"Buckled? Good." Eileen hit the undock button.

There was a slight lurch as the shuttle separated from the *Mary Ellen*, and a gentle shove as she pushed away under her own power. Slowly they floated away from the *Ellen* and the *Presidium*, where the work crews were already descending in to work on the ship. They passed the time in silence except for the purely functional communication of Eileen and Ben.

Once in clear orbit, they passed around to the day side of Venus, where the utter darkness of the night side transformed into the brilliant light of the day. The windows automatically polarized, blocking the bright sun and bright surface of Venus' never-ending cloud layer.

There were no visible stars, but there were occasional twinkles and flashes in the darkness that betrayed the location of Venus' vast manufacturing facilities. It was strange that so populated a place—there were many tens of thousands of people in orbit—could seem just as empty as the interplanetary space of the Solar System.

Eventually, one of those blinking lights burned steadily, and less than an hour later it resolved into a massive structure. An unbelievably massive structure.

Presidium was big. *Luna 1* was enormous. That would make Tarn Stefanovic's station absolutely gargantuan. Rather than a collection of modules and trusses with a few hab cylinders, the entire station was an enormous cylinder, a giant, soda can rotating in space, with one of the ends pointing to a shipyard a dozen time the size of the *Presidium*.

Inside each of those shipyard gantries was a ship *Mary Ellen*'s size or larger, either under repair or under construction. It was a tremendous sight, an awesome display of industry. No wonder UNASCA wanted to keep this place under their control, and no wonder Stefanovic was so reluctant to risk it.

All Joanna could think to say was, "That's big."

"It sure is. Welcome to *Agropolis*, Joanna. This is the legitimate part of Tarn's business empire. The semi-legit part, anyway. He owns it through holding companies and runs it from the background. Still, there's no way that UNASCA can't know who's in charge for reals, and they seem to put up with it."

"In other words, legitimate," Ben said sardonically. He tapped a few keys in to the radio console and got them permission to dock.

The small craft dock looked like an enormous Christmas tree studded with spaceship ornaments. Eileen slowly maneuvered the *Fisher King* in to dock, joining a few dozen other small craft of a variety of types. They had hard seal in just a few minutes.

They floated through the docking bay corridor into an even roomier, cylindrical space with a small info desk and enormous screens projected about describing the unique design of *Agropolis*, the sponsors who founded its construction, and the business people who kept it running. Perhaps unsurprisingly, there was no mention of Tarn Stefanovic.

There were quite a few people going about to and from the docking area, and as Joanna looked out the window she could see another triangular Shuttle Delta preparing for its docking run. There was just so much going on!

The exits from the transition area were a series of depressions on the walls. Inside these depressions were laddered holes leading outward into the rotating part of the station; these were set in a track that rotated slowly around the room.

"Hey, Joanna," Eileen said, gesturing to one of the lines that ran criss-cross the room. Joanna pushed off toward the line and grabbed it without too much trouble; she had been practicing her zero gravity maneuvers on the Ellen during her transit and she'd become at least proficient.

When she'd joined Eileen at the line, followed directly by Ben, Eileen said, "Be careful with those transition zones. You float over to one and lower yourself down, like you were climbing down the ladder to the bottom floor of a building. If you go down headfirst you'll realize a bit too late why it's a bad idea."

A thought of trying to stop a plummet into ever-increasing gravity made her cringe. "I believe you," she said with a chuckle.

They climbed down the ladders and Joanna noticed that the downward pull got ever stronger as they descended, just as it did in the *Mary Ellen*'s hab rings, and by the time they had passed through several landings and stood on the bottom most level they were at something a little less than Earth's gravity. Windows set into the floor showed the gibbous form of Venus sliding slowly around as the station rotated.

"You know," Eileen said, looking around the busy receiving area, "I had forgotten how incredible this place is."

The area around receiving was something of a mall and bazaar rolled together. Goods from the hundred factories orbiting Venus, rare gems found in asteroidal rock, zero gee crystals as big as Joanna's head, all were for sale. This was saying nothing of the tremendous variety of local artwork and music. There were even a few stores that she recognized from Earth, their advertising screens blaring over the noise of hundreds of shoppers bargaining and buying.

At the far end of the bazaar, they jumped on a slidewalk to reach the far end of the station. As they let the walk carry them along, Joanna glanced up through the transparent ceiling to the far side of the station's rotation; she could see the green and blue of a park. A space-suited crew with a small workpod hovered about one of the giant axial trusses, their suits flashing in the light from a catalytic welder. Behind them, the narrow central spire that joined all the trusses cast a shadow on the station's far side.

At long last they reached the side opposite the dock, the "south pole." The map on Eileen's handset identified it as the "entertainment district," but Joanna would've called it the red light district. This was the only area on the station that felt like a mob kingpin might be in charge of things, and it made up for what the rest of the station lacked in sleaze.

"If I remember right," Ben said, rubbing his chin as his eyes followed the curve of the floor up until it vanished, "he tended to make his home in a club called 'the Bordeaux'."

"Sounds like a classy place," Joanna said hopefully, and Eileen chuckled.

"It's okay. The drinks are criminally expensive, but high quality booze isn't easy to come by in space. It's not like you can brew the stuff up here."

The main avenue through the entertainment area was bordered on both sides by clubs, bars, inns, and what appeared to be houses of ill repute. Joanna tried not to decide what sorts of things might go on in there, this far from the laws of Earth.

The Bordeaux, Joanna was relieved to note, looked much better than most of the other places along the strip. It was done up in a veneer of old world charm, as though it had been transported whole from some English countryside four centuries past to the orbit of an entirely different planet.

They were waved in by the doorman, and Joanna noted that the interior didn't do much to keep up the pretense. Sure, the waitresses wore low-cut dresses and corsets, but Joanna was certain that the inns of the past had never bothered with lasers, holograms, or pulsing beats over a dance floor.

"There he is," Ben muttered in their ears, nodding across the room.

Tarn was a large man. He was dressed simply but elegantly in a low-collared suit, unbuttoned to show a silky white undershirt. The crowd around him looked a little more cutting edge, with the plastic clothing, no shoes, and smudged makeup look that was so popular in the western European Union.

They threaded their way through the crowd over to where he was sitting. Joanna couldn't help but notice that she and Eileen were drawing a lot of attention from both the male and female guests of the place. Surely she didn't look that far out of place? She tried to ignore them as she pulled up behind Eileen, but she could feel eyes on her back.

"Tarn."

"Eileen. Ben. Other friend," the man said, smiling conservatively. He was pretty average looking up close, thicker than most spacers.

"This is Joanna. Maybe you heard about our little adventure on Brighton?"

"Oh yeah," he stood up, gesturing for his table companions to step aside. They looked to be flunkies and hangers on, overdressed young men and women with too much makeup and too-beautiful faces.

"Joanna Newton," she said, not sure how else to start. She offered her hand to Tarn Stefanovic, who took it gently.

"The pleasure's mine. I hear that you and Eileen took a little walk outside near Brighton. Pretty much any news story about your little experience, that was mentioned. Fun stuff?"

"Not exactly," she said. In point of fact it had been one of the most horrible experiences of her life for a number of reasons, but this didn't seem like to time to get into details.

"I bet not." He turned to his companions. "Give us some space, guys."

They walked off and Tarn gestured for Eileen and the rest to sit. They did. Joanna felt a little uncomfortable that the seat was still warm from the tramp that had been sitting there before.

"Let's get right down to business, Tarn," Eileen said. "We're offering you twenty million in unclaimed, semi-refined ores right out of the *Ellen*'s holds. In return, you work the ship so that we can escape the planet unmolested, and you put us up somewhere while the work is being done.

Fair?"

"It's more than fair," he said, taking a sip of the amber liquid in his glass, "it's a damned steal." He carefully put his glass back down on the table's glass surface, fiddled with it. "Tell me about this data of yours."

Ben and Eileen exchanged glances. "Data?" Eileen said, giving Tarn a sidelong look.

Tarn leaned back, grinning. "Come on, Eileen. Of course I've heard about the disappearance of the *Atlas*, and of course I've heard that Belt Group and UNASCA are working together to get this data that points to the ship's current whereabouts. And now here you stumble into my lap and name-drop the ship. I might not be a detective, but that seems to be a pretty conclusive case to me."

"All right, fine," Eileen conceded. "I've got a datacube that we recorded back in the belt sixteen months or so ago, as we passed within a few hundred thousand kilometers of the *Atlas*. It wasn't until a year later that we learned we were the last ones to see the ship."

"Why does Belt Group think this data is going to help them find their ship? They have resources all across the Solar System; why not just use them?" Tarn asked, raising an eyebrow. "Come on, I know you know something."

"Well, not only do we have the last several weeks worth of full scope readings on the *Atlas*, we intercepted a few encrypted, low-power transmissions. They weren't calling home."

Tarn considered this for a moment, working his liquor glass around in his hands. "I can make things easy for you. If the data's valuable, I can unload it and spare you the trouble of trying to hide it."

"*No*!" The venom in Eileen's voice startled Joanna, and even Ben gave her a strange look. Eileen closed her eyes and took a deep breath, and continued in a much more reasonable tone. "No. I'm keeping this data, and I'm going to personally deliver it to whoever can hurt Belt Group the worst. You understand me?"

Eileen opened her eyes to find Tarn staring at her. The intensity of their eye contact made Joanna's skin crawl. "I want your best encryption expert to join us in your bolt-hole. Someone you can trust, mind," Eileen added.

To Joanna's surprise, Tarn didn't point out that Eileen was in no position to make demands. Instead, he laughed, and it sounded sincere. "All right, Eileen Cromwell. You drive a hard enough bargain, I suppose. And I can understand your desire for revenge; I'd feel the same way. And I have good people."

He hesitated dramatically. "All right, you've got a deal. I'll have my people send a maintenance order to *Presidium* to get your ship worked on, and I'll send over parts from a few key derelicts that might help. In the meantime, I think I have just the place to stash you. Naturally, you won't object to one consideration."

Eileen smiled sweetly. "What's that?"

"I want all the money up front, in ores."

"It's yours," Eileen said, still smiling.

"And I want a copy of the data once my hacker is done with it."

"Unacceptable." Eileen's smile faded.

Tarn held up his hands. "Relax, I won't hand it over. I'm making enough off this deal as it is. This would just be for the sake of my own curiosity."

Eileen's mouth worked for a moment, and Joanna could see the muscles in her arms bunch and flex. "Fine. But so help me, if you let that data free, I'll come back for you. In this life or the next. You understand?"

It wasn't a very reasonable threat, Joanna thought, but Tarn took in stride, nodding solemnly. "You have my word. For Stephen's sake, I'll do as you say.

"Now," he said, opening his arms to the three of them, "feel free to enjoy some hospitality on this house. You guys have had a rough flight, and if you're going away from the world for a while, might as well live it up for now."

It felt good to have some convincing gravity under her feet. Bronwyn stretched, feeling grateful to not have to worry about barking her hands in the tiny cabin that had brought her all the way from the Moon. She paced, thankful that *Agropolis*' slow rotation meant that walking spinward felt indistinguishable from walking antispinward. It was the small things that Bronwyn took so much pleasure in.

Bronwyn wasn't happy to be on *Agropolis*. She had looked forward to some relaxing Earthside work, something where she could be outside. Instead, she was waiting in a life support maintenance station with one of the people she liked least in the world: Keven Miletic. Most of the people that Bronwyn was forced to tangle with on the job, she had nothing personal against. Whether they had done something that hurt Belt Group, or just might do something, she didn't feel much about them one way or the other.

But Keven she could actively dislike. He was everything she was not: loud, large, and brutish. Why Forrester should trust him on the same level as her was quite beyond her ability to understand. Likewise, his orders for them to cooperate were intolerable. He knew how much Bronwyn disliked the other man.

"He's late," Keven said after they'd been waiting some ten minutes. "That makes me nervous." His voice seemed to be eternally stuck in a deep growl, as if he was trying to be intimidating in normal conversation. It was somewhere between pathetic and laughable. Bronwyn did not care for the man at all.

"Do not be nervous, friend Keven," she said, trying to keep her own patience with him. "This is not a professional we are dealing with, it is an informer. Furthermore, UNASCA operates differently. He is not bound by the same rules we are."

"Hmph," he said, staring down the maintenance passage from which their contact was supposed to approach.

They were in a rarely accessed life support control room. It was a pointless part of *Agropolis* unless the automated life support systems failed, and the semi manual overrides in the station's control room failed likewise. For that reason, and because of the continually rushing air through the massive conduits surrounding the control room drowned out most noise, it was a suitable if uncomfortable rendezvous point.

Keven appeared to be ready to burst into spontaneous growling when they finally heard the noise of a hatch opening down the maintenance catwalk. The sound came from slightly above them as well, thanks to the curving floor of the station. They saw a man walk below the crest of the station, and from the stooped back to the pallid demeanor, Bronwyn knew that he was their contact.

"Lamont Kinsey?" Keven asked, putting extra growling into his voice for maximum intimidation.

"Yeah, yeah," Kinsey said, looking completely uncowed. He had the appearance of a man who was too narcissistic to be properly intimidated, which would make their job more difficult. Already Bronwyn was developing a pronounced dislike for the man.

"You have information from UNASCA?"

"I told you I did, didn't I?" He turned to Bronwyn, his lower jaw jutting out. "Who is this monkey? I was talking to you. You know what I have, why didn't you tell him?"

Keven growled at him, and he just ignored it. Yes, he was completely uncowed. At least he wouldn't lie to them just to tell them what they wanted to hear. He might lie for entirely different reasons, of course, but Bronwyn would expect no less.

"I told my associate everything," Bronwyn said calmly, "but he merely wants to make sure that you tell a consistent story. I do not blame him."

"I suppose that's fair. Anyway, I've got what you asked for. It's over here," he said, gesturing vaguely behind him.

"'Over here'?" She repeated skeptically. "I asked you for information, not a physical object."

"I meant that I have your proof over here, blockhead." He made a twirling gesture next to his ear. "I swear, between you and your monkey I'm seriously starting to regret this setup."

Keven's fists were so tightly clenched that his knuckles were white. Bronwyn pressed her lips into a thin line, wondering if his obvious disrespect would cause problems if not punished. She decided that it wasn't worth it right now.

"I understand. We will follow you."

"Ah ah," he said, shaking a finger at her. "Monkey boy stays here."

"You do not give orders-" Keven started, jabbing a spearlike finger at Lamont's chest, but Bronwyn cut him off.

"He will stay, Lamont, but he will not be patient. Let us do what must be done."

For a moment it looked like Keven might be seized by his baser emotions and try to take Lamont's head off with a single giant fist. It looked possible; Keven was easily three times Lamont's mass, and it was muscle that made up the difference. The rumor mill suggested that Keven was continually juiced by Forrester just so hemight keep some leverage over Keven by controlling his supply. Like most rumors, there was most likely some nugget that wasn't entirely false.

Lamont gave one more skeptical look at Keven, then gestured for her to follow him. They left the control room and entered a small, undeveloped part of the station. It had an interface ring that allowed access to the station's central spire via the axial trusses. On one end of this spire were the docking facilities, and on the other end the control sections for the entire station. There were, however, a series of observation lounges scattered around the control modules, most of which were leased to astronomers and universities throughout the Solar System.

After a ten-minute float down the wide central spire, dodging out of the way of the massive quantities of cargo and supplies stored in it, they emerged into a fork that broke the tunnel up into innumerable smaller corridors. The largest of these led to the control room, but Lamont didn't use that one; instead he turned down a small, little used path.

This led to a locked hatch, which Lamont appeared to have hacked open previously. Inside the small chamber was an entire astronomy lab with multiple telescopes hooked up to a large controller. The entire assembly was a picture of sophisticated automation, so the lone non-interfaced telescope strapped to the wall seemed out of place even though it was a newer model.

Lamont retrieved that, socketed it into a previously aligned bracket, and made a grunt of satisfaction. "There you go, blockhead. I told you not to doubt me." He pushed away and let her float up to take a look.

She glanced into the eyepiece and immediately identified the object in the center of her field of vision: a small repair yard. A medium-sized interplanetary vessel was locked in the yard's main gantry, but at this distance it was difficult to tell anything more.

Bronwyn pulled away. "I am not certain that this constitutes the type of proof that we require."

Lamont rolled his eyes dramatically. "All right then, sister, check out the registry numbers on the hull there. Eh? Those match anything you might've read about or got briefed on? The *Mary Ellen* perhaps?"

"I will need confirmation," Bronwyn said skeptically.

"How's this for confirmation, then. That ship arrived yesterday, exactly when UNASCA's people said that it would. And just like they expected, they waited until the last moment to make arrangements with Venus orbital control. They waited, until Tarn had made arrangements with them. Cash exchanged hands, and I've got proof of that if you want it."

"Please."

Lamont flashed a condescending smile and pulled out his handset. He called up an audio file, and held the tiny speaker where Bronwyn could hear it.

Her gut tightened as Bronwyn recognized the first voice: Eileen Cromwell. The craven lunatic had almost killed her on the Moon. As much as she might want to relish in the anger, however, Bronwyn pushed it down and spread it out, waiting for it to dissipate. Strong emotion was her antithesis. Detachment was strength.

The second voice was Tarn Stefanovic. She recognized it from Forrester's briefing and her own subsequent research. They were discussing the exchange of goods for a hiding place, for a chop shop to work on the *Mary Ellen*. Belt Group didn't require judicial levels of proof. This would be good enough.

"Rest assured," Bronwyn said. "I am convinced."

"Yeah, well, color me reassured." Lamont rolled his eyes. "I should know where the girls are being kept by tomorrow; Tarn is meeting them back on *Agropolis* before taking them to their hidey place."

"As always, your information is of tremendous use to us. Will there by anything else?"

"Yeah, you bet. I want to be there when it goes down. I want to be right up front when you pull the trigger."

"I have not been authorized-"

"To kill him? Too bad. Still, I want to see the look on his face."

Bronwyn kept her patient smile, but Lamont was weakening her legendary self-control. He was a useless man: a traitor who was too afraid to act on his own will. "I will do my best, as I said."

"Good. Good." Lamont pushed away from the telescope, replacing it on the wall. Then, without any further instructions, he left. She followed moments later and returned to Keven in the atmosphere processor. As far as she could see, he had not moved in the twenty minutes she had been gone.

"It is as he said?" Keven said, straining against his baser instincts.

"It is. Their ship is here, and if Mr. Kinsey is correct, our marks have been meeting with Tarn. Lamont will let us know where they are going to be held tomorrow. We need but wait."

"If you trust him." It was obvious Keven didn't.

"I trust in his own greed. He will follow through."

"Good." Without another word, Keven strode forward and up, following the ring of the station, until he disappeared above the ceiling.

Chapter 9

Tarn Stefanovic had sent a ship for them. It was a Shuttle Delta, an older example of the *Fisher King*'s model. Joanna didn't know how old the Delta ships were, but she remembered seeing pictures of them in history books along with the first humans to visit Jupiter and Saturn. This might've been one of those ships itself; it looked well loved. As they were getting their gear stowed aboard it and securing themselves, Joanna whispered to Eileen, "It kind of smells like old sweat in here."

Eileen smiled conspiratorially and whispered back, "We're persona non grata to Tarn, even though he agreed to help us. He couldn't very well maintain plausible deniability if he was sending his best ships to ferry us around."

Floating into the cabin, Melissa said out loud, "Holy trinity, it smells like something died in here!"

"Hey, you don't like it, you can walk." The pilot was a gruff old spacer with a radiation-bleached beard and no hair. He also wore one of the darkest spacer's tans that

Joanna had ever seen.

"I'm just saying, don't you guys manufacture any enzyme cleaners here?" She snorted and took her seat, the one closest to the cockpit.

"Maybe I like the smell, eh, Ginger?" The pilot made a rude gesture.

Melissa returned it, "Wouldn't surprise me in the least." She chuckled as the man returned, cursing, to his work on the preflight sequence.

Ben and Almika floated in last of all, tossing some duffels ahead of them. "That's it," Ben said, gazing longingly out the side viewports of the shuttle at the *Mary Ellen*. After a moment, he tore himself away and started sealing the interior hatch.

"You okay, Ben?" Eileen reached a hand over to him from where she was strapped in.

"I'm fine. I'm, well, I'm doing just fine." He shook his head and floated over to the seat next to her.

The Shuttle Delta's cabin was large enough for eight people; the crash couches were aligned in two rows of four, with the pilot just forward and below them in the cockpit. There was a small rest station behind the cabin and a netted space for cargo just behind that. It wasn't designed for long-term comfort, and Joanna was more than a little happy that she wouldn't have to spend that long in it.

"We done crying yet?" The pilot said, turning to face the cabin.

Joanna and Eileen shot him matching glares.

"Works for me. Hang on." He muttered a few words into his headset and pulled a short lever, detaching them from the *Mary Ellen*'s rear dock. A moment later they were outside her docking gantry, and a few moments after that they were shoved back into their seats as the main engines lit.

Eileen just stared at Ben for most of the trip, who was in turn staring back at the dwindling pinprick of light that was the *Presidium* dock. Joanna had yet to suss out their relationship. They seemed to always be at odds, and yet Eileen seemed concerned for him now, just as Ben had been concerned for her when she'd been imprisoned on the Moon.

Well, there was no use asking them about it. Joanna could do little but observe and hope that someday they gave some unambiguous clues.

It was a couple of hours before they arrived again at *Agropolis*, just as they had before. They took the same route from the docking area to the transition zone, through the shops and offices, and into the entertainment district.

This time, however, the message from Tarn had said to meet him at his offices. Why those were in the entertainment district was anyone's guess, but sure enough just a hundred meters from the Bordeaux was an out-of-place structure that bore no flashy lights, no lasers, no OLEDs.

"You're in luck," Tarn said, smiling wide. "After a fashion, anyway. You're about to become part of history."

"Don't you have to be dead to be a part of history?" Eileen said, taking the drink that Tarn's steward offered her.

"Nonsense. Julliard Maximus is a major part of history, and he's plenty alive."

"Julliard Maximus discovered an entire new moon. He wasn't wanted by government agencies or private corporations, and even if he was, to get famous cost him five years of his life in deep space." Eileen raised an eyebrow. "That's a little more time than I plan to commit to this whole endeavor."

"We're waiting for things to blow over," Melissa said, raising her drink to Tarn as she took it, "not waiting for our pursuers to die of old age."

Tarn looked annoyed. "Anyway. I've had my man Lamont here," he gestured to a thin, almost emaciated older man with a snaggletooth and an unpleasantly intense grin, "looking into places to keep you. The place he found might surprise you." He looked over their faces, as if timing his reveal. "Hartley," he said calmly, "Aerostat."

"Oh!" Joanna exclaimed in spite of herself, and all heads turned to face her. "Oh, sorry. I double majored in history," she said sheepishly, wishing that she could fold into her own skin and disappear.

"Yeah, the real question," Eileen said as they turned back toward the table, "is how the hell you managed to get your hands on the very first Venus colony."

"I maintain the visitor's center," Tarn said evenly, meeting her expression. "And you're wrong. The real question is, are you going to take it, or should I try to give you your money back?"

Ben looked like he was biting his tongue. Eileen glanced around at the crew, and her eyes settled on him for just a moment. Then the hesitation was over and she turned back to Tarn.

"Your generosity, as always, is surprising. We'll take it."

"Wonderful!" Tarn clapped his hands, and Lamont

chuckled easily. Joanna could see Ben mutter a curse under his breath; she was quite sure that Eileen didn't miss it. "So it's settled then. Lamont already has some of my guys moving your stuff over to your lander, so you should be able to depart shortly."

He raised his drink. "Make sure you study the museum when you get down there," he said to Joanna in particular. "I was a historian in university too, and I'm pretty proud of what I've put together down there. It was my hobby for a number of years."

"And the decrypter?" Eileen asked, raising her drink.

"Will be there in a couple of days. Turns out finding one I trust as far as you need was non-trivial. They're all flighty bastards." Tarn chuckled at her alarmed expression. "Don't worry about it; I found someone competent *and* trustworthy."

They finished their drinks as casually as possible, keeping up the appearance of relaxed conversation. Melissa, ever the gregarious one, kept the flow up and covered well for the fact that Ben was almost entirely silent. And for the fact that Eileen's eyes were distant, and vacant like death.

Once the drinks were over and Tarn was able to get the *Mary Ellen*s out of his office, he slumped a little in his chair. When the door was sealed and the IDS was turned on, he turned to Lamont.

"What do you think?"

"I think that they suspect you, obviously," Lamont said. "It's way too damned risky to put them down there. If they manage to get some other sympathizers this could go very bad for you."

Tarn stabbed a finger at Lamont. "You're getting way the hell ahead of yourself. Way ahead. I don't have any plans to do anything right now. I just want to keep my options open."

"You've only got one option, dumbass," Lamont sneered. "Even if they accidentally let on to UNASCA that you're helping them, then you're screwed."

He turned back to the door where the crew had just left. "Speaking of which, I don't even know how that guy stands it, cooped up with four hotties like that. Damn! Probably they're all bent; I don't know."

Tarn rolled his eyes. "Hey, keep your head in the game. Don't get distracted. I want you to go down to Hartley with them, make sure they get settled, make sure they're legitimately comfortable, and then head back here in a few days. I'll have decided what I want to do with them by that point."

Lamont opened the door, but then paused cautiously, letting it close again. "Oh, I heard some of the guys saying that a couple of Belt Group enforcers from offworld showed up last week and have been poking around. Just rumors, you know. If I hear anything more concrete you'll be the first to know."

"Glad to hear it. Keep your eyes on the prize and be ready to act when I give the word. But for heaven's sake, don't act sooner than that."

Lamont walked out and let the door shut behind him.

"What did you think?

"He's nervous. Much too nervous." Leona King

moved aside the false wall and stepped out of the shadowed surveillance cubicle behind it. As she stretched her set of delightful-looking limbs, she continued, "I think that you should strongly reconsider sending him with Cromwell and the others."

"I meant about the miners," Tarn said, turning to give her a sidelong frown.

"Well, I think that they're the lesser of two threats to your organization."

Tarn felt a slight flush rise into his face, and he had to restrain himself from raising his voice. "I am dealing with Lamont. Please. I'm not stupid. Now, I would very much like to hear your opinion on those young people."

Leona sighed luxuriantly and sat down sideways in one of the chairs the *Ellen*s had just vacated. Draping her long legs over the armrest, she turned to Tarn with an appraising look. He jerked his eyes back to her face as she said, "I think that you're a big softie. Helping out those poor people just because an old friend of yours got greedy and died for it."

"Stephen Montgomery and I did very well together, thank you very much."

"I'm sure you did."

"And they were right. I owed him a favor. And," he sighed, "I am a bit curious about that data."

"I'm sure you are," Leona said, and Tarn felt his temper slip a touch at the condescension in her voice. Damned woman always knew how to push his buttons.

"Well, then what do you want me to say? Their data might not be this titanic revelation that Belt Group's convinced it is, but it's certainly valuable. The fact that they're running from the law proves that much."

Leona turned face-forward in the chair and leaned over the desk, glaring at Tarn. "I want you to tell me why we shouldn't rip them apart, find this data, and try to turn a penny off of it."

"It might come to that," Tarn acknowledged, "but for now, I've already offered them my protection. I don't go back on my word unless the situation changes. Right now, things are static enough." He hesitated, then continued, "Besides, with these rumors coming out of Jupiter, and all the unrest on the Moon...I think that the less attention that we draw from UNASCA, the better."

"But it's Belt Group. Rumor has it they're burning the candle at both ends," Leona frowned. "Ah, but publicly..."

"Right. And there's no public reward for the information, because they haven't even publicly admitted they've lost the ship. So you see..."

"Your hands are tied."

"Yeah," Tarn leaned back in his chair, lacing his fingers and resting them behind his head. "But go ahead and put out some quiet feelers for me, all right? If the situation changes, I want to be prepared."

"And Lamont?"

Tarn sighed and rubbed his temples. He hated dealing with internal security. Couldn't everyone just see how much more profitable it was to work together? Had he ever made anyone poor? Any of his friends, anyway? "Prepare a reception for Lamont when he gets back."

The silence of space slowly gave way to a whistling

rumble, more felt than heard. The deep back of Venus' night side, broken only by the few specks of light from her larger aerostats, took on a blood-red hue. That hue lightened to bright red to orange as the rumble increased from a barely audible sound to a roar loud enough to drown out all conversation.

Joanna clenched her armrests and closed her eyes as the orange glow turned to white-hot streamers that coursed over the viewport. She silently wished for the whole thing to be over as the ship rocked and vibrated, feeling as though it would tear itself apart at any moment. She'd traveled huge distances and lived in space for months, but this was her first atmospheric re-entry.

Suddenly, it was over. The roar and the vibration died away almost at once, leaving a quiet whistling noise that was not loud enough to disrupt conversation.

Joanna opened her eyes and was surprised to see the rest of her companions also looking a little pallid.

"You all right, Joanna?" Eileen muttered, her eyes closed.

"I'm fine. Are you okay?"

"Just a little space sickness. Re-entry always does that to me, no idea why." She opened her eyes. "Is it weird that flying in space makes me less sick than flying through an atmosphere?"

"Sure is," Melissa said, leaning back toward Eileen and sticking her tongue out.

"It is a little bit," Joanna said, trying to get caught up in the good humor and since they'd survived re-entering the atmosphere. It didn't work.

The horizon was still ever so slightly curved, and

most of the cloud mass was below them, but there were wisps of yellowish-white around tearing by them even now, painfully bright as they entered the day side of the planet.

"If this is any of your first times on Venus," the pilot said through the ship's PA system, "then you might want to hold on. We're in for some serious chop."

"Um, just how serious are we talking?" Joanna didn't relax her death grip on the seat's armrests.

"We're talking two hundred kilometer per hour winds with substantial wind shear. Plus, we're going to have to convert to atmospheric mode in order to make Hartley, which will make it all a little worse."

"Oh, great."

"It's not that bad, Joanna," Eileen said, "as long as you've taken classes as a stunt pilot or you really, really like roller coasters."

"I get sick on roller coasters."

"Then it's not going to be a lot of fun for you," she smiled, closing her eyes again.

"Also, I have a little rule," the pilot said again, "if you're going to be sick then you can do it on someone else's ship. Barf bags are directly in front of you if you can't follow instructions."

As the ship descended into the first cloud layer, Joanna could make out some textures and contours of its topside. The high-velocity winds sheared them into linear patterns that morphed and mutated before her eyes. They were nothing like the lazy fluffiness of Earth clouds.

And the rocking started. It was loud and violent, worse than the worst terrestrial turbulence that Joanna had ever felt. She could just feel her organs shifting and bumping into each other as the ship bucked and rolled. There was nothing to see outside but the bright yellowish white of the clouds, so Joanna kept her eyes screwed shut and prayed once more for it to be over.

The rocking seemed to last for hours, and eventually it got the better of her stomach. She opened her eyes and pawed desperately for the plastic bag in the seat back in front of her, barely getting it open before she was violently sick.

"Ah great, I thought you guys would make it. If it makes you feel any better, we're shifting to atmospheric mode," the pilot said after a short eternity. "Things'll get a little nicer in a minute. We're about twenty minutes from Hartley, by the way."

Joanna heard a mechanical groaning and opened her eyes. Out on the wings, large pod-like sections were splitting open, their shields retracting and four large blades extending from each. As soon as they were partway out Joanna could see them bite into the air and start to spin. Soon they were perfectly parallel to their path of travel and spinning like an airplane's propellers. In fact, Joanna was quite sure that's what they were.

"Weird," she muttered to herself. Thankfully, the turbulence had reduced itself to a much more manageable level and Joanna was no longer on the verge of puking, although the sour smell in the cabin was starting to get to her as well.

They dipped below the cloud layer and emerged into a space of clear air between the yellowish white clouds above and some darker orange ones hundreds of meters or more below. There was a blackish speck in the distance that grew more and more distinct until Joanna realized what it was: an enormous balloon. In fact, it was several balloons lashed together, with thick cables suspending the aerostat itself below. Hartley Aerostat.

Joanna had seen pictures of the station for years, and there weren't many other places like it, even a hundred years later. The trailing edge of the aerostat was a teardrop-like curve that broke the wind, and the habitable section nestled in behind it. It was modular, much like an older space station, but there was a lot more superstructure and other equipment that made it look a lot beefier than any space station that Joanna had ever seen.

There was a single docking node protruding from the parabolic shield, and the pilot called for complete silence as they approached ever so slowly up to it. Joanna wasn't quite sure why he was having so much trouble with an elementary maneuver until she remembered that they weren't in space. Both ship and aerostat were being pushed along at hundreds of kilometers per hour, and the ship was under power at that. She felt cold sweat break out all over her skin and she suppressed a shudder.

But they docked without a problem, and the pilot let out a sigh audible even without the PA system. "All right, thank you for flying Venus Express flight one eight two to historic Hartley Aerostat. Be sure to check your seat area for any personal belongings; this ship will be departing as soon as you're off."

They filed out the front docking port just above the pilot, the gravity making things a little cramped. Joanna had barely noticed during all the docking, but it felt a lot like Earth's.

Hartley Aerostat was small, almost as small as the Mary Ellen, but without the advantage of being in zero gravity. There were four habitation modules and two common areas, both of which had been converted into the museum and visitor's center. The accommodations looked like they'd been upgraded since the station was first build a hundred and twenty years previous, but not by much. Joanna distinctly turned her nose up at the toilet facilities.

"Well," Eileen said as they were taking the grand tour, "this is cozy."

"I have a really bad feeling about this," Ben said, frowning. "I sure hope that Tarn doesn't forget about us down here."

"Relax," said a new voice. The crew turned and saw Tarn's man Lamont Kinsey. "Tarn's been thinking about you guys a lot. My ship completely replaced the food supplies here and we brought you some fresh air and water too. What do you think of that?"

"Tarn's generosity is always impressive," Ben said, the frown not leaving his face. "But what are you still doing here?"

"Yeah, I asked the same question," Lamont said, "but Tarn wants me to make sure that you're settling in just fine. He said that it'd be a couple of weeks before the work is done on your ship, and he didn't want you to be worrying about it too much."

"That's awful nice of him," Ben said, his expression unchanged: he looked like he wanted to punch somebody. "Where the hell is his computer expert?"

"Not my problem," Lamont said airily. "Besides, Tarn doesn't tell me shit."

"Well then, um, where's the food?" Joanna said, smiling wide. The tension between Lamont, Eileen, and Ben was getting to be a bit too much for her.

"I'm surprised you're hungry, what with your performance on the ride down here," he sneered.

"Oh, um," Joanna said, feeling her cheeks burn. She revised her opinion of Kinsey downward by several notches.

"Hey, lay off," Eileen said, shouldering her way past Joanna. "I appreciate Tarn's concern, but guess what? You can leave any time you like. We don't need any of his toadies down here."

"Toady?" Lamont raised himself up to his full, considerable height. He was just barely taller than Eileen, which made him the tallest person in the room by far.

"You heard me. Is there a problem?"

Lamont worked his jaw for a moment, as though he wanted to say more, but he backed down a bit. "Nah, I'm just fine. Food's in the galley, this way." He gave Joanna an evil look as she passed him; she didn't bother to make eye contact.

"Fine, I guess I'll just head back, then," he called after them as they shuffled toward the galley. "Don't bother with anything! We've got you taken care of."

Venus was too far from the Earth for live communication, so Forrester's latest update came as a video recording. It was plain and simple in its language; Forrester was not a man to mince words. They all knew what their job was.

He put it this way: "Takedown at your convenience, Bronwyn. Belt Group will back you up. Make UNASCA feel as needed as possible but do not surrender any prisoners. Good luck."

Total running time, twenty four seconds. That was all she needed.

Their stateroom aboard *Agropolis* was tiny, but since all they had used it for was sleeping, that wasn't a problem. Keven stood staring out the viewport on the bottom of the deck; with the lights off one could make out the brighter stars as they lazily swung by under the station's rotation.

"Have you heard from Lamont?"

"I have not," Bronwyn said. She was about to dial him on her handset when it started vibrating. Sure enough, as you speak of the Augustus, he is at the gates.

"Bronwyn here," she answered as Keven crowded in close. With the volume turned up it was easy for both of them to hear without giving away that they were on a speaker.

"Hey there, blockhead. It's Lamont."

"We have been waiting for several days, Mr. Kinsey," she said, letting an edge of impatience bleed into her voice. "We expected to hear from you before now."

"Oh, goodness gracious I'm sorry. Turns out that Tarn wanted me to babysit your marks for a few days. Asshole," he spat. "I'm going to look forward to this operation."

"We do not yet have an operation, Mr. Kinsey, because we do not have the information from you as to where our 'marks' are."

"You in your room?"

"Yes."

"I'll meet you there in a minute. Gotta shake a tail

first." Click.

Keven frowned. "I do not like this man."

"I confess I do not admire him much either, but we are forced to put up with him just a little while longer." Bronwyn didn't say that she was very near to taking him out once his usefulness had expired; there would be nobody remaining to speak in his defense once their work was done. The man was annoying and his naked ambition made him dangerous.

It was a further quarter hour before Lamont tapped on the door to their quarters. When he entered, he was breathing heavily and smelled of sweat and anxiety.

"I think that Tarn is starting to get suspicious."

"Why is that?" Keven rumbled.

Lamont tapped him on the head. "Why do you think, dumbass? Because I'm about to put a damned knife in his back."

Keven pushed Lamont away a bit harder than necessary, slamming him back up against the wall. "You should be more careful with your tongue."

"And you should be more careful with your fucking hands. If this deal turns south I'll dump everything to Stefanovic. I've covered my tracks; you'll be the only ones covered in shit if I do."

Bronwyn stepped between them. "This is counterproductive. Before you do anything, tell me where the crew of the *Mary Ellen* is."

"No."

Bronwyn straightened, though she was still a good six inches shorter than Kinsey. "Pardon me?"

"I said no. I'm not so stupid as to cut my usefulness

this early. I'll send you there with my picked crew, and I'll have meatsack here with me, taking our Tarn. You can do your job but I'm not going to slit my own throat, you get me?"

Bronwyn screwed her mouth shut. His threat may have been an idle one, but if he believed that he could get some advantage by betraying their presence to Tarn Stefanovic...the risk was too great. Better to play along, and as of right now he had little reason to lie to them.

"Very well, Mr. Kinsey, we respect your wishes. Keven will accompany you to Tarn's place of business and I will go with your crew to the hiding place of the *Mary Ellen*s. When do we go?"

"Right the hell now. Even a couple of hours might be too long as far as Tarn is concerned, and there's no reason to delay on account of the *Mary Ellen* people."

"Very well. Keven?"

The man didn't look very happy about being picked to accompany Lamont, but he kept his tongue and nodded curtly. "I say we go."

They went.

Chapter 10

It had taken a full day for Joanna to grow bored with the Hartley museum. The artifacts were interesting, but there weren't many of them: an old deck of cards, a very old-model spacesuit that must've massed two hundred kilos, a piece of the original balloon manifold. One could only stare at them so long.

The crew had assembled in the galley. There had been an odd, unspoken sort of agreement that they would eat together, but even though the galley had been designed for a crew their size, she still felt crammed into it. Everything was small, in fact, and it was starting to make Joanna a little stir crazy.

"I feel like I need to run somewhere," she muttered as she spooned up some "turkey in cranberry sauce." It wasn't bad, actually, better than the *Mary Ellen* provisions. Unfortunately, it was just good enough that it made her nostalgic for the real thing.

"Ditto," Eileen said, polishing off the packet of

pasta she'd been toying with. "I had kind of assumed that Tarn would find a place in orbit for us."

"I think that he just wants us way out of the way," Melissa said. "Who would come down here looking for us?"

"Hopefully nobody," Joanna said, eating another bite. "What I hope is that the ship gets done quickly. I'm just about full of history."

Ben spoke. He had said only a few sentences to the rest of them the entire time that they'd been cooped up here; he'd kept to himself except for meals. "What I hope," he said slowly, "is that he doesn't decide that it's less trouble just to kill us and take our ship."

Joanna paused with her spoon halfway to her mouth. "What?"

"Don't listen to him, Joanna, he's just getting cabin fever," Eileen said, shooting a warning glance at Ben.

He ignored it. "Is that so? What, do you think that I wanted to tell you when we were making negotiations? Huh? That I thought we could do better? At least in orbit there would be some evidence if he went traitor on us. As for here, well, nobody would find us in the ninety atmospheres on the surface."

"But wait. I thought we trusted Tarn a little bit?" Joanna said, alarmed. What had been a latent case of stircraziness was blooming into full-blown cabin fever. The walls were a closing in, and her heart was pounding.

"We do," Eileen said. "He's not that kind of guy. If he thinks that we might put in a good word for him he won't just cut us off. He didn't get to be where he is by callous betrayal. It's bad for his long term prospects."

"But most of his prospects didn't dump a load in

his lap like we did. If we hadn't dragged Stephen's name into this and paid him good with it, you think that he even would've answered our call?"

Eileen nearly dropped the datacube she'd been working at obsessively with her fingers. "What did you say?"

Ben frowned. "I said that if it wasn't for Stephen's name he wouldn't have even answered our call."

"No, that's not what you said," Eileen was standing now, and Ben hopped down off the food processing unit that he'd been using as a seat. "You said that I paid Tarn off using Stephen's name."

"I guess so. Who cares?"

Eileen was almost shouting now. "I care! If you think I'm trying to profit off of his death..."

"Now just a damned minute," Ben said, holding his hands up. "That's crazy."

"Eileen," Joanna said softly, reaching for her shoulder, but Eileen shoved her hand away.

"How dare you. I haven't even had time to grieve, and if you think that I'm so mercenary as to try to profit off his death...he died in my arms, Ben!" There were tears in her eyes, but there was also fire behind them.

Joanna was starting to panic. It seemed like the walls were very close, like they were crowded together. She was suddenly very aware of the station's slow swaying in the wind, the howling that just barely penetrated the hermetically sealed windows, the slight jostling as the station pulled on the balloon cables. It all seemed so...fragile.

Then there was an abrupt bump, like something big had hit the station.

"Come on, my friends, you can do better than that!" Tarn yelled, throwing the dice again. They landed on seven and eight, losing him another twenty five. It was just a friendly game with some of his companions at the Bordeaux, but he still didn't like losing.

"It looks like you should play with dice with fewer sides," said Chomsky, the club owner and his trusted lieutenant.

"It looks like maybe I should choose not to play at all," Tarn snorted, raising his highball glass. "How about another scotch, eh? I think I remember there being something from the forties in your lower cabinet. A good decade. For losing, anyway."

Chomsky barked an order at one of his servers. His other trusted companion at the table, Leona, handed the dice back to him, kissing his hand as he took them. "Come on, Tarn. You're not that big of a screwup, are you?"

"I'd have more luck throwing them *at* you," he said, laughing at her mock hurt expression. "Still, no bad luck unless you try, right?" He placed a few chips and threw them again. One and nine.

"See, Tarn? My help, obviously." Leona smiled as she handed him a small pile of chips.

"I should never have doubted you," he said, kissing her on the cheek. He started to pull away but she held him close for a moment, breathing in his ear. "Don't trust Lamont. Saw him with those Belt Group agents." She let him go, smiling as if she'd just trusted him to some sexy secret.

Tarn smiled back, feeling the hollowness in his cheeks as he did so. "So, you've seen your old friends?"

"Not personally, but a, ah, sister of mine did. Lamont said hello himself."

"Well. Good for him."

Chomsky pushed the dice back toward him. "How about once more to even the score?"

Tarn shook his head, standing. "Sorry, Ned. Leona and I have some important errand to attend to. Family business, you understand."

Chomsky smiled thinly. He understood. "All right, Tarn, be careful. See you back for happy hour?"

"It'll be a happy one, all right," he said, excusing himself from the anonymous admirers that always clustered around his table. Leona followed close behind, her slinky blue dress swishing around her utterly perfect legs.

Her face lost some of its perfection when they left the club, melting into a scowl. She reached into her purse and tweaked something. Tarn's suspicions that it was the interceptor beam were confirmed when she said, "What are you going to do about Lamont?"

"I thought I told you to have a reception ready," Tarn whispered, trying to keep his temper.

"I did. Chomsky fouled up."

"Damn. If I asked him to come see me personally he'd refuse and he'd know for sure I'm onto him. If he doesn't already," he said, stopping on the concourse and raising his eyebrow to Leona.

She shook her head, brunette trusses swaying as she did so. "He knows. But it's confirmed; he met with the Belt Group agents just as soon as he got back from Hartley."

Tarn resumed his swift walk back toward his office. Once he got there he'd be safe. "Then we don't have a second to lose. Lamont isn't known for playing his cards this close to his chest—if he's come that far already he'll make his move really soon. Today, probably."

Leona stopped, grabbing his arm urgently. "Tarn."

He looked at her, at the frightened expression on her face, then followed her gaze forward toward where a few men were walking out from a cheap gin joint on the promenade, just across from his office.

They were all wielding weapons openly and looking directly at the two of them.

"Leona, run."

"Tarn-"

"Just run!" He shoved her back, and dove to the side, reaching into the pocket of his waistcoat as he did. His assailants opened fire, just as the sound of fighting back by the Bordeaux reached him.

"Is that someone docking?" Eileen said, frowning as she left the galley. "We're not scheduled to get any visitors."

"Maybe it's the cryptologist?" Joanna said, not really expecting it to be true.

"They would've called first," Eileen said. "I have a bad feeling about this."

"And we're trapped here like roaches," Ben cursed. "I bet that asshole turned us right in."

Eileen turned on him so suddenly he almost tripped. "This conversation ends right now," she said, stabbing a finger into his chest. "We're in a situation, and I need you on my side. Get it?"

Ben swallowed hard, then averted his eyes. "Yeah. Yeah, I get it."

"Good. Now go find a weapon, all of you. Just in case, okay?" She turned to Melissa as sounds of the aerostat's docking hatch echoed through the hull. "Mel, go back to that galley with Joanna, and if they reach you try to delay them as long as possible. I don't think they'll use lethal force."

"Reassuring," Melissa said, moving toward Joanna.

"No, wait, I don't want to split up again," she said, pleading.

There was movement from the front of the station. Whoever it was, had come inside without announcing themselves. Eileen's face twisted in concern as Ben returned with a couple of emergency rebreathing tanks, each ten kilos or so. "Good enough. All right, stay behind me. We need to attack before they can get their bearings. Ready?"

"Ready as I'll ever be." He handed a tank to Eileen and one to Melissa, leaving himself empty handed.

Joanna felt her heart pounding in her ears. The stations still felt tiny, and she had nowhere to go. Her own death once again seemed imminent, and it was even less fun than the first time.

Eileen faced toward the front of the aerostat and shouted loud enough for whoever was there to hear her. "Let's roll!"

With a shout, the five of them ran through the first museum module, then into the second as three men and two women that Joanna didn't recognize walked through the hatch from the docking area on the far side. They seemed surprised that all of their targets were already there.

Her mind seemed to be operating on a different plane than her body. Joanna noted in quick succession that there were multiple people, and none of them looked like a computer expert. The second thought, trailing the first by microseconds, was that all of these people were armed with actual weapons, whereas the best weapon the *Ellen*'s had was an oxygen tank.

Her third thought was that the woman leading the party was Bronwyn.

Joanna didn't want to fight. She hated fighting. But as soon as she saw that one of her opponents was to be Bronwyn all of her courage drained out as though someone had opened a valve on her feet. She halted her movement and slid to a stop behind a display case containing an ancient space suit.

"Do not resist; we come with a warrant from UNASCA," Bronwyn was shouting. Joanna risked a peek over the display case, and she saw Eileen and the others tried to square off with the intruders, but those people had no interest in fighting clean. There was a loud crack and Almika fell, hit by an electrolaser bolt in her center of mass.

Luckily there wasn't room for them to keep their range, and a few more bolts went wild, setting off the environmental alarms in the cabin. A screaming warble filled the room as the brawl continued.

There was a crack of fire again, this time directed toward their attackers, and Joanna could see why Ben had left himself empty handed—he had his own pistol. He had never mentioned it or showed it to anyone, but why wouldn't he be carrying it if he was expecting a betrayal.

One of the assailants went down, meaning that the *Ellen*s were outnumbered two to one. The only reason that any of them were still standing, Joanna was sure, was that

Bronwyn had been trapped behind her own people, and was fighting to actually enter the fray.

Eileen swung her heavy tank at her attacker, who stumbled back into a case displaying a scale model of Hartley, bouncing off the hardened plastic. He fired his electrolaser from the hip and hit Eileen on the leg, staggering her; his second blast went wide as she fell, bringing the tank down on his face. He didn't move after that.

There was a flash of movement to her left and Joanna was startled to see one of the large women standing just next to her case.

"Come on, girl," the woman growled, leaning in to grab her. A frantic glance about confirmed the obvious: there was nobody to help. She ducked back, the screaming alarm melding with her own thoughts to create a sort of living nightmare. The woman took a few steps toward her and reached out with a grasping claw.

A electrolaser blast missed both of their heads by centimeters. Across the room, lying where she had fallen, Eileen was aiming her attacker's weapon with her off hand.

The woman recovered, but Joanna recovered first, finding a rebreather mask and emergency tank on the wall. She swung with all of her might at the woman, knowing that the tank was far too light to cause any serious damage, that she was just going to annoy her attacker and lose anyway.

The tank hit and the woman stumbled. There must've been a projection, a sharp piece on the tank that caught skin. Blood sprayed and the woman fell backward onto her butt with a yell of pain and fear.

Joanna had an instant to decide whether to run or

fight. She wanted to run, but out of the corner of her eye she could see Bronwyn finally working her way into the module. No, damn it, no!

Joanna fell on the woman, bashing away with her tank and not stopping until the woman's movements had long ceased. It was as though she was watching herself from outside her body. She could see her lips curled in rage, the burning incandescence in her eyes, the savage way her hand grabbed the tiny air tank, the merciless way that she brought it down hard on the woman's face. For a single moment, she wasn't Joanna, the scared puppy, but Joanna, the brave warrior.

It felt good.

"Help!"

Joanna blinked, staring at the bloody mess that had been her attacker, the dripping blood on her hands, and then turned to see the source of the shout.

Eileen was backing away from Bronwyn, who strode toward her with calm grace. The heavier gravity only seemed to make Bronwyn's movements even more graceful and purposeful, and there was no doubt in Joanna's mind that Eileen was as good as beaten.

Eileen's eyes met hers. There was a look of such powerful desperation in them that it touched the dying ember that had been her rage just a moment ago, and lit it once more into a conflagration.

Without a single articulate thought entering her mind, Joanna charged for Bronwyn. She'd taken her once, she could do it again.

Bronwyn must have heard the footsteps, and turned just in time to easily deflect Joanna's charge. The blow took her on the side of the head and deposited her, ears ringing, balance shot, on the grimy deck.

Eileen had charged at the same time, and had actually reached Bronwyn, only to get shoved back the same way. Bronwyn took another step toward her, only to duck with supernatural reflexes as Joanna chanced a throw of her only weapon, the air tank.

It didn't come close, but it brought Eileen the instant she needed. Bronwyn had shoved her into the cupola that joined the two museum modules together; Eileen just hit the emergency close button and the door slammed in Bronwyn's face.

There was a hoarse shout. From her place on the deck, Joanna could see Ben get shoved back against the space suit case, his mouth and nose bleeding, see the weapon get knocked from his hand by one of the male intruders. Another blow brought him low, and a third put him on the deck.

That was the moment that Joanna noticed that Ben's gun had landed right next to her on the deck. It was the same moment that she noticed that Bronwyn had turned toward her.

The weapon was in her hands in a second. Bronwyn saw her, nobody else did.

Her ears were ringing and the room was spinning, but Bronwyn was still in the cupola. She had nowhere to go.

Yet she went. Bronwyn threw herself forward just as Joanna's beam went over her head and wide. The woman landed right next to Joanna on the ground, and she didn't even have time to blink before a sharp blow sent the weapon flying from her numbed hand.

Bronwyn, still on the deck, was rearing back with an opened palmed blow that looked to remove her head from her shoulders. Joanna couldn't help it—she closed her eyes.

The blow never landed. Instead, Joanna heard a staccato burst from an electrolaser.

Joanna opened her eyes. Bronwyn, eyes closed peacefully, was still on the deck, her open palm resting centimeters from Joanna's eyes.

"Gotcha," Melissa said, and Joanna turned to see her standing, propped up against a display case with a bunch of small artifacts sitting on the bottom, jostled from their pedestals.

"Hi," Joanna said, blinking in disbelief.

"I think we're square," Melissa said, pointing her weapon at a target Joanna couldn't see, firing a couple of times, and then joining her beneath the display case.

"Eileen got away."

"I saw it. I think one or two of them went after her. There's still-"

A sharp crack cut her off, and a solid bar of lighting hitting the wall by her face dazzled Joanna's already overloaded senses. The ringing in her head seemed synchronized with the alarm buzzing.

"There's still one over there," Melissa continued. "If we can just hold him off, we might stand a chance."

Chapter 11

Tarn slammed into the doorframe of the cheap hotel, pressing himself into the tiny space while the door ever so slowly accordioned open. He heard the reports of weapon fire and he saw chips being blown out of the frame across from him. So they weren't interested in taking him alive, eh? Just as well. He wasn't all that partial to non-lethal weapons himself.

The door open, he spared just a second to check on Leona, running into a bar several doors down and across the concourse, and then ducked into his own building. They had to be right behind him.

There was no desk clerk at the hotel, just a checkout kiosk. The electronic greeter started chiming, "Greetings, Mr. Stefanovic. Might I interest you in one of our finest rooms? We offer free breakfast and complimentary passes-"

"Not interested. Shut up."

The greeter shut up, just keeping the visual display.

Tarn's mind was wheeling. There wasn't anywhere to go from here, unless...

The first-floor rooms opened off a narrow corridor. He followed the curve up the station's deck for several doors until he found one marked "Maintenance."

It wasn't unlocked, but that didn't matter—you built something on Tarn Stefanovic's station, you made damned sure that Tarn Stefanovic had access to secured areas. It was just good business.

The door opened into the space inside the enormous circumferential partition that divided the entertainment district and the administration and office area. It wasn't wide, but if you didn't mind ducking around conduits and other projections you could go around the entire station in this space.

Just as he pushed his way past the mops and brooms into the maintenance space, he heard the electronic greeter start up again, "Greeting, Mr. Glandis. Might I interest you-"

The report of a gunshot quieted the greeter, but it had told him enough. Glandis was one of Lamont Kinsey's good friends. As if he'd needed additional confirmation that the bitter old man was after his blood. At least Glandis wasn't one Tarn's best men, far from it. All the skilled ones were loyal.

Tarn was running down the corridor, wondering if he'd shut the door to the maintenance area behind him, and then realizing with a sharp stab of anger that he had not. The door crashed open some ways behind him and he heard shouting.

There was a crack of weapons discharge, but he was

already far enough up the station's curve so as to be out of range. But it wouldn't last forever—he'd been slacking off on his cardio workout. An easy thing to do in space, even with gravity. He might not make it all the way around the partition to the Bordeaux at this rate.

He hoped that some of his best men would escape the abattoir. Tarn, still running, snagged his handset from his pocket and hit the first address on speed dial, below Leona's: Tom Oberlin, his chief bodyguard. A dozen paces later, he was expecting the worst; there was no response. Ditto with the next address, Tari Yu, his accountant. The third address connected to Toyotomi, his chief intelligence man.

"Toyotomi!" Tarn whispered into the headset as he squeezed between two conduits, continuing to run.

"Tarn? I thought you were dead," he whispered back. "I can't talk long—Liang and Tymoshenko just tried to kill me!"

"It's Lamont, Toyotomi. His thugs just about caught me napping."

"You might be on your own, Tarn. Looks like he bought out people all around the planet—heads are rolling as we speak! Rumor is, he has offworld help."

"I know," Tarn said, sparing a glance behind him. He could still hear his pursuers, if not see them.

"Sorry, boss. I screwed up—I knew something was brewing but I didn't figure he'd act so soon. I knew he was angry, but he's just an impotent old chicken."

"We'll talk about this later. Stay alive and spread the word that I'm alive, on *Agropolis*, and I need as much help as you can get me." He paused. "And take care of Leona. If she's got half a brain, she'll be heading your way.

With a sinking feeling, Tarn hit the disconnect button. There would be no help for him now, just like in the early days. It had been years since he'd been in a fight for his life, and even though he was older and softer now he thought he just might still have some chicanery left.

The men behind him had gone silent, doubtless running as fast as they could after him. He couldn't tell how close they were, how soon it would be until he was within weapons range. His chest was heaving, his lungs burning.

Damn it!

The next exit from into the entertainment district, he took. The door accordioned open and he flew through it heedless of the space he was entering. There was a small closet just inside, and then he burst through another, manual door.

Two things hit him right away: the smell of expensive, subtle incense, and the sight of naked women. A lot of naked women, and real ones at that. This was the Venus Underworld, one of his finest massage parlors slash brothels. Of all the places to end up.

There were shouts of alarm as he entered the room, ones that calmed as soon as the women saw who he was. He waved and smiled, his chest still heaving, aware that he was flushed and sweaty, a far cry from the controlled appearance that he liked to maintain in public.

The madam, Sonja, ran into him as he tried to leave from the front entrance.

"Mr. Stefanovic, I didn't see you come in?"

"I used the back way, Sonja," he said, looking out the ornate glass window in front, trying to see if there was anyone waiting for him out there.

"Well, do you want your usual today?"

"No." He turned to her, urgency in his voice and his movements. Lamont's men were seconds behind him. "Some men might follow me. Slow them down if you can, but don't do anything too risky. They're armed and crazy."

Sonja took a nervous step back. "Mr. Stefanovic, I don't understand..."

"Don't worry about it," he said, deciding that it was more dangerous to stay than to continue, shoving his way out the front door.

He was about half a rotation away from the Bordeaux or his offices. He gave his weapon a once-over as he jogged up the concourse, keeping to the sides where market stalls were conglomerated, selling jewelry or engraved glass or bits of Venusian rock for the tourists. Just three rounds left; he regretted wasting so many just to cover his end run.

Might as well get some use out of them now. He walked, calm as he could manage, up to a cart selling a local variant of the hot dog, interposing it between him and the entrance to the parlor.

Just on schedule, three men burst from the parlor's front door, looking back and forth, trying to spot him. They were about thirty, forty meters away and moving toward him. Hearing the tourists and merchants shout in alarm as he pulled his gun from his pocket, he took careful aim down the curvature of the station and pulled the trigger.

"Joanna, we need to help Eileen," Melissa

whispered harshly. There was still the occasional crack as an electrolaser beam fired by their remaining attacker whipped against the display case that they'd taken cover behind.

"Well, you're the one with the gun," Joanna whispered back.

"I know. Can you shoot it?" Melissa said, raising an eyebrow.

"Um," she hesitated. Her ears were still ringing with the alarm and the module seemed to be growing tinier by the second, but it had at least stopped spinning. That was something. "Maybe?"

"Okay, well, we're going to find out in a second, because I'm going to run interference for you. When he tries to hit me, you hit him, got it?"

"Okay. Melissa?"

"Yeah?" she said, bracing herself to run, ducking a bit as near miss from an electrolaser beam ionized the air around them.

"Thanks for saving me."

Melissa shook her head, forcing smile. Then, with that, she pushed off.

A beam narrowly missed her a moment later, so narrowly that her hair stood on end. Joanna peeked around the display case, willing herself to focus, willing the room to stand still.

The guy was standing just behind the space suit case that Ben was lying at the foot of, the one that she'd lately taken cover behind. He was peeking his gun hand around to shoot...

With as calm a squeeze of the weapon's tiny trigger as she could manage, Joanna hit his hand square on. The electrolaser was most effective when it hit the center of mass, but Joanna was only aiming for "good enough," and she hit it. Even tagging his hand caused such a tremendous spasm that it put him out right on his rear, and Joanna's second beam nailed him, center-of-mass.

She was getting to be a pretty decent shot.

Melissa picked herself up from the floor, groping around until she reached the weapon that Bronwyn had knocked from Joanna's hand. She then walked over to Bronwyn, tilted her head as if considering a work of art, and then pumping another beam into her. She twitched, and then lay still but for the slow rise and fall of her chest.

"She's lucky I'm such a nice lady, or she'd be dead," Melissa said, pumping a second blast into Bronwyn for good measure.

Joanna was about to respond, but Ben did so first. "Where's Eileen?"

"She's leading at least one of them on a merry chase. Here," she handed him the weapon that Joanna's last target had dropped. "If any of them move, hit them again. You okay?"

Ben paused for a moment, regarding her with a swollen, bloodied face. Then he spat dark red saliva and said, "I think I'll manage."

"Great. Come on, Joanna."

Joanna gave Ben a sympathetic smile and followed after Melissa. The second museum module had some small evidence of a struggle. The far hatch, leading toward the crew living area, had been thrown up like someone had been chased through it.

That was when they heard the sounds of shouting

and a struggle from somewhere toward the back of the station. The galley, workout room, labs, and crew quarters described a circular path, starting at one end of the living area where Joanna and Melissa stood and ending at the other.

"You go left, I'll go right?" Melissa raised an eyebrow.

The absolute last thing that Joanna wanted to do was split up. That ember of rage that had kept her alive during the fight was turning to ash. Yet, she found herself saying, "Yeah. Sure."

"Okay. Break."

Joanna opened the left hatch and entered one of the crew modules. Bunk beds were stacked on one side, with desks and storage areas on the other. The bifurcated clouds of Venus being whipped along by the planet's eternal gale were visible through a window at the end of the module, just next to a hatch that read "Labs A."

Holding her electrolaser in front of her like the soldiers in the movies, she hit the open button for the Lab A hatch.

"Joanna?"

"Don't move!"

The two overlapping voices, one Eileen's, one her captor's, hit Joanna as soon as the hatch was open. A scar faced man was holding her in a standard sort of hostage position with one arm around her upper body, blocking her arms, and another pointing a weapon at her. Joanna noticed with sinking, horrifying dread that it was not an electrolaser.

"You shoot her, and I'll kill both of you," he snarled. "Now back up!"

His face was such an inviting target. She kept the laser pointed forward in the man's direction, afraid to drop it and afraid to fire. She didn't want to die.

Where was Melissa?

"I said drop it! I'm supposed to bring you in alive, but I won't hesitate!" He brandished his pistol.

"Joanna, careful!" Eileen's fear was painted on her face in broad strokes.

"Dr-drop your, ah," Joanna started to say, feeling a horrible lump catch in her throat, seeing the gun waver in her hands. There was no way that she could do this. She might be a decent shot, but...no way. Not with her hands shaking with adrenaline and fear.

The man was looking angrier and angrier. "Damn it!" he snarled, and fired.

The instant between him pulling the trigger and the bullet hitting her in the chest seemed like a dark, regret filled eternity. Why hadn't she done what he had asked?

Then the bullet hit, and there was pain. It was like a knife of fire had buried itself to the hilt in her belly, tearing things, important things, as it went. Like a switch being thrown, all of her strength left her and she fell to the deck.

The man swore. Through the pain, it was as if she was hearing him through a great distance, and likewise could hear Eileen emit a startled, strangled sound as he hauled her away. Joanna could do nothing for her now, another regret in a moment so full of them.

No. Joanna realized that, as long as she had the slight bit of strength to lift it, the laser still clutched in her hand was still a useful weapon. And the man had been so anxious to move on that he hadn't bothered to separate her from it. He might have killed her, but there was no way that he was getting away unscathed.

As he fiddled with the hatch in the crew module, he had to open it with one arm and also to keep Eileen at bay. She wasn't making it easy for him, and for at least a brief moment it was taking up more of his concentration than he could spare. And his back was to her.

Joanna fired. And fired, and fired. If she hit Eileen, who cared as long as she hit her target?

After ten or so shots, she could see through the darkness entering her vision that the man had fallen. Eileen had too, but she was picking herself up and running over to Joanna, saying something vague and indistinct, impossible to interpret. She looked down at Joanna's crumpled form, and Joanna realized that what had been a burning fire on her insides was now expanding into a cold, numb void.

Tarn fired, and fired, and fired.

He could see that he hit at least one of his attackers, but he didn't wait for the rest of the results. He ducked low and ran, ducking between the carts affixed to the deck. More rounds whizzed overhead or buried themselves in the deck—frangible rounds, so they didn't blow a hole right through the hull.

He could see the Bordeaux just a quarter-revolution away, but there was no obvious way to get there. The crowd's panic had rolled ahead of him and people were clearing the streets, greatly reducing his cover options.

The two survivors were getting close, and his weapon was now so much dead weight. He tossed it aside, feeling a slight tug at his elbow as he turned to run. He realized a moment later that he'd been winged by a round, and was dripping blood.

No time to worry. He gritted his teeth and ran on, ducking into doorways and through the colorful awnings of the concourse kiosks as he did so. His lungs were burning, his elbow felt like it was on fire, and he was out of ammo. Worse, his pursuers were gaining and he had little chance of any backup showing up.

A lesser man might have given up. Then again, a lesser man would never have found himself in Tarn's place.

There she was, straight ahead! The Bordeaux stood like a gleaming edifice, a sanctuary where he might find rest! He risked a glance behind, and saw that his attackers were falling back.

Ha! So he was out of breath, sore, and feeling old. How about them? All this time he'd been so terrified.

And yet.

No longer fearing for his life, he slowed to a fast walk, taking a moment to wrap his handkerchief around the laceration on his arm, and taking in the scene. There were no civilians around; the gunfighting had scared most of them off. He could hear music coming from inside the Bordeaux, the same house beats that he'd been listening to just a short while before.

The entrance to the club was up a few wide, sweeping steps beside an empty bouncer's desk. Its computer still checked his identification as he stood in the entrance, hearing the music but not seeing the activity that he was used to seeing inside.

Had Leona made it? She must've, and barricaded the place down. If there were any of Lamont's men, he would've been gunned down as soon as he set foot inside.

But it didn't quite seem right. Still, keeping his wits about him, he took a step inside. Then he saw Toyotomi, sprawled on the ground in a pool of blood.

He also saw the men, just as they attacked. Tarn still knew his way around his fists—his first blow caught the man on the side of the head, laying him low where a kick to the face put him out. He whirled, fumbling to block a blow from the other attacker, an athletic woman. He knew her name: Kendal.

"How much did he pay you?" Tarn spat, throwing a flurry of blows that backed her up against the wall.

"More than you!" She shouted, going full power, trying to force her way out of a clinch. She didn't make it; even tired, Tarn still overpowered most boxers and when he got in close, the game was over. Thumb, elbow, knee, and she was on the ground, bleeding from a bloody nose.

The blow from behind took him by complete surprise. Pain radiated out from the back of his neck and he felt the energy drain from his body. It was all so unfair, he raged as he fell to the floor. He hadn't even heard anyone come up behind him. He felt himself being rolled over, and a large, European-looking man that he did not recognize put a booted foot firmly against his windpipe.

"That's enough, dumbass. Don't kill him!"

Lamont Kinsey.

Sure enough, the man must've been hidden in the back room. To think that Tarn had been that close to twisting his blister of a head off his scrawny neck. He came into view, a leering sneer on his face.

"How this, Tarn? Or should I call you 'Mr.

Stefanovic'? I'm rather enjoying this little reversal of fortune. And the spoils are *wonderful*," he chuckled, reaching out of Tarn's field of view and pulling Leona up against his filthy body, running his fingers through her hair as she stood trembling.

"You son of a bitch!" Tarn wheezed. The European pressed his foot down until Tarn gagged, and left it there until Lamont gave a signal. And then a little longer.

"All right, all right! Damn it, you dumbass, I said not to kill him yet." Lamont leaned down. "Call me old fashioned, but I just wanted him to know how badly I had beaten him. Oh, and I've got some more news for you, Mr. Stefanovic—not only did I turn your entire damned operation inside out, but I've also been selling information to UNASCA on the side. Did you know that?

"Yeah, you remember those failed business ventures on Europa and Oberon? Couldn't figure out why those kept running out of supplies or having legal difficulties? It's because I was spoon feeding all of your contraband info to Portland! So sorry," he chuckled.

Tarn groaned. The bitter taste of defeat was lingering in his mouth, but it was washed aside by the even filthier bile of failure. He had thoroughly underestimated Lamont's greed and intelligence. But there was nothing to be done about it. He just wished that the European would kill him and get it over with.

"And just in case you think that I was working with Belt Group too, you were only half right. See, I make my own rules."

He grabbed a pistol from the thug nearest him, cocked it, and pointed it, not at Tarn, but at the European standing on his neck. Tarn saw the surprise register for a microsecond before Lamont opened up, tearing his chest open with a three-shot burst.

The pressure on Tarn's neck vanished as the man staggered backward. He tried to stand, but his limbs weren't responding. Out of the corner of his eye he could see a second burst open up the European's head like a melon.

Then the gun turned back to Tarn, and he realized that it was over.

As Lamont fired, Tarn won a final, albeit small, victory. Rather than the last thing he ever saw being Lamont's sneering mug, it was instead the genuine fear and anguish in Leona's eyes. At least she had remained true to him until the end. His failure had *not* been complete.

Chapter 12

"She's not doing well," Ben said, sounding worried, though not as close to true panic as Eileen felt. They'd left Joanna where she was, afraid of moving her, and Melissa had run after Ben, the only one among them with any sort of medical training.

"Gee, you think so?" Eileen said, hearing her voice almost break. She couldn't look down; seeing Joanna's innocent face lying framed in a crimson pool was almost too much for her. Melissa was standing back, hugging herself, looking overwhelmed.

"Let's get her on the ship."

"I'm not even sure that I know how to fly this," Eileen said, feeling trembling wisps of panic start to edge in on her consciousness as she took up the pilot's station. The ship was designed for both atmospheric and spaceflight, which wasn't unusual, but it also had a variable geometry hull and solar power for use in the atmosphere, which was.

"You'd better figure it out pretty damned soon,"

Ben shouted from the passenger area. "She's fading fast."

"Ah, the hell with it," Eileen said. The atmospheric components were probably optional, anyway.

She threw the undock lever and with a loud clank their ship separated from Hartley Aerostat. Melissa was strapped into one of the seats behind and above her. Over the increasing roar of the engines, she shouted, "Where are we going, by the way?"

"Not back to Tarn's, that's for sure."

"You think he was behind that attack?"

"For sure. Belt Group must've paid him off. You know that woman that almost did you in? That was Bronwyn Calleo."

Eileen brought the ship around to due east, adding Venus' sluggish rotation to their ship's velocity, helping boost them into orbit. Any help at all would be useful now.

"How do you know that she didn't just get our information from one of his people?" Melissa sound unconvinced.

"I don't, but we have just one chance to get Joanna somewhere safe, and I don't want to risk Tarn or whoever trying to finish the job."

Ben worked his way forward and sat down next to Melissa, in front of where they'd stashed the recovering Almika and the dying Joanna. Oh, Joanna. Eileen's heart clenched a little bit whenever she thought of the girl bleeding out. It was her fault that Joanna had gotten involved at all; that was impossible to forget.

"For once, I think we see eye to eye on this, Joanna," Ben said. "I'm pretty sure that it was Tarn behind this attack. So, what's our course?"

Eileen gritted her teeth. "Sagan Hospital."

There was silence in the ship, except for the muted rumble of the engines. They climbed above the uppermost cloud deck, emerging into a dark brown sky illuminated by brilliant cloud layers below. The brown was giving way to black as Ben said, "Eileen, that's a UNASCA hospital. It's a public building. They'll let us land, sure, but there's no way that they're letting us take off again."

"Yeah, I know."

"You realize," Ben said, his voice rising, "that we're wanted by UNASCA? That we went through this entire dog and pony show to avoid getting nabbed by them?" He was almost shouting now. "You realize that the reason that Joanna got shot was because we were trying so damned hard to avoid UNASCA? And now you're going to deliver her into that nest of serpents?"

Eileen's hands gripped the controls with white-knuckled intensity. One of her screens was a video display of the passenger section, showing what she could not see from her seat at the pilot's station: Ben had just about lost it. Melissa was looking between them, horrified. And with good reason. If they'd already been in orbit, Eileen would've beaten some sense into Ben until he would've needed hospital treatment as well.

Instead, she just gritted her teeth and said, "Yes, Ben. I know that."

He deflated a little bit. "So, it's over then?"

"Yeah, Ben. It's over. Sorry." In truth she was feeling sick in the pit of her stomach. They had risked so much to get away, to keep their secret data safe, to stay out of the hands of people that had been responsible for the death of Stephen, but it was all over now.

Oh, damn it. Stephen. Just before they'd been boarded, she had been seconds away from just losing it at Ben over some slight or other to him. She just needed to mourn. Maybe if she was in jail she'd at least get that chance.

"Maybe it won't be so bad," Melissa said, a sort of artificial hope coloring her voice. "Maybe once they have the data they'll leave us alone."

"Yeah, sure," Ben scoffed. "They seemed to anxious to do that back on Brighton, right? No, they want that data of Stephen's, but more than anything they want it contained."

"You can't 'contain' data," Melissa said, scoffing right back. "What is this, the nineteenth century?"

"Well, they know that we can't spread it around if we're going to try to sell it. I guess they'll just lock up anyone that they think might have had access."

"Ben's right," she interjected, and the other two fell silent. "They'll take the data, and they'll put us away." The other two stayed silent. For the moment, there was nothing to say.

The sky was now the deep black of space, and around them Venus was acquiring a distinct curvature as they climbed. With the cockpit lights dimmed, the brightest of the stars were just visible, along with the bright light reflected off of the evidence of Venus' massive orbital industry. How strange that it all seemed so remote.

It all seemed so remote, now that Eileen knew that she was alone. Ben and Melissa couldn't help her now, and Joanna was in need of plenty of help herself. As for Almika, well, she was a nice, capable woman, but she was new to the crew. She had no reason to stick her neck out on Eileen's behalf.

And so it was just as it had been since Stephen's death: Eileen was on her own. And once again, she'd been hurt by a cause that she didn't even want to get involved with: the stupid data.

When they had been settled in at Hartley, Eileen had given serious consideration to just broadcasting it around the entire system. Hundreds or thousands of people on Venus alone would have known all that there was to know about the *Atlas*, that ship, and Eileen would've been okay with that. She had no plans to sell the data. It would've been a giant "screw you" to UNASCA.

But it wouldn't be personal enough. She wanted to stick the knife in herself, feel UNASCA's blood herself.

After a twenty-five minute burn, they were in orbit. Ben reported that Joanna had been stabilized, but at such a low level that she might tip over at any second. Worse, they were still at least two orbits from the hospital.

On the first, they burned to align their orbital planes, thrusting through a dozen degrees of orbital inclination. Then another full revolution to synchronize their orbits, trading as much fuel as they needed for speed.

At last, almost three hours after departing Hartley, the hospital loomed large in the viewport. It was one of the brand new non-modular stations, just like *Agropolis*, although this one had a giant caduceus painted on the rotation portion, and despite being somewhat smaller, an even more extensive docking assembly than *Agropolis*.

The controller was polite, directing them to their proper docking slots and advising them that emergency personnel were en route. She didn't say so, but Eileen knew that she must also be calling security. She reached into her pocket, felt for the familiar shape of the datacube. May it cause UNASCA and Belt Group as much trouble as it had caused her.

When Bronwyn regained consciousness, she ached all over. Even in her top physical condition, it took a moment for her to regain command of her body. Her rubbery limbs had to be beaten into submission.

This was the second time that she had been taken down by a neophyte, a helpless individual. There would not be a third time.

What was worse: her ship had been taken. There was a trail of blood leading through half of the aerostat, littered with the dead or unconscious bodies of her assistants. They were coming to, albeit slower than she, but Bronwyn ignored them. They'd proved less capable than she had expected, even worse than she had feared.

There was an emergency escape craft attached to the aerostat, worthy of the name "spacecraft" only in the most technical way. There were room for two people, but when she closed the entrance hatch the other seat lay empty.

The controls were simple: they were set for a predetermined destination, which in this case was *Agropolis*. Simple enough, for that was her destination anyway. She selected the launch control option to wait for optimal launch conditions; they would arrive within the hour. Otherwise, she would be left in the proper orbit but perhaps on the opposite side of Venus from the station. Given that she had nobody to come after her, she decided not to get stranded.

She passed the time by composing a quick status update back to Forrester, and trying to check up on Keven and Lamont's other team. There wasn't much interference, and after a quarter hour of trying, she received news that Lamont's insurrection had been successful. Stefanovic was dead.

Of course that meant little now that the crew of the *Mary Ellen* had escaped, but at least they were without support. What was more, they no longer had access to their ship. They weren't leaving Venus yet; she was careful to emphasize this to Forrester. She would get them yet.

The stupid clods that she was leaving behind hadn't even realized that there was a ship they could use until she thundered away from the platform, borne aloft on a small but powerful liquid fuel rocket.

Bronwyn passed the time in meditation until she arrived at *Agropolis*. The controller was automated, and accepted her credit information for a short range rescue. An hour after launching, she was striding—still stiff—into the entertainment district.

It was a mess. Many of the clubs looked as though they had been looted, and there were a number of dead bodies in the streets. Perhaps one of them was Stefanovic's.

The Bordeaux appeared to be Lamont's base of operations, if the guard detail outside was any indication. The guard gave her one look and waved her inside.

"So, you're alive," Lamont said, sitting up from an elevated table that must've been Stefanovic's. His alarmed expression proved to Bronwyn's satisfaction that he hadn't expected to see her again.

"I am still alive," she confirmed. She didn't mention that as soon as she had a weapon, that would no longer be true for Lamont.

"And you were successful, I'm sure?" he asked, his voice quavering a bit. He knew what she knew.

"No, we were not successful. Several of your men will require rescue."

"Yeah, maybe. Plenty of good they were, failing to capture those unarmed, untrained spacers. I'll give them some time to think things over. You will notice that we were successful up here, though."

"I did notice." Bronwyn was standing just below Lamont on the middle of what had been a gaming area, but the tables had been pulled aside and replaced by what appeared to be loot from this club and others nearby. The larger part of it was alcohol, but there was some art and high tech in the mix as well.

"Maybe you should've been a part of our fucking team, eh? Not that dumbass you saddled us with. Didn't do us much good."

Bronwyn took an impatient step toward Lamont. "Yes, he failed to respond to my communications on the way up here.Tell me where he is."

"Sure, in a minute. Have a drink, eh? No hard feelings?" He held a bottle of expensive looking liquor out, and Bronwyn started by reflex to extend a hand to grab it. That was when she noticed the men moving into position behind her. They were all armed, but their weapons were as yet holstered.

She grabbed the bottle and made a show of removing the stopper. "While we are enjoying this drink, will you tell me where Keven is?"

"Yeah, he's performing some additional duties, I guess. I had a special job for him."

"Oh?"

The first thug went for his weapon, either on his own initiative or at some unknown sign from Lamont. He never reached it.

The bottle smashed against his face, but not before his face smashed underneath it. He went down in a moaning heap, and before he even reached the ground Bronwyn chopped at the throat of the man next to him.

The blow staggered him, revealed the snub-nosed pistol at his belt. Bronwyn smashed at his solar plexus, and when he doubled over she put him down with an elbow to the face and a kick to the inside of one knee. His pistol was in her hands before he was on the ground.

The women were scattering behind Lamont, deciding that running was less risky than chancing his anger. The guards near them were going for their own weapons, and Bronwyn decided that she had no choice but to use lethal force: two shots for each thug and they were down. The men outside were running in, confused and blinded for a moment in the dim interior of the club, and they were likewise dispatched.

Perhaps five seconds after she had first moved, six guards were down, Lamont's harem had scattered to side rooms, and the man himself, for the moment alone, was staring at her with ill-concealed horror.

"You, uh, what?" He said, his wide eyes taking in the carnage.

"The incompetence of your men on Hartley

Aerostate nearly cost me my life," she said, throwing the pistol aside as she stepped right up to Lamont. She was within one pace; at this distance she could kill him before he could draw any weapon. "And these fellows were prepared to kill me before I even arrived. I sense you are not being entirely honest with me, but I will give you one more chance," she had, grabbing him tightly by the throat and staring up into his eyes. "Where is Keven?"

Lamont's eyes flicked about in panic, as if he was coming up with a new lie just as fast as his brain could work. "That asshole turned on me!" he said, trying to keep his voice from cracking. "He must've had special instructions. I figured you were in on the game. Obviously, right? How the hell was I to know that you were innocent?"

"This conversation is over," she boomed, and shook him once, hard. "Come clean now, and agree to provide all necessary resources to tracking down the crew of the *Mary Ellen*, and I will submit you to the proper authorities for persecution. If you dissemble again..." She flexed a veinous, muscled hand in front of his face.

He went ashen.

"He killed your man in cold blood." In an instant, Bronwyn had Kinsey in a hostage hold and whirled so that they were both facing the new voice. It was a woman in a dirty blue evening dress, one who would've been gorgeous save for her frazzled hair and smudged makeup. Instead, she looked like death itself.

"He killed in cold blood," the woman repeated. "Your man and Tarn both."

"You are?" Bronwyn said, frowning.

"I'm Leona King. I'm...I was Tarn's executive

assistant. That, and other things," she said, the brief burst of fire from her eyes making it clear what she was referring to.

"Do you have access to Mr. Stefanovic's resources?"

"She's a damned liar, she-" Kinsey choked as Bronwyn's fingers closed around his windpipe.

King gestured to Lamont as he struggled. "Assuming he hasn't already screwed everything up. He'd just started the loyalty purges on *Agropolis*, but he hasn't had time to tie up all of Tarn's resources. Tarn was a good man, had lots of friends. People worked with him because they liked him, not because he bribed and flattered them. Not like this...this scum." She looked near tears as she gestured to Kinsey.

"Now, you and your man might've had something to do with Tarn's death. Right now, I don't care, because I know that this scumbag is ultimately responsible. Let me kill that traitor, and I'll help you in whatever way you want."

Bronwyn's frown deepened. "If you think that I may have been responsible for your associate's death, then I cannot trust you."

"Maybe not, but you know that Lamont will just try to ice you the second you're out of reach. You know what kind of man he is. You want to try to take over Tarn's operation yourself? Good luck. It looks like I'm your best hope." Leona walked with enviable grace over to one of the guards that Bronwyn had been forced to kill and pulled the half-drawn pistol out of its holster.

"Or," King said, pointing the weapon at Bronwyn and Kinsey, "Or I can kill both you. It's kind of a win-win for me."

Bronwyn considered for a moment, and released Kinsey. The woman looked more than capable of murder in her present state and Bronwyn could deal with her if she was unencumbered by Kinsey.

"Lamont, I hope you freeze in hell for a thousand years," King said, trying not to cry.

"Leona, damn it, please!" Kinsey said holding out his hands in a desperate plea for his life.

Crack. Crack. Then Lamont hit the floor, eyes still open, and it was all over.

King dropped the pistol, sighed, and turned to Bronwyn. "Now I need to do a little house cleaning, but I can get you the type of access that you need."

The actual interrogation wasn't half as bad as the waiting, Melissa decided. At least she knew that this whole ridiculous business would be over soon. Holding an icepack against the swollen eye she'd received on Hartley Aerostat, she answered Bronwyn Calleo's questions.

"No, I didn't have access to the actual data. I never did. Stephen Montgomery kept it with him at all times, and when he died, Eileen took possession. I swear to you, that datacube is the only copy in the entire Solar System, and I have no idea how to decrypt the important parts. Not even Eileen does."

Bronwyn looked on in calculated disbelief. What an unpleasant woman. She looked as though she were carved from stone—never smiling, never frowning. Melissa had to wonder what sort of past could harden someone like that.

They were seated in one of the hospital conference rooms, across an empty steel table. The room wasn't guarded, and more than once Melissa was tempted to try for the door, just to see what Bronwyn would do. But then again, she knew all too well what Bronwyn *could* do. Still, even in this stressful situation, part of Melissa was curious why Bronwyn was acting so furtive.

"Would it be possible to recover any portion of the data from your ship's memory cores, using data recovery tools?"

Melissa shrugged, eyes on the middle of the table. "You're welcome to try, but I doubt it. Crazyhorse has standard instructions to regularly wipe empty space on our drives."

"Who is Crazyhorse?"

"The *Mary Ellen*'s expert system."

Bronwyn paused a moment, and as she did so, her handset chirped. "Excuse me," she said in a mockery of common courtesy. "Please do not leave this room." A few steps, and she was out the door.

Oh, it was tempting to run for it. Or at least to check if Bronwyn was right outside or not. Something strange was going on with the other woman; she seemed furtive, almost anxious. Melissa had a few theories as to why that might be, but for the moment, she didn't have any evidence.

But she didn't have any time to act as Bronwyn re-entered the room. Stony-faced as always, she nonetheless managed to convey something like worry. It was unsettling.

"Our plan has changed," Bronwyn said, stepping just to the side of the door. "We need to leave the station right now."

"What about the rest of my crew?"

"They are being assembled. Please," Bronwyn said, gesturing to the door. Melissa left the room and Bronwyn followed right after her, keeping an iron hand on her shoulder. A door several meters down had a portable maglock installed; Bronwyn tapped in the code, and the door opened.

"Just what the hell is going on?" Ben thundered as he stepped out. "You have absolutely no right to-"

Bronwyn grabbed him hard by the shoulder, cutting him off as he winced in pain. "I apologize, but there is no time to discuss this right now. We must leave the hospital at once."

"And what about Joanna and Eileen?" he asked, as Almika exited the room behind him.

Bronwyn hesitated for a fraction of a second, but that fraction told Melissa quite a bit. "They are beyond our reach for now. Please, let us hurry."

"What's the *hurry*?" Melissa asked, as Bronwyn marched them along toward the hospital's central axis.

Bronwyn didn't answer, but the situation became much more clear when they reached Sagan Hospital's more populated areas. Their awkward appearance would warrant a few stares, sure, but as they passed examination rooms and offices, Bronwyn hurried them ever faster, ignoring the extra attention she was drawing. When they reached the admitting and processing area, the situation fell into place.

A few UNASCA security officers were chatting against one of the admitting kiosks, watching over patients with bored eyes and restless bodies. When their gaze happened to track across Melissa, Bronwyn, and the others, however, they started and called out, "Bronwyn Calleo!"

They started to shout some legal jargon, the gist of which was more or less, "surrender," but Bronwyn was whispering harshly as she increased their speed once again. "If you slow us down at all, UNASCA will capture you. They will not be as kind as Belt Group."

"Go to hell," Ben said, jerking against Bronwyn's iron grip. Only Almika wasn't being restrained, but she looked far too cowed to try anything.

"Benjamin Riley," Bronwyn said, not bothering to restrain her annoyance as she dragged Ben along, "Belt Group wants to bring you to Earth. UNASCA will send you to their prison on Mars. Surely you can see where the advantage lies!"

"Ben, don't be stupid," Melissa said, watching with trepidation as the guards jogged toward them, weapons out and at their sides. "You want to jump out of the frying pan and into the fire?"

Ben glanced back at the security officers, now spreading out just a few paces distant, fingering their electrolasers. He looked like he was about to boil over with rage. "Fine," he spat.

"Thank you," Bronwyn said.

What happened next, happened in the time it took Melissa to draw a sharp breath. Bronwyn dropped Ben's arm and pulled her own electrolaser. She was already squeezing the trigger as she pointed it at the first guard, and the blast took him right in the chest. The second guard just had time to jerk in surprise before an identical shot hit him. The few patients and hospital workers still in the admitting area shrieked and ran for cover further inside the hospital, crowding the other security officers that Melissa could see rushing to reinforce their fellows.

Without any further words, Bronwyn pulled them toward the central axis.

As they were floating in zero-gee, pulling themselves toward the Belt Group ship, Ben whispered to Melissa. "What the hell was that? You pulling for Belt Group, now?"

"I think UNASCA already has Joanna and Eileen," she whispered back, glancing at Bronwyn. She didn't appear to hear them, but who knew? "I think that I trust the government a little less than Belt Group, no matter what they've done."

"I sure hope you're right about this," Ben muttered, pulling ahead of her.

Melissa rather hoped that she was. Swallowing hard, she tried not to picture what full-scale interplanetary war might look like. The two most powerful groups in the Solar System, at each other's throats? It was going to be horrible.

Forrester waited quietly while Rosetta finished reading his report's précis. She reached the end, frowned, turned back a couple of pages, furrowed her brow, and set down the dataslate.

"Rather questionable, wouldn't you say?" Forrester said, when she didn't respond.

Rosetta kept staring out her office window for a moment. It was a beautiful morning; the sun was just burning off the morning clouds, promising a clear, crisp day. Pity she wouldn't be able to head out into the country to enjoy it. She'd be lucky if she got to breathe some fresh air at all today.

"I said, rather questionable, isn't it?"

Turning back to him, Rosetta straightened her shoulders. "You mean our contact turning on your agents?"

"Yeah. I'm wondering if it was just our bad luck, or if there was someone else involved. It seems a little too coincidental."

Rosetta didn't say anything, but flicked to a new file on her dataslate. Forrester took it, frowning, and read for a moment. She could see the moment that he reached the important part; he just about dropped the slate.

"What the hell is this?" Forrester said, gesturing with the slate, trying to keep his face impassive.

"It's exactly what it looks like. I got it a few hours ago. It appears that UNASCA thinks that our 'special relationship' is no longer necessary. They think after that coup of Venus, they're holding all of the cards."

"But Bronwyn captured several of the *Mary Ellen*'s crew! And Tarn Stefanovic might be dead, even though from what I hear his second-in-command is no pushover. What's Yessenia thinking?" Forrester sat down heavily in front of her desk, massaging his temple.

Rosetta shook her head. "Pruitt didn't have anything to do with this, except rubber-stamping it. This is Israel Moen making a hard move. It's got to be." She chuckled, a dry, humorless sound. "Well, if he thinks he can turn back the clock, let him. Some minor victory for UNASCA isn't going to change a damned thing."

"Let me sic Bronwyn on them. She'll steal that data back right under their noses, I'm sure of it."

"Oh, definitely." Rosetta nodded. "But according to Chen, we're not going back to the negotiating table with

UNASCA. If they think they can act in bad faith, then let them. We're through."

Forrester sighed. "I'm not arguing with you. You understand that? But I don't think this is the best way to get the *Atlas* back. This Free Jovian thing is going to get out of hand."

"Robert." Rosetta picked her words carefully. "Let me worry about that. I'm leaving the *Atlas* situation in your hands; this goes beyond that. Working with the Free Jovians might just help us accomplish what we were trying to do with the *Atlas*: get out from under UNASCA. Don't lose sight of our goals."

"Meanwhile, helium-3 production is way down and investors are getting nervous. If we make the *Atlas* a low priority and someone finds out..."

Rosetta leaned out and touched Forrester's shoulder. "I know we're living on borrowed time. And we're not making the *Atlas* a lower priority, not by any means. You've still got carte blanche. Keep on these *Mary Ellen* people, and let me know if you have any new leads, all right? Give me regular reports."

Forrester smirked. "Thanks."

"Anything else, then? I need to prepare a response for UNASCA."

"Yeah, just one thing: I do have a new lead on the *Atlas*."

Rosetta raised an eyebrow.

"There's a group on Mars, the Saekir. They're like an independent smuggler's coalition with some unusual tendencies, but whatever. They've been putting out their own feelers about the *Atlas*, and my analysis section just traced them back to it a few hours ago. I'm activating Martian assets."

"Do it," Rosetta nodded. "Anything else?"

Forrester grinned. "Pin UNASCA to the wall for me."

Chapter 13

For maybe the sixth or seventh, maybe the hundredth time, Eileen screamed at the top of her lungs.

"Come *on*! I need to talk to someone! Come on!"

Of course, nobody answered. And why would they? Just as she had predicted the staff at Sagan hospital had ripped Joanna away, making worried faces. Then the security folks had shown up and hurried Joanna into intensive care with worried faces. The rest of the crew had been separated, and Eileen had been locked in a tiny examination room but otherwise ignored.

It had been at least four or five hours, maybe a day since they'd locked her up. She'd been fed just once, but it had been that a high nutrition sludge that provided enough calories and nutrients for three meals. One or two servings a day would keep her alive forever, given how little she was moving.

Eileen was sick of being in prison.

"Someone, please, for pity's sake!" She shouted, and

once more her voice seemed to bottle up in the cell. There was a tiny window in the door, all she could see through it was a bare, white wall.

Eileen slumped on the mattress, pulled her knees up to her chest, and tried to control her breathing. At least Joanna was safe. Probably. Hell, at this point they were all probably safer than they had been since she'd first seen Bronwyn. Now that they were captives there was no point in chasing them any further.

When someone did come to Eileen's room, she was a little surprised—not displeased, of course—that it wasn't Bronwyn. The fact that the UNASCA security officer seemed almost jovial as he escorted her to the small guard's office was even more surprising.

When they arrived, the guard shut the door behind her and stood outside. Eileen wasn't restrained at all, and she was just starting to wonder if there were maybe any weapons in the disused-looking office when the computer started up.

A telecom program opened and connected to a familiar-looking remote address. Eileen sat at the rolling chair before it, and frowned as a similarly familiar-looking woman with gorgeous eyes and a sad aspect appeared on the screen.

"Eileen Cromwell?"

"Yeah." She raised an eyebrow.

"I'm Leona King. I was Tarn Stefanovic's executive assistant."

Eileen remembered the woman from his club, the Bordeaux. "I see. Awfully bad luck that those Belt Group thugs found us in Tarn's 'hiding' place. Awfully, awfully bad luck."

The woman met her gaze. "Tarn's dead, Eileen."

"Wait, what?"

"He's dead, and his organization is in shambles. It looks like it was an inside job; the traitors even killed one of those Belt Group agents."

"Shit," Eileen breathed.

"No kidding. Their other agent is very much desperate to get you, but I managed to throw them off your trail for a few hours."

"So what-"

Leona cut her off. "Listen, we don't have much time. Tarn's network is a mess; the traitor faction wasn't big, but they were surgical. They've been dealt with, but...not fast enough. Eileen, I'm losing control. There's just one reason I haven't been shuffled off: I promised to help the Belt Group agent find you."

Eileen raised an eyebrow and forced herself not to look around in a panic. Nobody was gunning for her in here. "Well, thanks for the warning."

"Hey!" Leona barked, and Eileen's head jerked back toward the screen. "Let me finish. I need to get offworld, you need to get offworld. I'm willing to take you with me, in Tarn's memory. I figure he'd hate it if he knew you'd suffered so much under his protection."

"What's the catch?" Eileen was still trying to look in every direction at once, straining to hear every minute sound over the steady drone of the environmental unit in the office. She swore that she would never be sent to prison again.

Leona shook her head. "No catch, except that we're

taking your ship. I don't trust any of my captains right now. Is that acceptable to you?

"You've got that right. What about Joanna? What about my crew? What about my *datacube*?"

"Check the table in front of you. Who's Joanna?"

"The girl who was with me. The one in the hospital," Eileen said, frowning and running her eyes over the desk. There: a small plastic box with her name on it. She popped it open and the datacube—her datacube—dropped into her hands. Miraculously, the integrity seal was intact. Her data was still secret.

Leona arched an eyebrow. "Are you joking? It's going to be hard enough getting just you out; there's no way that I can spring anyone in the hospital's security ward. As for your crew...I'm sorry, Eileen, but it's too late."

Eileen's started. "What?"

"They were kept in a lower-security section of the hospital, and Belt Group found them before I could do anything. Eileen, I had to feed them to Belt Group to keep them off your back for a little while." There was the sound of a tone on the far side of the transmission, and Leona looked down offscreen in concern. When she looked back up, her teeth were gritted and she spoke quickly. "Sorry, Eileen, no time to talk. I have to tell this Bronwyn woman that you're-"

Eileen sucked in air as if she'd been shot. "Bronwyn? You're working with Bronwyn?"

"I hardly had a choice, did I?"

Eileen felt herself starting to tremble already. She'd meant to kill that bitch while she was unconscious; no way she would've hesitated to kill someone so dangerous in cold blood. Pity she hadn't gotten the chance.

"That name is ill luck. Very, very ill luck," Eileen said, standing. She paused, then sat back down, leaning in close to the screen. "Where do I meet you?"

"I'll have one of my men meet you down in the docks."

She nodded. "Now get going." Without saying anything else, she closed the connection.

Joanna realized that someone was talking to her. Right on the tail of this realization was a second one: she was awake, and she wasn't dead. The dead don't hurt.

After a good long moment she opened her eyes. A hospital suite. So Eileen *had* saved her. Oh, praise the Lord.

But Eileen wasn't there, and neither were Ben, Melissa, Almika, or any of the other people that she knew. Instead, there was a serious-looking female doctor and several even more serious-looking men in what appeared to be security outfits. Of course Eileen wasn't there; she was in a hospital, which meant that she'd had to turn herself in to get Joanna treatment. Joanna was still trying to work on the ramifications of these revelations when the doctor spoke again.

"Joanna Newton?" When Joanna started to talk the doctor put a hand on her shoulder and shook her head. "Don't try to talk, dear. You sustained a pretty serious wound, but don't worry, the tissue lattice is holding well and you'll be good as new before too long.

"You'll need your rest," the doctor said, as much to the serious-looking men in the room as to her, "but these gentlemen want to ask you some questions. Don't strain yourself, but try to do as they ask, okay?"

Joanna shook her head, trying to work just a word or two past the dryness in her throat. "Where...where is Eileen?"

"If you're referring to Eileen Cromwell," the doctor looked uncomfortable, shooting a glance at the two others in the room before answering, "well, she's under arrest, Joanna. You had to realize that there was a warrant out for her arrest as well as yours."

Joanna just exhaled and leaned back, closing her eyes to try to block out the thoughts that were coming unbidden. Eileen had thrown away everything for her. Her injury was serious; she would've died, but Eileen insisted on her being treated even if it meant failing at her own mission to stay away from UNASCA, Belt Group, and others.

Oh heaven. She didn't deserve that sort of treatment.

While one of the security men escorted her doctor out of the room, Joanna spared a moment to analyze her physical situation. She was weak, very weak, but there was no pain except for a rasp in her throat. IV lines snaked down into her arms, and there was a complex-looking device strapped to her stomach, right where she'd been shot. There were a variety of tubes and cables attached to it; Joanna decided that it was maintaining the tissue lattice that was rebuilding her shattered insides.

"Joanna Newton," the darker-haired security man said. It wasn't a question, and it made for an annoying introduction.

"Yeah," she rasped, feeling a little surge of energy catalyzed by her annoyance. "What is," she swallowed hard and started again, "what's your name?"

"I'm Sanderson," he said, and indicated his somewhat fatter partner, "and this is Pauls. We just need to ask you a few questions."

"Go ahead," Joanna said, and started looking around for something to drink. Her throat was killing her.

"You've been traveling on the Mary Ellen from Brighton, haven't you?"

"Yes," she said, finding a bottle of water on her nightstand and greedily sucking it down. The water was like a soothing cascade of relief for her parched throat, and Joanna felt a bit of energy start to seep through the rest of her body.

"Can you tell me where you first met Eileen Cromwell?"

"Yes."

The agents waited for her to finish, and when it became clear she wouldn't, they exchanged a longsuffering look and Sanderson, rubbing his forehead, said, "Could you expand on that a little bit?"

"I first met her on Brighton when her boss was trying to sell something to my boss."

"What was he trying to sell?"

"Information." She wasn't going to be able to get away with telling the agents nothing, but she took a perverse bit of pleasure in frustrating them.

"What sort of information?"

"I don't know."

"It didn't have anything to do with a ship? Maybe out in the belt?" Sanderson said, fishing.

"It looks like you know more than I do," Joanna

retorted, all but sticking her tongue out at the man. It was childish, she knew, but couldn't help it.

Sanderson exchanged another glance with Pauls. The other man shifted his weight a bit and said, "Listen, Ms. Newton, you and Ms. Cromwell are wanted for serious crimes against the United Nations Space Colonization Authority. I'm sure that you're aware of that."

"Yes," said Joanna, feeling some of the impishness drain out of her.

"So we think that you have certain information that we need. This informal interrogation is just out of consideration for you, so if we feel like you're being intentionally unhelpful, we can just stop, wait until you're feeling a little better, and break out the thumb screws. Do you understand me?"

He stared at her with unbroken intensity, and despite her earlier brazenness she felt herself shrink a little bit under his gaze. "Yes."

"Good. And you should also know that, since we have Ms. Cromwell in custody, trying to protect her right now would be misguided at best. Just tell us the truth and this whole unpleasant episode will pass before you know it." He leaned back against the wall and Sanderson cleared his throat.

"Now then, what do you know about the information that Eileen Cromwell and the crew of the *Mary Ellen* collected in the Belt?"

Joanna leaned back and stared up at the screen in her room that was dedicated to entertainment programming. It was streaming news headlines at the moment, but she just stared past them. Decision time.

In retrospect it was an easy decision to make, not even worth deliberating about. If they had Eileen in custody then they didn't need her to say anything, they'd just get it out of Eileen. Unless they couldn't, in which case she *shouldn't* say anything. Either way, not talking seemed like the best choice.

And she owed Eileen. Owed her life twice. Prolonging the discomfort and anguish that had been the last few weeks for a little while longer seemed like too little payback.

Joanna wasn't looking forward to getting back to Earth anyway. That would mean talking to her family, including her mother, and that made it a simple decision: don't talk. And she didn't; she just shut her mouth and didn't move it no matter what, not even as the agents raised their voices, not even when Sanderson started shouting threats at her. She just stared at the ceiling until the two men left.

It wasn't until the next day that Joanna made two discoveries: first, she was, just as the agents had promised, going to be subject to additional interrogation, and just as Eileen suspected they weren't keeping her anywhere heavily populated. She was going to Mars.

The second thing that she discovered was that Eileen *wasn't* in custody. Her doctor, feeling sorry for her after the agents' treatment, had whispered that the rest of the crew had escaped several days before, right under UNASCA's nose. There would be hell to pay for that one, if rumors were to be believed.

So, less than a week after awakening, Joanna was put on a transport for Mars. Her ultimate destination was the UNASCA Aquifer Prison facility near Olympus Base, a place of dark reputation. UNASCA needed a lockup that was completely under their jurisdiction, which meant off Earth and not subject to oversight.

If Joanna hadn't known that Eileen was free, it would've been too much to bear.

Rosetta walked ahead of her escort and threw open the door to the UNASCA conference room. The view over the Willamette was socked in with an odd afternoon fog; it fit Rosetta's mood. Scanning the room, she saw only Israel Moen; Yessenia Pruitt was nowhere to be found.

"What the hell is going on, Moen?"

Moen nodded in greeting, not rising from his seat at the large conference table. "Afternoon, Rosetta. Can I get you some coffee? Or maybe something more stimulating?" His idiot grin boiled Rosetta's blood.

"What you could offer me is an explanation. We had an agreement in good faith, and then I get this?" She threw a hardcopy of UNASCA's warning to Belt Group on the table. "I have zero patience for your games right now, Moen. I'm trying to run a business, and UNASCA isn't making it easy. No wonder people across the Solar System are getting fed up with you."

Moen's eyes flashed, but that condescending grin never left his face. "Well, I'm trying to run an interplanetary government here, Rosetta. We did agree to help you find *Atlas*, yes. We agreed on a special relationship, yes. But you talk about good faith...was sowing chaos throughout the Solar System part of that? Hmm?"

"Chaos?" Rosetta choked the word out. "What?"

"Shall I list the dead on Venus for you? Shall I show you the overwatch footage of your people raising hell on space station and aerostat? Well?"

Rosetta closed her eyes for a moment, marshalling her calm. She couldn't afford to let the little man push her buttons. "We made contact with your agent, as promised, and we were pursuing information related to the *Atlas*. Like we agreed."

"While they were there, your agents also decided to take down Tarn Stefanovic. Which we didn't agree to. You can see where my problem is here."

Rosetta frowned, and sat. Something here wasn't making sense. According to Forrester's report, it was the UNASCA agent who had first suggested the takedown, and Bronwyn had only gone alone with it quid pro quo. Which meant that either Moen was playing some sort of second-order game, or...

"Oh. I *do* see," Rosetta nodded. "Forrester was right; your 'agent' wasn't working for you when he decided to take down Stefanovic, hmm? He came up with that himself?" Moen's eyes flashed again, and Rosetta echoed Moen's condescending smile, which had since become a like a dead rictus. "But now you're making the best of a bad situation, are you? Stefanovic's out of the way, so you think you have Venus locked down. You've got the *Mary Ellen*'s elusive crew under arrest, so you think you've got us locked down too, hmm?"

Rosetta chuckled quietly to herself and stood once more. "I think this meeting is over, Mr. Moen. Belt Group doesn't make agreements with snakes."

As she turned to walk out the door, Moen spoke

with quiet menace. "Snakes? Let's talk about the Free Jovians, shall we? Let's talk about Belt Group's other 'special relationships'."

"I don't know what you're talking about," Rosetta said, holding her head high and not turning back to Moen.

"Don't you? You're right. Controlling the Solar System's resources is crucial to UNASCA's influence. Resources like Venus, yes. The *Atlas* eroded that, but we tolerated it because it was such a shining example of what the offworld economy offered people. But if you're going to brazenly support Solomon Gracelove, then we have a problem."

He didn't have any proof. He couldn't have any proof, because there wasn't any to offer. Belt Group's support for Free Jove was so far under the table it was in the basement. They'd exchanged promises, nothing more.

Rosetta turned slowly back to the table and cleared her throat. Moen looked at her with a raised eyebrow, that asshole smile replaced by something much, much darker. "I would say that we both have a problem, Mr. Moen. Because controlling the Solar System's valuable resources, at least the important ones, is also crucial to Belt Group's business interests. And frankly, we're not in the mood to put up with UNASCA interference any longer. Now, good-bye."

She turned once again, and she made it all the way to the old-fashioned brass doorknob before Moen called out, "Just a damned minute, Rosetta. You walk out that door, you're going unleash hell. I had hoped that you could cooperate, but if you can't, you'll find out just how much influence UNASCA still has."

"I guess you're going to have to surprise me, then."

Rosetta turned the handle and walked out of the room.

Her knees were shaking so badly that she had a hard time making it back to her car. The driver held the door open for her and she collapsed into the back cabin. They were airborne over the West Hills before she trusted herself to make a phone call.

When Chen came on the video link, Rosetta realized that she must look as bad as she felt. "What's wrong?" he asked, concerned.

"Nothing's wrong. We're just going to have to activate the Jovian contingency, is all."

He sighed and nodded. It looked like he was in his bedroom, and Rosetta felt a stab of guilt for interrupting him at home. "Your meeting didn't go so well?"

"It went about as well as expected." She paused, then related the high points of Moen's conversation.

Chen was silent for a long time, he dark brow furrowed. Rosetta felt her chest tighten; if she'd screwed things up, if he decided to be angry...

But when he spoke, he was more thoughtful than mad. "Well, what's done is done. Perhaps the tipping point came sooner than I expected, but no matter. Forrester is working on the *Atlas* situation? Good. In the meantime, we need a trusted agent to visit Jupiter in person. Free Jove is going to stage an out-and-out revolution soon, and we must be prepared." He sighed. "I know that you won't appreciate it, but we may need to send Mr. Forrester himself."

"Whatever you say," Rosetta muttered, relieved. As long as he wasn't sending her. "And I'll let you know what his people turn up on Venus and Mars."

"Yes, Rosetta. You will."

PART III: MARS

Chapter 14

The message arrived at the very end of the day. Galen Rojas typically stayed in his office at least a bit late; his position as Security Chief of Olympus Base had enough duties to keep him busy for nine or ten hours straight. Especially since, thanks to their recently Earth-appointed governor, "Chief of Olympus Security" was more and more often meaning "Chief of Martian Security," a thoroughly unwelcome, if unsurprising, development. UNASCA was consolidating everywhere, for all the good it would do them.

He almost didn't read the message out of principle. Rojas tried to segregate his life and his UNASCA business as sharply as possible. The odds were that it would be something inconsequential that could easily wait until the next day, but if he didn't read it, it would nag at him when he was trying to relax. With a sigh, Rojas tossed his coat on his desk and called up the message, rotating his screen so he could ready it from the front of his desk.

Two sentences in, he sat down heavily. A few more

sentences, and he was wishing that he had waited until the next day after all.

Moments later he was shoving his way through the door into the bullpen. Officers Cruikshank and Ojedo were on duty; most of the staff had gone home and the lights were dimmed. Often duties in Olympus Base were slow enough and the population peaceful enough that a heavy workforce was not required. That was about to change.

"Come on you two, up and at 'em. Get Marla and Grantsville on the phone and have them come into the office."

Cruikshank raised a bushy eyebrow. "But Marla's on-"

"I don't care if she's on vacation, I need her in the office, right now!" He pressed his index finger against Cruikshank's desk to emphasize the point. "We've got important orders from Portland and I need all hands on deck. Ojedo, better call the missus and let her know that you won't be home for a few hours."

Ojedo rolled his eyes and started to protest, but Galen cut him off. "Hey! I'm not thrilled about this either but things are about to get real. Get those two, and you two, in my office. You have thirty minutes, you understand? Half an hour."

With that, Galen turned his back to their objections and walked the ten meters back into his office. They were good people, and rare were the times that he had to so much as raise his voice; now that he had, they looked like they were taking him more seriously.

Sure enough, they did. Twenty-nine minutes later, the four of them were in his office; Marla and Cruikshank, as senior officers, got the two chairs and the other two stood behind them.

Galen started talking without preamble. "Just as I was about to leave, I got a message from UNASCA security headquarters tagged as high importance. I'll give you one guess what it says."

Marla chuckled. "Has it finally come down to martial law? Who's going to win the pool?"

Galen shook his head, not laughing. "It's not martial law but it's close. Too damned close. UNASCA's issued the latest version of its undesirables list, and it's suspending section twelve rights for all of them. What's more, it wants them in custody at once."

There was no dramatic reaction from the assembly. They'd been expecting it for weeks; UNASCA's dispatches from Earth had contained more and more bad news of late. The Free Jovians were starting riots somewhere just about every other day now, it seemed, and it didn't take much reading between the lines to see that UNASCA was losing control—first labor disputes with the mining companies, then a prison break on the Moon, trade disruptions on Venus, now Jupiter.

And so they were responding at last. The response, to Rojas complete lack of surprise, was to tighten their control everywhere else, and there were more Free Jove supporters on Mars than anywhere else in the system, even in the Belt.

Cruikshank broke the silence. "Well, damn."

"You said it," Ojedo agreed. "What's their timeframe?"

"Pretty much, yesterday," Galen sighed. "They're

getting desperate. I'm sure they want to show the colonials that they're still as powerful as they used to be, but I don't think that this is another Titania—they're not going to reach a settlement here. It gets better, too: looks like UNASCA is done turning a blind eye to the Saekir. There's a meeting in just a few weeks, and they're issuing an a priori warrant for anyone found there."

The assembled group stared, dumbfounded. Heaven knew most of them had gotten tired of the Saekir's quasi-legal activities being consistently ignored and overlooked, but they were still trying to put it all in context. As was Rojas himself; the times were changing, and all the little activities that UNASCA might not have considered worth public response a few months or years ago now had to be crushed lest they agglomerate into something more serious.

He shook his head in annoyance. Politics wasn't part of his job, just following orders. "All right, enough talking. There's nothing to discuss anyway." He gestured to a UM card on the table in front of him. "That's got the list on it. Most of those folks are probably under surveillance already; Marla, I want you to bring in as many patrols as you can spare, and try to round them all up tonight."

He turned to Ojedo. "Just glancing over it, it looks like there are a few unknowns on the list. Try to assemble as much data as you can, and if you have a confirmed match you call Marla and have her round them up too. Any you can't find, you turn over to Grantsville and he'll get digging. Understood?"

A chorus of murmured affirmatives indicated they did. "Then let's get it done. Marla, I'm sorry that your vacation got cut short; looks like the wife and I won't be making it to Valles this weekend either."

She nodded. "It's all right. Was bound to happen sometime."

"Sure. Sure. All right, folks, let's get it done." He clapped and they filed out of the office.

As soon as they were gone, he felt himself slump a little bit. Not for the first time, Galen found himself wishing that these sorts of assignments could fall to someone else. He wasn't looking forward to walking down the Aquifer Prison blocks tomorrow and seeing all those innocent faces, all those mournful looks. Sometimes he felt like he would rather join them than fight them.

Eileen started as she felt someone behind her, nearly bruising her eye on her telescope eyepiece. She jerked around, saw that it was just Leona, clad in a shipsuit, staring out the observation port window beyond Eileen. The red disc of Mars was visible to the naked eye now, a thumbnail-shaped red smear against the deep black of space. Perhaps it wasn't quite blood-red, but she was in a bad enough mood that she was willing to give it the benefit of the doubt.

"I've been meaning to ask you," Leona said, pulling herself into the tiny observation cupola with Eileen, "what your plans are when we arrive."

Eileen sighed and turned back to her telescope. "My plans right now are to get an accurate fix after that last plane adjustment burn. I think at least part of the *Mary Ellen*'s scan platform is misaligned."

"Mm," Leona said, making it obvious she wasn't really listening. "I ask because I have an idea if you find yourself unsure."

Eileen took a generous moment before answering, tapping her telescope reading into her handset, interpreting the results, and then plugging them into the small standalone navigational terminal that took up much of the cupola's usable space.

Leona had turned out to be a better shipmate than Eileen had presumed. Moreover, Leona's people knew their business and the woman kept to herself most of the time, leaving Eileen plenty of time to sulk. She sighed. If she was honest with herself, that was pretty much all she'd been doing for the last few weeks. Sulking. She was torn up about Stephen's death, torn up about leaving Joanna, torn up about being alone again. It had not been a fun trip.

"Leona," Eileen said at last, "I'm not sure if I'm in the mood for this right now."

Leona cocked her eyebrow. "And when do you expect to have the time, Eileen Cromwell? Before or after you crawl out of this dark pit you're in?" Eileen glared at her but the damned woman just took it in stride. "Yes, I've noticed. I know that you're in a bad mood, and I understand why. Tarn was," she sighed, "more than just a boss to me. And now he's dead, and it's just as much an outrage as anything that's happened to you."

Eileen wasn't sure yet whether she wanted to punch Leona or break down into tears. Or both. If that self-serving whore thought that she could talk down-

"The whole point of this expedition," she continued with some force, "Is to rebuild Tarn's...to rebuild my contact network. They tore everything to pieces at the first smell of blood, even some of Tarn's most trusted lieutenants." Leona sighed loudly and pinched the bridge of her nose. "Anyway, my point is, I'm moving on. You should do the same. Build your future, don't mourn your past. That starts, for both of us, on Mars."

"Mars."

"Yes, Mars. You of all people should know that for the next few months, Mars will see a lot of mining and freighter crews stopping over between Ceres and Venus. It's those people that I need to talk to."

"Okay, slow down." Eileen settled her back against the observation window, trying to put a little space between her and Leona. The woman had such a narrow definition of personal space. And, she didn't quite trust herself yet; her fists were clenched so hard her knuckles were white. "If you think that you can come in here, on *my* ship, and castigate *me* for *my* personal issues, then we need to work something else out right now."

"This is an opportunity for you, Eileen. What else are you going to do?"

"Hurt UNASCA. Hurt Belt Group. Whatever...I want to make them pay for what they've done to Stephen, to Joanna, even to Ben and Melissa. You understand?" Eileen stopped, swallowing hard. She was not going to lose it in front of anyone, much less Leona.

"Then come with me, if you want. These people are no greater friend of UNASCA or the conglomerates than you are. You'll be among like-minded people. And you'll be doing me, and yourself, a big favor."

Oh, it would be nice to be among kindred spirits. She was tired of running, even tired of sulking. Perhaps Leona was right, perhaps it was time to start doing something again. At the very least, she wouldn't be alone, and that sounded like a pretty damned good bargain.

"You know what? Maybe you're right." She sighed, letting out a long ragged breath. Flicking a few commands into her handset, she closed down the system. The course was set, they just needed to make another burn.

She felt the familiar shape of the datacube in her breast pocket. It stayed there like a talisman for the last twelve weeks, as the *Mary Ellen* drifted silently through the deep space between Venus and Mars. Leona knew that she had it, of course, but she'd never mentioned it. Eileen hadn't felt the need to bring it up either; she didn't even want to think about it herself.

Then she had an idea.

"These 'business associates' of yours, they've got good resources, right? A variety of contacts?" Eileen rubbed the datacube in her pocket.

"Of course. Why else would I bother with them?" Leona raised an eyebrow. "Why?"

"No reason. We'll be ready for orbital insertion in about a hundred hours."

"Good." Leona's face rippled through a number of expressions, from suspicion to confusion to flat, affected disinterest. "Thanks."

Eileen was already halfway down hatch to the ship's hub. She didn't respond. Shortly, she hoped, Leona would no longer be a consideration.

There was a slight jolt as the prison ship eased into the dock at Mars. Joanna didn't know what the name of the dock was. She didn't even know what the name of her ship was, or what it looked like. She'd been trapped in a ten by ten by ten cube for weeks, with just a few hours to stretch in the long tunnel outside, the one with dozens more cells just like hers opening onto it.

The hatch to her cell swung open. The warden floated outside, his scowl deep as though it were carved onto his face. It deepened when she glanced at him.

"Prisoner Joanna Newton. Come forward please," the warden barked. He floated impatiently, one hand on a rung and one hand holding his handset as she pushed herself out of her cell into the common area of the prison module.

"Reporting." Joanna stepped forward, keeping her eyes down. They didn't like it when you made eye contact; the procedure had been made plenty clear to her the first time he'd let her out for exercise.

"Prisoner Joanna Newton, number 2-182957, I have your planetside assignment."

Sighing, Joanna continued their little game. "Warden, what is my planetside assignment?"

He nodded in approval of her demonstration and said, more softly, "Newton, you're headed to Aquifer Prison, south of Olympus Base. There, you'll stand for interrogation and processing. Do you understand?"

"Yes, Warden."

"Good." He flipped to the next screen. "Okay. Once you're off the ship, you're in the hands of local security. " He gestured down the corridor. "Be good, Newton."

"Yes, Warden. Thank you."

He pushed himself aside and allowed her to float up

into the transport's axial corridor. Sure enough, there was a dour-faced local security officer waiting for her there. The warden on the prison ship had been unpleasant enough, but she'd gotten used to him. Now there was a new person and a new procedure to learn.

The security officer moved aside, allowing her to go first toward the airlock. Joanna reflected that this sort of intense scrutiny was going to be the order of the day for the rest of her "sentence" on Mars. The trip over had been surreal enough. Limited contact with others (not much of a punishment for her, not in prison) but a perfectly adequate entertainment selection. Plenty of time to think over where she'd gone wrong on Venus, on the Moon, even back on Earth when this whole adventure would have been inconceivable.

The transport must've docked to a special airlock, because even though Joanna could see a sprawling transfer station outside the lock windows, the space that she entered on the far side was dark and cramped.

She hesitated, and then started as the security officer barked, "All right, move along!" He made her follow a short curving corridor to a reception area, where she was scanned into the system. Beyond that was another airlock, and inside it, a lander.

The guard waited for her to take her seat before saying, "You must've screwed up good to get your own little transport to the surface. Isn't that just special?" She didn't respond, and the guard huffed.

"Fine, whatever. Closing up!"

The airlock snapped shut, and Joanna was once again alone. The lander's pilot was in separate section ahead of her, leaving her to the hum of the air conditioner, and the occasional flashes of the red planet outside the plate-sized viewport.

Alone, it seemed, was to be her lot in life, Joanna mused darkly. There wasn't anyone on Mars to help her; there was no way that she was going to let anyone in her family know what had happened to her, not after her father. Her father—how many times had she been humiliated when some new person, some potential friend had found out he was in jail? The irony left a bitter taste in her mouth.

And the only person off of Earth who could help her was who-knows-where. Even if Eileen was following her, she almost dared to hope, there was no way that she could single-handedly spring Joanna from prison.

She hadn't thought about it that way at the time, since they'd been under so much stress and subject to so many tribulations, but it was now obvious that her time with Eileen and the crew of the *Mary Ellen* had been one of the happiest times of her life in recent memory.

A jolt woke her from her reverie: the lander was pulling away from the station. Time seemed to pass slowly—the pilot never spoke to her and she had no instruments in the crew area. They seemed to float forever until at last she felt, then heard, the rumble of re-entry. From that moment on she felt like she was truly trapped, now by gravity as much as by any intangible part of her situation.

Rosetta wished that Forrester were here. She really, really wished that she was just about anywhere else. But this job couldn't be trusted to one of his lackeys, not by a long shot.

The night was that peculiar mix of cool ambient temperature and warm winds cascading down the urban canyon that Rosetta was standing in. The Sun had set an hour ago, leaving the Vancouver borough of Portland dark and less than inviting.

Not that Vancouver was an inviting place. The garish neon from the casinos, off-track betting parlors, pachinko rooms, and a dozen other types of lower class, semi legitimate entertainment flooded the street, replacing the light of the Sun with an entirely different type of noon.

Rosetta was wearing a beat up pair of running pants, a simple top, and her oldest, rattiest pair of walking shoes. Her face felt naked without any makeup, and she couldn't help running a hand through her carefully disheveled hair. She hated this cloak and dagger business, and wished once more that Forrester wasn't offworld.

She was hiding near the loading dock of one the larger casinos, a squat pyramid covered with ever-changing geometric patterns that pulsed as if to some hidden music. It was an attractive effect, she had to admit, or at least it was from the air—from the smelly, dirty loading dock it just seemed artificial.

There was a rumbling hum, and Rosetta looked up to see a robot lifter positioning its cargo module above the loading dock's flat surface. It seemed to be having a difficult time getting itself aligned properly; Rosetta was wondering if maybe its computer needed upgrading when she heard the footsteps behind her.

Very close behind her. She whirled, managing to avoid reflexively drawing the electrolaser in the pocket of her coat. As it was her fingers had it in a death grip as she stared at her visitor.

"Hey, you're kind of pretty," the man said, winking. He was short, fat, and balding, and smelled like a potpourri of semi-legal drugs. Forrester's type if anyone was.

"Not what you were expecting?" she said, scoffing.

"Not really. Most of the people I meet with are either ugly, or pretty and terrifying. You're pretty, but not so scary."

Wonderful. Rosetta tweaked her wish and pictured herself nice and safe at home. Maybe in a sonic bath. "You have some information for me?"

"I sure do, if you're the one I'm supposed to be giving it to." He winked at her again, and Rosetta managed to avoid rolling her eyes.

"Maybe this will convince you, then." She pulled an envelope out of her left jacket pocket and dropped it on the ground. It hit with the satisfying heaviness of a large number of unmarked, non-sequential NORPAC dollars.

He took the package, inspected the contents, and then smiled at Rosetta. "Consider me convinced." Nodding toward a dark side alley not far from the loading dock, he said, "Come on. Let's you and me go somewhere more private."

"Yeah, right. Come on, you've got your money. Spill it."

The man shrugged. "Suit yourself. What I've got is well worth your money, believe you me."

Rosetta tapped her foot and stared expectantly at the man until he threw his hands up. "All right, all right. You want the short version first, right? Well, I have here in my pocket a UNASCA dispatch. Not just any dispatch, mind, but a very special one. A very secret one. Not to be shared with just anyone."

"And what's it say? Damn it," Rosetta blurted, and then tried to calm herself, reminding herself that losing one's control during sensitive black-market dealings was seldom a good idea.

"Well why don't I just read it." He pulled out a thick sheaf of hardcopy from the inside of his jacket; Rosetta wasn't sure where someone his type had acquired that much of the stuff.

Dramatically clearing his throat, he lifted the paper before his eyes and said, "From UNASCA chief of security, blah blah blah, to all stations, high importance, blah blah blah," he scanned down a bit and started again. "We hereby order that protocol thirteen be initiated at once in relation to the members of the 'Free Jove' movement. The code phrase is 'Elysium.' Confirm these orders according to usual processes, blah blah blah." He looked back at Rosetta. "Satisfied?"

"What's this 'protocol thirteen?"

"Unlucky number thirteen, right? Well, back on Jupiter, we knew something about protocol thirteen." He handed her the wad, and she glanced at the top couple of sheets.

The man looked like he was expecting a big reaction, but Rosetta managed to keep a straight face. Somehow. "You say you're from Jupiter?"

"Yeah, I worked the helium extractors in the atmosphere. Lived out of Foundation Home on Europa; did contracts for Belt Group, Skyhook, a few others. So, big news, huh? Not that anyone on this planet will give a damn, and the folks back around Jupiter will just ignore it. Worst for Mars and Venus, I think."

"This calls for the suspension of civil liberties," she exclaimed. Abashed by her loudness, Rosetta glanced around, as if she would be able to spot a spy beam or covert surveillance drone.

"Ain't that a bitch."

Rosetta glanced at the date on the memo. It had just gone out the previous day, so it was quite possible that she was the only person not connected with UNASCA security who knew of its existence.

Glancing back up and her rather self-satisfied looking co-conspirator, she shook her head. "How the hell did you come up with this?"

"I have my contacts back there." He shrugged, full of false modesty.

"The real question," Rosetta said, realizing another angle to this story, "is this: can you confirm it?"

"The checksums are all there, but I don't think I need to," the man said, shrugging elaborately. "Just read the news from Mars and the Belt. If you can read between the lines at all..."

"I see what you're saying."

"Good times then. Well, be seeing you." The man spun on one foot with reasonable dexterity, stopped after two paces, and spun back. "Say, whatever happened to the usual fellow that asks for this type of stuff?"

"He's on a, ah, business trip."

"Good. Good, I hope he has fun." With no more information than that, the man spun about once more and walked away, whistling a commercial jingle for Squid Fries.

As soon as he had passed to the darkened street, Rosetta looked back down at the sheaf in her hand. This was big. If Free Jove was going to be their secret dagger, this would be a huge broadsword. It would bring everyone into the game against UNASCA.

On the other hand, they knew that their backs were up against the wall. An enemy was always the most dangerous when it knew it was trapped.

Chapter 15

"I realize that it's not actually illegal, but aren't you a little worried that this exotic course of yours is going to draw notice?" Eileen glanced at the orbital display which showed the icon for their ship, alone and conspicuous, far from the normal orbital lanes.

There were still high above Mar's atmosphere, the tenuous, unbreathable mix of carbon dioxide and trace gasses almost invisible as it blurred the limb of the planet beneath them. Leona had ordered her ship into a polar orbit, which was unusual enough for an interplanetary craft, and the *Fisher King* was burning hard for what looked like a polar landing site. It was bound to draw attention.

"I'm sure that some computer deep in one of UNASCA's orbital complexes is logging it as we speak. Maybe some human someday will take a look at it, but I doubt they'd find it more interesting than the computer. Besides, we're hardly the only ship headed this direction."

Eileen frowned at the scopes. Despite her earlier

appraisal, there did appear to be a number of tracks converging on their projected destination: an ice shelf close to the north pole. Most of them were a fair bit discrete, but even so. Whoever these smugglers were, Eileen hoped that they had an escape route planned. Meeting like this was hardly inconspicuous.

"They're called the Saekir," Leona said without preamble. "It's a conglomerate...no, that's too strong a word. More like a loose confederacy, I suppose, of ships and owners with similar goals."

"And those goals would be..."

"Well, money, of course. But see, they don't care much for UNASCA monopolies on hauling and mining. I'm sure you can identify with that," Leona said, looking at Eileen expectantly.

Eileen took some small pleasure in disappointing her. "I don't know about that. The *Mary Ellen* is..was strictly a company ship, and I didn't make many business decisions."

Leona gave her a sidelong glance. "That surprises me, considering the circumstances we met under."

"That was an exception. A big exception. And it certainly had nothing to do with business."

"Hmm. Anyway, Tarn had a longstanding agreement with the Saekir. Informal as it was, it was great for everyone involved. When word got around that Tarn was dead, and that vultures were already picking at his corpse," she spat, "there was suddenly a lot of reluctance to do business." She shook her head. "Things went from perfect to horrible in days. Days. And now I have to redo years of work, if it even can be redone."

"Stand by for the interface," Eileen mumbled, and their shuttle pitched up, jerked, stabilized, the windows glowing orange with plasma streamers, the bright light filling the cabin and the growing roar drowning out any attempt at normal conversation.

When the roar abated and the bright light faded away, the horizon had lost the pronounced curve of orbit, and now cut a sharp, straight line across the sky. The sky was clear enough to see the ground far below, and although the details were lost to height and atmospheric blurring, Eileen got the impression of gently sloping hills with a few large boulders and small mountains. The entire planet had been worn smooth, like a rock in a desert.

Ahead of them, against the horizon, the character of the land shifted. The smooth red desert gave way to a thick sheet of dirty white, like a cotton rug on a stone floor. Eileen could make out striations and fissures in the ice, but compared to the desert and the space above it, it seemed exceptionally brilliant.

"Do the Saekir have some sort of meeting space here? Or is it just on one of the shuttles?" Eileen asked.

"There's a geological outpost dating back from the first explorers. It's cramped, and the amenities aren't outstanding, but it has air and heat, and it's very private."

"I can imagine," Eileen murmured as the ice sheet swept beneath them. They were losing altitude by the second, and she could see the massive cracks that split the ice. Many of them were dusted with red; it appeared that there was truly no place on the planet that could escape that tenacious dust. Eileen remembered that every indoors space on Mars, no matter how pressurized and otherwise hospitable, carried that faint odor of rust and gunpowder, and how every surface, if left unattended, would develop a dusty red coating.

"Oh, look to starboard. See that cloud?" Leona pointed.

"I do. A dust storm?" Eileen squinted, but it was hard to get a perspective on the cloud. There was no way to tell where it began or ended, or how far away it was. Still, it was impossible to mistake it for anything else.

"Certainly. It might be localized. I hope so; I'd hate to have to fly through it. Ah," Leona said, pointing ahead of the ship now, at a dark spot on the horizon. "That's our destination just up there."

In short order, Eileen kicked in the hover jets and the reverse thrusters fired, killing their forward momentum and leaving them fixed in the air a dozen meters above the hard ice. There were a few other vehicles here, most suborbitals and aircraft, although there was one other orbital shuttle: a Shuttle Alpha, its characteristic cargo pods painted with a livery that Eileen didn't recognize. When Eileen set the *Fisher King* down on the ice, it gave just a centimeters or two, and then held them steady as stone.

After an uneventful moment, Eileen started the shutdown sequence and called for a suit check. She went through the very familiar routine of affixing her helmet and checking her gloves, and nodded when she heard the hiss as her backpack tank pumped life-giving air into the helmet, and checked the pressure readings on her wrist. Steady, no leaks. Eileen and Leona gave each other's suits a quick once-over, and as soon as they gave the thumbs-up, Eileen depressurized the cabin and cracked the hatch.

The icy surface of Mars was surprisingly brittle, as though the top layer of ice had warped and cracked, while the ice below remained firm. It was not quite white; what had seemed brilliant from a few kilometers up was less so here; that omnipresent red dust cut the white, sprinkled about like nutmeg on a custard.

Leona was walked ahead, and Eileen jogged to catch up. The gravity took a little getting used to; an iota less than ship's gravity, more than the Moon's, and much, much more than Ceres'. Every planet seemed to have its own gravitational particularities, and even someone as well-traveled as Eileen took a few moments to find her planet legs.

They reached the outpost, and Eileen could see that it was as old as Leona had claimed. The exposed workings looked positively primitive, with pumps, valves, and conduits exposed to the thin, dusty atmosphere. The main module was a geodesic dome, half buried, with several smaller modules attached with flexible tunnels. Wear and radiation had turned the metal a dark gray, with lighter patches revealing more recent repairs. It was old, but it was still used: the dust and ice had been worn away near the entrance.

There were footprints in the ice leading up to an airlock module, and Leona was already working its controls as Eileen arrived. They stepped in, waited for the door to close, waited through an annoyingly long pressurization sequence, and cracked the inner door.

The airlock led into the geodesic dome's main room. It was a living space, with a large table in the center and a few chairs and benches. A kitchen unit filled out one wall, and storage modules the rest of them. There was no decoration, no sense of being lived in, but it was hard to tell given the crowd of people clustered in the center.

There were a half-dozen of them, seated at the table or leaning against the storage modules. They were all wearing helmetless, gloveless pressure suits of widely varying models, and no less consistent were their appearances: tall, spindly women obviously used to low gravity, squat men who looked uncomfortable in Mars' one-third gee, radiation-darkened faces, the pale skin of one who lived deep underground, and everything in between. They were, Eileen decided, one of the most eclectic-looking groups she had ever seen.

It seemed that Eileen and Leona had interrupted their conversation, for several of them were leaning forward, caught in mid-gesture. As Leona popped her helmet and stuffed it under her arm, one of the seated men, a dark-faced, easy-looking man with broad features, gestured at her while addressing the others.

"For those of you who aren't familiar, this is Leona King, lately of Tarn Stefanovic's operation on Venus." Then, to Leona, "I was sorry to hear about Tarn. We all were. We did very, very well by each other." His voice was melodic and sounded as easy-going as the man looked.

"No more sorry than I was," Leona said, tipping her head to him. Then, as Eileen removed her helmet, she said, "This is a friend of mine, Eileen Cromwell. She was partly responsible for a little incident on the Moon awhile back that I think we're all familiar with. She was also involved in the situation that got Tarn killed."

"It looks like more condolences are owed," said a

pale, gawky, red-haired woman leaning against the wall. "I knew Stephen Montgomery; he and I worked together on the *Godspeed*, what, fifteen years ago? I was sorry to hear about him."

Eileen wasn't sure what to say, so she just muttered a, "Thank you," and let Leona continue.

"I presume that we're waiting for a few others? I was expecting twice this many," she said, moving to the table and setting her helmet down on it.

"They'll be here presently," said the easy-going man, his expression flicking between Eileen and Leona. "They'd better—I'm sure you saw the storm brewing."

"Naturally."

"Naturally. So, you can speak your piece whenever you want, but I've got other business to discuss here as well. Business you might not want to get involved with. Dangerous business."

"How dangerous?" Leona narrowed her eyes, trying to take in the whole room at once.

"Very dangerous, possibly. UNASCA's suspended civil rights for Free Jovians and their sympathizers. They've got to have their crosshairs on us, too."

The Aquifer Prison wasn't what Joanna expected. There were no wide cell blocks like she'd seen in her father's prison (when she'd decided to visit him), no bars, almost no people. Those people she did see looked like those her father had been in with, though: normal-looking people carrying haunted expressions.

The cells were quite familiar from her trip on the prison transport. She was in her own tiny room with a tiny window and a heavy, solid door. It was clean, thankfully, but quite spare. The hallway outside lead to a sort of common area where she'd first been processed, which was the complete extent of her knowledge about this place.

As Joanna sat on the hard cot, she realized that she wasn't sad, or scared, or worried, or any of things she'd felt when UNASCA had first locked her up in Sagan Hospital, months ago. She was grateful. Thankful. Thankful that the door to her cell was opaque, so that she couldn't see anyone else, and that nobody else could see her. Thankful that, if she stayed on Mars, none of her family would stop by for a visit, even if they found out where she was. Thankful, most of all, that Eileen wasn't here.

She laid down on her cot's single blanket, turning that thought over in her mind. Yes, she was most thankful for that. There was no chance of a rescue of course, but even if there was one, would she take it? Maybe this was where she belonged. Maybe being in prison was in her genes.

The ceiling of her cell was a flat sheet of shiny metal, unbroken except for a flat light fixture. She stared at it for awhile, because it was preferable to the thoughts that she was avoiding. Thoughts of her father trying to hide his tears in the prison meeting room at St. James. Thoughts of her mother chatting with another woman, artfully avoiding mentioning where Joanna's father was, that little way she teased at her hair when she was dodging the questions.

It was too easy to imagine her mother doing just that same thing when some well-meaning relation asked, "How is Joanna doing, Martha?" "Oh, just fine. She's in space, you know," would be the response, and then the conversation would get steered toward the weather, or the elections, or the latest episode of *Trespassers*, or something otherwise innocuous. She could barely imagine how her father would react.

There was a loud banging on her prison door that pulled her out of her woolgathering. She propped herself up on her elbows as the hatch slid into the wall with a hiss.

"Prisoner 2 dash 182957? Come with me." A guard stood in the doorway, arms at his side, an electrolaser at his belt. Without waiting for a response, he stepped to the side to allow Joanna out.

She stood, still adjusting to the gravity, and walked where he indicated. "Where are you taking me?" He cleared his throat and she added, "Prisoner 2 dash 182957 would like to know where she is being taken."

As they started down the narrow corridor, the guard said, "To the catacombs." She could almost hear the sneer in his voice.

"Prisoner 2 dash 182-"

The guard interrupted her, and this time he didn't bother hiding his pleasure at her discomfort. "You'll find out what it is soon enough."

The prison was constructed like a living being, with the tiny capillaries containing the cellsbranching off from a few main arteries. These arteries were connected to the main organs of the dining area, the recreation rooms, and the medical center. She had seen all of these on her way in.

They turned into one of those main arteries, stopping to allow a line of prisoners flanked by guards to pass. The prisoners were both men and women, all wearing that sort of hangdog of guilt that Joanna knew all too well from her younger years. It was the same sort of expression she'd had glued on for the past months, in the space between worlds.

The man at the end of the line of prisoners wore a different expression, one with less contrition and more calculation. And he was staring right at her. It was Thomas Gabriel.

Joanna blinked, and he was past. "Wait," she half-shouted, taking a step toward that retreating column of prisoners. She didn't have a chance to take a second step before her escort was there, his viselike grip around her arm. "Prisoner! Stand down," he growled.

Joanna yanked against his grip once and realized that she'd sooner escape the Sun's gravity. "That's Gabriel, damn it..." A floating riot drone was hovering overhead, probes and manipulators extended, waiting for her to make a move before suppressing her.

"Prisoner! Resume your march on the double or it's night-time when you get back to your cell." Joanna wasn't sure what that meant, but she was suddenly feeling very small. There was a lot of attention focused on her, and what could she do? She relaxed, the guard let go, and she walked where he indicated, feeling like scum.

That had been Gabriel, though. There was no mistaking that appearance, that look of calculation. How had he ended up here? The Moon had its own detention facilities, and with the Earth so close Joanna assumed he'd just be recalled so that they could throw the book at him there. Joanna decided she would not have been more surprised to see St. Peter and Johannes Kepler on Mars.

Before she knew it, though, they were past the

dining room, the rec center, and the medical bay, standing before a large, open-mesh elevator. Joanna could feel a waft of cold air coming from below, sending a shiver up her spine.

"Get on the elevator. The processing team will meet you at the bottom." The guard chuckled. "Good luck."

The wire door opened with a clatter, and Joanna took tiny steps until she was just past its threshold. She was afraid to go on, afraid not to. As the elevator started down, though, she wasn't worried quite so much about her impending interrogation. Gabriel's presence had just about forced it from her mind—wherever Gabriel went, things went badly for others. Last time, of course, they'd gone really badly for *everyone.*

So much for quietly serving her own time.

"Perfect time for a storm," Cruikshank muttered. "It's going to play hell with our satellites."

Rojas stared at the projected map in the security office bullpen and chewed at the inside of his lip. It was a live satellite image of the north pole with the geological research station centered in the display; the various craft landed around it had call-outs indicating their registration and ownership. The Saekir didn't intend for their meeting to be secret. Perhaps they hadn't heard about Rojas' special orders? Or they had heard, and they were flaunting it. Whatever. Rojas was a lawman. He didn't deal in subtleties. If they wanted to set some scheme in motion, they could work it from a prison cell.

"They're in for a surprise," Marla muttered, a corner of her mouth twitching upward.

"Yes," Rojas said, casting her a stern glance. "Let us hope that nobody acts too rash."

She lowered her gaze, and he turned his back to the map. He felt bad for even such a minor snap, but he felt like he wanted to smash something. If he were honest, he should've recused himself from the entire crackdown after the first day. A good officer is able to separate his personal opinions from his job performance; Rojas was being forced to conclude that he wasn't a very good officer.

"Looks like the last of them have arrived," Cruikshank said, pounding his fist on his desk in enthusiasm.

"What's meteorology have to say about that dust storm?" Rojas called to nobody in particular.

Ojedo answered. "Looks like a pretty big one. It should cover most of the pole, but it'll move south again after a day or two."

Rojas nodded in approval, never removing his gaze from the display. He wasn't sure what he was waiting for. Whatever they did would not make his decision for him, nor would it ease his guilt if he made the wrong one. Or the right one. Assuming there were even such at thing.

"Ojedo?"

"Yes, sir?"

"Make sure that our entire fleet is powered up and ready to fly, but they're to hold until I give the signal."

Marla frowned at him. "Are you waiting for something in particular?"

"As a matter of fact, yes. I've just received word that UNASCA has an agent inside the Saekir; they'll give us a go-code when we can strike."

A gravid pause settled on the team. Glances were exchanged, silent except for the periodic tapping of keys and awkward shifts of weight. It was Marla who had the courage to break it. "*UNASCA* has an agent, sir? Not us or one of the other cities?"

"Yep," Rojas said, drawing out the syllable.

"So the administrator told you-"

"The administrator didn't tell me anything," Rojas cut her off, still staring at the meteorology report on the main screen. "This was a coded message direct from Portland."

A frustrated sigh rippled around the room. They all felt the same way: when being a UNASCA citizen was just doing taxes and filling out paperwork, it was annoying enough. When it meant being a puppet for someone on another planet, it was far worse. And lately, Rojas hadn't felt very much in control of his own strings.

Marla opened and closed her mouth, fishing for the right words, finally settling on a simple, "Okay," that did little to alleviate the tension in the room.

"Listen," Rojas said, tearing his eyes from the displays and looking his men in the eye, "we do our jobs, okay? We don't have to like it, but we have to follow orders. Now, get the damned strike team armed up. I'll be down in the squad bay." He was lashing out because of his own guilt, he knew that. He felt sick.

"You're leading the team yourself?" Ojedo didn't sound very surprised.

"That's right. Any problem with that?" He let a hard edge into his voice, and Ojedo raised his hands in silent acceptance. "Good. I'll be down in the squad bay," he repeated, "and I'll let you know when I get that go-code."

As he walked out the door, he felt Marla fall into step behind him. She waited until they were alone, walking down the half-underground corridor between the security offices and the city proper. The hazy sky cast a purplish light through the skylights, the first signs of a new sol starting.

"You want to tell me what's going on?" she said, keeping her voice low.

"You know what's going on. UNASCA's running the whole show from Earth now. We're just pawns being shuffled around." He hoped he didn't sound as bitter as he felt.

"It was the same thing during the Titania crisis," Marla said, her voice soothing. "They're just nervous."

"No, it's different. There's too much cloak-and-dagger stuff going down. They might've been anxious of other independence movements after Titania, but this Jupiter business is making them more than anxious. They're terrified, and they're overreacting." He shook his head. Why was he telling her this? It was something he needed to get off his chest, but he was afraid of how far he'd go if she let him. "It doesn't matter. We do our jobs. I just want all this over with."

"And you're leading the strike team?"

"I've got to command *something*, don't I? Now that UNASCA has taken over everything else." He tried to chuckle at his little joke, but it was barely out of his mouth before his gravity smothered it.

"Right," Marla said. They reached the hatch leading to the city's administrative section and Rojas keyed for the airlock. Both sides were already pressurized, so it opened after just a moment. Rojas stepped in and blocked Marla from accompanying him.

"You're needed in the office. I'll be fine. I might go work out or something." He frowned at her obvious disbelief and added, "I'll be fine."

"Sure thing, boss," she said as the airlock swung shut. The last thing Rojas saw before it closed was the disbelief in her expression morphing into even more obvious concern.

The storm was starting to pick up. Dark swirls of mist-like dust beat against the side of the geological outpost with a scratching, rasping noise that seemed to be everywhere at once. It wasn't loud, but it was persistent and difficult to ignore, like hearing one's name called in a crowd.

Based on the intensity of the conversation, however, it didn't seem to be ruining the atmosphere much. Leona was holding forth with some animation, while Bucholz, the easy-going fellow, was leaning back and listening with an air of cultivated disinterest.

"Fifteen percent. Fifteen percent! With that kind of increase, you could hire a few more folks to take the edge off those long flights. For that matter, you could lay in a few more supplies, upgrade your old ECLSS systems for longer duration, you could do anything. Think about it. My outfit could add an entire ship for fifteen percent—think of what you can do."

Eileen was pacing along near the outside walls of the dome, listening to Leona and Bucholz go at it. It seemed like a lifetime since she'd last been concerned with mere business matters. She'd been consumed by them, same as everyone in her line of work. Now they seemed vapid and meaningless, and she was losing her patience listening to the two of them spat like children. Eileen had started the day in a dark mood, and if she was honest with herself for just a moment, she wanted someone else to take it out on.

Leona finished and gestured for Bucholz to respond, which he did with gusto. "Sure, we save money by going around UNASCA's monopolies. Everyone knows that. I think that you're emphasizing the benefits over the risk, however. UNASCA's centralizing their administration; what makes you think they're going to keep turning a blind eye to your little outfit? Suppose they stage a crackdown while one of my ships is docked at your precious *Agropolis*?" He leaned forward, raising an eyebrow. "Suppose you've already lost *Agropolis*, eh? I hear things haven't been what you might call status quo since Tarn died."

Eileen saw Leona's jaw set, saw her bite her tongue. She understood the feeling, thinking back to her last conversation with Ben and Melissa. She felt the new cocktail of guilt and grief rise up in her gut, but she shoved it back down with a practiced air. Not the time. Not yet.

"Are you doing all right?"

Startled at having her internal ritual interrupted, Eileen whirled on the new speaker. It was the young, gawky red-head who'd known Stephen; Eileen hadn't caught her name.

"What? Why?" Eileen tamped down on her sputtering, took a deep breath, and started over. "I'm sorry. Yes, I'm doing fine."

"Good. You just looked a little miserable over here. I'm Clara Canady, by the way." The woman smiled, showing a lot of very white teeth, and extended a thin, bony hand.

Eileen took it. "You served with Stephen on the *Godspeed*?"

"Sure did. We did some of the first material runs to the *Robert Hunt* under construction. I'm still nostalgic about those days," she sighed, looking far away for a moment.

"I understand," Eileen said. She understood it too well; it wasn't something she wanted to get in to. To bring the conversation out of painful past, she said, "So, what are you doing now?"

"Oh, I'm mostly doing low-orbit work now, hauling material down from Newport Orbital, and doing some freelance work unloading Belt Group bulk carriers and asteroid miners." She shrugged. "It's all pretty routine, but it pays the bills and I get to meet a lot of people."

"You do freelance? So you have your own ship?"

"Bought and paid for," Clara said with a smile of pride. "It's an old Invictus D90 lander, but I picked up some brand-new Kobuta SSWR-VB engines at a fire sale. Given how much iron I'm hauling down, they were a pretty solid investment."

"I bet. Wow." Like most pilots, Eileen had always dreamed of owning a ship outright, but even the smallest orbital jobs were far out of her reach. A ship like the *Mary Ellen*, necessary for interplanetary work, was so expensive that only a consortium could afford one, even if it was old and well-used. "Where'd you get the money for that?"

"A loan, from Bucholz' group," Clara said, nodding toward where the man was still sparring with Leona. "He's a good person, appearances occasionally to the contrary."

"I'm sure he is," Eileen said. She must've let too

much sarcasm into her voice, because Clara suddenly became very quiet. Eileen, kicking herself, tried to find a way to resuscitate the conversation.

"I hear you've got something that UNASCA wants," Clara said, leaning in toward Eileen and speaking quietly. She wasn't smiling anymore. "Something they want very badly."

Fighting the reflex to feel for the datacube in her pocket, Eileen frowned. "How'd you hear that?"

"Like I said, I talk to people a lot. You've been declared a person of interest by UNASCA, and the rumors are that Belt Group is after you too. Their security men have been talking about you and your ship."

She had to force down a brief moment of panic for the *Mary Ellen*, reminding herself that Leona's people had done a very thorough job obfuscating the ship's true identity. They had seemed very practiced at it.

"And have they said why I'm a 'person of interest'?"

"They have. I guess you're in possession of some sort of secret data. Is it true?" Clara raised an eyebrow.

Eileen leaned against the dome's wall, anchoring herself to the solidity of it. At least for this wall, the storm was roaring *outside*. "I've got something, yeah. I'm not sure what it is, but going by Belt Group's reaction it must be something important." She narrowed her eyes. "Why?"

Clara took a step back and smiled warmly. "I think I might be able to help, is all."

"I haven't had such great luck with getting help. I'm sure you heard about Venus."

"I did." Clara picked at a seam in the wall with a short fingernail. "Trouble does seem to follow you. It always followed Stephen, back then."

"Really?"

"Yeah, although he brought a lot of it upon himself. He was always a bit of an armchair captain, and our actual captain never appreciated it. He kept swearing that he'd put Stephen off at the next port, but after we brought in one of those huge hauls and lived easy in port for a few weeks, Stephen would just show up at the next muster and the captain wouldn't say a thing."

Eileen had heard the story before, but coming out of Stephen's mouth rather than his shipmates, it had a rather different slant. In spite of herself and the surge of emotion that it brought up, she was curious to know more.

"Why was that?" she asked.

Clara shrugged. "He was good crew. He knew his stuff, but more than any of us, he took real responsibility, owned his assigned tasks. Reliable. Of all of us, he was the only one that I could see getting his own ship."

"He was very proud of his ship," Eileen said, glancing skyward for a moment. Somewhere far above, the *Mary Ellen* was orbiting the planet, a testament to that pride. She felt like she needed to sit down. "I just want to do right by him."

"That's why I made my offer," Clara said, joining Eileen on the plastic crate she'd claimed as a seat. "I know a datajack that might be able to help you. If it's UNASCA data that you're having trouble with, you won't find a better guy on the entire planet."

"Is he trustworthy?"

"You can never be sure, of course, but datajacks work on their reputation. If they resold data on a routine basis, word would get around, and word on this guy is that he's laser-straight."

Eileen gnawed on a knuckle. She started to ask herself what Stephen would do, but the answer presented itself almost before she asked the question. After all, he'd risked trying to sell the data to Gabriel before he'd even had any skin in the game. Would he try to do something even more risky with it if he had a personal stake? Of course; just like Clara had said, he owned his responsibilities. And now she had a responsibility to him.

"How do we find this guy?" Eileen asked, standing abruptly. Now that she'd made a decision, she felt anxious to be away from that place and those people.

"What about Leona King?" Clara glanced at the animated group in the center of the dome. They were consumed in their negotiations. It sounded like things were going well for Leona, but who could tell?

"I'll come back for her. Come on, let's get out of here." She hefted her helmet and secured it on her collar. Conversation over.

Chapter 16

The questions hadn't been kind. There hadn't been any beatings or any drugs, but her guard had sneered while leading her down there for a reason. They held her life in their hands, and they knew it. Her interrogator was an older man, one who might have been kind-looking except for hardness of his expression, and he was very good at his job. He knew her family history, he knew what she feared most.

He had said that it would be inevitable that her parents—especially her father—would find out about her imprisonment. That can be avoided, though, if only you cooperate. Tell us what you know about the *Atlas*.

I don't know anything about the *Atlas*, she'd said. It was true. In those weeks she'd spent with Eileen and the others, spend aboard the *Mary Ellen*, she didn't know what Eileen knew, what had gotten her involved with UNASCA in the first place. She'd asked, but Eileen had never said, and in the end it hadn't mattered.

Her interrogator didn't think so. Back and forth

they went, questions and promises, but the session hadn't been long. The man was enough of a professional to realize that not only was she telling the truth, but that she would've been incapable of lying to him. It wasn't her way.

So, he'd signaled the guard, who'd led her back to her cell, and there she was. It had been perhaps a few hours ago. She was under the impression that they were making her sit here alone, rather than in the common area, until she became more cooperative. At this point, Joanna didn't care. What more could they do to her? It was strange to feel so numb—she wasn't tired, hungry, or sad, but just empty.

Oddly, the last time that she could remember feeling that way was when her father had first been convicted. It had been a fast trial; the evidence against him was so good, and he'd been caught so red-handed, that his advocate hadn't been able to mount much of a defense. They'd brought out some correspondence indicating the higher-ups at his company knew he was taking all of that money and not doing anything, but it hadn't stuck, and the justices hadn't been convinced.

So before they knew it, it was time for tearful goodbyes at the prison, with the mass of a fifteen-year sentence filling the air. At least, it had been a tearful goodbye for her mother; Joanna had just stood there, not getting in the way, wishing that the goodbyes were over and that her father was already in his cell, and then feeling guilty for that. And then the numbness of the ride home, a numbness that had persisted for weeks. How long would it last this time? Without school and friends to pull her out of it, would it ever end?

A chime sounded from some invisible public

address system, and a smooth, digitized voice announced, "Sixteen hundred hours. Report to dining for dinner count." Then there was a thud from her door as the locks disengaged.

Joanna just stared at it for a moment, wondering what would happen if she refused to get up. The packet she'd been forced to review on the transport over here indicated a wide variety of possible punishments for interrupting the counts, but at least they couldn't take away visitation rights, could they? Who would come visit her?

But then she remembered Gabriel. In the unpleasantness of the interrogation she'd hardly thought about him, but he had been there in there in the prison, had met here eye. The numbness started to wear off a bit, replaced by a deepening curiosity. Even if she wasn't hungry, she'd have to leave the cell anyway; might as well do it now and figure out what Gabriel was doing here.

The door opened at the press of a button and let her out into a narrow capillary she shared with a five other cells. There was nobody else here, but she could see people walking down the main artery. Following them, she could see that most of them were the same type of person she'd seen just before her interrogation: quiet and bearing that appearance of guilty suffering that she couldn't stand. A few were having loud, good-natured conversations, but these were the exception to the general rule.

They were filing into the dining area and standing military-style along tables with attached benches. There was a serving line along one side, empty now, but the smells coming from it reminded her that even if her brain wasn't hungry, her belly was. It looked like there were almost more inmates than there were tables, however, and more were filing in every moment, she picked up her step, searching for the one face that she recognized.

Just as she was starting to feel exposed, walking slowly into the dining room, she saw him. Standing at a corner table that wasn't yet full, Gabriel cast a significant look her direction. She felt a brief rush, knowing that she hadn't just been imagining things, but it was short-lived. After all, Gabriel was actually here.

So she walked slowly over to his table, standing at the seat across from him. He was still looking at her with a slight smile, but just as she opened her mouth to speak, a loud tone sounded through the room.

"Count beginning. Please do not move," the digital voice said. There were a few human guards near the door, and a human serving staff, but the count appeared to be being conducted by those floating riot drones. She felt a powerful downdraft as one flew overhead, tossing her hair into a nimbus about her head.

"Count complete," the voice said a moment later. "Tables one through five to the serving line. All others may sit."

Her table had a large "thirteen" stenciled in the middle, so its occupants sat as one. Gabriel was still staring at her, still saying nothing, but she guessed that by the way a smile kept teasing at the corners of his mouth, he was enjoying her discomfort.

Damn it. "I'm in here because of you." The words burst out all at once, and to her surprise, they kept coming. "I'm being interrogated because of you. You just couldn't bear to take blame for anything without bringing everyone else down with you. I'm surprised that you're the only one from Brighton here; you weren't the only guilty one, that's for sure. I, for one, am not guilty of anything. At least I wasn't when you had an warrant out for my arrest."

Joanna took a deep breath, and the next words came out in an angry jumble. "So what do you have to say, huh? We've got plenty of time to talk, thanks to you." She glared what she hoped were daggers at him, and his smiled slowly evaporated before he spoke.

"It's good to see you too, Ms. Newton." He glanced across the room as the next batch of tables were entering the serving line. "How have you been?"

"I've almost died. Twice!" She blurted.

"I don't suppose that it ever occurred to you, my dear, that I issued an arrest warrant for you because I thought you were actually guilty?"

"Not really."

"Or, more practically, that I had no choice? I'm sorry, but my own life was in danger. If you'd been in my place you would've named your own grandmother."

Joanna just set her jaw. "Well, aren't you a hero."

Gabriel snorted. "You know better than that." He leaned back and gestured at the room, at the others at her table that were trying to hide their obvious interest in their conversation. "But that's all water under the bridge, now. I'm not your boss anymore, you're not in possession of classified documents anymore." He steamrolled over her protests. "Now we're comrades. Equals, eh? Might as well work on our future together."

"*Our* future? How dare you, you damned opportunist!"

He shrugged elaborately. "I just believe that most inconveniences are opportunities in disguise. I didn't become a UNASCA administrator by rolling over at the first setback."

"And what opportunities do you see here, exactly? What are you doing here in the first place?" She snorted, looking around the bare facility. He wouldn't be able to import his usual gambling-and-booze operation from Brighton.

"Same as you—UNASCA thought I knew something. And when they found out I didn't, they hid me away so that nobody would know that I flaunted them. Politics, you know?"

"And we just happen to go to the same prison? It's on a different planet."

"You know how the public is—out of sight, out of mind. We're not the only people here just to be shut up."

Their table was called before she could respond, and Joanna grabbed her tray from the table in front of her as she stood. Gabriel hurried to be next to her in line; she tried to get away from him, but she had to admit that she wasn't trying too hard. What else would she do if she weren't talking to him? She noticed her increased heart rate, the flush on her face—she was angry, and it was delicious.

"I'll tell you what kind of opportunity I see here if you think you'd be interested in being a part of it."

He whispered in her ear as they took their place in the line. Feeling his breath on her neck was a vile thing, and Joanna let it feed her anger. "I'd rather clean the toilets with my tongue."

"Okay. But take a look around you. This prison

hasn't always been so full, and hasn't always had such a high ratio of inmates to guards."

She had noticed that, but attributed it to the riot drones overhead. As she slid her tray along, taking the protein sludge and the greenhouse vegetables as she moved, she had a brief impulse to dump her tray onto Gabriel's head.

"And what's more, most of these people aren't even guilty of anything. They haven't even been tried. They're just political prisoners that UNASCA was able to associate with the Free Jovian movement. I'm sure you've heard of it."

Everyone in the Solar System had heard of it. She was starting to get impatient.

"There's a lot of dissatisfaction here, a lot. Even the guards are feeling it. I've made a few friends, Joanna, and I think that I can make a difference here. *We* can make a difference, that is."

A harsh bark of laughter escaped her unbidden. She didn't even answer until they were sitting back at their table. Gabriel ate as he spoke. "I was going to act without you, but with you here—we're better together. Nobody can dislike you, for one thing. You've got such charm."

She raised an eyebrow, silently shoveling a few bland forkfuls into her mouth before answering. "What about these folks?" She gestured to the people sitting next to her, still feigning disinterest in the conversation. "Won't they tell on whatever scheme you've got going?" She hoped that they would. She hoped that she could ruin everything just by talking a little too loud.

To her surprise, Gabriel didn't react with distress, but he smiled almost thinly. "Oh, don't worry about it, my dear girl." He exchanged that grin with the others sitting there, their interest no longer concealed. He even glanced at a guard standing a few tables away and exchanged that same grin with him. "I told you, I've made a few friends. I'll introduce you in a short while."

Joanna noticed that theirs wasn't the only table listening to their conversation. She saw people at the next table over, a few of them chuckling to themselves. Gabriel was no longer speaking quietly. Her whole perception of the situation was flip-flopping—this wasn't some stupid gambling scheme, or one of Gabriel's little rackets.

"We're not happy with the current prison situation. Not happy at all. And I'm going to do something about it with a few hundred of my friends." Gabriel smiled wide, and she felt a sinking feeling in her stomach, a very familiar one.

She felt the room constrict around her as he chuckled, a sudden need to run, to run forever burning in her guts. Tom Gabriel was planning a prison break, and he wanted her in the middle of it.

The radio-blocking envelope of superheated atmosphere gave way to a quiet hum as the *Fisher King* glided down toward the rust-colored canyons of Acheron Fossae. Eileen grimaced; what had seemed gently sloping walls from space were actually cut through with narrow, steep-sided canyons. Worse, as they descended, Eileen could see large boulders littered across the landscape. It wasn't inviting.

The signal came in, a complex series of pings, sent once and never repeated. Clara scrambled with the navigation panel to get the inertial guidance system a course before the signal stopped. She managed it, however, and they rode the non-existent beam into one of those narrow canyons Eileen had been eying with suspicion.

The *Fisher King* wasn't designed to navigate tight spaces; quite the opposite, she was always intended to give everything a wide berth. Eileen had to slam the master caution and warning to make it shut up with the proximity alerts before they gave her a headache.

It took a few moments for Eileen to find a space with enough open, unbroken space for her to land, but she managed to wedge the ship into a tiny flat area centimeters wider than the ship's wing-span. As she went through the post-landing checklist, she took a more detailed look at where they'd ended up.

The canyon had been carved by water late in Mars' geological history, but it was still ancient, and millions of years' worth of dust storms had softened all the edges and rounded the sides of the canyon. Even so, it was deep, and only a narrow slice of the dark pink sky was visible. As night came on, anything down here would be just about undetectable all the way up to orbit.

Eileen and Clara checked each other's suits with quick, professional ease, and popped the hatch. "Signal came a quarter kilometer to the west, though the canyon," Clara said as they clambered out of the ship's nose airlock. "This datajack works out of a mobile lab. Originally, it was used for geological research, I hear, but he's rigged it up with the latest in DSN uplinks. Moves it around to keep UNASCA from shutting him down." Clara flicked on a flashlight and gestured up the canyon with it. "Let's go."

The trudge wasn't easy in pressure suits. Eileen's in particular was designed for orbital work, and the legs weren't quite flexible enough to provide enough dexterity to get over all of the rocks and through the sliding sand. She felt paranoid about falling and cracking her faceplate—unlikely, but still—and so she moved slowly. The walk seemed to take an age, and she was worn to the bone when at last she saw a glint of her flashlight beam off of metal.

The lab was huge. It was a boxy vehicle the size of a medium house, articulated in the middle and nestled on four pairs of sizable treads. An elaborate collection of antennae and dishes pointed skyward, and Eileen could see an overlapping set of cameras monitoring the outside. The rig wasn't running any lights or signals, and when the flashlights were moved elsewhere it melted into the darkness of the canyon.

"You know your way in?" Eileen asked, looking for a hatch or other entrance.

"Certainly do. Set your radio to 951.7." They synchronized their radios, and Eileen heard Clara shout, "Open up, Dmitri. You've got visitors!"

For a moment, there was no response. Then, "I told you not to come back here." The voice was male, heavily accented in eastern European Union fashion. It also sounded quite tired.

"Dmitri, I have work for you. Paying work."

"Not interested," Dmitri said, and yawned.

"Then I'm going to tell UNASCA where you're hiding, Dmitri. You think you'd like them to know that?"

A brief pause. "You don't scare me."

"Just let us in!" Clara barked.

An exterior airlock popped open near them, and Dmitri sighed. "I will see money right away, or you are leaving."

"Understood." Clara gestured for Eileen to follow her into the airlock. As soon as they were inside, however, Eileen pulled Clara close and pressed their helmets together.

As the air began to hiss into the sealed chamber, she said, "Are you sure this is a good idea? I thought you were friends?"

Clara chuckled. "We are friends. He just gets into these little moods; it'll be fine. Show him the shiny stuff and he'll forget whatever he's upset about."

The inner door opened onto an airlock anteroom, and beyond that, into a large, exceptionally tidy workshop. A series of screens lined one wall, and the others were packed with communications gear in neat stacks, with cables neatly secured and workspaces cleaned.

At the far end of the rectangular room, in the midst of all the screens, seated upon a large inflated ball, Dmitri was aiming a submachine gun at them.

Clara held her hands up and chuckled. It sounded a bit forced, and Eileen caught the way her eyes danced around before she said, "You've got us; we give up."

Dmitri ignored her, indicating Eileen with the stubby tip of his weapon. "I know you," he said, furrowing bushy eyebrows. "From the *Mary Ellen*, yes?"

Eileen frowned back. "Yes. How'd you know."

A grin tugged at one corner of Dmitri's mouth. "You'd be deaf not to hear the rumors. You are high on UNASCA's wanted list. Some data they want, yes?"

Swallowing hard, Eileen nodded. "Yes."

"Give it to me."

"The important parts are encrypted," Eileen said,

cracking her suit seals and rummaging through an interior pocket. "Clara said you could help me."

Her fingers found the cube, and she realized that she was trembling. It wasn't the weapon; Dmitri no longer looked like he had much intention of using it. It was the irrevocable step. It was the knowledge that once she tossed him the cube, everything she'd fought to protect was out of her hands. Dmitri could do whatever he wanted with the data, and she wouldn't be able to stop him.

"Well?" Dmitri hefted the weapon a little higher.

Eileen closed her eyes, pulled the cube out, and hesitated just a moment before tossing it to him.

"Thank you," Dmitri mumbled, dropping the weapon to catch the cube. As he slotted it into a machine on his workbench and the two women relaxed a bit, he continued, "I don't trust you, Clara Canady. But you, Eileen Cromwell, I trust. We have the same goals, you and I. UNASCA is a yoke upon all of us, a yoke that must be lifted." He started tapping commands into his computer faster than Eileen could follow, his lips moving silently.

"I just kind of fell into this game." Eileen felt like she had to respond. "I'm not a revolutionary."

"Not a revolutionary?" Dmitri laughed, turning from his screen to eye her up and down. "Well, there are only two kinds of people today, and you are not a loyalist. UNASCA would lock you up in a very tiny place if they caught you. Therefore, you are a revolutionary."

He turned back to his gear. "Now, please relax and let me work. Coffee is on your left."

Eileen saw the pot but her stomach was far too jittery to stand any caffeine. Clara moved toward it, but

Eileen caught her and leaned close to her ear. "You sure about this guy?"

They both glanced briefly at Dmitri as he plowed through the cube's data. "I told you, stop worrying." She smiled and squeezed Eileen's shoulder and moved to get her coffee.

However, she barely had it in the cup when Dmitri scoffed in surprise.

"What? What?" Eileen said, restraining the urge to run up to his screen.

"Easy. Very easy. You are the only person to have this data, Ms. Eileen. If anyone else had it, it would've been cracked many months ago. Here," he said, pointing to one of the screens, and Eileen moved closer. "An old code, one I cracked some time ago."

"Belt Group?" Eileen asked, trying to figure out what she was looking at in the mess of alphanumerics.

"No. Free Jove." Dmitri stared at her. Trying to gauge the impact of his words?

"That doesn't make sense; that communication came from the *Atlas*," Eileen said. Then, realization hit her all at once like an asteroid impact. She felt suddenly disconnected from her body. "No. Wait," she muttered.

"I think we know what happened now to the *Atlas*," Dmitri said, pulling file after file out of the decrypted directories. "Belt Group has lost their toy." He chuckled and rubbed his hands together. "Ooh, so many people can do so much with this information. It will be fun!"

"No," Eileen said, feeling flush with panic. "No, you can't pass this one. I *need* it to stay secret."

"What? Why?" Eileen saw Dmitri's eye stray toward

his weapon.

"No, it's..." It's a pathological need to take revenge, she didn't say. I'm the one that needs to hurt UNASCA, Belt Group, everyone. I need to find some way of using this to somehow make them *pay*.

"Don't worry," Clara said, her voice stilted and strange. "It'll stay a secret."

"See, even Clara agrees," Eileen said, straightening to face her.

And then she stopped, still half-crouched by Dmitri, that sense of unreal disconnection flooding over her with redoubled strength. Clara was standing with her back against the wall, legs spread in a shooter's stance, an over-under heavy pistol pointed at Eileen's brain.

"Sorry," Clara said, and Eileen could barely hear her over the roar of her own heartbeat. "But both of you need to move away from the computer. Right...now."

The moment the signal came in, Galen Rojas made his way to the armory adjacent to the motor pool. Ojedo, Cruikshank, and Marla followed him down there.

"Origin of the signal?" Cruikshank asked, throwing open his locker and pulling out a section of armored spacesuit.

"In the Acheron Fossae. Make best speed; you've got a couple of hours at least until you're in range." He turned to Marla. "You'll follow up in the transport. Keep well behind the strike planes, and don't land until the situation reports secure. I'll be in the transport. Ojedo, I want you to grab another plane and run high-altitude coordination."

"How high?"

"High enough to keep us in constant contact. I wouldn't put it past the Saekir to have tapped the comm satellites, so I want broadcast traffic only; keep off the network. Understand?"

A chorus of acknowledgments followed, and he nodded. "All right, let's do it."

They donned their armored suits by the numbers, secured weapons. The security forces, by UNASCA policy, kept a monopoly on the legitimate use of force and they took that duty very seriously. Submachine guns and shotguns were doled out to the strike teams; each weapon had an electrolaser attached for non-lethal takedowns. A breaching gun and vortex cannon were retained for special circumstances.

They went through the armory's quick-cycling airlock and out into the hanger, the dusty Martian air lanced with beams from the setting sun. The strike teams lined up in parade-ground order and Rojas ran down the line at a brisk pace, inspecting suits and weapons. At the end of the line, he nodded in satisfaction.

Then the unavoidable horror at what he was doing crept into the military mindset he'd tried so hard to erect. He shook his head and keyed his radio to broadcast. "All right, pay attention. You did good work during the initial crackdown, and I need you to maintain that same light hand today. No mistakes. I want you all to come home, but by heaven all of those perpetrators had better come with you. Alive." He paused, and couldn't quite bring himself to issue the traditional benediction: "good hunting." "That is all," he finished lamely.

The line broke and the squad turned toward their waiting vehicles. Even in the thin Martian atmosphere he could hear the powerful engines starting up, and moments later the wasp-like shapes of the strike craft were taxing out of the hangar. Their delicate-looking wings unfolding from their storage configuration, they pulled out onto the long, flat runway.

There was a chirping on the command frequency as Rojas strode toward the fat, beetle-like command craft. "Rojas."

It was Ojedo. "Boss, I just sat down and logged into the command network, and there was priority alert. Looks like trouble at the prison. Serious trouble."

Rojas' step dragged just a bit. He quickly tapped on his wrist computer and called up the situation report. His heart leapt into this chest.

"A riot? What the hell? How did this happen?"

Rojas could nearly feel Ojedo's shrug. "You know what I know. The warden just got a generic SOS out before communications went offline altogether."

Damn it. He knew the other boot would drop eventually; there would be some response from the crackdown. But not now, not like this. Innocent people were being put in a lot of danger; UNASCA would demand a very visible response to a very visible challenge.

"Damn it, all right. Ojedo, take off right now and see what you can see about that prison. If you can establish contact with any guards over short range frequencies, let me know.

"Roger."

Rojas picked up his step toward the transport plane

and keyed himself into the general frequency. "Quick change of plans. There's a serious situation at the prison. Cruikshank, you're headed there right now. Keep your second team on the way to deal with the Saekir. I'll follow behind that team, and Ojedo will keep in contact with both of us. Understand?"

"Roger." Cruikshank's voice crackled over the radio. "What's the situation at the prison?"

"Unknown. Ojedo will give you the details."

"And what are my operating instructions?"

Rojas sighed. He gamely restrained himself from taking his frustrations out on Cruikshank. "No casualties, but I want order restored."

"Those might be contradictory instructions."

That joking bastard. He'd get his hide tanned for that later. And on the general frequency, too. "Lieutenant Cruikshank, I expect you to use your discretion, do you understand me?"

The voice came back contrite. "Yes, Chief."

"Good. Keep me informed." Rojas reached the transport plane and jogged up the ramp just as it was raising. Marla was already there and patted him on the back of his pressure suit as he sat. She made a gesture and he turned off his radio.

Pressing her helmet to his, she smiled and said, "Not exactly what you were expecting?"

Rojas shook his head. Marla would understand feelings that he didn't dare express to Cruikshank or Ojedo. "These past few weeks in general haven't been much of what I expected."

Marla nodded in sympathy. "Sorry. Sounds like I'm

not the only one that's going to need a vacation after this."

"Not at all," Rojas sighed. "I hear Valles is nice this time of year."

"Not many Free Jovians or Saekir in Valles, if the rap sheets are anything to go by."

"Bingo." With that thought, he leaned back and closed his eyes. Beneath him, the transport started to roll out onto the field. Maybe he could catch just a few of the winks that the past week had robbed from him before Cruikshank's men reached the prison in, what, half an hour? Things were going too damned fast.

Too damned fast altogether.

Chapter 17

Rosetta felt her hands shaking unaccountably as she waited just off the press room stage. The auditorium on the ground floor of Belt Group's headquarters, and the anterooms outside it, were packed. The closed-doors meeting of the Mining Consortium had turned a few heads, and now that it was over, many of the high-powered networks and a huge number of bloggers wanted to know what was going on.

But that wasn't why her hands were shaking. Her hands were shaking because today, Belt Group declared war.

Chen had masterfully teased a few of the well known and predictable press agents outside that meeting. He'd also dropped a few discreet lines in the meantime with other media personalities, and then there was all the high-profile traffic that poured through Belt Group's building over the course of the day. The larger the audience, the better.

"You're not feeling nervous, are you?"

Chen looked resplendent in his tailored European tuxedo. As he straightened his bow tie, Rosetta could see that his cuff links were made of a platinum-iridium alloy mined by one of their own ships in the Belt. A subtle statement.

Rosetta smoothed out her conservative dress and clenched her hands at her sides. "Not in the slightest."

He smiled knowingly. "I'm not either, although if you happened to have any good news about the *Atlas*..."

"Nothing new, I'm afraid," she smiled back. It was becoming a running joke of sorts, of the laugh-so-you-don't-cry variety. After those folks Bronwyn captured turned up worthless, Rosetta, and Belt Group in general, had had a very bad week.

"So," she said, turning serious, "because I know I'm going to get asked, exactly what went on inside that meeting?"

Chen shook his head. "Closed doors means closed doors, Rosetta."

"Even for me?"

"Even for you. But rest assured that even though our decision wasn't unanimous, the corporations that didn't go with the majority have at least agreed to stay quiet."

"Thanks for that."

"Not a problem." He glanced at his watch, an expensive analog model. "I also told them about the *Atlas*."

"What?" Rosetta goggled. "Do you have any idea what's going to happen to our market share-"

"As it happens, I do. But UNASCA will let release the info regardless, and I don't want it to seem as though I was holding information back." He gestured to the stage.

"Besides, what you say today is going to completely overshadow it."

"Ah," Rosetta said, feeling her hands start to shake again. Not what she wanted to hear just before a press conference.

Then, sooner than she liked, she was in front of the lights. They were kept muted; this was to be a somber conference. The camera drones hovered about the room, taking in the scene in three dimensions. Members of the press filled out the, simple room. She stepped up to the podium. Lights flashed green down among the attendees as recorders were turned on. Chen and a few prominent members of the Mining Consortium sat just behind her; she could feel their stares on the back of her neck. Just as she had always done, she didn't allow herself a chance to be nervous, she just plunged into it like the first dive of a roller coaster.

"Ladies and gentlemen of the press, people of Earth, and Belt Group employees from across the Solar System, welcome."

She took a sip of water, a ploy to build tension, and continued. "Here at Belt Group, Limited, we have come into possession of some disturbing evidence. Sources within UNASCA have revealed to us that, given the current climate of unrest on Jupiter, Venus, and elsewhere, they have made the decision to suspend all civil rights of UNASCA citizens that they deem 'in opposition to the common good.' Belt Group cannot condone this activity.

"No longer is the United Nations Space Colonization Authority dedicated toward protecting the interests of Earth or its citizens, but rather toward furthering its own authoritarian agenda. They have abandoned the republican ideals that we on Earth hold so dearly, and as a result, Belt Group—and the rest of the mining consortium—cannot continue our relationship with them."

There was a brief stir among the reporters. Rosetta pressed ahead. "UNASCA has existed in its current form for more than a century. During that time, the world—indeed, the Solar System—has changed around it, but rather than adapt, they have only worked to cement their old powers.

"Earth-bound corporations, such as those that comprise the Mining Consortium, have long tolerated UNASCA's monopoly on goods mined, harvested, manufactured, and refined in space. Their margins have long been fair, they insisted, but I am here to tell you tonight that their price can never be fair; indeed, we declare that this monopoly is inherently unjust, not just to Belt Group, but to the people of Earth in general and most of all, to the UNASCA citizens that see no direct share in their labors. The members of Free Jove and the colonists on Titania know this well, and to them I wish to say, 'Belt Group stands with you.'"

"Therefore, effective immediately, Belt Group," she paused for the briefest moment in spite of herself. The enormity of what she was saying caught the words up in her throat for a moment. "Effectively immediately, Belt Group shall unilaterally abrogate all of its UNASCA contracts, and shall instead negotiate them directed with representatives of the miners and harvesters that gather them out in space."

That caused quite the stir. Most of the assembly were expecting big news, no doubt, but this was big.

Rosetta smiled to herself, and when the clamor had died down, she raised a hand for silence. "Now, I will take some questions from the assembly."

As the clamor started up again, she turned back to Chen. He smiled in approval and nodded toward the crowd. That same determined grin glued to her face, Rosetta turned back to the crowd.

After their dinner meeting, Joanna had resolved to have nothing more to do with Gabriel. She would never have gotten involved in this entire situation in the first place except for his interference, and she was hard-pressed to find any compelling reason to work with him now. If he was lying or deluded, then there was no reason to even be associated with him. If he was correct about his assessment of the prison, well, that didn't improve her situation much either.

Much better to just serve her own time. It could be a long time, but the odds of it being fatal were low, far lower than they had proved to be on the outside.

The next day Joanna remained in her cell during the elective recreation time, laying on her cot and trying to fall asleep. She drifted in and out, trying to keep her mind a blank and formless thing, trying to forget about Gabriel and his vague promises.

"The time is twelve hundred." That now-familiar digitized voice spoke over the public address system. "Report to the dining area for lunch count." With considerable regret, Joanna stood, stretched, and left her cell.

She didn't notice anything was amiss until she

entered the main travel artery on her way to the dining area. This was just her third full day in the prison, but she'd been starting to get a feel for how things worked inside. This felt different.

Many people were wearing the same expression. Whereas the day before it had been that look of guilty shame that she knew so well, today it was something altogether different.

It was gleeful anticipation. Something was going to happen.

The people were moving in large groups toward the dining area, walking in almost deliberate quietude. She fell in with one of these groups and as she entered the dining hall, was surprised to see that a large number of guards were present, far more than had been there for dinner the day before. Most were spread out to guard the exits, like Joanna had expected, but perhaps half were standing in a corner as if guarding it. From whom, it wasn't clear.

There was once again an open place by Gabriel. She ignored it, taking one close to the door with a random group of men and women.

After a few moments, the murmur of quiet conversation was interrupted by the doors to the room rattling shut. That digitized voice spoke again. "Stand up for the count. Please do not move." Joanna glanced at Gabriel, and was disheartened to see him wearing that calm, controlled expression that meant he was not only planning something, but that it was going exactly as he had expected.

"Count complete. Thank you. Tables one through five...stand by." Joanna blinked at the pause. There was a general murmur of anticipation in the crowd before voice resumed. Then, with a surreal tone that it took Joanna a moment to process, it said, "The day of revolution is at hand."

Joanna started as if struck. But if she was surprised, she could see that nobody else was—they sprung into action the moment the computer had uttered the first syllable of the word, "revolution."

She could now see what the guards in the corner had been standing watch over—it was a crate of weapons, including electrolasers and firearms—which were now being handed over to the gleeful prisoners. The gate to the dining area rattled open again, just an alarm started wailing in the cell blocks. The lights shifted from white to red, casting long shadows from the tables.

Gabriel was standing on one of the tables and shouting. "For Jupiter! Down with UNASCA!" His cries were being echoed throughout the room. "But first, down with the Warden!" That elicited the most riotous response of all, and the prisoners started streaming out of the room.

As the alarm wailed, Joanna forced herself against the outgoing tide, moving toward where she could still hear Gabriel shouting, and when she reached him, she shouted as well.

"What the hell are you doing?"

He looked down at her, grinning from ear to ear. "Taking over the prison, Joanna. I told you that I had a great opportunity here."

"You're going to get people killed!"

He reached a hand down to her, but she refused it, preferring to yell up at him. He shrugged and replied, "You think that I just invented this sentiment?" He gestured to where the last of the prisoners were fleeing, leaving just a small number of the less courageous or convicted ones in the dining room, milling about uncertainly. "Read the news, Joanna. This was a volcano that was just ready to erupt. As it happens, I was just the instrument, and a very small one at that."

Joanna wrinkled her nose as Gabriel finally hopped off the table. In the distance, they could hear shouting and the sounds of a scuffle. "Come on," Gabriel said, holding out a hand.

She should've refused it. On the other hand, what was the alternative? Going back to her cell and waiting patiently? Besides, despite what Gabriel had assumed, she did read the news. She knew what the Free Jovians were fighting for, what kind of people they were. They had a way of making an impact wherever they acted.

There was chaos in the main prison artery. Men and women were running to and fro, mostly toward the end of the cell block that joined with the prison administrative section. Joanna could hear the very familiar sound of electrolasers firing, even some gunshots. The sounds were distorted and diffused by distance, adding to the unreality of the situation.

"Come on, sounds like things are wrapping up," Gabriel muttered, and strode toward the chaos. It did indeed sound like it was starting to wane a bit.

Indeed, the shouts transformed into cheers as he approached. There were bodies all over the ground, some in prison jumpsuits, some in guards uniforms. The mob ignored them, forming a dense clot against the main blast doors to the administrative area.

"Come on, let me through!" Gabriel shouted at their backs, and dove in when they seemed unwilling to acknowledge him. "Come on, make way," he grumbled, pulling Joanna behind him.

She was pressed up against him by the mass of the crowd. While she had his ear for the moment, she muttered, "How did you manage this? You've been a prisoner for months! And I can't believe you could ever make this many friends without bribes."

Gabriel ignored her as he reached the front of the crowd. The mob had made a bubble around two (former?) Security guards, sweaty with exertion, as they tried to force the lock on the heavy blast doors at the end of the ward. The doors were labeled, "Administration," and more ominously, "Unauthorized access will be severely punished."

"Any luck?" he asked the two guards.

One of them, hands deep in a bypass panel, just muttered something rude-sounding. The other one answered, "No, they changed the access codes quickly. Almost too quickly," she said, giving Gabriel a sidelong look.

"There have been rumblings. They must've been on alert," he said, meeting her gaze without flinching. That gaze Joanna remembered well. It was one of Gabriel's most powerful assets.

"And why would they be on alert, Gabriel?" The woman asked, matching Gabriel's tone. The crowd shifted, and Joanna realized how much could hang on this one encounter. Mobs weren't known for their ability to reason through competing viewpoints.

"I have no idea, Tania. Maybe the fact that we just

got a crate of firearms smuggled in here set off a few alarms. It won't be a problem," he said soothingly. "Just relax."

"And who the hell are you?" The woman narrowed her eyes, shifting her gaze to Joanna.

"I'm an old...colleague of Gabriel's," Joanna said, striving to adopt the same pose and narrow her eyes the same way. "From the Moon."

"Oh," the woman said, drawing the syllable out. Joanna felt the tension ease just a bit, letting her breathe again. "Well, nice to know that we're not the first ones he's promised the world to. Glad to know it always works out so well for people."

"Look, Tania," Gabriel said, stepping out in front of Joanna, "she's right. We have other problems right now. I told you that I wouldn't be able to deliver until we had control of the administrative section. I need to make a call offworld and your little radio," he gestured at her earpiece, "can't just replace the orbital maser array, right?"

"Mmph. I've got it," said the other guard. He jerked once on something deep in the bypass panel, and the blast door shuddered once, and then opened without any additional fuss.

"Sure thing, Gabriel," Tania glared. "But as soon as we've got control..."

"Don't you worry about a thing," he said, patting her on the shoulder. He turned back to the crowd. "I deliver on my promises. You take this base, and Free Jove won't ever have to worry about money again. Just take that control center. Go!"

The prisoners surged, shouting as they tried to shove their way through the opened door. Their guard allies, with clubs and firearms, tried to move their way to the front, and the whole mass seized for a moment. But just for a moment; the front few prisoners worked their way inside, and their removal opened up a flood behind them. The attack had begun.

Alarms were still blaring inside, and a voice was calling for reinforcements over the PA system. It sounded more than a little haggard, and as the mob swarmed in, shouting, jostling, firing, it cut off abruptly with a curse.

"You promised them money?" Joanna said, staring at Gabriel, mouth agape. "And just how the hell are you going to manage *that*?"

"These are political prisoners, Joanna. They're in here because of what they believe."

"Gabriel, you're missing my point. How do you even *have* any money?"

"Don't worry about a thing," he said, putting a hand on her shoulder and using the same condescending voice he'd tried on Tania. "Trust me. I have some outside help."

"And the guards?"

"Not all of my money is going into Solomon Gracelove's accounts." He took a few steps after the mob and beckoned her on. "Come on, Joanna. We're missing all of the fun."

Once they'd breached the administrative section of Aquifer Prison, their job was pretty much done. As Joanna followed Gabriel into narrow corridors lined with offices and supply rooms, she could hear the occasional shout or scuffle deeper in, but the sounds of chaos and combat were surprisingly absent. In fact, for the most part they seemed to be alone.

Until they reached the control center nexus, that is. The mob had swarmed through here, smashing what it could, crashing against security's defenses. There were bodies here, and blood. A few prisoners and guards were tending to their wounded comrades, and laying sheets on the dead ones, but the fighting here had been fast and brutal. In the end, the prisoners numbers had won out, though not without cost. A high cost.

Tania was standing watch over one of the consoles, its screen shrunk so that one couldn't read it without getting close. A few of the prisoners were going through the pockets of the loyalist guards, and Tania only intervened if they got close to her console. When she saw Gabriel and Joanna approaching, she laughed. "You all right, girl? Never seen combat before?"

Joanna narrowed her eyes at Tania, the reaction feeling more authentic this time. "You have no idea." She consciously stopped herself from scratching at the tiny scar on her belly where that bullet had nearly killed her on Venus. "I'm just surprised that it was all over so fast."

Tania shrugged and stepped away from the console. "Those Free Jovians are maniacs. It was a mistake to keep all of them in one place together." She turned her attention to Gabriel. "Here, I've saved one for you. I sure hope you're not forgetting your end of the bargain already?"

Gabriel made a soothing gesture as he sat. "You worry too much. I just need to make a few transmissions to Earth and the Moon. Figure on twenty or thirty minutes, accounting for the speed of light."

"It better not be much longer than that. They're not

going to just let us keep the prison."

"Tania, I'm not sure where you got this low opinion of me," Gabriel said, and Joanna could see him struggling to maintain his famous composure. More was the pity that Tania seemed immune to that steely gaze. "I said I'm doing it."

Tania huffed and took a few steps back, staring at some of the other consoles that had been smashed in the mob's frenzy.

"Excuse me." Joanna started, nearly stepping on a woman crouched right near her feet. She was laying what appeared to be a towel over the upper body of a man lying on the ground, a dark red pool around his head and neck.

"Oh. Sorry." Joanna numbly took a step back, her eyes not leaving the man until the towel obscured his features and the pool beneath them.

"Don't be," the woman looked up at her, smiling a sad smile through loose strands of brown hair. "He died fighting for what he believed in." She sighed heavily, looking back at the towel-covered body. "We should all be so lucky," she said, as if to herself.

Joanna felt an almost overwhelming urge to say something, to do anything. She knelt next to the woman and gently laid a hand on her back. "Well, I'm still sorry. What, um," she cast about for a polite way to ask, "was he fighting for?"

"For his freedom. For our freedom." The woman's eyes didn't waver in the slightest.

"From prison, you mean?"

"No." The woman gave Joanna a strange look. "No, from UNASCA. You don't know about Gracelove? About

Free Jove?"

"Of course I do, but...on Mars?"

The woman nodded. "We're all the same under UNASCA's thumb. Once things started getting bad on Jupiter they had us rounded up. All we had done was go to rallies and held protests, but they must've had our names—our faces—on some kind of file." She sniffled. "Those bastards. They broke down our door in the middle of the night, hauled us away. By the next morning we were prisoners here along with the thieves and fraudsters. No trial or anything. Way to prove our point, I suppose." She chuckled a few times, but that laughter gave way to sobs after just a moment, and the woman lapsed into silent tears. Awkward as it was, Joanna forced herself to keep her hand there, to be at least some comfort, to do at least some good for someone.

At last, the woman blew her nose into her sleeve and wiped her eyes. "Sorry."

"Don't be. At least you have some freedom now, right?"

"Well." She nodded toward where Gabriel was working on the console, intent on whatever he was doing. "Provided he comes through like he said he would. He said that he'd be able to arrange our release. He said that he had money, and that he'd be more than willing to spread it around if we helped him escape."

"And you believed him?" Joanna couldn't keep the surprised disbelief out of her voice.

"Of course not," the woman scoffed. "But then the next batch of prisoners arrived, and they said that our disappearance had been covered up. Nobody had known where we'd gone. We realized they were never going to let us out, not as long as Jupiter was still in uprising. So we decided that we had only the one shot, since he had some of the guards on his side. He'd better come through. If he doesn't, I'll..." she didn't finish her threat, but just returned her sad, longing gaze toward the body on the floor.

"He will, I promise you. I know him. I'll watch him."

The woman smiled. "Thank you. You're Joanna, right? I heard him say your name."

"That's right."

"I'm Emily. That...was Farouk."

Joanna nodded, her throat tight. "Farouk won't be disappointed," she muttered, and gave the woman a final pat on the back before standing.

She felt like an idiot. Here she was, pissing and moaning about how the universe had done her this grave disservice, about how Gabriel was pulling one over on these people, not even stopping to think if they might be more than just lackeys or fops. They were willing to fight for something, to die for it, and a few minutes ago, she had been more than willing to just walk right back into her cell and let things take care of themselves.

Well, not any more.

As soon as she'd made that resolution, she heard Gabriel curse and stand up. Immediately, Tania was back in the room, shouting, "What? What?"

"They're coming. They're already coming!" He gestured vaguely at the console.

Tania frowned and gestured at the screen, enlarging it so that it could be seen across the room. Joanna couldn't immediately make out what was going on—it appeared to be some sort of scanner display—but she saw Tania's eyes widen and could make a guess at what it meant.

"By Jude and all the saints. That was fast. Way, way too fast." At that moment Joanna saw a look of realization cross her face, and she whirled on Gabriel, pulling her sidearm. "It was you, wasn't it! You set us up." Gritting her teeth, she raised her weapon. Joanna found herself flashing back to that moment on Hartley Aerostat.

Gabriel raised his hands and pointed at the screen. "Come on, give me some credit! I already did part of what you asked!"

At that moment, a new message notification flashed across the screen, and Tania pulled it up. It appeared to be some sort of bank authorization, recognizing Gabriel and indicating that some money had been transferred to a local account. Some money, hell—he had millions of dollars in his accounts. She clicked her jaw shut, realizing that she shouldn't be surprised.

Tania lowered her weapon and shook her head. "Damn it. Fine, fine. You just worry about getting that divvied up between all of our offworld accounts, and I'll worry about holding the line. We won't last long if they're bringing assault troops, but we'll buy you a moment." She took two steps, then appeared to notice Joanna and Emily for the first time.

"Come on, you two. No time for crying if you want all of this to mean anything. It's time to act." Without waiting to see if they followed, she jammed her gun back into its holster and fled the room.

Emily didn't hesitate before following, allowing

herself one last look at where Farouk sat on the floor. Joanna only paused a moment before trailing after her. She didn't care for Tania's mercenary motivations, but she couldn't just stand aside this time. Ever since Brighton, she'd only been thinking of herself and at most Eileen as well. But now, here were these Free Jovians, fighting for something bigger than themselves. Neither she nor they were friends of UNASCA, but regardless, there was something to fight for.

And Joanna decided that this time, she would fight. She didn't spare a glance for Gabriel as she left the room.

Chapter 18

When Joanna and Emily caught up with Tania, she was standing in the blast door that she'd helped force open, the one that defined the boundary between the cell block's main artery and the administration section. There were a number of armed prisoners here, most of them working to manhandle heavy equipment into place as cover. Joanna stood back for a moment, unsure of what she should be doing.

"No, not out there! Fools," Tania shouted at a group of men and women creating barricades outside in the artery itself. "Everything and everyone, inside!"

One of the men looked at her in defiance. "If we're trying to slow them down, then we need to create a defense in depth-"

Tania shook her head and cut him off. "Well, it's reassuring to know that we have a couple of armchair guerrillas serving with us. But guess what—we're not on Earth here, and the main prison complex is above ground.

They'll crack every seal from the landing bay down to this blast door, and unless you can breathe nothing but a couple of millibars of carbon dioxide, your defense isn't going to have much depth. Come on."

She didn't want to see if they complied. She just grumbled as she turned back to the rag-tag bunch of defenders just inside the door. "They're right about defense in depth, though. Make sure that you have a couple of other defensive points between here and the control center. We can't stop them forever, but if we don't stop them long enough..."

Tania trailed off as she noticed Joanna standing there. Emily hadn't hesitated before pitching in with the other defenders, but Joanna hadn't felt quite right doing so. It seemed like a familiar thing to do, and she had never been that great at just throwing herself into other's conversations. Especially when those conversations were about things like lines of fire and angles of cover or whatever.

"Looks like Gabriel's 'good friend' decided to pitch in with us normal folks. Is that satellite lined up yet? Is he working to get us our money?"

"I'm not his good-"

Tania didn't let her finish. She seemed to enjoy being the only one allowed to finish a sentence. "You know what? I don't care in the slightest. They'll be coming down that corridor in half an hour, probably less. Maybe much less. And we can't surrender until your good friend finishes up with his emailing."

Joanna tossed around a number of sarcastic replies, and she hated that she lacked the courage to make any of them. "What do you want me to do?"

"Go fetch as many emergency air kits as you can find, and then work on securing the command center with Gabriel. Thanks." She turned back to a group that were trying to lever some sort of desk into place as cover. "No, you idiots—their shots will punch right through that. You need something heavier—at least an inch of solid metal."

Joanna didn't hang around.

The emergency air kits were scattered throughout the administrative complex in recesses painted bright yellow. She pulled away the metal panel of each, grabbed as many kits as she could carry from their charging stations, and moved on. Unfortunately, the lower gravity of Mars didn't make the tank-and-mask combinations any easier to carry, and by the time she finally reached the command center she was dropping almost as many as she was picking up.

Gabriel was still at the console when she dropped the pile of masks next to him. "Any luck?" Joanna asked.

"What?" he jerked as if he hadn't noticed her walk up, and then relaxed a bit when he saw who it was. "Oh. Some. It'll work out," he said, like it was a comforting mantra.

"Great." There were a few defenders here already, working to create or shore up whatever cover they could. Joanna was pleased to see that Emily was among them. "Here," she said, trying a smile and handing her an air kit.

"Oh. Thank you." She tried her best to return the smile before gesturing at the table they were moving to cover the door. "I don't know if this is going to make even a tiny difference. If they use electrolasers, maybe, but if they turn those weapons on full automatic..." She shrugged. "Well, what's done is done, and here we are."

"So, when Gabriel has his confirmation, we're just going to surrender?"

Emily grinned, but it wasn't a happy expression. "Joanna, we're never going to surrender."

She was cut off as the PA system squealed. It was Tania's voice. "This is it; we've just heard that two police assault craft have landed at the prison. That means at least fourteen troops, armed and armored." She paused, then mumbled, "Good hunting."

Emily was staring at Joanna wide-eyed as the PA system cut off, but she made a visible effort to harden her expression, none of the rising fear that was clenching Joanna's insides visible on her face. "Good luck," Emily said quietly, and, accepting a sidearm from another one of the defenders (who likewise wished her the best) took up her defensive position.

"Joanna!" Gabriel whispered from his console. She turned to see him gesturing frantically at her. Joanna felt a bit of guilty pleasure in seeing his control slip at least a little.

"What is it?" she asked, joining him.

"If they're attacking, we need to get the hell out of here." He turned back to his console and pulled up a series of video feeds, flipping through them rapidly. "I took the liberty of having a ground shuttle made ready for us. No sense in not padding our bets, right?" He chuckled nervously, not looking at her. "Ah, here we go."

Gabriel selected an image and maximized it. There was no sound, but it was obvious what was going on; a few nervous-looking folks in prison outfits were pacing around a worm-shaped ground vehicle with enormous, bladed tires and a segmented middle. Gabriel nodded at the display.

"That's our way out. What do you say?"

Joanna stared at him. She wasn't sure if she was surprised or fulfilled to hear him so baldly express a desire to flee this confrontation he'd started. "So, you're giving up, are you?" She raised an eyebrow. "Going back on your word?"

Gabriel, looking somewhat strained now, answered, "No. I said I'd take care of it, didn't I? I'm not sure what I did to deserve this reputation as a cheat and a hack."

"Do you even need to ask?"

"Fine," he sighed. "Now that I have satellite access, I can finish up on my handheld, but I really, really don't want to be here when the fighting goes down. It's not exactly-" He was cut off by a muted thud that seemed to reverberate through the prison's very structure. Emily and the others defending the control room looked about, worry fighting with resolve on their faces. "It's not my style to be in the middle of a conflict unless I already know how it's going to end," he finished.

"I'm not going," Joanna said, watching Emily and the others settle back into position with looks of resignation.

"What?" Gabriel half-stood in surprise.

"I said I'm not going, and neither are you." She put a hand on his shoulder and forced him back down, hard. "You finish up what you said you were going to do. I am not going to let you mess everything up for anyone else, Gabriel. Never again, you understand." Pointing at the console, she said, "Get back to work. *Now*."

"Damn it, Joanna," he pushed the hand off of his shoulder and tried to stand again. She tried to shove him back into his chair, but he caught her hands and deflected her into the console itself. Righteous anger boiling through her veins, expanding her strength, narrowing her vision, Joanna surprised herself by lashing out with a fist, solidly connecting with Gabriel's temple and sending him to the ground.

He held the side of his head in surprise as much as pain, just as Joanna stared, open-mouthed, at her aching fist. It hurt, sure, but it felt good. Better than just wrestling with someone, better than firing a weapon. It was real power.

She vaulted the chair, landing with a foot on each side of Gabriel and shoving him back down as he tried to stand. For too long Joanna had been jerked around by forces that she couldn't control, forces that she couldn't even see. Now, here was Gabriel, showing up out of what she'd hoped would be her forgotten, irrelevant past, trying to do it again.

"Never again," Joanna said, pointing a spearlike finger at his face. "Never, you understand? Not to me, not to anyone."

"Joanna, what the hell is wrong with you?" He didn't try to stand this time.

Laughter bubbled up through her, unbidden, and she grabbed the front of Gabriel's jumpsuit in both hands. In the one-third gravity of Mars, he was more than light enough for her to manhandle him back into his chair. He tried to turn away from the console back to her, his mouth open as if to speak, but she shut it promptly with a slap. The loud cracking noise drew the attention of those guarding the door, but they looked back down the corridor as they saw her expression.

"You finish what you started," Joanna growled,

pleased to hear venom dripping from every word. "You do what you promised, and then we'll leave. Not a microsecond before, you understand?"

"Right," he said, nodding his head with a jerking motion, turning back to the screen as if afraid to take his eyes off of her. Let him be afraid—Joanna had always known that his famous steely gaze was nothing but an act. He was a coward beneath it all.

There was a crash in the corridor outside, and Joanna turned to see a half-dozen red-faced, terrified men and women in prison jumpsuits run through the door and vault over the impromptu cover. "It was...so fast," one of them panted, and another added, "They're coming. We only have a minute or two." The lot of them turned back toward the door as a series of loud, familiar crackling noises echoed down the hall. Electrolasers.

Joanna, her heart still pumping that righteous high, was next to the defenders. "Give me a gun," she said. "We're not giving up. Not now."

Emily nodded, fear competing with courage on her face, and handed Joanna a gun from a small pile next to her. It was not an electrolaser, she noticed. She might have to kill. So be it.

Behind them, Gabriel grunted and sat up in his chair. "I think we might have something here." He started jamming on keys, moving screens around. "Just a few more minutes."

"Look!" One of the defenders shouted, and Joanna turned back to the corridor just in time to see an armored head duck back behind a corner, barely escaping a hail of bullets.

"Not long now," one of them muttered, and Joanna hunched down with them. She *hoped* it wouldn't be long. Righteous as she was feeling, she knew that it wouldn't last forever. May it just last long enough.

A small object, tossed from around the corner, rebounded off the far wall, came to a halt right in front of the barricade. A grenade! Joanna ducked behind the cover, heard the pop and hiss, and realized as her nose and eyes started to tingle that it was gas rather than some explosive. Those who had retreated from the forward positions already had their air kits on; Joanna grabbed one and shoved it over her face, pressing the button to seal it to her face with negative pressure while she tried to get the straps on.

"Fire, damn it, fire!" someone was shouting, and almost as one they leaned out and opened up on the first of the police to charge down the corridor. Bright actinic beams lanced over their heads and into their barricade, leaving spots in their eyes, but they heard a scream and that first guard crumbled. Behind him, the other police were pressed up against the walls. Their pressure suits made them look inhuman, their robotic eyes showing no mercy or compassion. There would be no surrender here.

Joanna swung her weapon around to face the nearest one just as his weapon flashed.

Her own shots worked themselves over his armor as he tried to pull back.

"Yes. Yes! I got it!" Gabriel shouted.

Then something exploded behind her. She could feel a wave of air lift her up like a hand, dropping her hard back on the barricade. Her head swimming, she thought she could hear shouting and screaming. Her arms weren't answering, they couldn't get her weapon up, couldn't move her back under cover. Then a robotic face filled her vision, and there was searing, blinding flash as everything went dark.

"You can't be planning to just watch us for three hours." Eileen tried to stretch her shoulders, but the limited movement did little to relieve the burning ache. She and Dmitri were tied to the workbench chairs in his lab using the bindings most readily available to Clara: fiber-optic cables from the mass of comms equipment that lined the walls.

"I'll watch you all day, if I have to." Clara was trying to keep her voice even, but Eileen could hear the edge of strain in it, faint but noticeable. "Stop talking."

Antagonizing someone with a firearm is not a smart thing to do; Eileen didn't need police training to know that. All it took was one momentary slip of control or will on Clara's part, and important bits of Eileen would be decorating the unplugged lab equipment.

But Eileen was *angry*. She could feel it bubbling up in her mind like superheated liquid; it was all she could do to keep her own voice even. "So that business about Stephen...that was all a lie? Just a little game to get me sympathetic."

"For your information," Clara said, enunciating every word, "no, and yes. Respectively." She gestured with the over-under in her hand. "Now. *Shut up*."

"So you're going to just turn that information over to UNASCA, huh? Or is Belt Group signing your paycheck? Or maybe it's someone else. Thomas Gabriel of Brighton, maybe? Who's tugging your strings?" Eileen reveled in the feeling of delicious abandon. If it was all over—and it was, if that datacube was sitting in her palm—then what was she saving herself for? What did she have to lose?

"Eileen, I don't want to have to hurt you," Clara said, and Eileen could tell by the waver in her voice that it was true, "but I will if you don't bite your tongue *right now*!"

Ignoring the dangerous, desperate look in Clara's eye, ignoring the alarm that was overtaking Dmitri's own simmering anger, Eileen charged ahead. "If you didn't want to hurt me, then you've made a big damned mistake, because right now I *really* want to hurt you. It wasn't the lying or the betrayal; I've dealt with enough of that before. But you're taking away the last little bit of Stephen that I had, Clara." The quicksilver-slick danger in her voice surprised even Eileen. "So help me, if I get out of these restraints I will flay you *alive*."

Clara took three rapid steps forward and slammed Eileen across the jaw with the barrel of her pistol. The side of her face exploded in pain and she tasted the sharp tang of blood where she'd cut herself on her own teeth. Still Clara was standing there, hands at her sides, staring down at Eileen, emotions flicking across her face.

"You really *are* unsure. You really *are* a puppet." Eileen shook her head. "Why, then? Why do this when you don't have the guts to go through with it?"

"Not all of us," Clara said, her voice reflecting its own brand of quiet anger, "are committed to overthrowing the government. Some of us are on the side of order, not chaos."

"I don't give a shiny damn about your preferences,

you two-headed snake," Eileen spat. "The only side that I give a damn about is doing right by Stephen. I held him in my arms as he was dying, and I swore to myself right then that the only way I could mourn him was by getting back at those that had done ill by him.

"Well, guess what," Eileen tossed her head toward the still-open screen of decrypted messages, "that was my last chance. You've got it now, and I'm helpless. Nothing to lose, not even my own life. So let me be perfectly damned clear: you're going to have to kill me, because if you don't, I'm going kill you instead, and I'm *not* going to be *fast* about it."

Eileen swallowed hard and held her chin up. "So just go ahead and do it, why don't you? Put the muzzle of that thing against my neck and blow my spine out."

Slowly, with a thousand emotions playing across her face, Clara brought the gun up. As it entered her field of view, Eileen surprised herself by not caring. She hadn't meant everything as bravado, but even so her genuine acceptance came as a pleasant surprise. At least it would all be over soon—the running, the hiding, the burden of responsibility—and she could rest for a while.

"Eileen. I don't..." Clara started, and swallowed. The barrel of the gun wavered. She was almost straddling Eileen now, her tortured emotions radiating in an almost physical way. "I didn't..."

"*Do it!*" Eileen shouted, and jerked her head toward the gun.

Clara was weak. Disappointing. She recoiled in horror as the muzzle touched Eileen's neck.

Her legs were bound to the chair with the same

cord that bound her hands. But, the chair wasn't secured to the floor in any way. Eileen acted without thought or intention, just out of pure reflex.

With one leg she jerked the rest of the chair forward. It was a move that could've only worked in low gravity, but as Clara was stepping back, Eileen's own leg jammed into hers, throwing her off balance. As she started her own slow fall downward, Eileen kicked with both feet and slammed into Clara.

Clara hit the ground on her back, and Eileen was right there before she could spring back up. She didn't have any way to slow her own fall, but whatever. She slammed into Clara with her face, her body and her chair keeping the other woman from righting herself.

Now Clara was scrambling for the gun. Eileen shifted her weight, trying to pin Clara's arm, and as long as her face was on Clara's chest, bit down as hard as she could. Clara shrieked, more in alarm than pain, and tried to bring her gun to bear.

But suddenly, there was Dmitri.

He must've worked his legs loose, because he was able to kick the gun away, and shove Eileen likewise with his foot before body slamming into Clara. They both let out a painful *whuff* as they collapsed in a pile. Dmitri started to get up a moment later. Clara didn't.

Working with her toes, Eileen pivoted her chair around, trying to feel for Dmitri's bindings with her own painfully stiff hands.

Chapter 19

"Oh, no." Rojas suppressed a groan as he entered the prison's administrative area. "Oh, hell." As he regarded the blasted-out mess that was the prison's control center, he was filled with a now-familiar stab of profound frustration, mingled with a brand-new, substantial dose of regret.

He resisted the urge to take Cruikshank by the collar and instead turned to him with exaggerated calm. "Did you use a grenade on it, Sergeant Cruikshank?"

At least the man had the good sense to look contrite. "Yes, sir. But we were taking fire, and felt it necessary to return-"

"Thousands of rounds?"

"We had no cover, sir." Resistance flashed for just a moment in Cruikshank's eyes, then he looked back toward his boots. "This will all be in my report, sir."

"In that report," Rojas bit off the words, "will you also explain how this failed to prevent the serious injuries to Officer Suree?"

Cruikshank's head jerked up, his jaw set, but Rojas shook his head. "No, I'm sorry, Cruikshank." He looked back up the command center. "How many dead here alone?"

Marla was standing beside him, maintaining a respectful quiet. "Four, with two injuries. This was where the most hardened prisoners made their final stand."

Nineteen dead prisoners and who knows how many serious injuries. Over-zealous officers destroying a ground shuttle in the motor pool, a fire started that almost overwhelmed environmental control. An officer wounded so seriously that he might already be dead.

What a fiasco.

"There's going to be a reckoning for this," Rojas muttered.

Marla, bless her heart, jumped to his defense. "Sir, we're not trained for riot control. UNASCA will understand, if only you—"

He shook his head, cutting her off. "I'm not talking about us, I'm talking about UNASCA. Those damned arrest orders. They overwhelmed the system, they gave political activists more than enough opportunity to become terrorists." He closed his eyes and sighed. Olympus Base: such an easy post.

He opened them again and turned to the staff following him. "I want to see the survivors of this mess in the control room. They're in the prison hospital, I suspect?"

Marla nodded. "It was in decent shape, except for the controlled substances locker. For rioters, they were pretty restrained."

Rojas leveled a gaze at Cruikshank. "Well, it's nice

to know that someone was." Cruikshank opened his mouth to respond, but Rojas shook his head, turned, and strode out of the room. When Marla tried to follow, he just waved her back. "I'm not in the mood for company."

The prison hospital was small, but full. The prison had its own staff of doctors, and Rojas admired their professionalism in treating patients who had run them out of their own offices hours before. The patients needed it—the five beds were full and there were at least twice that many people on the floor or sitting on counters. The smell of antiseptic and unwashed bodies was thick in the room.

"Who's in charge here?" Rojas asked the room at large, and an orderly gestured to a serious-looking man in a lab coat.

The doctor introduced himself, delivering a firm handshake and sizing Rojas up with a granite gaze. "Bit of a mess on your hands?" Rojas asked once they'd disengaged.

"You could say that. Your men did a number on the prisoners. Beams at close range, and all that."

Rojas was wishing more and more that he was home, asleep, and that when he woke up, he'd be waking up to a different planet.

"Some of these patients are going to need transfer to Cadeucus," the doctor continued, "back at Olympus. I understand that your wounded man has already gone there; he was in bad shape."

Rojas nodded. "Do you mind if I talk to some of the wounded?" Gerhardt shrugged in dismissal, and turned back to his task of hooking some sort of machine up to a man with serious burn injuries in one of the beds.

He didn't want to bother the worst injured of the

prisoners, but a few of those standing or sitting appeared to have relatively minor injuries, however, and he approached one of these. She was a young woman bearing a bandaged arm and forehand, and a thousand kilometer stare.

"What's your name?"

Joanna started, not even realizing that someone had approached. It was a man in a police uniform with cropped black hair and a nameplate that said "Rojas."

"I'm Joanna Newton," she said, narrowing her eyes. So far the police had been happy enough to leave the wounded alone, and Joanna had just resolved to savor her last moments of freedom before being locked in some new underground box for the rest of her life.

"I'm Galen Rojas, chief of Olympus Base security."

"A pleasure," Joanna spat, and turned her back to him. Not easy, considering that she was sitting on a counter, but she hoped that he'd get the hint and leave her alone.

"I want to talk to you about what happened."

"Which part?" Joanna asked without turning back, "The part where you imprisoned a bunch of people illegally, the part where they fought back, or the part where you killed a bunch of them?"

There was silence for a moment, and it felt good. So nice to get some anger off her chest. It was only a drop in the bucket, but she'd take what she could get.

"Some of my men may have been...overzealous." Joanna snorted in derision, but Rojas forged ahead, "But that's why I'm here. I want to know what happened."

"What happened?" Joanna turned back, incredulous. "What happened is that your guys shot a thousand bullets into that room, plus grenades, before we were even given a chance to surrender." Joanna could see Gabriel lying on his bed halfway across the room, unconscious.

"They were fired upon."

Joanna shook her head and turned away again. "I think that you should go away for now. I'm sure I'll meet you again at the trial."

"What trial?"

"Um, the trial for the prison riot?"

"Right." He sounded unsure of himself, so Joanna sighed and turned back to him.

"Listen, as long as you're here, I might as well ask—what's your plan for us? You're not going to put us right back in our cells, are you? There aren't enough of them." At least, there hadn't been; Joanna realized darkly that there were likely to be at least a few vacancies now.

"I'm not sure. It'll have to go to the UNASCA judge, although there's likely to be offworld interference."

"Offworld?"

"From Earth. They're the ones calling the shots, these days. Heaven alone knows what the local administrators think about that."

That took Joanna aback. It wasn't surprising news, but it was surprising that the police chief of all people was telling her, of all people. Did he know her file? Did he know that she was as guilty of conspiracy or treason or whatever UNASCA was calling it as anyone else around?

She decided to ask. "Why the hell are you telling me this?"

That seemed to startle him almost as much as the

thought had startled her. "Well. It affects you, I suppose." He paused. "I guess I'm not sure." Another, longer pause. "Guilty conscience, maybe."

"Well, maybe you'll keep that in mind the next time you feel like arresting political dissidents. I think I'm done talking to you." Joanna couldn't bring herself to feel the least bit sorry for him.

"Ms. Newton, I didn't just wake up one morning and feel like arresting people whose only crime was getting themselves on UNASCA's 'don't like' list. Those orders came from Earth; I'm sure that the colonial administrator saw them only a little bit before I did. Maybe you've been in prison too long; UNASCA is calling pretty much all the shots from the head office now."

"Ha!" Joanna laughed humorlessly. "Surprise. That's because UNASCA's control is slipping away. Did you know that I worked in Brighton for almost a year for an administrator who ran an entire black market operation on the side? Or that when I was on Venus, it was that stupid smuggler calling the shots? I never heard anything about the administrator."

Rojas' mouth was screwed shut tight.

"I guess there's a bright side to all of this. I can just hang out wherever you put me until UNASCA tightens their grip so much that everything just falls apart and I can go home again."

After a moment, Rojas said, "Maybe that's already happening."

"What?"

"I haven't had the least bit of support since this operation started, and just before it did, there was a big press conference where a consortium of mining companies all came out and condemned UNASCA for this mess."

"Are you serious? Was...was Belt Group one of those companies?"

"It was. Why?"

Joanna felt her head spin. She'd been chased by UNASCA and Belt Group across two planets as though they were of a singular mission. Now, if that had changed...

"What was UNASCA's response?"

Rojas smiled, but he didn't look happy. "They issued a press release saying that they were working with local authorities. But they aren't. At least, not around here."

"Wow."

"So, to be honest, I'm not sure what to do with you. With any of you."

Joanna shrugged, still feeling a bit unsure of herself. If UNASCA and Belt Group were on the outs, then maybe UNASCA would rescind the charges against her? After all, she'd been imprisoned on the Moon because she was supposed to have had information about Belt Group's new super-ship. Of course, she'd escaped from prison and all that, but still, if they wanted to make a point...

But it was just wishful thinking. There was no way that UNASCA was going to let her walk away, not now. If they were worried about appearing weak, they couldn't afford to be lenient to anyone, much less a rioter who actually deserved to remain in prison.

"I guess that we're all on our own, then." She finally said, weakly.

"Yeah," Rojas said. "I guess so." He sighed. "Get some rest," he finally said, and walked away. He didn't speak to any of the other prisoners, just walked out of the room as though he had a purpose.

For her part, rest sounded great. She wondered if they'd let her back in her cell, where there was a bed.

Chapter 20

The Free Jovians had the *Atlas*. All this time, rumors be damned, the Free Jovians had the *Atlas*. They hadn't even stolen it; Captain Constance Kelley had turned the ship over to them as a political gesture. Where it was now was anybody's guess, but the reason why it had stayed secret was much easier to guess: they were milking Belt Group for assistance on the side.

The *Mary Ellen* had only been in position to intercept a few messages from the *Atlas* before their relative positions had shifted. But there, in just a few dozens of kilobytes, was the situation in the Solar System right now. There was going to be a confrontation on Jupiter, and shift lines of allegiance all the way from there to Earth.

Eileen almost wished that Dmitri hadn't decrypted the data. She was sitting on a nuclear bomb and she had no idea what do with it.

She glanced at Clara, tied double-secure in the corner and dozing nicely on a hefty shot of downers from the medical kit. Poor woman. Now that the stress and rage had burned through all of Eileen's energy, she felt a little sorry for Clara. They were all puppets now, directly or otherwise, but at least Clara could see the strings.

"So what are you going to do with this?" Dmitri asked, taking a pull on a bulb of coffee.

"I imagine Free Jove wants it suppressed just like anyone else."

"I imagine so. Nobody wants their secrets spoiled." Dmitri took another drink. "You can be certain I will not distribute your message."

"No, I expect not." Eileen sighed. "Fine. Delete it. Delete it all."

"But you said-"

"I said, *delete it.* Purge your memory. Write zeroes, whatever. Just leave it on the datacube. I want it as a...a memento."

Dmitri opened his mouth to protest, glancing at Clara, but changed his mind and dropped the cube into Eileen's palm.

"Sorry, Stephen," she muttered. Her strength, already sapped, seemed to leave her altogether just then, and she slumped back into one of Dmitri's chairs.

There would be no revenge, now. She might have a nuclear bomb, but she couldn't detonate it. It would hurt too many people, most of them either friends or enemies of enemies. Eileen was forced to conclude, much as she hated the idea, that Stephen wouldn't like it.

The empty feeling that followed on the tails of that realization brought tears to her eyes. She'd failed. There would be no revenge, which was bad enough. But what was worse...there was nothing left to fill that void. She'd burned every bridge to do right by Stephen, and now that she couldn't, she was surrounded by water on every side, alone on her little island.

"Are you all right?"

Eileen wiped at her eyes and forced herself to look directly into Dmitri's. "Yes," she said. "I'm fine."

"Do you want some advice?"

"I suppose." Anything would work.

"I have heard rumors that Free Jovian sympathizers across the Solar System are heading to Jupiter. It's a convocation. Mr. Gracelove is going to declare independence."

"So?"

He shrugged, his discomfort obvious. "You look like you need something to do."

Eileen swallowed and nodded. "I suppose UNASCA wouldn't like it if I worked for an independent state."

"They probably would not," Dmitri agreed.

"And Belt Group might not either," she added.

"Not when they see this data, or discover the truth through some other means. As they will inevitably."

"Well then. Why not?"

"You will need a crew, yes? I know that Leona King's men crewed your ship on the way over here, but I suspect that you will not be leaving with her." Dmitri raised an eyebrow. "I know of some people who would gladly work for passage."

No, she would definitely not be leaving with Leona. Best of luck to that woman, but her aims were too personal for Eileen's tastes, too selfish. Even if Leona would take her on—and she very well might—the work wouldn't suit her.

"I think," Eileen said, "I guess I should call Leona and tell her just that."

An awkward pause descended on the room, the type brought about when one conversation runs its course without suggesting another. Dmitri finally broke it. "You can use my quarters, if you wish."

"I'm sorry?" What an odd question.

"For your, um," Dmitri fumbled, gesturing at her head. Her eyes. Her eyes, still puffy from her desperate attempts not to burst into wracking sobs.

After a moment, the urge to cry began to wane. She had a mission now, a method of revenge after all. It didn't involve the data, but it involved hurting UNASCA, in ways big and small. Once that was done, once Stephen was avenged, then she'd let the tears come. Then, not a moment before.

"I'm fine," Eileen said, and was pleased at the firmness of her voice. "We both need to make some calls," she said, standing. "Let's do this."

Joanna was a little embarrassed to admit the extent of her relief when Gabriel finally opened his eyes. The blast that had landed her in the infirmary had left her with a few scratches and some tinnitus, nothing serious. Thomas Gabriel, on the other hand, had taken the full brunt of the fragmentation grenade, and if it hadn't been for the quick action of the surviving Free Jovians, he would've died on the floor of the command center.

"Oh," he moaned. "What happened?"

"Olympus security happened. You almost died."

Gabriel took a moment to digest this. "And am I going to die in the near future?"

Joanna chuckled, a nervous sound that she quickly clammed up. "Not according to the doctor. Sounds like you had a concussion, plus they had to dig some shrapnel out of you."

"And the money..."

"As I hear it, your traffic got out. A few of the other prisoners have been able to check their accounts, and they're certainly singing your praises."

"And you?" He said, smiling weakly. It was odd to see him looking so weak, somehow even more odd now that he was awake. As much as Gabriel irritated her, he had always worked from a position of strength. Seeing that undercut by his wan coloration, the hospital gown, and the machines clustered around the bedside seemed a little embarrassing, as though she were intruding on some private part of his life.

"Well." Speaking of embarrassing. "I guess I was wrong about you. At least a little."

His smile widened a bit, though it seemed no stronger. "Not entirely wrong, Ms. Newton. I was only working in my own self-interest, after all. Just like you said."

"But you helped out all those people..."

"They're not-" he broke off, coughing. She handed him a cup of water, watched him drain it. When she took the cup back, he started over. "They're not mutually exclusive. I still got my ticket out of this place. And I got yours, as well."

"What?" She blinked. Gabriel had done something

nice for her? When it was his fault that she was here in the first place? Joanna bit back her instinctive response—he was still weak, after all—and just said, "Why?"

He shrugged weakly, as if unsure, and Joanna had to look away. Somehow that made it even more awkward. Gabriel said, "This is going to sound a bit...odd coming from me. But, I think that you're my only friend."

"Gabriel. I'm not really your friend." Joanna grimaced at how harsh it sounded, spoken to anyone in Gabriel's condition, but it was the truth. At the very least, he'd earned that.

He chuckled, and the chuckle turned into a hacking cough. Joanna refilled the cup and handed it to him, watched him greedily drink it down once again. "That's what you say, Ms. Newton. Joanna. But I'm not sure if you realize how low my standards are, of late."

Joanna let out a long breath. "I guess you're not the only one. Okay, fine, but I hope that you didn't buy me a ticket back to Earth."

"I haven't bought anything yet, just arranged for a future purchase. And anyway, we're still in prison. Aren't we?" He tried for a moment to look up, look around the room, but his strength failed him, and he sagged back into the bed.

"We're still in prison, at least for now. But things are changing, probably even more than UNASCA realized. I talked with their security chief when he came to visit the hospital, and afterward most of the guards pulled back. We have complete run of the prison now; no daily counts, no lights-out, nothing. Rumor is—and it's a strong rumor—that those of us who haven't yet stood trial are going to be released. That includes you, and it includes me."

Gabriel smiled again. "Lovely. So, if you're not going to Earth, where-"

"Jupiter. Without question."

His smile faded somewhat. "Ah. And why is that?"

"Because..." Because she didn't have anywhere else to go. How sad was that? An entire Solar System, and she had nowhere else to go. Most places, she still ran the risk of encountering less sympathetic UNASCA officers. And Earth, well. Earth had its own problems for her. "Because I've seen how dedicated these Free Jovians are. I guess I want to be a part of something like that, something I can believe in. I've been running for so long. I want to take a stand now." She shook her head. "Sorry to get a little intense there."

"Oh, Joanna. It's been a long few months for you, hasn't it."

"You could say that."

"Well, I'm happy for you, Joanna. I honestly am, even though I'd hoped to travel in your company. As soon as our release is confirmed, I'll see to it that you get your wish."

"Thanks." She swallowed hard. "Um, well. I'll let you get your rest."

"Yes, rest." Gabriel shifted a bit in the covers and let his eyes fall closed. "I feel like an old man. Also, I think I'm going to need a long vacation." He opened his eyes again. "Back on Earth, that is."

Joanna nodded. "Yeah." She shifted uncomfortably as Gabriel settled back into his bed. Her life would be a lot simpler on Jupiter; no need to run from UNASCA and Belt

Group in a place where they had no influence. And if the Free Jovians there were welcoming of someone who fought with the ones here on Mars, then maybe she could solve two problems at once.

"Well. Goodbye, Gabriel. Let me know when you get home safely."

"And you, Joanna." He grasped her arm, gently, as though he were an entirely different person. Too bad he had been such scum in the first place, or things might've been very different. "Just let me know what arrangements you need via the DSN, and I'll set everything up. I promise."

Surprising herself, Joanna believed him. She squeezed Gabriel's hand and left him to sleep. If the rumors were true, there wasn't much time to arrange things. She set off to find Emily.

Galen Rojas knew that his men were avoiding him. And why shouldn't they? He was acting irrational, even he could see that. He had disobeyed orders and not even given his men the courtesy of a lame excuse. Nobody had yet asked him to explain himself, which was just as well seeing as how he could scarcely decide on an explanation.

He was packing up his desk. Even if he wasn't sacked, Rojas was no longer sure that he wanted his job. Olympus police chief was a fine job when all it meant was keeping the peace among peaceful people. When he stopped being the chief of police and started being the thought police...it wasn't the same.

He was deep into feeling sorry for himself when the door tone sounded. He wasn't sure if he wanted to talk to anybody, but there wasn't going to be any running away from this. With a sigh, he gestured for the door to open.

Marla stepped in and looked around in surprise as the door closed behind her. "Did you already get this message?"

"What message? Oh, and it's good to see you too."

Marla smiled thinly and gestured at the room. "The message from UNASCA. About your suspension."

Rojas shook his head. "I don't need people to tell me what I already know."

"I suppose not." She took one of the chairs in front of his desk and sat in it, regarding him. "I don't suppose you're willing to tell me why you did it?"

"Would it make a difference?"

"It might. I've been chosen as your interim replacement, so if you're privy to any special knowledge..."

"No, not really."

"Okay." She chewed on her lip for a moment as Rojas opened the next drawer and started picking items out of it. "So why did you do it?"

"Because my job is to keep the peace. When UNASCA issued those orders, they were starting a war."

"Someone might argue that your job is to obey orders, regardless of your personal feelings."

Rojas looked at her in surprise. Her tone was mild, but her words were cutting. Calculated or not, it hurt. "I suppose someone might," he admitted. "Would you?"

"I think so. I'm sorry that you're getting the short end for your decision, if that helps at all, but you have to understand the magnitude of what you've done."

Rojas placed a set of files into his duffel bag to give himself a moment to think. Finally, he said, "I think you'll have to make a similar decision yourself. It won't be long, I have a feeling. Is being UNASCA's pawn more important than following your own conscience? If you can make that choice easily, then well. Maybe you're better at life than I am."

"It *would* be an easy decision; that's what I'm trying to say. I'm not content to let the Solar System slip into chaos."

"I wasn't-"

"Yes, you were. Galen," Marla sighed, "when a corrupt administrator tries to thwart UNASCA, they can always chalk it up to an isolated incident, you know? Suppress it in the media. But it's already more than that. First, that sad incompetent who administrates Venus has a gang uprising under his nose, and now you, the very picture of professionalism-"

"I see where you're going with this."

"The very picture of professionalism," she continued, glaring at him, "blatantly and publicly disobeying a set of system-wide orders. It's going to catch fire, Galen. I'm asking out of honest curiosity: what were you thinking?"

Rojas frowned at her. "I sympathize with the aims of the Free Jovians, but that's not the big part of it. More than anything, I think that UNASCA's orders were unjust, and it would've been unjust of me to follow them without protest, even before I saw the havoc that they were already wreaking." He slumped into the wire chair behind his desk and rubbed his temples. "Was it the right thing to do? Who knows. But I did it, and I'd do it again."

Marla didn't look convinced, but she didn't argue. She just sat on the edge of the desk, looking tired. "Well, that's fair I suppose that's enough. I presume you're not going to fight your termination notice?"

"I'm not going to fight it; I can't do this job anymore." He shook his head. "This whole business has been bad for my health. I think Karen and I might head back to Earth. Get some fresh air where UNASCA's draconian ways won't hurt us." He placed his uniform cap into the box, realized what he was doing, and pulled it back out again. "I guess this is yours. I suppose I should ask what you plan to do with those prisoners."

"I'll re-institute the crackdown, of course, but don't worry. Most of those prisoners went to ground or got out while they could. It's mostly for show now, I'm afraid." Marla picked up the hat and looked it over. "I sure hope this isn't as heavy for me as it was for you."

"You would be surprised how much a little nylon can weigh on Mars." Satisfied with what he had retrieved from his desk, Rojas slammed the last drawer shut and lifted the box containing his personal possessions. He wasn't sure if it was just the Martian gravity, but it seemed much lighter than he would've expected. "I guess this is it. Enjoy your new job."

"Sure," Marla said, and as he turned to go, she added, "I respect you for what did. I just think there's still room to disagree."

"I suspect, one way or another, that's going to change soon." He tapped the door button and smiled back at Marla with genuine warmth. "I really mean this: enjoy it while it lasts."

PART IV: JUPITER

Chapter 21

The *Mary Eileen's* command center was both the ship's bridge and the operations center during her mining operations, and was large enough for a half-dozen foremen and operators to work with room to spare, in addition to the ship's pilot. It was a familiar space, one that Eileen had spent countless hours in over several years. But somehow it seemed like a different place when it was run by a different crew, the second new crew in the same year.

It was good to see the ship packed again, like they were on a job. They'd crammed as many Free Jovians aboard as they could find, mostly Dmitri's friends from the smaller colonies and outposts. Leona had not been thrilled that her ride back to Venus was heading in the exact opposite direction, but her negotiations with Bucholz had gone well enough. Odds were, one of his people was going to be heading back in-system before long.

The unfamiliar, amateurish crew hadn't helped what had turned out to be a very dark voyage for Eileen. The weeks had passed at a blur, in the same unattached state that Eileen always entered in deep space. But where it usually passed like a dream, this time it had been more like a feverish nightmare, full of self-doubt and personal anguish. At times, she doubted whether things would ever get back to normal.

There was just one bright spot in the entire trip: the *Mary Ellen*'s new pilot was an old associate of Stephen and Eileen's, a man that they'd been trying to get on the crew for years. Piet Magnus could make a funeral seem cheerful. Despite a steady diet of ship's rations and regular exercise, he was a tremendously large man, and his shaved pate made him look like an egg glued to a much, much larger egg. And yet, he was a competent pilot who knew his business, and an excellent shipmate on account of his good humor.

Eileen treasured the times they spent in the same room. He seemed to keep the darkness at bay just a bit, just enough. So she had responded quickly to his summons, and floated into the bridge.

"Ah, Eileen! Glad to see you. Heartily glad." Magnus' booming voice begged to be thick with some ethnic brogue, but was disappointingly average, the same generic accent that most born spacers had to make do with.

"Well, you called for me," Eileen slid into the only other harness in the tiny compartment.

"I suppose I did, but that doesn't make me any less glad to see you. I'm hurt."

Eileen rubbed her eyes. "Magnus, did you have something to say? I was taking a nap and I'm still half-asleep."

"Fine, fine. Check the forward scope."

Still blinking the sleep out of her eyes, Eileen called up the requisite screen, adjusted a few display parameters, and stared at the resultant picture for a moment. Maybe it was the fog in her brain, but for some reason what the display was actually showing was taking a long time to resolve.

"I don't get..." Eileen trailed off. It clicked. "It's...it's like a mass migration."

"Or an exodus." Magnus' voice was more reflective than before, and its booming quality had subsided. "Most of them were running silent, or hadn't filed flight plans. They've been lighting up for course correction over the last few hours. It was like they all planned to arrive at the same time."

Eileen realized why she'd had such a hard time deciphering what was going on—the scale was all messed up. There were often a cloud of transports, freighters, mining ships, and shuttles throughout the Jupiter system, most of them just outside the killing radiation of the planet's magnetic field. There were always a few inside, heavily shielded vessels doing pickup runs on Jupiter's extractors or shuttling between the colonies on Europa, Callisto, and elsewhere.

But now it looked as though everything had been reduced one step. There was only a relatively small cloud close to Jupiter, just outside the radiation belts. It was small, though, only in relation to the much larger formation of vessels days to short weeks outside the system. Space was vast, and usually it was rare to be in scope range of more than a few ships at once when not in planetary orbit.

But the *Mary Ellen* was still two weeks out from

Jupiter, and she had something like two hundred ships on scope. Nearly that many again were outside of scope range, but visible by their massive power output as they made course correction burns. It was, without exception, the most ships that Eileen had ever seen—probably, that anyone had ever seen—within such a small space.

"And we know why, too. You've heard of Solomon Gracelove, right? Of course you have. Everyone has."

"I've heard of him, sure. I don't know anything about him, really, except that he's the leader of the Free Jovians and has worshipers throughout the Solar System. Not that I would necessarily count myself among them."

Magnus laughed, a deep sound that brought to mind childhood images of Santa Claus. "You were right to use the word worshipers. Ha! Truth is, it's not far off. The man is popular, and high on UNASCA's hate list. I'm sure they'd love to treat him to some classical space discipline. You know, send him walking home."

Eileen winced. "I'm sure."

"But this came over the radio and DSN during your nap. Listen." He tapped a few controls, and the tiny compartment filled with a rich, velvet basso as the now-familiar image of Gracelove appeared on the main screen.

"Greetings, people of the Solar System, and especially to the people of Earth. I am Solomon Gracelove, spokesman for the Free Jovians."

"I've been listening to a lot of chatter from the inner system. People are confused about the Free Jovians. What are our goals? How far will we go to accomplish them? How will it affect the peace and prosperity of mankind?"

"Let me answer the simplest question first: simply put, the Free Jovian's believe that a man is entitled to a share of profits from his own labor, and that he is entitled to a say in his own future. These are tenants that nobody on Earth would disagree with—they are the foundation of every nation. And yet, their brothers and sisters off-world have long been denied these rights.

"Oh, don't get me wrong. Here on Europa, we elect our own colonial council, and we are allowed to elect the judges that preside over our courts. Furthermore, we are generally kept fed, warm, and safe. Generally.

"In the last two decades, UNASCA has been faced with a stark realization: they are no longer necessary. No longer does it administer tiny, disconnected colonies, and no longer does Earth face any preventable existential threat from outer space. Instead, most UNASCA colonies have hundreds or thousands of members. We no longer need the helping hand from Earth. We no longer need someone else's control.

"Instead, we demand the right to self-actualization. We, not UNASCA, will work with other governments and corporations for the benefit of all. We, not UNASCA, will decide on our own laws and govern our own futures. We, not UNASCA, will reap the benefits of our hard work."

Gracelove's voice had been rising in volume and when he paused Eileen found that she was holding her breath in sympathy. In spite of herself, she couldn't argue that he was a rapturous personality.

When he spoke again, he was quiet, almost contemplative. "If we get what we want, the people of Earth will scarcely notice. Things will continue much as they always have, save that the people of Europa, Ganymede, Callisto, and the other moons of Jupiter will know that they're working for themselves—they now have a share in the products of their labor.

"We will go to any length to accomplish our goals, people of Earth. We hope that we can reach a peaceful solution, but if it's necessary we will not hesitate to use force."

He smiled that grandfatherly smile again. "It is only with your support that we can pull this off, and my heart was warmed by the news that the members of the Mining Consortium pronounced support for the Free Jovians on Mars, and condemned their illegal imprisonment. Others have rejected their mistreatment on Saturn, on Venus, and elsewhere. With such overwhelming support, our future cannot help but be secure."

"Now that so many of my brothers and sisters are safe, and so many more are about to arrive, I feel confident delivering a message that has been swelling in my bosom for many a long year." Eileen could hear his deep breath over the mic, and realized that she was gripped by what he might say next, even though she was pretty confident she knew what it was.

"As of today, the fifth day of August, 2189, the colonies of Jupiter have voted to declare secession from UNASCA, and do abrogate all contracts and agreements with that body. No longer will the people of Jupiter be ruled by offworlders. Today is the first day of our new destiny, the first day of the Jupiter Cooperative."

"That is all."

It wasn't possible to slump in zero gravity, but

Eileen felt herself go limp nonetheless. She had known it was coming; it was almost obvious. There had been prison issues on Mars, open flaunting of UNASCA on the Moon and Venus, but to actually hear the words herself was unbelievable. And yet...

"UNASCA isn't going to let them get away with this," Eileen said, by way of response to Magnus' look of expectation. "This isn't Titania, a useless colony on the edge of the system. Jupiter is...fundamental. The economy of the entire Solar System depends on it. There's going to be bloodshed."

"Yes." Magnus nodded slowly. "There probably will be."

"And we're flying right into it," Eileen muttered, glancing again at the crowded scope view.

"Yes," Magnus replied. "We are."

As Bronwyn's shuttle descended toward Foundation Home, the largest colony on Europa, she noted with some consternation that much of the population appeared to have the same idea: there was a steady track of ships heading toward Foundation Home's substantial spaceport, and the collections of ships that were loitering in orbit were much increased.

No surprise. Jupiter was not a healthy place to be now, not if one wished to maintain good relationships with UNASCA. There were still many who wanted to do so.

The shuttle was an unusual model. It lacked the aerodynamic surfaces of most general purpose landing craft, instead being a rough sphere with tanks of oxygen and propellant strapped to the outside, much like an asteroid lander or a larger interplanetary vessel.

More unusually, it had no windows, and the outer skin was thick, made of exotic materials. During the slow period of their descent, Bronwyn asked the pilot about it.

He looked at her in a condescending fashion that she found herself not appreciating. "It's the radiation. You think deep space is bad—the surface of any of Jupiter's moons would cook you like an egg in a day or two. Magnetic flux is pretty intense down there. That's why we make a high power approach, much higher than you'd see on one of the outer moons."

The pilot frowned at his readouts. "Speaking of high power approaches." He pressed a few switches. "Shuttle gamma one oh nine, be advised that you are in my approach vector. Change course at once." He turned back to Bronwyn. "Local space control is all shot to hell nowadays. UNASCA did some things right, I say."

A few moments passed in silence, then the pilot swore feelingly. "Shit, hold on."

Bronwyn was pressed back into her seat as the roar of the engines filled the cabin. "What is happening?"

"It's a UNASCA gunship. They're on an intercept course."

"They can intercept us in orbit?"

"No, but...hang on." He jammed on the controls and Bronwyn felt her body spin and jerk against her restraints as invisible forces tried to pull her out of her seat.

In an instant, the tension released and they were in free fall again. The pilot sighed and wiped his forehead. "Yikes."

"Will you please tell me what just happened?"

"Yeah, I'll tell you. UNASCA doesn't want anybody else landing and adding to that mess they've got in the colony. That was a crazy, illegal maneuver; they're trying to scare us off." He muttered something else under his breath that Bronwyn didn't catch.

"Why do you say that?"

"Well, they were transmitting," he said, tapping his earpiece. "'Stay away, under UNASCA order blah blah blah quarantine zone.' You can't get just anyone to take you down there nowadays."

Indeed, that was true. Bronwyn had spent several days at Mitsubishi Orbital trying to hire a pilot to go to Europa, but the vast majority of them refused to even speak with her. Too dangerous, too uneconomical. A lot of them seemed to be toeing the line; few seemed to be UNASCA boosters but there were few in open support of the new Jupiter Cooperative.

And UNASCA was everywhere in orbit. It seemed that what control they'd lost on Europa had been redoubled everywhere else. And its people were visible, armed and armored, a plain sign that UNASCA didn't intend to just step aside.

"But don't you worry," the pilot was saying. "That little spin didn't mess our orbit up too much. I'll get you there just like I said." To Bronwyn, he sounded somewhat shaken.

The rest of their trip was uneventful, and a few hours later they touched down at Foundation Home.

The entrance to the landing pad had been carved at a laser-straight angle into the ice. Bronwyn had access to the external cameras at their seat and was able to watch as they drifted down into the granite-hard ice tunnel, its size dwarfing her small shuttle. At the very end stood a blast door, open to reveal a number of ships already on the pad itself. Most were heavily armored models like the one that she was riding, but there were a few inner system transports and dropships. After a brief search, she spotted the sleek, arrowhead shape of Forrester's shuttle parked in a prime spot near the gate.

This place was going to hell.

She thumbed the pilot's invoice, billing the transport to Belt Group, and proceeded into the colony.

Foundation Home was very much an industrial complex, unlike Brighton or Sagan Hospital or most of the newer colonies. There would normally be no tourists here, no one at all that wasn't somehow involved in the profitable, essential business of harvesting helium-3 from Jupiter and transporting it to the rest of the solar system. That helium-3 was the lifeblood of the Solar System's economy; without it there would be no interplanetary travel, no free power on Earth, Mars, or the outer colonies.

The colony itself was laid out in several levels, with each level comprised on hexagonal modules connected by wide corridors. The hexagons were prefabricated and identical, although each was subdivided and equipped according to its intended purpose: living quarters, machine spaces, common areas. The industrial simplicity of the design was doubtless an asset in the outer Solar System, but it was also disorienting and easy to get lost in.

Worse, the base was in chaos. Equipment was strewn through the corridors, and people seemed to be hurrying wherever they went. And there were a lot of people, more than she would've expected to see in a colony this size. Some handled themselves like spacers, while some were plainly having difficulties handing the colony's one-tenth gee.

Bronwyn wandered the base for a few moments, trying to get her own handle on the gravity, not sure how to go about meeting up with Forrester or any other persons of interest. Somewhere in the base was Solomon Gracelove himself, but Bronwyn was somehow certain that he wouldn't be here in the common areas, with the ad hoc shelters and the refugees. It did not look safe.

"Bronwyn Calleo!" As she was wandering through the camp, she finally heard the voice that she was waiting for: Robert Forrester.

She turned and saw him approach, confident in the low gravity.

"Forrester. It is good to see you."

"Pretty good to see you too. Come on, there's a lot to do here. Shit is picking up." He started maneuvering his way through the small shanties that had been set up in the common area/mess hall. "Just about everyone with an ounce of revolutionary or iconoclastic blood in their body has managed to find their way here. It's like the marshaling of the armies just before the war starts."

"I am certain that you are not referring to actual war."

Forrester shrugged. "I wish I could say that I was certain of that as well."

Bronwyn opened her mouth, but was not sure how to respond. War was a little bit beyond her usual training.

Forrester didn't appear to notice her speechlessness

as they cleared the shanty town and reached a second cluster of elevators. He thumbed the keypad and pressed a button marked "L3."

"At any rate," he continued, "I know that Gracelove's people have rounded up pretty much anyone who's continued to profess UNASCA loyalties. What he's done with them, I'm not sure, but I do know that not all of them have made it offworld."

"Dead?" She raised an eyebrow.

Forrester shook his head. "I haven't found out yet. That's one job I have for you. Belt Group has put a lot of their political capital into this arrangement with the Free Jovians, and if they turn out to be as bad as UNASCA, well, I'd sell off your stock options early."

The elevator door opened before she could respond, and they emerged into a much more organized section of the base. If the section above looked industrial, this looked merely Spartan. The combination of low corridors and low gravity meant not hitting her head when she took a step took some work. Still, there was less debris to avoid, and no shanty-dwellers.

"Where are we going?"

"I want you to meet Gracelove himself. Once you've done that, well, I have a few special assignments for you."

"Assignments on whose behalf? Belt Group, or Gracelove and his Free Jovians?"

Forrester gave her a sidelong look. "An astute question. The technical answer is both. But make no mistake, we want Belt Group to come out ahead in this game." He spoke in quiet tones as they passed others in the narrow corridor. "It's not a zero sum endeavor, but things are still very, very touch and go. UNASCA has a lot of strength focused on Jupiter, and I don't doubt that they'll go down fighting."

"I'm starting to think this might not have been the best idea." Joanna said, trying to keep the nervousness out of her voice.

There hadn't been much trouble landing at Foundation Home, despite the crowded press of other ships. But now that they had actually landed and disembarked from the *Trenchant*'s shuttle, things weren't looking so good.

The little capsule description of Foundation Home that she'd read on the DSN made it sound like it was pretty much just a small, underground living area for the people who maintained the helium extractors in Jupiter's orbit. From what she could see, that had been pretty accurate. However, the capsule description had not been updated to reflect the unprecedented influx of refugees choking every available space. There were tents and lean-tos thrown up against every available surface. There were people sleeping on and under tables and desks. Confused-looking itinerants meandered through the narrow, underground corridors of the colony. And she hadn't even gotten through customs into the actual living areas yet.

"I'm starting to agree with you," Emily murmured back. She huddled close to Joanna, and Joanna fought the urge to cuddle back. The press of humanity was a shock after the flight over, not to mention her stay on Mars. Aquifer Prison had been downright roomy for an offworld colony, and the *Trenchant* had been roomier still in spite of carrying almost two hundred passengers.

The line of people waiting for customs was more like a mob, and she could hear shouting coming from the mass of people near the front of it. The life support systems in the customs area—little more than a cargo receiving area, just off the landing pad—were simply not equipped to handle this many people, and the sour smell of their bodies hung heavy in the air.

The light gravity wasn't helping things. It was lighter than the Moon, lighter than she had ever felt short of freefall, and every step threatened to send her into the low ceiling. She wasn't the only one having problems; each time the crowd surged several people were sent flying or floating away.

And then there were the guards. Joanna had gotten used to being stared at by people with heavy weapons back in Aquifer Prison, but these people didn't have the air of detached professionalism of those guards. They looked more like predators: hungry and dangerous. Joanna tried to lose herself in the crowd, not to stare, not to draw their attention, but she could still feel eyes on her.

So far, Foundation Home was a mighty unpleasant place, but it was far, far too late to back out now.

It took several hours for them to work their way to the front of the line. There, Joanna could see that the customs desk wasn't even a permanent fixture, but just a folding table that had been bolted to the deck. The screens on it were being projected from dataslates and the officials were seated on wire chairs.

Emily and Joanna approached the middle of three

officers, an overweight, ugly man, and Emily presented their paperwork. It all passed for legitimate, and Joanna felt a huge weight lift from her shoulders; in spite of his late transformation, she hadn't been sure if she could trust Gabriel's motives, much less his judgment. The man took the slip and held it up to his screen, watched the data transfer over. He mumbled quietly to himself as he tapped a few keys.

Joanna heard him mutter the word "Mars," and he let out a loud exclamation. "Mars!" he repeated, loud enough for the entire nearby mob to hear. It got people's attention.

"Mars," he said a third time, and looked up at the two of them in wonder. "Were you in prison?"

Emily's eyes went wide. "What? How did you know that?"

Joanna just nodded. "We certainly were. For the whole uprising and suppression, and everything else," she said, gesturing to the crowd at large. "A few of these people were with us. We saw a lot of unjust things there, and we were hoping to make them right, here."

There were murmurs of assent from the crowd, and the customs man looked at Joanna with something approaching awe. Joanna felt heat rising into her face, and she felt the need to smooth out her shipsuit. "What?"

"I think...I think that Mr. Gracelove will want to see you. I know he feels just like you do. An abortion of justice is about right," he nodded repeatedly in a strange, birdlike way. "Brom. Korus. Come on."

Two of the guards—nicer looking ones, Joanna was pleased to see—stepped forward and forced the crowd aside with liberal application of harsh language and the business ends of their weapons. "Take them directly to the operations center, and give this to Mr. Gracelove. Tell him I'm sorry for interrupting, but I'm following his instructions." He handed Joanna's chip to the first guard, and gestured emphatically at her, that expression of awe still on his face. "Go. Go. Please, do good for us."

As they made their way through the crowd toward the elevator bank into the colony proper, flanked by the guards, striding deliberately in the low gravity, the customs official followed them with that awestruck gaze. And Joanna could see that he wasn't the only one; more than a few of the press of refugees were looking at the with an odd look that vacillated between curiosity and appreciation.

And yet, if Gracelove's reputation was to be believed, Gabriel might just have met his match here. Few people commanded such instant loyalty as Gracelove, the stories went. It was all media hype, but as the elevator doors closed around them and they felt its acceleration overcome the weak tug of Europa's gravity, she smiled thinking about how that confrontation might look.

The guards escorting Emily and Joanna into Foundation Home kept a respectful distance, and they never tried to use force to get them to cooperate. But they were very insistent nonetheless; when Emily paused for just a moment when an onlooker called her name, they stopped and very deliberately placed themselves between the two women.

"If you please, Mr. Gracelove is waiting," the taller of the guards said, his polite veneer making it very clear that he wasn't making a request.

"Well," Joanna said, "lead the way." She tried to

match their deliberation as he kept walking.

Joanna had assumed that the interior of Foundation Home would be less crowded than the customs area, but as they walked she could see that was not the case. Haggard and desperate looking people filled every available cranny, and bedrolls, tents, and personal items were stashed wherever there was room.

The narrow, industrial corridors and small modules of Foundation Home weren't designed to house so many people, and its environmental systems weren't designed to process all of their waste. The air was clogged with the smell of unwashed human, dirt, and a slight edge of rot that Joanna realized she hadn't smelled since leaving Earth. As they strode past a particularly bad pile of garbage—another thing crammed wherever there was room—Joanna flashed back to her medieval history class in college. Cities were breeding grounds for disease.

They arrived at a small cluster of open elevators, little more than platforms with wire mesh sides. The deck around them was clean for several meters, and guards armed with automatic weapons glared daggers at anyone who paused to look at all the unused space with longing.

"In here," their tall escort muttered. "Mr. Gracelove will meet you below."

"Won't we get a chance to change first?" Joanna frowned. "We're still in our ship suits."

The guard threw back his head and guffawed, a laugh so enthusiastic and unaffected that Joanna couldn't help but chuckle with him, as if she'd made a ridiculous suggestion. Then the guard hit the lift controls, and they were headed down.

They descended just two levels, but the air wasn't quite as close, and far easier to breathe. As the doors opened, the smell of bodies had given way to the austere, mechanical odor typical of a space station or ship. It was easy to see why: after the packed bustle of the upper levels, the corridor they were entering seemed almost abandoned, except for a single guard.

That guard opened a door, and the corridor was flooded with light. They had arrived at the operations center.

The room was small, but crowded with people and gear. Unlike above, the mass of people here all moved with purpose, and the gear wasn't trinkets and garbage, but spaceship-grade scope consoles, massive screens showing video from throughout the station, news tickers from Earth and the other planets and, in the very center of the room, a massive three-dimensional display of Jupiter, its moons, and the ships that buzzed about them all like fruit flies on a rotting orange.

Joanna couldn't tell if it was deliberate or not, but somehow the activity in the room seemed to draw the eye inward toward that console, and then toward the man behind it. When he looked up and met Joanna's eyes, she had to fight the reflex to take a step backward.

It could only be Solomon Gracelove.

He wasn't tall, but he gave the impression of great height. He was a bit overweight, but he carried it with elegance. Even though he was just wearing ship suit, he still radiated dignity and presence such that Joanna had never seen. Gabriel had a way with people, but Gracelove made people want to have a way with him.

"Joanna Newton and Emily Cherenkova?" he asked, his voice a deep, rich baritone. "A very profound pleasure to meet you."

Joanna was very proud of herself: she only had to swallow a single lump in her throat, and she was able to respond. "The pleasure is mine," she said, and was doubly pleased that she said it loud enough to be heard.

"Likewise," Emily said, beaming ear to ear. Emily, it seemed, was less skeptical of the DSN's adoration for Solomon Gracelove.

"Now, let me apologize for hauling you into my presence like some sort of criminal. I assure you, you are not a prisoner here, you least of all." Gracelove's formal pose relaxed somewhat, and his voice lapsed into a thoughtful tone. "We know what happened on Mars. It was a grave injustice, a direct insult against everyone who stands for the cause of freedom. We're sorry that you had to get mixed up in it. The Earth media and the DSN don't know the truth, just yet, but I hear that you're the woman who might be able to tell them." He was favored Joanna with a sidelong but nonetheless intense look.

Joanna made a grateful-sounding noise and Gracelove continued, "But if it makes you feel any better, it was a windfall for our cause. We've had some public sympathy for years, especially among our fellow spacers, but it wasn't until after UNASCA announced their suspension of civil rights that the actual supporters came out of the woodwork. Now we have a little support even at the highest level, not to mention the PR from the 'traitor' Galen Rojas.

"I don't mean to ramble, so I'll just get to the point. Thank you for your sacrifice. It has done tremendous good for the cause. And yet, we want to give you a chance here do even more for the Jupiter Cooperative."

Joanna had been getting more and more fidgety during the conversation. For some reason, she found it hard to even look at Gracelove; something about him was engrossing and repellant all at once. Even so, if Gracelove had been mistaken on why she'd been forced into prison, she wasn't about to correct him. Despite her discomfiture, she had definitely thrown herself on the Free Jovian side.

"What would you like us to do?" Emily asked, trying to match Gracelove's dignified tone.

"A series of broadcasts. Our followers are streaming to Jupiter from throughout the Solar System. They want to see that we're a strong, vital force. We can't very well let many of them down here; Foundation Home is already overtaxed. So we provide a focus for them to participate virtually over DSN and radio."

"You want me to talk about my time in prison, then?" Joanna asked. "Why me? There are hundreds of other prisoners upstairs, waiting in customs."

"I have a reliable source who suggested that you have a certain...spirit. And we have material prepared; there's no need to make it too autobiographical. We want to deliver a consistent message, and we want you to do it."

"That, um, makes sense," she agreed.

"Excellent." He gestured toward the back of the room and started walking their direction. "I'll have some quarters set aside for you; they're damned uncommon these days. Hard to find for yourself. And, for your own safety, an escort, courtesy of our friends at Belt Group."

Belt Group? Joanna followed Gracelove's gesture

toward the crowd at the back of the room. There were maybe two dozen others present, but compared to Gracelove's charisma and presence, they were more like background than individuals. But as Joanna first examined them as individuals, one in particular stepped forward and as Joanna glanced at her, a bolt of electricity shot through her body, rendering her catatonic as if she'd been hit by an electrolaser.

It was Bronwyn Calleo. Joanna hadn't seen that face in months, and even now she only remembered the circumstances as a stressful blur. A blur, except for that face, that face that had been burned into her mind as though by a red-hot iron.

As Joanna shook Gracelove's hand, she could hear herself saying something trivial and worthless, desperate not to let her true state of mind show through. They were in way over their heads if Bronwyn was on *their* side now.

Chapter 22

It had been surprisingly easy to get into Foundation Home. Her shipful of refugees had functioned marvelously as a calling card, and Piet Magnus had graciously volunteered to watch the *Mary Ellen* in orbit to let her head planetside. And now she was here, ready, willing, and able to help the cause, ready to do whatever she could to undermine UNASCA. Except there was nothing for her to do.

Well, there was work to be done, but there were far, far too many people to do it. Foundation Home was a smallish colony that, in normal times, was given over to the courageous few who maintained the robotic helium-3 extractors in Jupiter's upper atmosphere. Even figuring in the people who supported *those* people, the colony only had a few hundred.

But those few hundred, and the few hundred on Callisto, and the few hundred scattered throughout the outer moons, had started a system-wide revolt. And now they'd declared complete independence. And their sympathizers were showing up. In other words, the colony of a few hundred had swollen to a few thousand, with more arriving every hour. Every job was filled and had a waiting list. More so for the living spaces; most of the new inhabitants were living under tarps and blankets in the heretofore common areas.

And so Eileen had nothing to do except sit and go quietly insane. This had been a terrible, horrible idea. She could've done more good going back to Venus with Leona; at least she'd be *doing* something. As it was, the sheet-metal walls of the common area—where she could see them between the shanties and people—seemed to be closing in.

She had to go. She had to move. She shoved through the small crowd filling the rest of the module and ignored their protests as she took off down the corridors. The labels above the module entrances informed her that she was moving past life systems, living quarters, offices, but it was all maddeningly identical and disorienting. As she shoved her way through the crowd after crowd of similar people, she could feel a scream bubbling up inside her. That, or tears.

Another turn, another corridor, and Eileen jumped aside as a door accordioned open right next to her. In the low gravity, she leaped off the floor and hit her head painfully on a ceiling conduit, but that pain didn't even register compared to the shock she felt when she recognized the face of the woman who had just stepped into her path.

"Bronwyn Calleo," Eileen breathed, and the other woman stared back at her in plain recognition. Venus. Hartley Aerostat. Joanna Newton, lying in a pool of her own blood, a slug buried in her guts, Bronwyn's hired thug falling in a blast of electrolaser fire. Joanna's eyes as they'd closed, for what Eileen had feared would be the last time.

Bronwyn started to say something, but it didn't register. Her fear, anger, sadness, and madness compressed into a single pulse, a roar of terrible rage, a symphony of hot blood that sang in her ears. The animal knot in her hindbrain begged for release, and Eileen was all too happy to grant it.

A savage growl burst from her throat as she leapt, fingers outstretched like the claws of a jungle cat. Bronwyn threw up an arm with uncanny speed and tried to bash Eileen aside, but there was nowhere to go in the narrow constraints of the corridor. A shout went up from the civilians that surrounded them, a crash as they tried to clear a space where there was no room.

Eileen's strike had enough inertia to knock Bronwyn off of her feet in the low gravity, and their two bodies, locked in mortal struggle, sailed to the next intersection before coming to a skidding stop against its far wall. She was peripherally aware of dozens of bystanders scrambling to get out of their way.

Bronwyn might've been a fighter of incredible skill, but Eileen more than made up for her inadequacy with ferocity and speed. She clawed at Bronwyn's eyes and throat, pulling herself too close for Bronwyn to block, entangling their legs to keep from getting kicked off.

A powerful blow rammed a dull spike of pain into her kidneys, and Eileen's grip loosened of its own accord. Bronwyn was calling for help, her voice calm as she tried to guard her face and beat Eileen into submission. A second powerful shot against her kidneys and she was on the floor next to Bronwyn, scrambling away to keep from being pinned.

She poised to leap again, but never made it. Powerful arms gripped her from behind, and a male voice was shouting for her to calm down. The man locked her arms behind her and shoved an elbow into her back, pinioning her with impressive strength. She hissed and spat, trying to free herself, trying to get at Bronwyn, to tear and rend that stony face down to bone. Eileen could see that Bronwyn's face and neck were bleeding from dozens of scrapes and tears, and Eileen could feel skin under her nails.

"I'll rip your face off. Die, bitch!" Eileen mustered her strength for one last lunge, and all it got her was a tightening of the death grip on her arms.

"I said calm down or I'm going to shoot you!" The man was shouting in her ear, and slowly the fury ebbed, replaced by simmering anger and a dull, throbbing pain in her side. Relaxing a bit in the man's grasp, Eileen glared at Bronwyn, wishing just once that she could kill someone that way.

"Surprised to see me, eh?" Eileen said to Bronwyn, keeping her chin high. "Thought I was dead on Venus? Or under arrest."

"If you wish to hold me responsible for what happened on Venus, then I cannot stop you," Bronwyn said, and Eileen was sure that the calm in Bronwyn's voice would drive her mad. "But factors beyond our control held sway there. It was not my intention that anyone should get hurt, and I certainly think that Joanna did not deserve the injury she received."

"Don't you talk about her in that familiar tone, you soulless beast! You wooden-hearted she-devil!"

"She did not seem to mind when I used it in her presence."

Eileen felt like a dog jerking at the end of its chain, as Bronwyn's words forestalled her utterly. "Wait, what? When?"

Raising an eyebrow, Bronwyn said, "Moments ago." Her confusion seemed genuine. "You did not know she was here? That would explain your surprise at seeing me here."

"Joanna's *here*?" Eileen felt her breath coming in short gasps, and she felt the muscles in her arms cord and bunch.

"Of course she is here. I assumed that you were looking for her." Bronwyn looked confused.

"Let me go. I have to see her. I have to..." to apologize, she didn't finish. Someone like Bronwyn didn't deserve to know something that intimate.

"If you will agree not to attack me," Bronwyn said, "Forrester, let her go."

The arms released, and Eileen slowly brought her arms around in a broad stretch, knuckles brushing the walls of the narrow corridor. She tried to calm her breathing. "Please," she said. "Tell me where Joanna is."

"The media lab," Bronwyn said, pointing down toward the elevator and beyond to one of the corridors Eileen hadn't yet explored.

Without saying anything further, Eileen took off. She watched her gait to avoid hitting the ceiling, she rebounded off of the corridor walls and hit her head twice. She could just make out the words "media lab" above a module hatch in the midst of the corridors when the voice started.

"I was on Mars, and I'd like to tell you my story," Joanna heard herself say.

"Like so many others, I was arrested purely on hearsay, and imprisoned without trial, just because of who I chose to associate with. There were professionals, homemakers, teachers, and others who had never broken a law in their lives, but were thrown into jail just because of what they believed, and what their friends believed.

"Naturally, we couldn't tolerate that."

Joanna listened with a bit of trepidation, trying not to think of the facts that she was distorting. None of it was really untrue *per se*, but it she couldn't deny that it gave the listener the wrong idea, and wasn't that the same thing? Gracelove and others had just patted her arm when she'd pointed out the misleading parts, saying that she was really speaking for all prisoners, and at any rate, people needed a morale boost right now.

She didn't feel any better about it, though.

Jolene Xiu, the technician responsible for taking her speech and working whatever magic put it on the speakers, seemed to pick up on her discomfort. "You did great, Joanna," she said, patting Joanna's arm. "You have a natural voice for public speaking."

"Yeah, I don't know about that," Joanna demurred, tapping her hands on the desk as the recorded Joanna talked about the Aquifer Prison riot. It was like listening to a different person; she wondered if Gracelove had asked for the timbre and inflection of her voice to be changed in post-production. She didn't doubt for a minute he'd try it.

There was a slam at the door, like a body had smashed into it, and both women started. The hatch was locked during the broadcast, but someone was trying and failing to open the door, first with the control panel, and second with brute strength.

"Are we being attacked?" Joanna asked, wondering if she should sound the alarm.

"Probably not," Jolene said slowly. She tapped the button on the interior panel that unlocked the door, and it flew open.

For a split second, Joanna didn't recognize the haggard, haunted-looking woman standing in the door, staring at her in unbelieving wonderment. Then, the short, dark hair, the thin, tall build, the dark, flashing eyes all triggered the same memory at once.

"Eileen!" Joanna barely had a chance to stand before Eileen, her friend and one-time savior, enveloped her in an embrace that seemed to come from the very center of her being.

Their embrace seemed to last for a thousand years, and Joanna never wanted it to end. It was as though the previous months and her imprisonment had never happened, that she was back on the *Mary Ellen* flying as fast as she could from a Moon that had betrayed her. Before the Free Jovians, and before her new job here on Foundation Home.

"Oh, Joanna." Eileen murmured into her ear. "I am so sorry. I am so, so sorry." She sounded like she was near tears.

"For what?" Joanna murmured back.

Eileen pulled back just a bit so she could see Joanna's face, a look of slight confusion coloring her features. "What do you mean, 'For what'? For letting you get shot. For leaving you in the hospital. And now I hear you've been in prison, and I was only a few hundred kilometers away from where I was? What the hell kind of friend am I?"

"Hey, hey. I saved your life, didn't I? And I was under guard anyway. You couldn't have done anything," Joanna said, pulling Eileen closer again.

"But-"

"But nothing," Joanna said, and laughed.

After a moment, Eileen let out a choked laugh of her own. "Well. I guess I'm glad I let you stay in prison, if it got you to grow up a little bit." Then she laughed again, and Joanna felt her tears soak into the shoulder of her ship suit, and after a moment they were both laughing and crying, their entwined embrace once more never-ending. In the background, Joanna could hear herself talk about her escape from Mars over the broadcast radio.

After untold eons, Joanna's arms and back were getting sore, and she patted Eileen gently and disengaged, wiping her face on her sleeve.

"I am so surprised to see you here," Eileen said, sitting in Jolene's seat. The other woman seemed to have disappeared at some point during their public display of affection.

"I'm pretty surprised to be here, so I understand," Joanna said, taking her own seat again.

"So, how much of this is true?" she asked, pointing at the ceiling to indicate Joanna's broadcast, which just wrapping up.

"Well, none of it is out-and-out false, but it's maybe a little distorted. Don't blame me, I didn't write it." Joanna took a deep breath, and launched into a heavily abbreviated version of her convalescence and imprisonment, the riot and Gabriel's part in it, and her surprise release and escape to Jupiter.

As Eileen listened, her eyes got wider and she leaned forward more and more. The moment Joanna finished with her story, she blurted, "Thomas Gabriel is here?"

"No, *he* decided to go back to Earth. But he paid for my ride here, so be nice."

"And what's this about Bronwyn Calleo?" Eileen asked, sounding a little more concerned. "I just about killed her a few corridors over before I found out that you were here. She said that you were on 'familiar terms'."

Rubbing her forehead, Joanna tried to put her thoughts in order for her friend's benefit. Her friend. It was so nice, wonderful even, to have someone to talk to. Gabriel had been a poor substitute. Despite the months that had passed since they'd last spoken, it seemed like only moments now that they were together again.

"I was surprised as could be to see Bronwyn again, too. And you had better believe I was angry." Joanna chuckled nervously. "But, I don't know. We're not friends, not even close, but it's hard to say that I hate her anymore."

"She almost got you killed. Twice!"

Joanna shrugged. "Yeah, but she was just doing her job."

"Just...what?"

"Just doing her job," Joanna repeated. "For

Bronwyn, that's all it is. I'm not even sure if she even has a personality, Eileen. She definitely doesn't hold grudges or let it get personal. She's told to hunt us down, she does. She's told to make nice, she does." Joanna thought for a moment. "I wish *I* could switch mental gears that easily."

"Yeah, well. No promises I won't lose my temper someday and do her in at long last. Gabriel too, maybe."

"Oh, be nice to Gabriel."

Eileen goggled. "What the hell did you just say?"

"I said be nice to him. He's like a little puppy. Just because he piddles on the floor, doesn't mean that you can get all that angry. He can't help it."

"Joanna, you wouldn't even be in this situation if it wasn't for him! Speaking of people who have almost gotten you killed..."

"I also would've never met you," Joanna said, tapping the desk for emphasis. "Besides, he did all right for me back on Mars, and he's the only reason I'm here right now."

"If you say so," Eileen said, sighing heavily shifting in her seat. "What horrible, horrible luck. So," she said, her voice brightening a little, "you're a Free Jovian now, huh? You fall in with them in prison?"

"Yeah, I don't know. I've never cared about 'the plight of the worker' before, you know? And I definitely don't have much stake in whatever happens here. At least, I didn't. But their dedication to their cause, their willingness to die for it," she waved her hands in confusion, "it struck me, I guess. It was nice to have something to believe in, something to work toward, rather than running all the time."

"Why not just go back to Earth, then? Surely Gabriel could've arranged it if he arranged to get you here."

Staring at her feet and toeing a scuff on the floor of the module, Joanna muttered, "Personal reasons."

She could tell that Eileen wanted to know more, but she didn't feel like going into it. Joanna had never told anyone offworld about her father, her mother, growing up with them both in their own world. It was still too painful, even for someone that she trusted.

"Hey, you need a room?" Joanna asked just to break the silence, trying to throw a little levity into her voice. "I've got one, and there's plenty of extra space. We can throw a cot in there, it'll be just like old times."

"I absolutely need a room, and I'd rather bunk with you than live in one of those upstairs shanties. I was hoping to swing one by finally unloading this data about the *Atlas*, but I don't think it's worth much now." She took the datacube out of her pocket and rolled it around on her palm.

"When I was in prison, they were certainly curious about it," Joanna said. "They picked up on the fact that I didn't know anything pretty quickly, though."

"I don't think it's worth much now," Eileen repeated, and dropped the cube back into her pocket. "Certainly not to the Jovians." Joanna gave her an odd look, but she couldn't bring herself to explain any more. Even now, many weeks after Dmitri had cracked the encryption, it was a sore spot too uncomfortable to expose.

"We can deal with that later," Joanna said at last. "I might be able to mention it to Mr. Gracelove when I see him. He's a very personable sort of guy, and he at least pretends to listen to pretty much everyone."

"Everyone who makes it past the elevator, I suppose," Eileen said, raising an eyebrow.

"Yeah, it's no good up there. I hope it's just temporary."

"Me too."

There was a lull in the conversation, both women's thoughts turned inward. Joanna broke it first.

"If you need, I can get your stuff moved into my room."

Eileen chuckled. "I don't have any 'stuff.' You weren't the only thing I had to leave behind on Venus. I've been wearing Leona King's clothes for months now."

"Who? Oh, the lieutenant of that guy on Venus."

"Leona King. She got me to Mars. Long story." Eileen nudged Joanna. "At any rate, I suppose I wouldn't mind getting into your room. A good sleep is just what I need right now." She stretched, then winced and gingerly probed her side. "Bronwyn kind of did a number on me."

"I'll get you settled, and we can talk later. I still have some things to do here."

"Thanks, Joanna." Pause. "I'm really glad that you're okay."

"Me too." They hugged again, with less intensity than before, but with a familiarity that sent Joanna's heart into a bit of a flutter. "Me too."

UNASCA headquarters was not looking too good, Rosetta noted with some satisfaction as her car floated down toward the landing pad. The Portland police had long since set up temporary barricades to ward off the protesters, and Rosetta caught a distinct glint of moonlight off of the hovering riot drones. Things were going to get quite interesting here.

As soon as she landed, a guard gave her a curt nod and escorted her down into the depths of the building. He didn't take her to the conference room with the impressive view, but rather to a much smaller and more austere one. One with fewer distractions.

The guard opened the door and allowed Rosetta inside. She made it two paces before noticing that there was only one other in the room with her.

As the door behind her whisked shut, Israel Moen smiled from his position by the coffee cart. "Evening, Rosetta. Sit back, relax."

Rosetta didn't take a seat, and she didn't relax. "I was told that I was going to be meeting with Yessenia Pruitt and your esteemed self. I can't help but notice that we're alone." She narrowed her eyes at Moen, but he just chuckled.

"Yessenia's a bit busy, as you might imagine."

Rosetta smiled, sitting gingerly behind the conference table.

"Now. I figure that you were coming here for an eleventh-hour negotiation, since you had just made some profound realizations." He held out a hand while holding forth as though he were relaying some unimportant bit of trivia. "I thought that maybe we could reach a mutual sort of understanding."

Rosetta sighed. She was starting to regret this little errand. Still, there had been some realizations. She'd been working with NORPAC's energy ministry, and they had made numerous demands. Simple demands, ones that might not be a problem if they had guarantees of production like in the old days. However, the Jupiter situation had been too unstable to meet production quotas for several quarters in a row. The investors were getting nervous.

"Well. Since much of this situation is out of my hands, I'm not sure what you want me to do." Rosetta folded her hands on the hardwood table and raised an eyebrow to Moen.

"Oh, lay off it, Rosetta," Moen shook his head and started pacing. "You're not Solomon Gracelove. You don't even care about his plans for the liberty of the workers or whatever the hell. You just want workers who will maintain your precious extractors in Jupiter's atmosphere and allow you to dictate contract terms out of gratitude."

Rosetta raised a finger. "That's not entirely-"

"Yes it is," he sneered. "And you're just now realizing that if you topple UNASCA—which, I'll admit, is a distinctly possible bit of fallout here—then you're erasing the type of stability you'd need to create contracts in the first place. Rosetta, you're burning down the house because you don't like the furniture." He chuckled. "And you're asking NORPAC to buy new furniture for you."

She froze. Someone had been talking. The negotiations with NORPAC were supposed to be top secret.

"That's quite the analogy," Rosetta said, hoping her emotions didn't show on her face.

"You like it? I just came up with it on the fly." Moen stopped pacing abruptly and yanked out a chair, sitting down with heavy finality. "So, it's deal time."

"What are you even asking for? We're not retracting any statements."

"Then don't retract anything. Your public relations are none of my concern. You've put us in a very difficult place, Rosetta. A very, very difficult place. We're beset on all sides by groups I would've called allies a year ago. Our back is against the wall. A government has a right to act to preserve itself, Rosetta; that's something that anyone from NORPAC should be very familiar with."

Rosetta leaned back. There was something indefinable in Moen's voice. Regret? He was a manipulator; she found it all too easy to second-guess her read of him. Even so, there was a lot going unsaid, more than usual.

"And a corporation has a right to make the decisions that are best for it as a business, and for its stakeholders," she said at last.

"Indeed." He paused, picking at a bit of lint on his lapel. An affectation, one more obvious than she would've expected from Moen. "Listen, I'm more than willing to let you sleep in this bed you've made for yourself, but the Council has decided to be generous. So, consider this," he said, looking her in the eye again. "UNASCA is willing to pay Belt Group and other interested parties a ten-percent bonus on existing contracts if you'll refuse to abrogate them. Consider it carefully; it's more than you deserve."

That would run Belt Group hundreds of millions of dollars. Not a bad investment, at least, in the short term. "I'm not sure that Gracelove would appreciate us taking up your suggestion."

"Gracelove's a problem." Moen shrugged. "He has a lot of public support, but without your *business* support, his organization will starve. And there are...other plans in the works for dealing with him.

Rosetta scowled. It didn't take someone familiar with Moen to read what he was saying. There was no way that Gracelove would last on his own if UNASCA made a concerted effort against him. The only reason he was still afloat and popular now was that Belt Group had been supporting him for months.

And yet, she knew a lesser leader than Chen might have been tempted by Moen's terms. There were certain to be a lot of smaller Consortium members tempted by it. But Chen had thought about this ahead of time, and Rosetta hadn't even realized it. Even though Moen had nailed her true concerns right on the head, he hadn't nailed Chen's.

"Sorry, Mr. Moen, but we're not interested."

"Disappointing. How about fifteen percent instead? And I'll take you and Mr. Chen out for a fancy dinner to negotiate it."

"Blah. Now I'm definitely not interested."

"Funny."

Rosetta shook her head. "UNASCA's usual solution isn't going to work this time, Moen. This isn't a problem that's going to be solved by throwing money at it."

"What do you mean?"

"Isn't it obvious? What I mean is that we've dug ourselves into a pit with our loud pronouncements to the press. I've got to give Chen credit, because he sticks to his word. There's no way that we can back out on what we've cast as a firm conviction bordering on self-righteousness."

Moen nodded as though she had just told him the relative humidity, and said, "Well. I suppose it was worth an effort. You should know that I'm going to have to recommend drastic action to the council, and they're going to agree with me."

"I'm sure they will."

"I'm sorry about this, Rosetta. Those folks on Europa aren't going to have a good day tomorrow. UNASCA's gotta stick to its word here, too. See, you're not the only one in a pit with the marketing department. We back down, we lose. Plain and simple. You tell that to Chen. See if he thinks that it's worth all of those people's lives. Your people's lives."

He wasn't sneering, or chuckling, or maintaining that haughty look that he always reserved for her at their meetings. Instead he was entirely, deadly serious. He wasn't bluffing

"Well then, Mr. Moen." In spite of herself, she could feel a lump in her throat. "Have a good night."

"And you too. Get some sleep. I have a feeling that tomorrow will be a busy day for all of us."

Chapter 23

Seeing Joanna again had been...unexpected. Amazing. It had been enough to wrench Eileen out of the pit she'd dug for her mind, or at least enough to give her a solid hand-hold on the pit's edge. The quiet voice of despair was still nagging at the edge of her awareness, but at least it wasn't front and center any longer.

Seeing Bronwyn had also been unexpected, but far less encouraging. That woman had a special talent for showing up where she was least wanted, which is to say, anywhere within a light-year of Eileen. It also meant that the rumors of Belt Group's collusion with Free Jove were far more than just rumors. Having the friend of one's friend be one's enemy was awkward at best.

At least Joanna's connections had guaranteed her food, water, air, and a place to stay. Many of those other spacers in the colony lacked these basic essentials. It was a good thing Gracelove had such a cult of personality, or there would be chaos in Foundation Home.

As a consequence of all this, when Eileen awoke one morning to the sound of persistent commotion outside, her first emotion wasn't fear, but relief. At least it would mean something to *do*.

It wouldn't be busy-work, even. It would be survival. Chaos had erupted in Foundation Home.

Refugees who, the day before, had been cooperating even in their hardship were now fighting over scraps, pressing against each other in mobs, stealing and looting. Gracelove's guards were trying to break up the fights, it seemed, but there weren't many of them and they seemed reluctant to use their weapons. Eileen eased back into her tiny cabin, shut and sealed the door. Best to get some intelligence.

She flicked on her handset, and just as quickly switched it back off. The DSN signal was at zero; only the local network was available, and that had been locked down for days. Europa got most of its DSN feed from Callisto, outside Jupiter's radiation belts where the signals were easier to untangle, so an outage couldn't be unprecedented. And it couldn't be solely responsible for the chaos she saw outside.

Eileen eased the cabin door open and slipped through, quickly sealing it behind her when she saw the coast was clear. She had to get down to the administration levels; she wasn't going to leave Joanna behind again. Ducking through the mobs, avoiding the sounds of fighting, and trying her best to keep a low profile, she worked her way through the corridors to the main elevator leading to the administration sections where Joanna worked.

When she saw it, though, her heart sank. There was a tremendous mob, one of the largest she'd seen, trying to beat back the guard contingent. As she watched, they guards, invisible behind the crowd, cut loose with a blast of electrolaser fire that beat the mob back a few steps. In the moment before they surged back in, Eileen could see Bronwyn go to work.

She had drawn a line in the sand, so to speak. Everyone who approached was shoved back, beaten, disposed of. People in the crowd were calling out to Gracelove for mercy, for help, but their motive didn't seem to matter to her or the guards. Bronwyn kept her line in the sand, and anyone who escaped the electrolaser fire to reach it was quickly added to the groaning pile at her feet.

Watching Bronwyn, Eileen had a sickening feeling she knew what her best chance for getting to Joanna was.

The crowd surged in again, got beaten back again, and Eileen made her move. She slammed her way into the outer mob that formed a semicircle around the elevator, where the people were clustered thick, and worked her way in between a large, sweaty man and a tiny, equally sweaty woman. In the low gravity, it was easy to smash her way through, and in a moment she was in the sparse inner crowd, where the few die-hards that were crazy enough to mix it up with Bronwyn were rushing in on the attack.

"Bronwyn!" Eileen called, and dove for the invisible line she was guarding. She could see the surprised expression on the other woman's face, but Bronwyn didn't try to stop her. With a floating kick, Bronwyn sent another of the mob flying an almost comical distance, lofting him almost to the ceiling in the one-tenth gravity of the moon.

Still frowning in surprise, Bronwyn snapped, "Get behind me," as the crowd came on again.

There wasn't much room for them to operate at this point; bodies were clogging the floor and those in the front of the crowd didn't seem all that happy about being pressed forward by those in the back.

As they reached Bronwyn, she set herself to receive them and shouted, "Sergeant!"

Eileen, standing just a few feet behind, saw Bronwyn set her feet and deliver a shove powered by her entire body to the nearest man. He flew into the crowd behind them, stumbling the entire mass, while Bronwyn turned and, before Eileen could react, pulled her to the ground just as the guards opened fire.

Before, the guards had fired quick electrolaser bursts to scare back the crowd. Perhaps they had noticed that wasn't working so well, because this time they held down their triggers. Searing blast after searing blast washed over the crowd, though Eileen couldn't see, squeezing her eyes shut against the blinding light of the beams.

After a moment, the guns went silent. Eileen opened her eyes to see Bronwyn offering her a hand. She took it.

"Thanks," Eileen muttered, dusting herself off and looking about. The crowd had half fled, and the other had been dropped where they stood. A few of the earliest individuals to be stunned were twitching and groaning as consciousness returned.

"I presume you did not seek me out to attack me again," Bronwyn said, hands on hips, looking placidly at Eileen.

"Um, no."

"Then why?" she demanded.

"Because I need to get to Joanna. Well. First, I need to figure out what's going on, and then get to Joanna." And then she needed to get Joanna as far from this place as possible, but she somehow doubted that Bronwyn would be gung-ho about that plan.

"The short version is this: UNASCA has issued an ultimatum. If Gracelove does not retract his claims of independence and submit to the presence of UNASCA troops in Foundation Home, then they will use an orbiting warship, the *Teutoburg,* to destroy our oxygen generator plant. This will force his hand."

"Force his..." Eileen blinked, trying hard to process. "That's an atrocity!"

"Technically, as the attack itself will not kill anyone, it is merely an act of war."

Figures that that Bronwyn should have memorized UNASCA wartime regulations. "How long did they give?"

Bronwyn licked her lips. It was quite possible the first time that Eileen had ever seen Bronwyn show the slightest signs of hesitation or nervousness, and it caught Eileen off-guard. "Forty-eight hours."

"Shit."

"Yes," Bronwyn nodded. "And Gracelove has ordered that nobody shall leave Foundation Home. He fears that a mass exodus of his supporters would unduly damage his cause. He believes UNASCA will not follow through."

"That's ridiculous. There are two hundred sympathetic ships up there. Why not use them?"

"I cannot answer," Bronwyn shook her head. "My orders are to enforce Gracelove's edict."

"Whatever." Eileen shook herself. "Like I said, I

really need to get to Joanna."

"So you can leave?" Bronwyn asked, tilting an eyebrow.

"So I can keep her safe," Eileen frowned. "Why the hell do you care?"

"As I said, I have orders." Bronwyn checked the charge on her own electrolaser before returning it to her belt. "And Gracelove's orders says that no unauthorized personnel are to be allowed below."

Eileen opened her mouth to protest, saw Bronwyn's determined look, and closed it again. Bronwyn was as implacable mentally as she was physically; she couldn't be browbeaten.

On the other hand, she wasn't a robot. And there was no way she was looking out for Free Jovian interests over Belt Group's, not now.

"All right, listen. I propose an exchange." Good thing she'd held on to that datacube. "Information for access to the admin levels."

"And what information are you offering."

Eileen gritted her teeth. "Information. Aboutthe *Atlas*."

Bronwyn raised an eyebrow. "You have information on the *Atlas*? I would have simply taken the information if I had been directed."

"Well, then I'm sparing you the need to take it! Are you interested or not?" The mob was starting to rally behind Eileen, and the noise in the module was getting louder. She could see the guards double-check their weapons and move into firing position.

After an interminable pause, Bronwyn answered.

"Very well."

Eileen fumbled for the datacube in her pocket and slapped it into Bronwyn's hand. "I had better not regret this."

The other woman didn't answer. She just gestured at the guards and they reluctantly parted to allow her to pass.

The crowd was reforming. They were shouting, screaming for Gracelove to release them, to come to their rescue, to come up with some plan to save them, to just say something or make a statement. Bronwyn hammered on the elevator button, and when the cage opened, she shoved Eileen inside. As the elevator began to descend, Eileen could see them surge forward.

Rosetta didn't wait for Chen's expert system to finish its typical greeting. "Is Chen in his office?" she demanded, trying to keep her voice steady. "Is he there now?"

"I'm sorry," came the contrite reply a few seconds later. The speed of light was so damned inconvenient sometimes. "Mr. Chen is out of the office and cannot be disturbed. If you'd like to leave a message, it will be routed to his central mailbox."

"Damn it," Rosetta swore. The expert system wouldn't care, but it made her feel better, at least. "Can I set my message as high priority?"

"Yes, Rosetta Lovelace. Your identification is confirmed."

"Thank you. Yes, high priority message for Mr. Chen: see me as soon as you can. I have urgent data regarding the fate of the *Atlas*. Thank you."

"Will that be all?"

"Yes, that will be all, damn it." Rosetta hung up and slumped back in her chair. In the window on the floor of her hotel room, the Earth slowly rotated into view. Rosetta was unaffected by the magnificence of that white and blue globe. Her mind was elsewhere, on Jupiter.

After all that Belt Group had done for Solomon Gracelove, after all she personally had done for him, he'd been pissing all over their deal from the very beginning. Not only did he have the *Atlas*—the *Atlas*, the multi-billion dollar flagship spacecraft that carried her company's future for cargo—but he'd had it for over a year, a year during which Belt Group agents had been tear-assing around the Solar System following up the most insubstantial leads. He'd had it for months during which she'd risked placing her most capable number-two man in his service.

She was going to kill him, even if UNASCA didn't.

The timing was even worse, because she wasn't on Earth in her office, someplace where she could act effectively. Instead, she was light-seconds from everywhere on a damned PR stunt, inaugurating a statue for the hundredth anniversary of the construction of the *Luna-1* space station. Not that anyone wanted to talk about the space station, of course, they all wanted to talk about Europa and UNASCA's damned warship, the *Teutoburg*.

In two centuries of manned spaceflight, and a full century of ubiquitous deep space travel, there had never been an interplanetary war, but that's what UNASCA seemed to be aiming for. Orbital bombardment of one of their own colonies...a Pyrrhic victory would be the best they could expect. Moen hadn't been bluffing when he'd called it "extreme measures". If their measures were this extreme, then UNASCA must be really and truly desperate.

The Free Jovians had to be equally desperate. There was no way they could take on a warship with their cloud of mining vessels, container ships, and fast couriers. That's why they'd cultivated a relationship with Belt Group: they needed offworld support. And now Gracelove had made a mistake of tremendous proportions. He'd stolen the *Atlas*, and Rosetta was going to nail him to the wall right when he needed her most.

It was a tremendous opportunity. Assuming, of course, that Chen gave her permission to make a hard move.

Rosetta received a call back from Chen's office in the middle of her speech. Cutting a giant swathe out of what she was going to say, she hurried back to her hotel room, plugged her scrambler in, and called him back.

When Ronaldo Chen's grim face appeared, she felt an almost palpable sense of relief.

"Good evening, Rosetta. I received your message, and I have to say...the *Atlas*? Surely there must be some mistake."

"Forrester confirmed the data was legitimate, sir." Rosetta strained to keep the impatience out of her voice.

There was that damned two second pause while her transmission was beamed over the 380,000 kilometers separating the Belt Group headquarters from *Luna-1*, and his reply was beamed back. "From Forrester?" Chen raised an eyebrow. "I thought all DSN access from Jupiter was being interdicted. All we've received here have been second- and third-hand reports."

"This didn't come over DSN, Mr. Chen. Forrester managed to route a transmission off of one of our collector stations in Jupiter's atmosphere. A line-of-sight burst to one of our microwave collectors in lunar orbit. It actually came in several hours ago, but my expert systems took awhile to piece together the fragmented bits." She shook her head and took a deep breath. "That's neither here nor there, though. My point is that we now know the location of the *Atlas*, or at the very least what's left of her."

"In Gracelove's possession."

"Yes, at least according to the transmissions that the *Mary Ellen* intercepted in the belt."

Chen looked pensive, and his pause was too long to be explained by speed-of-light delays alone. Finally, he said, "Can you send a message back to Forrester using that line-of-sight burst you mentioned?"

"Yes, we set up a system of data dumps before the DSN went down." She didn't mention that they'd done it in case Gracelove himself had removed Forrester's DSN access; it remained to be seen whether that would be relevant. "Why?"

"Have him go to Gracelove. I want an explanation, and a damned good one, or so help me there's going to be a shift in public opinion."

"With respect, sir, I think it's time for a harder move than that." She took a deep breath. "Sir, I recommend that we abandon Gracelove and repossess the ship immediately." Rosetta paused, but Chen didn't answer. "Anyway, if we decide that it's still worthwhile to bargain with Free Jove, we stand a better chance of dealing with the *Teutoburg* from orbit."

After a moment: "Rosetta, we've invested a lot of PR in our support of Gracelove; if we flip-flop, the damage to our image will be incalculable. This Free Jove business has been a godsend in *covering up* the *Atlas* situation. We don't want to reverse that."

"Frankly, Mr. Chen, we have greater concerns than public relations. I know that sounds strange coming from me, but we have very limited time, and if we can kill two actual birds with one stone, who cares how we describe those birds later. I apologize for the metaphor, but you understand what I'm saying."

Chen licked his lips for several moments. He didn't look happy, which was good; it meant that he understood how precarious the situation was. At last, he sighed deeply. "Rosetta, I trust your judgment. I think you're underestimating the potential fallout from this decision, but it's the kind of decision I hired you to make."

He sighed again. "Do what you will."

Rosetta nodded, tried to say something reassuring, and realized there was nothing reassuring to say. She settled for a lame, "Thank you," and cut the connection.

She sat still on the hotel bed for just a moment, willing her racing heart to settle down. A clear mind, that was what she needed. The company, the Free Jovians, the Solar System, it could all hang on the clarity and effectiveness of her instructions to Forrester. She wondered what the investors would say.

"It's up. It's up!" Joanna just about dropped her dataslate when the DSN indicator changed from "no signal" to "full connectivity." She slapped the commands in to open her mailbox and download new messages from the local server.

There probably wouldn't be anything for her; it was impossible to keep all DSN servers synchronized across interplanetary distances, and the cache-burst method that was used to provide the *illusion* of synchronicity only worked when connections stayed up for more than a couple of minutes. Thanks to the UNASCA warship in geosynchronous orbit, getting a connection for a fraction of that time was something to be celebrated.

"See if you can get the headlines, too," Eileen mumbled from her bunk, her shifting form under the blankets barely visible in the dim light put out by Joanna's slate.

"I'll do what I can." Her heart caught for just a moment—new messages! Most likely junk, the way her luck went, but still.

It wasn't junk. She held the dataslate rigidly in both hands, could feel herself trembling. The message header said that it was from Earth. From her father.

Her father, who was languishing in a NORPAC prison cell in the Rockies. Her father, who she hadn't spoken to since she had told him she'd be working on the Moon. Years ago. A *lifetime* ago, it felt like.

"You get anything?" Eileen asked, but Joanna barely heard it. She was staring at the message preview, the first hundred-odd characters. All pleasantries, nothing of substance. What if the entire message was like that? What if it wasn't?

What a stupid thing to be worried about. Angry at herself for feeling so emotional, she stabbed at the message indicator, opening it up full-screen.

She read.

"Hey, you all right?" Eileen sat up, bleary-eyed, her hair a mess. "Hey?"

"It's from my father," Joanna muttered, going back to the first line to read again.

Eileen's hesitation was obvious. "Isn't your father...in prison?"

"Yeah."

"I got the impression that you two weren't so much on speaking terms."

"No."

"Okay," Eileen said. They sat in silence for a moment. Joanna went back to the first line to read the message one more time.

"He says," Joanna started, and swallowed hard. This was so stupid. Why was it so hard to say? "He says he's proud of me." She could feel tears welling.

The expression of utter discomfiture on Eileen's face was so comically at odds with her usual assurance that Joanna couldn't help but choke out a gasp of laughter. "It's okay, Eileen. It really is."

"Good." She looked reassured, but only just.

"It's fine. You want me to read part of it? Here, he says." Joanna paused, swallowed hard once more, and continued, "He says that he understands why I was in prison. He says he's been reading about UNASCA and about the Free Jovians. He says that I was in prison because of what I believed, because I was sticking to my principles. He says that I'm so much better than him; he says he's only in jail because of his own selfishness."

She had to stop. Stupid or not, she felt like she was going to cry.

"I never told you why he was in prison in the first place, did I?" Joanna asked, once she'd regained control of her faculties.

"Not really."

"Embezzlement. He was an insurance agent and skimmed their largest contract for years. You know, it's funny," Joanna said, "but I never wondered why we could all of a sudden afford all of these trips and new things. Aerodynes and so forth. It wasn't until he was arrested that I had the slightest inkling. After that, Mom was never really the same again. I was seventeen; I left home as soon as I graduated."

"Sorry." The honest concern that Eileen was radiating warmed Joanna's heart. In fact, it wasn't just that. She felt as though this huge weight she'd been carrying, one she hadn't even been aware of, had been lifted. If her father was okay with where she was, and was still proud, and Eileen was here and so honestly concerned...

Warships, UNASCA, Belt Group, Free Jove: for the moment, none of it mattered. Joanna felt *good.* The tears welled up again, and this time she let them come. She heard Eileen get up, felt her sit down next to Joanna, offer her shoulder.

By the time the tears stopped, Joanna felt even better. "Thanks, Eileen. I just...I'm glad to be here with you."

"I'd be glad to be anywhere, if you were around," Eileen smiled.

Gosh. She was happy. What were the odds?

And then, as if she'd summoned it with her happy thoughts, the door chime sounded. Frowning, Eileen went to open it, and her frown only deepened when she saw Bronwyn outside.

"What the hell do you want?" Eileen hissed.

Bronwyn raised an eyebrow at her tone, but said, "I want you to come with me. The situation has changed; we are leaving the colony."

Chapter 24

"Will you please tell me what's going on?" Eileen hurried to keep up with Bronwyn's steady, long-legged stride, and more than once she had to push herself off the ceiling. They were in the lower administration level, beneath the operations center and Joanna's editing bay, and wherever Bronwyn was going seemed to be well off the beaten path. Eileen was not in the mood to put up with any of Bronwyn's bullshit at this point.

"As I said," a note of impatience was creeping into Bronwyn's heretofore flat voice, "the situation has changed." She said nothing else, but redoubled her pace such that it was hard to match in such low gravity.

At length they reached a hatch marked "Secondary Power," and Bronwyn opened it without hesitation. As they entered, Eileen could see that it had been hastily converted to a type of office, with screen projectors mounted on the walls of the tiny space and a wire chair set on top of what appeared to be a capacitor bank. There was a man in the chair, a man that look familiar to Eileen.

As the three of themselves crammed into the room, Bronwyn shut and sealed the door, and the man turned to face them.

"Greetings," he said, his voice deep. He was tall and fit-looking, not what she would've expected from a spacer, although his pale skin and close-cropped blond hair were typical of an offworlder. A air of confidence surrounded him like a garment, and Eileen had to admit that he was no less attractive for it.

"I'm Robert Forrester," he continued, "special attaché from Belt Group. It's a pleasure to meet you." He paused. "Or meet again in your case, Ms. Cromwell. I'm glad I don't have to pry you off Bronwyn again. Anyway," he continued, ignoring Eileen's glare, "I have to say that I'm rather surprised we're meeting like this. Bronwyn has been chasing both of you at my order for the better part of a year, and here you are voluntarily."

"I don't know if I'd call us 'volunteers'," Eileen said, glancing at Bronwyn. Her stance made it obvious that she was guarding the door from both sides.

"Actually, you are," Forrester said, then raised a hand. "That is to say, you can feel free to refuse my offer if you like."

"Then I refuse!" Eileen scoffed. "You tried to kill me, to kill *us*, and I gave you the data you were looking for anyway. I don't want anything else to do with you."

"You did give us the data voluntarily, which proves you can be reasonable. That was all we were ever looking for, Eileen Cromwell. If you would've handed it over on the Moon, this whole situation could've been avoided." Eileen was at least gratified to see that this Forrester character wasn't quite as implacable as Bronwyn. He looked angry; his face was flushed.

"Go to hell. My best friend died because of that data."

"Not my fault," Forrester said, leaning forward in his chair, his voice rising. "We killed nobody. You almost died because of your own resistance, and you almost killed Bronwyn at least twice. I'd say that we're square on that count."

"Eileen," Joanna said, putting a hand on her arm, but Eileen bucked it off.

"I don't believe your nerve," she muttered to Forrester, debating taking a swing at him. Maybe he was right, maybe he hadn't killed Stephen—Gabriel would face a reckoning for that someday—but she still yearned to claw the smug-ass look off his face.

"Eileen, please!" Joanna said, jerking Eileen around. Surprised, Eileen didn't resist. "You can be as angry as you like, but we might as well listen. We don't have much of a choice."

"Joanna Newton makes a good point," Forrester said. When he continued, his voice had lowered in volume and gained a seductive edge. "Orders from the top: we're making a clean break with UNASCA. You want to get revenge on them, I know. This is your chance.

"You don't have to like me or agree with me, Ms. Cromwell. But this opportunity fits right into your own interests. I'm giving you two the chance to join us because you've done Belt Group in general and me in particular a tremendous service. This is *strictly* voluntary. If you don't like it, you can go right back to that editing bay and we'll never discuss it again." He paused. "Of course, we'll likely never see each other again, because if that warship follows through with UNASCA's plan—which it will—then you'll die here. Do you understand?"

Eileen glared at him, wishing that she could strike him dead with her gaze. It didn't work, but that didn't lessen the sheer hatred burning in her gut. "Joanna," she asked, not looking at her friend, "what do you think?"

"Well." Joanna sounded...*confident*, far more so than Eileen was feeling. "I don't like you, Mr. Forrester. I think that you're not a very nice person and you're not very sympathetic. You can try to avoid the responsibility if you want, but we've been through a lot because of you." She sighed. "But I don't want to die here, and working for Mr. Gracelove hasn't worked out for me. At least tell me what your plan is."

Eileen let out a heavy breath and stifled her objection. Biting her tongue, she leaned up against the wall, crossed her arms, and waited.

Forrester stared at her for a long second before turning to Joanna and saying, very politely, "Thanks to the data provided by Ms. Cromwell, as well as information from a few secondary sources, we believe we've located the *Atlas*."

Eileen cocked an eyebrow. "Really? Already?"

"Yes, of course. We wanted that data for a reason."

"But the data wasn't *that* specific."

"No, it wasn't. But it did fill in a few missing holes in our own data, and then a search with an optical telescope on Europa's surface did the rest. The *Atlas* is here, ladies. It was never lost; thanks to those transmissions you caught, we know that Gracelove bought out the captain and senior officers, bought them out using funds skimmed from *our* helium-3 operations, and brought the ship here. According to senior Belt Group officers that have been in touch with Mr. Gracelove," he almost spat the name, "he was using it as insurance, a way to guarantee that neither Belt Group nor UNASCA nor any of the other gas extraction firms could put down his little revolution."

Joanna frowned. "But Belt Group's supporting Free Jove."

"I know!" He almost shouted, then closed his eyes, taking calming breaths. "I'm sorry. Corporate politics. But if we've found the ship, then it doesn't matter. We knew it was here, hidden somewhere. It had to be concealed by one of the moons, otherwise it would've been detected long before now. So, after Bronwyn, ah, acquired telescope access for me, I did a little survey." He gestured at one of his screens, enlarging it so it filled the entire wall.

It showed a dark, heavily artifacted image that Eileen couldn't immediately resolve. But she was determined not to give Forrester the satisfaction of asking for an explanation, so she stared at it for a few moments, looking for a frame of reference. There was a line of lighter gray that might be the limb of a moon. Behind it, a mass of shapes that looked like a digital artifact but might in fact be...

"A ship." Eileen said. "Is that...is that the *Atlas*?"

Forrester nodded, smiling. "And the moon is, well, not really a moon. It's a captured asteroid in a unstable orbit. Only two kilometers across, minimal gravity, and an albedo not dissimilar from the *Atlas*'. I found it just because I happened to notice a secular reflection as it fell behind the limb of Jupiter." Forrester shook his head. "I didn't want to believe it, but there it was right in the telescope, next time the asteroid swung around. Damn Gracelove."

"You still haven't told us your plan, though," said Joanna.

"It's simple: we're going to take her."

Forrester glanced from Joanna to Eileen. The whirring of the life support system was the loudest sound in the room.

"And how are you planning to get there, Mr. Forrester?" Eileen asked. "The landing bay has been secured by Gracelove's guards."

"Leave that to me," said Bronwyn, and Eileen didn't press for details. The enforcer might not have been her best friend, but there was no denying her abilities.

"Can I talk to Joanna for a minute?" Eileen asked, resigned. She hated it, hated like poison owing Belt Group anything. And yet, what were the alternatives? As Joanna marched out the door ahead of her, Eileen vowed that when this mess was over, she was going to go far, far away, as far as she could find a ship to take her.

When they were alone, Joanna said, "I think we should do it."

"You don't think they might be trying to trick us? You think it's a good idea to throw our lot in with them, the ones that have been nothing but serious trouble for us for months?" Eileen shook her head. "I'm so tired of being in these situations."

"Me too, Eileen, me too. And he looks like a snake; I don't trust him." Joanna said, grabbing her friend's arm.

"But I don't want to get caught between UNASCA's desperation and Gracelove's pride. He plays for keeps, Eileen. Those notices I kept reading weren't just bluffing; he's ready and willing to die, and he'll be perfectly happy to bring everyone else with him."

"If he's honest, then he's one step beyond Belt Group or UNASCA," Eileen grumbled, but despite her bellyaching she knew that there wasn't much alternative. "Fine, let's do it."

"We agree," Joanna said as soon as the door had shut again. "We'll go with you, but I have one question."

"Sure," Forrester said, standing carefully.

"When you get your ship, if you have the chance, will you help the people on Foundation Home? I don't mean helping Mr. Gracelove. I'm talking about the people."

Forrester smiled, but the only emotion behind it was predatory calculation. "Don't worry, Ms. Newton. We fully plan on extracting Mr. Gracelove from this quagmire." He tapped a few keys, and a moment after his computer shut down, Eileen saw a flash charge burn its way through the console. "Now, I think we're done here."

Eileen frowned at his back as she followed him and Bronwyn out of the door. Bronwyn was capable, lethal even, but honest. This Forrester seemed equally—if differently—lethal, and far less honest.

Joanna felt a fluttering in her stomach as they walked through Foundation Home. The mobs had settled down; their anger seemed to have given way to weary resignation. Joanna would've preferred them angry; as it was, the confident stride of their group through the upper levels of Foundation Home was going to stand out.

"We'll play it safe as long as we can," Forrester had said, "but when the fighting starts, we're going to have to run and gun all the way to the landing pad."

"What will we do with the guards there?" Joanna had asked. Forrester had just looked significantly at Bronwyn.

Fingering the electrolaser he'd handed her and that she had hidden in her jumpsuit pocket, Joanna tried to look everywhere at once. The tension, the stress was bringing back extremely unpleasant memories, and she thought more than once about asking to turn back. But if Eileen was going ahead, then so was she. After all, she'd survived all the other times that she'd felt stressed, right? So she was going to survive this one, right?

It didn't make her feel any better.

Bronwyn, leading their little formation, made a subtle gesture and Forrester stopped right behind her. They paused for a moment, exchanging silent glances. After a moment, they exploded into action, hurrying Eileen and Joanna back against the wall and into an empty shanty formed from a blanket and some spare packing materials.

"Guards," Forrester whispered harshly. "Mercenaries."

Feeling the flutter in her stomach turn into a small tempest, Joanna did her best to act casual, forming her face into the tired, listless expression that a lot of the upper-deck mob seemed to have adopted as their badge. The space they were in had once served as a laboratory, but the workbenches and tables had been cleared, and most of the instrumentation was nowhere to be seen. Instead, like everywhere else, the shanties and their occupants were prolific.

Joanna had just managed to marshal her expression when the guard formation strode in. Forrester was right; they were plainly mercenaries, not volunteers. Even in the low gravity they put on an impressive marching display, moving in a line from the corridor leading to the docking bay into the room.

She breathed a shallow sigh of relief as they gave them the most cursory of glances before moving on. They did seem to have a particular mission, perhaps searching for someone, but it wasn't them and that's all it took for her to feel thankful.

"We move," Bronwyn murmured, and they took off again. Joanna risked a glance behind them, in the direction that the mercs had moved, but they had passed through the next corridor, out of sight.

"Will Joanna Newton please report to the editing bay, please?" They all—except Bronwyn, of course—jumped when the mellow, digitized voice of the public address system called her name. "Pass the word for Joanna Newton, report to the editing bay please."

Forrester shot her an angry, questioning look, but all she could do was shrug. She wasn't supposed to read another script for at least an hour. He growled and gestured to Bronwyn. They increased their pace.

"Pass the word for Robert Forrester. Robert Forrester, please report to administration." This time none of them were startled. They just hurried.

As far as Joanna could tell, they made it about two thirds of the way from the administration elevator to the landing pad elevator before the situation started to deteriorate. Just a few minutes after Forrester's name was called, she could hear a disturbance behind her; shouts and cries of anger echoed through the corridors. The upper-deck folks that they passed looked back in confusion, and then at them with some curiosity. Wouldn't be long now. That tempest in her stomach was gaining strength and persistence.

Eileen fell back a little bit and grabbed her arm, whispered in her ear, "You okay?"

Joanna just nodded. She didn't trust herself to speak. The next corridor, the next set of shanties passed; this time they appeared to have been built in a recreation room whose game tables now covered bedrolls and makeshift sleeping pads.

"There they are!"

Joanna jerked around. Behind her, a squad of mercs, the same squad that had overlooked them before, were marching back toward them out of the corridor they'd just left.

"Hurry!" She threw herself forward, just about cracking her head on the ceiling, and shoved against Eileen. But Eileen was moving too, moving quickly. Forrester had taken the lead and Bronwyn was falling back, putting herself in position to engage the mercs. As Joanna passed Bronwyn, the other woman nodded to her, perhaps wishing her luck. Joanna could see that the weapon that she carried was no tiny personal defense weapon like Forrester had handed her, but was instead a stubby, two-handed over-and-under weapon. If the clip was any indication, it wasn't just an electrolaser.

"Come on, damn it," Forrester shouted, and as the shooting started, they ran.

They rounded the next corridor at speed. Running was difficult, but after a few moments Joanna fell into a gait that pushed her more forward than up, allowing greater speed without the risk of cracking her head on the ceiling conduits.

The room behind her erupted into combat. She couldn't see what was happening, but she could hear the reports of multiple weapons firing rapidly. Fortunately they sounded more like electrolasers than gunshots, but if Bronwyn fell now it wouldn't matter if she survived getting hit or not.

The sounds of combat came to abrupt end, though there seemed to be some more activity. As they moved, Joanna strained her ears but couldn't quite make it out.

She was concentrating so hard that she almost plowed into Eileen's back as the other woman abruptly stopped.

There were more guards in front of them.

They two groups noticed each other simultaneously. Forrester, his weapon in hand, fired a snap shot and dove, while Eileen and Joanna fumbled for their weapons while falling back.

Neither side had any cover except for the curve of corridor that Joanna had just emerged from. She fell back behind the curve, firing blindly and waiting with intense dread for the shock and encroaching darkness of a direct hit.

"Joanna!" Eileen shouted a moment later. At that moment, Joanna realized that while she was still shooting, nobody was shooting back. She let up on the trigger, staring in some awe at her weapon, and then at the pile of bodies just around the corridor. Bodies that she'd helped pile up.

Something clicked. The fight for Aquifer Prison, the confrontation in Hartley Aerostat, the fight in the Brighton Depot, all these blasted back into her mind. She'd fought like this before, and survived. She'd do so again. The tempest in her stomach disappeared, and it felt as though she were standing just a bit taller.

"You okay?" Eileen raised an eyebrow. She looked a little flushed herself.

"I think, um," Joanna said, taking a deep breath. "I think I'm fine, yeah. How are you?"

"Just fine, thanks," Eileen said, a little grin tugging at the corner of her mouth. "Just fine."

In two steps, however, her mood took a hit.

"Ah, hell," Eileen said, staring at Forrester's unconscious form. "That's just great."

"Do we carry him?" Joanna asked, glancing around. Most of the people who'd been occupying this section had taken cover behind whatever they could and didn't seem all that excited about leaving. She saw several heads poke out from behind tables, desks, piles of crates, examining the scene and retreating quickly.

"I don't know," Eileen said, chewing the inside of her mouth. "Let Bronwyn take care of him. You think he'd wait for us?"

"Are you sure?" Joanna started to say, but her words were cut off in a gasp as someone touched her back. As she turned, Eileen's sharp intake of air echo her own.

"You will carry Mr. Forrester," Bronwyn said between breaths, oblivious to the fright she'd given Joanna.

"And I will take the lead. We only have a few more compartments to go, and the elevator compartment is heavily guarded."

Beneath them, Forrester groaned and started moving. Bronwyn knelt and checked him over quickly, saying, "This discussion can wait. We need to move, now. I sealed an emergency bulkhead behind us and disabled the manual override, but the group chasing us can still reach us through secondary compartments. It will take time, but not much time."

Bronwyn nodded to them as she helped Forrester up. "The elevator should be only two compartments away. I will investigate; make sure Forrester is fit to move by that point."

Eileen closed her eyes and put her hand to her temple, giving a great sigh, but she grabbed Forrester's other arm and helped Joanna. They got him fully to his feet, and steadied him as he swayed there. "Been a long time since *that's* happened," he murmured, rubbing his chest. A section of his suit was warped and discolored, and crumbled in his fingers. "Ow."

"Not sure this was the best idea," Eileen muttered.

"It's not like we had a better one," Joanna said, sighing in resignation.

As quickly as she had left, Bronwyn returned. If anything, she was hurrying more than before. "The elevator compartment is locked down. Guards have set up a defensive position. They guessed our tactics. Mr. Forrester will wait here and recover while we fight to secure the department."

"Wait, we're going to fight a force of guards that

know we're coming? With these?" Joanna asked, dangling her stubby electrolaser between two fingers.

"We have no choice. We must get to the landing bay, and there's no alternative. We must fight. To delay is to risk being attacked by those following us."

"There's an alternative," Eileen said, massaging her hands and working her fingers gingerly. "We can use maintenance access to get to the surface; if they follow standard emergency procedures, then pressure suits should be nearby."

Bronwyn's mouth twitched. "That is ill-advised at best. The surface radiation is intense."

"I didn't say it would be pleasant," Eileen said with forced patience, "but they'll have armored pressure suits for surface work, and we can always take heavy doses of triexitine when we get to safety."

Bronwyn just stared that implacable stare for a moment. Joanna found that she had been unconsciously squeezing her fists and forced her hands to relax. Was that the sound of commotion in the near distance? At length, Bronwyn said, "I know of an access way that should suit us." Without further comment, she turned toward a heavy hatch mounted in the compartment bulkhead, far from the primary corridor.

They had entered a secondary corridor that appeared to double as a maintenance tunnel. The narrow space, choked with pipes, valves, conduits, and manual gauges, wasn't wide enough for them to walk two abreast. Eileen took the lead, and Joanna had to nudge Forrester in ahead of her before taking up the rear position. She tried hard not to think about what would happen if they were discovered in here. There was nowhere to run.

Several minutes passed before Joanna remembered that she had not closed the access hatch. Damn it, damn it.

Bronwyn seemed to have memorized the layout of these tunnels, but as they took several turns, Joanna instantly became lost. Sounds boomed all around them, some mechanical, some unidentifiable, and she couldn't tell if they were being followed. Fighting against an enemy she could see was one thing; this was going to drive her crazy.

At last, Bronwyn gestured for them to halt, and Joanna paused to listen. It sounded like there might be some commotion in the tunnels somewhere, but with the pipes and the echoes it was impossible to tell where.

"Perfect," Eileen said, moving ahead of Bronwyn. The tunnel opened up into a sort of airlock anteroom. Massive, oddly articulated pressure suits were mounted on racks against the wall, with tools and parts slotted into compartments all around them. The far wall had been replaced with an airlock, much heavier-duty than the kind Joanna had seen in space.

As Eileen and Bronwyn started to inspect the suits, and Forrester sagged against the wall, Eileen said, "These are more like construction suits than deep space ones. They take a few minutes to put on."

"I'm not rated in space suits, no matter what the type." Joanna took in the massive armored forms with some apprehension. They reminded her of diving suits, the kind that the construction crews of deep ocean habitats would use. Rather than the tight-filling plastic and synthetics of most spacesuits, these were plated with metal, with only a thin visor slit in the helmet. Mechanical linkages connected the joints, augmenting the user's strength. Even in low gravity, that suit had to be unwieldy as hell.

"That's fine," Eileen replied, stopping at the rear of her suit and pulling the entry hatch open. "I'll walk you through it." She paused. "Do you hear something?"

Joanna strained her ears, but Bronwyn—who, Joanna noted with annoyance, was having no problem with her own suit—replied first. "Several people are moving through the maintenance tunnels."

"Then it won't be long until they find us," Eileen said, climbing into her own suit.

Bronwyn had temporarily abandoned her own suit and was helping Forrester into his; at least Joanna wasn't the only one unfamiliar. She felt a pang of sympathy as he walked, uncomfortable even in the low gravity. The first few minutes of waking up from an electrolaser blast were incredibly uncomfortable; your brain felt like gelatin and your limbs like they were a thousand miles away.

"All right, Joanna. Open up the rear hatch. Climb in backwards, so you're facing the rear of the suit. Hurry, girl."

Wrenching her eyes from Forrester's attempts to move, Joanna scrambled to obey.

The space suit was more like a space *ship*. There was room to move around on the inside, a hatch to seal, systems to power up, controls to learn. It was a lot to take in for such a short time, but when the adaptive padding expanded, the suit felt a lot more snug and moving felt almost natural.

Bronwyn was last into her suit, and as she was climbing into the rear hatch, Joanna saw her pause, frown slightly, and then continue even faster than before. Joanna would've called her frantic, but her motions were as smooth and controlled as a dancer's.

"Radio check," Eileen said, her voice crackling to life in the suit helmet.

"I hear you," Joanna said.

"Yeah," Forrester muttered, sounding tired.

"We need to move," Bronwyn said. "Now."

There was a tongue control—disgusting idea—that lowered the suit racks and disengaged the locks keeping them in place. Released from its supports, Joanna's almost fell before she stomped forward and recovered her balance. It was easier than she expected; there had to be a gyroscope in the suit helping out.

Bronwyn had just hit the airlock controls when their pursuers arrived.

There were four of them, and they burst into the room in semi-controlled fashion, weapons up. The suit completely isolated her from outside sounds and there were no audio pickups, but their leader's body language was unmistakable: "Surrender."

"Keep moving," Eileen said. "I've got this." She was closest to the entrance, closest to the guards. Joanna watched in horror as she braced herself and charged into them. "Go!" she shouted, scattering the group in the small anteroom.

Forrester and Bronwyn were already inside the airlock. One or another was gesturing for her to follow. Joanna looked back and saw a few electrolaser blasts hit Eileen, not even staggering her in the heavy suit. Gracelessly, but effectively, she charged the next group. One didn't get out of Eileen's way fast enough, and the massive bulk of Eileen's augmented body check sent him crashing into the wall. He didn't get up.

Joanna was in the airlock. "Come on, Eileen. Hurry!"

The other woman turned toward the airlock, disregarding the continual electrolaser bursts. Bronwyn hit the close control, and the massive door started swinging closed as Eileen ran for it.

"What the hell are you doing?" Joanna shouted, moving toward the controls to halt the door.

"She will make it," Bronwyn's voice crackled.

The door was almost closed when Eileen reached it. Her suit's armored gauntlet wedged itself between the door and the frame, forcing a larger gap. She heaved against the tiny opening, forcing the door aside as she fell in. The door sealed behind her, and the indicator on the control panel showed that the pressure was decreasing at last.

Joanna patted Eileen on the back, seeing her heave with breath even through the heavy suit, hearing her frustrated exclamations over the radio. Then, what she said next turned Joanna's blood into ice.

"I think I got shot."

"What?"

"Are you injured?" Bronwyn asked quickly.

"Not bad. Frangible rounds, must've been. Fragmented when they hit the suit armor, but I think, ah," she paused, "I think I've got a slow leak."

Joanna's heart leapt into her throat. "Can you fix it?"

Eileen turned to face Joanna, and she could see Eileen's face through the tiny visor, her dark hair plastered to her face. "Sorry, girl. We'll just have to hurry."

"Eileen, be honest. How bad is it?"

Eileen didn't answer as the exterior door swung open. There was a small, open elevator platform just beyond, its rails set into a perfectly smooth, round shaft of white material. It must've been melted right through the surface ice. They all piled aboard, and Eileen hit the button for the top level.

The tunnel shot past them for what felt like an eternity, but when it began to slow and Joanna's head reached the surface, she gasped.

Ahead of her, the laser-sharp horizon of Europa seemed close enough to touch. Unlike the Moon's jagged peaks, the limb of the Europa seemed smooth, as though the entire thing were cut out of white marble.

But it was the sight beyond that caught her eye. The massive bulk of Jupiter, banded in red, orange, and white, dominated the sky. It felt as though it were mere kilometers away, and her stomach leapt into her chest. She got the sudden impression that it might fall on her at any moment. She could see the tiny orange sphere of Io cutting off the limb of Jupiter, and the brown point of Ganymede just cresting the opposite side of the planet. It was a magnificent, unsettling sight.

"We need to move," Bronwyn said, and started off.

The elevator had surfaced near a collection of antennae, transmitters, and telescopes mounted on a platform set into the ice. A few small structures clustered around them, but Bronwyn ignored all of this, heading off on her own tangent. Joanna, hoping that the woman knew what she was doing, started off after her.

Walking for any distance was tiring. In the heavy

suits, it felt more like she was leaping off the ground with each step, skipping along in an awkward gait. She could hear ragged breathing over the microphones, and wished that she knew where the volume control was.

They walked for about twenty-five minutes according to the clock display in Joanna's helmet. It felt like she'd run a dozen kilometers, and she was exhausted, but when Bronwyn stopped and Joanna could see a broad, perfectly rectangular opening in the ice, she felt jubilant nonetheless.

Until she realized that at least one set of haggard breathing hadn't stopped.

"You doing okay, Eileen?" she asked, trying to keep the worry out of her voice.

"I'm fine," came the spare response, and the breathing continued. "But we need to hurry."

"Where's the way in?" Forrester asked, peering over the edge. The opening continued into a rectangular tunnel that bored down into the ice at a 45-degree angle; the tunnel was more than wide enough to accommodate even large landing craft.

"There is a heavy door at the bottom. It will be sealed, so you will need to use your Belt Group authorization to open it," Bronwyn said with confidence.

"Belt Group authorization?" Joanna asked.

"Belt Group helped fund construction of Foundation Home," Forrester said, following Bronwyn down into the tunnel. "We demanded certain concessions."

"From what I hear, Belt Group concessions are the only thing keeping this place afloat."

"I suppose that we'll find out," Forrester said

quietly.

As they half-walked, half-fell into the tunnel, Joanna started to fear for Eileen in earnest. She was lagging behind, stumbling, but every time Joanna asked if she was okay she got the same sparse response. Several times, Joanna had to double back to help her up after she'd fallen.

By the time they reached the door, a massive wall of articulated metal, Joanna had to support most of Eileen's weight. Even in the light gravity, it was a heavy burden.

"Bronwyn, we need to hurry. We need a ship."

"My ship should still be here," Forrester said. "It's big enough for all of us."

"Big enough for the suits?" Joanna asked, and was not encouraged by his silence.

"Maybe," he said at last, and moved to the control panel set into the door frame, a diminutive point of color against the unending gray and white.

"Eileen, you okay? Please, tell me something. Don't brush me off here,"

"I'm...okay," Eileen said, and she sounded out of breath just from standing. Joanna bit her lip. It wouldn't do any good to lose it over the public radio channel.

She felt a vibration in the ground, and looked up to see the door rolling silently into a recessed ceiling compartment. In the vast, cubical space beyond, dozens of ships were crowded into painted slots of tarmac.

"Looks like I picked a good parking spot," Forrester chuckled as he approached a ship near the gate, a large, arrowhead-shaped craft that appeared to be about half engine. Joanna was relieved enough to see it that she didn't even feel annoyed at his flippancy, and moved toward the airlock as he opened it.

The tiny airlock. It would fit one suit, *maybe* two. It would be tight.

"Step aside; let me go first. She's wounded." Without waiting for a response, Joana pushed ahead of Forrester and starting working Eileen into the airlock. She was helping, but barely. "You still with me, Eileen?"

"I'm here." Her voice was breathy and weak.

"Wait just a damned second," Forrester barked, climbing the first few rungs of the ladder. It was too late, though; Joanna had already started the airlock cycle. It'd recycle soon enough and he could have his precious ship.

Unless...

Joanna had a terrible thought. She rejected it, but that didn't make it go away. "Eileen?" Joanna licked her lips. "You feel like you can fly this ship?"

For a moment, there was no response. The air pressure monitor ticked up. Then, finally: "Yeah, probably." A deep breath. "Wouldn't be fun. Why?"

"Then let's do it. We're leaving Bronwyn and Forrester." The airlock pinged, and the inside door opened. Joanna slapped the "exterior lock" button and moved into the cramped cabin, bending in double so the huge suit would fit.

"What?" The strength in Eileen's voice was reassuring.

"Because they're untrustworthy scum. Because they tried to kill both of us, and because I'm sick of getting led around by the nose. And because I'm sick of being afraid." Joanna gritted her teeth and popped the suit hatch. "Now, get out and help me start this thing up."

Eileen opened her suit as Joanna was stuffing hers in the rear living area. Joanna turned back and let out an involuntary gasp. Eileen was covered in sweat and blood.

"Holy shit," she breathed.

"It's not as bad as it looks. Flesh wound." Eileen tried to smile, but she looked so ragged it made her overall impression even more concerning. "Good to see you taking a stand."

"It's about time," Joanna said, smiling tightly. "Now, I'll get you the medical kit. You get us out of here."

Eileen stumbled toward the cockpit, and Joanna felt her stomach clench, perfectly at odds with the appearance she was trying to project. She very much hoped she wasn't making a terrible mistake.

Chapter 25

Eileen made it all the way through the orbital burn sequence before lapsing into unconsciousness. They were both dripping with sweat, but hers was cold and clammy. Her skin was even worse, bearing the bluish tinge of hypoxia. After securing her in a sleeping bag mounted to the wall, she pressed an oxygen mask against Eileen's face and watched her chest rise and fall.

"Come on, Eileen. Say something." She was drifting in and out of consciousness; all she'd done was groan and murmur since being removed from the suit.

It wasn't dramatic, but Joanna immediately noticed that the woman seemed to be breathing a little easier, and her skin seemed to be warming up again. Her heart rose into her throat as Eileen's eyes blinked open ever so slightly.

"Hey," she managed to groan out, the faint sound muffled by the mask. "I'm alive?"

"Barely," Joanna said, feeling a grin rise unbidden to her face, squeezing Eileen's hand. "That was...intense.

Thanks for clearing the way for us back there."

"Now...now we're even," Eileen said, and Joanna could see the barest hint of a grin tugging at the corner of her mouth. "You got yourself shot for me...and now I've done it for you," she finished, the last words wheezing out in one breath, as if taking another would've been too much effort for her.

"Come on, none of that." Joanna squeezed her hand again. "But thanks."

Suddenly Eileen's eyes went wide. "How much time do we have? We have to make our retrograde burn-" she forced her way out of the sleeping bag, disregarding Joanna's firm hand on her shoulder. "We won't get another chance at this." Wincing with the motion, she pushed herself toward the cockpit. "And how long until UNASCA's ultimatum is up?"

"About three hours." Joanna followed after her, gritting her teeth in sympathy as Eileen slowly strapped herself in.

"Then it's going to be close, if we're going to do anything. Strap yourself in; it's just a few minutes until we burn."

Joanna worked her way into the copilot's seat "Are you sure you're going to be all right? Can you take the acceleration?"

The pause before Eileen responded tore at Joanna's heart. "I'll be fine," Eileen said at last, but not so that Joanna believed her.

"You sure-"

"I'll be fine," Eileen barked, then gritted her teeth. "We don't have a choice."

And so, with Joanna watching in helpless anxiety, Eileen programmed in the burn that would sync their orbit with the *Atlas*, and suffered in sympathetic pain as they were slammed against their seats by Forrester's ship's powerful engines. Fortunately, the bullet wound that Eileen had sustained had been minor; the hardsuit had taken the brunt of the force. But Joanna was no doctor. Who knew if there might be complications?

Seconds turned into minutes, and Joanna started to worry about Eileen. She wasn't looking so good. Then, as the minutes started to draw out, Joanna started to worry about herself. She was getting fatigued just sitting, and she was afraid what might happen if she fell asleep.

Finally, the roar of the engines cut off, and the return of microgravity made Joanna feel like she was a balloon, stretched taut by internal pressure. To be able to move her limbs felt almost novel.

"Hell of a ride, huh?" Eileen said, her voice stronger than before. Joanna felt the most wonderful perfusion of relief through her entire body.

"You can say that again. How are you feeling?"

"I'll be okay." She tapped in a few commands, glanced out the forward viewport, took a longer look. "Will you look at that? A perfect burn."

Joanna was busy stretching after the tension of the burn; she hadn't even looked outside.

It was as though that fuzzy telescope picture that Forrester had shown them on Foundation Home had come to life. They appeared to be holding position some distance away from the ship, though it was hard to get a real sense of scale in space. The ship was hovering in the shadow of a large, bright rock, and beyond that, Jupiter shone in all of its glory.

The rock must've been that asteroid that Forrester mentioned, the one that was two kilometers long. If it was that big, then the *Atlas* must be...

Joanna felt her jaw drop. The ship was nearly the size of the asteroid it clung to, as if one were looking at the before-and-after picture of a spaceship sculpted out of stone. She'd seen pictures before, of the *Atlas* and other large ships, but seeing it in person boggled her mind. The *Mary Ellen* would've floated next to it as a remora floated next to a shark.

"That ship...is *huge*," Eileen breathed.

The grand majesty of the ship only grew as they got closer. They could see habitation rings—four of them, each one with greater area than both of the *Mary Ellen*'s put together—clustering around the forward section of the ship, just aft of the shielded control modules and just forward of what appeared to be a mobile factory. The refinery, Joanna remembered. It had been all over the news just before she'd left Earth. They wouldn't need to send their ores back to processing, they could just take care of everything themselves.

Eileen shook her head. "Seeing it through a telescope doesn't do it justice." She tapped a few keys. "It looks like primary power is offline, but backup solar power is working. So's emergency life support; there's air and heat inside, sort of." Joanna felt the shuttle start to move. "I'm moving us to the forward docking port."

Then there were the engines. Massive thrusters and tremendous radiators projected from the reactors at the rear of the ship, a wall of asteroidal iron protecting the crew forward from their radiation. It was an awe-inspiring sight; knowing that man was capable of such things sparked a tiny glow in Joanna's heart.

It all disappeared behind the bulk of the ship's asteroid shield as they slipped in toward the forward docking port. The maneuver was simple and quick, and before five minutes had passed, the nose of Forrester's former spacecraft was kissing the *Atlas*. The airlock was below the shuttle's cabin, and they spent a few moments in its anteroom suiting up for their expedition. The life systems had been kept online, the *Atlas'* computer reported, but it was very cold and the air was very stale. Better safe than sorry.

In terms of internal area, the *Atlas* was more like Foundation Home than the *Mary Ellen*. In microgravity, it seemed even more massive, and Joanna was sure that hundreds wouldn't feel crowded within its habitable spaces. When it was completely empty, however, that emptiness seemed redoubled by the craft's sheer darkened volume.

Their shuttle's infrared scope had proved that people couldn't have been living inside the *Atlas*. With her life systems in auxiliary standby, the ship's internal temperature was only slightly warmer than the interstellar background temperature. There were a few hotspots where the algae vats were kept warm for when the crew returned, but the ship was invisible in infrared. Good thing they had brought their suits.

Joanna followed Eileen as she entered the *Atlas*. The ship hadn't been abandoned in haste; gear was neatly stowed, hatches were closed, computers were in standby.

Joanna wasn't sure if it would've been more or less eerie if the ship's crew had trashed it on their way out.

"It's like a ghost ship," Joanna said, awed.

"You don't believe in space ghosts, do you?" Eileen chuckled.

"Not until now."

They moved through the crew processing area at the front of the ship into the operations section in the core of the ship's habitable space, near the storm shelter. The *Atlas*' bridge, Forrester explained, was a small space only used during maneuvers. The operations center oversaw most ship activities, including mining, refining, and most importantly, crew support.

The operations center had been as neatly secured as the rest of the ship, and it took them just a few moments to get a few screens back online. "Lucky us. The passwords from Forrester's ship still work—you'd think Gracelove would've had them changed." She tapped a few more commands. "How long until UNASCA's deadline?"

"Two hours and twenty minutes. You okay?"

"I'll be fine. Let's just get this ship up and running. I have an idea of how to deal with Gracelove's problem."

Rosetta Lovelace desperately wished she could violate the speed of light. She'd fly all the way out to Jupiter, land in front of Robert Forrester, and hit him so hard they'd feel it on Callisto. Then she'd move on to Gracelove, suplex him deep into Europa's icy crust, and then find the *Mary Ellen*'s crew and bring them back to Earth. Them, she'd deal with more slowly and more painfully.

Considerably more painfully. Because they'd stolen

the *Atlas*.

Rosetta sat in her office, quivering with unfocused rage. Forrester's message, just reassembled by his own analysis section, was open on her screen, but she was looking into the far distance beyond it.

The *Atlas* had been stolen. *Again.* There would be a reckoning, and soon. There were two paths ahead, and neither would be fun to walk.

She could cut and run. Dump her stock, have a few friends in financial sector do their magic to hurry the money to safety, and blow off to the Moon until things turned around. If she waited six months or a year until the piranhas were in the middle of skeletonizing Belt Group, she could probably offer her services to the firm that stood the most to gain, and be welcomed with open stock options.

Rosetta sighed. It was tempting, and it might even be the better idea, but she couldn't bring herself to do that. Not after everything she'd put into the company, after everything Chen had done for her. It might be smart, but it wouldn't be right.

The second path would be even harder. She could compartmentalize the damage; try to pin as much of it on Forrester as she could. Forrester deserved better, but he'd screwed up, *hard.* Maybe she could get Bronwyn to testify against him in exchange for immunity. Then, they'd turn everything over to the marketers. Their core assets in the belt and Jupiter's atmosphere were still intact. They'd survive, but depending on the press they got, they might just be surviving to die a slow death later.

But she'd feel better about it. Forrester wouldn't, but if he didn't have a secret golden parachute stashed somewhere, then Rosetta didn't know him at all.

So, there was still UNASCA to deal with. And, offense was always the best defense.

The UNASCA warship *Teutoburg* hovered high above Europa's equator just south of Foundation Home like a vulture above the desert. Unlike most civilian ships, which tended to be long and spindly, the warship was fat and spheroid, maximizing the amount of damage it would take to disable her. Stubby missile pods and armored plates girded the ship's main hull, while the domes of fusion-pumped laser emitters clustered around the rear reactor section.

The *Teutoburg* wouldn't need any of these weapons to destroy Foundation Home. They would just turn so that their fusion drive pointed at the oxygen plant, buried half a kilometer below the surface, and go to full thrust.

For all their ubiquity—every interplanetary ship had one—a fusion drive was still one of the deadliest weapons ever invented. A spear of coherent plasma ten thousand kilometers long, it would boil away the surface ice of Europa and blast through the oxygen plant without stopping. Thermal expansion of the ice-turned-steam would cause moonquakes across the planet, quite possibly causing direct damage to Foundation Home.

All that was less than two hours away from happening. And it would happen, Eileen was sure. And Gracelove wouldn't let people leave. There was far too much to lose for both sides. It was going to be a tragedy.

The *Atlas* was a remarkable ship; she had a crew of hundreds, but could be operated in an emergency by just a few people from this one room. Her computer, Carnegie, was a high-end billion-node expert system that could just about run the ship by itself. As long as nothing physical broke, as long as they didn't actually need to do any mining, and as long as their luck held Eileen, Joanna, and Carnegie could take this ship anywhere in the system.

But leaving wasn't on Eileen's mind. She and Joanna were staring at the forward telescope display in rapt attention, each lost in their own thoughts. Joanna surprised Eileen by being the first to break the silence.

"We need to do something."

"For Gracelove?" Eileen didn't try to hide her skepticism.

"For the people. For Jolene and Emily and the others who don't deserve to die because of Gracelove's foolishness." Joanna sighed. "I feel bad enough for leaving them down there."

"We didn't have much of a choice."

"I know."

Silence reigned again for a moment. Eileen watched the gibbous surface of Europa through the wide telescope view and the beetle-like UNASCA warship through the focus view. How the hell had she gotten here? The last year seemed completely unreal. She'd flown across half the system, desperate to exact her revenge on UNASCA, on Belt Group, on anyone who'd gotten in her way, and what had actually happened? They all seemed bent on destroying each other without her help. Had she made even the slightest impression?

The darkness she'd felt since Mars, pushed to the background when she'd found Joanna, threatened a resurgence. She could feel that familiar welling of emotion behind the iron gate in her mind, the familiar void just beyond that.

As she watched Europa, the *Teutoburg*, the hundreds of other ships on the scope, something clicked into place.

"Here's my chance."

Eileen's sudden exclamation startled Joanna out of her reverie. "What?"

Eileen could feel an idiot grin spreading across her face. "This is exactly what I've been looking for." She turned to face Joanna, saw growing concern there. "Ever since Brighton. I've wanted to take revenge for Stephen. I didn't want him to just get quietly shuffled off."

Joanna frowned. "Revenge? Eileen..."

"No." Eileen shushed her with a motion. "Not now. Here's my chance. We have this ship, we have UNASCA's ultimatum...we can make an impression. For *Stephen*, Joanna."

Looking from Eileen's face to the telescope view and back, Joanna's frown deepened. "You mean, you want to destroy that ship?"

Eileen was riding on a wave of giddy, if ill-colored happiness. "Not just that ship, Joanna. Think about it."

She did. Her expression shifted from concern, to confusion, to dawning comprehension, to horror. "You're joking."

"Not joking. The *Teutoburg* has enough weapons to stop a hundred ships like the *Mary Ellen* if they tried to pull something. But the *Atlas*...that's another story. She's an order of magnitude more massive. There's no way the *Teutoburg* could stop her."

"Stop her from what?" Joanna asked slowly.

"From colliding." Eileen raised an eyebrow, trying to contain a mirthful chuckle. At last. Her chance.

For a moment, the whir of the life supports systems was the loudest sound in the room. At length, Joanna said, "Why?"

"Don't you see? UNASCA wants to hurt the Free Jovians? Well, whatever. Losing their ship hurts UNASCA. Belt Group wants the *Atlas* back? Well, losing their ship hurts Belt Group. At long last, some damned just desserts.

"We've been fugitives, Joanna, fugitives for an entire *year* because of their political wrangling. I'm sick of it. Damned sick. This is our chance to *act*, not just *react*. For this brief moment, we control everything. Let's take advantage!" Eileen was breathing hard. She felt either laughter, tears, or both welling up with impossible force.

Joanna swallowed hard. Her genuine concern was sobering. A *little* sobering. "Fine," she said at last. "Fine. As long as we help the Free Jovians, that's fine with me. What do we do."

"Carnegie?" Eileen said, struggling to keep her voice under control. "Warm up the engines and plot us a collision course with the UNASCA warship, scope track 183."

"I'm sorry," Carnegie replied, his digital voice inflected with artificial concern, "but my safety interlocks prevent me from establishing a collision course."

"That's fine. Warm up the engines anyway, will you?"

"Of course, Captain."

"Captain?" Joanna raised an eyebrow.

"I have root access," Eileen shrugged. "I made a

few changes." She tapped a few more commands, and nodded. "All right, time to go."

"We're leaving?" Joanna struggled out of her restraints. "I thought the computer wouldn't plot your course?"

"It wouldn't. I'll have to fly it in manually?"

Joanna froze. "You're staying aboard?"

"Of course not, silly," Eileen laughed. Joanna's voice had almost enough genuine concern to open the gate. "I'll fly the ship by remote. I've just established a handshake with Forrester's ship. How long to UNASCA's deadline?"

"Just under two hours."

"Just enough time. Let's go."

The trip back through abandoned modules and corridors passed in a blur. Everything in this one moment was so perfect, Eileen was almost afraid to think about it too hard, as though it might pop like a soap bubble if she poked at it with her mind. Soon, though, it would all be over.

They jumped back into Forrester's ship, sealed the airlock. One hour, fifty-one minutes. Without bothering with her restraints, she undocked, pushed away from the *Atlas*' bulk with reaction jets.

As soon as she had some distance, she flipped all of her MFDs to remote control, and authenticated with Carnegie aboard the *Atlas*. A computer could be programmed to refuse to do things, but a similar safety measure kept them from trying to stop the things humans did. It'd help guide the *Atlas* on its final voyage, whether it liked to or not.

"Engines up. You might want to watch this,

Joanna." She tapped a key, and nothing happened. The *Atlas* hung in space. Eileen double-checked her readouts.

Except something was happening. There was no exhaust, no jerk of acceleration. Imperceptibly at first, then plainly even to the naked eye, the *Atlas moved.* It was a graceful thing, a fine ship, one that Belt Group had every right to be proud of.

How long would it take the *Teutoburg* to notice that their ship was being targeted? Eileen brought the *Atlas* around, aiming for where the *Teutoburg* would be in exactly an hour and forty-nine minutes. There would be no chance of a course correction; the margin for error would be too narrow. She just had to hope that the *Teutoburg* had orders not to give under any circumstances.

The *Atlas* vanished into the distance, her reactor section flaring white-hot as the engines heated up. She had disappeared from sight, remaining visible only on the scope screen. Joanna sat next to her in silence, engrossed in her own thoughts. Eileen did not disturb her.

The next hour passed in a haze of giddy joy skirting along the void. She could see the collision in her mind's eye a thousand times, but the moments afterward were dark. How would she react? She couldn't say.

Forty minutes until the deadline. "Something's happening," Joanna said, and Eileen realized she was looking at the scope screen.

The little indicator that represented the *Teutoburg* and the oval line that represented its orbit were shifting. "She's moving," Eileen muttered. "Not going to get away, though. Not today." She tapped in a few corrections on the *Atlas*' controls, and watched.

It was a slow dance, writ large across the moon's orbit. The *Teutoburg* knew that she was being chased; every move that she made, the *Atlas* echoed. Calculations flew through Eileen's mind as she timed burn durations and angles to keep the ship's prograde marker firmly on the invisible point in space where the *Teutoburg* should be when the *Atlas* got there.

It was a guessing game, a mental challenge in the extreme. Eileen found herself thankful that it crowded out other, darker thoughts.

"Missiles!" Joanna shouted, leaned forward.

Hundreds of thousands of kilometers away, the *Teutoburg* was launching its main anti-ship ordinance. Chemical rockets the size of a small spacecraft burned out of their launch cells, reoriented themselves, and pushed their engines to maximum, each one playing the same guessing game as Eileen. Where would their target be when they got there? Behind them, the *Teutoburg* continued her own part of the dance, and in front of them, the *Atlas* did the same.

With each moment, as time passed and momentum built up, the game involved less and less guessing. A ship could only move so far in a given amount of time, and the faster it was going, the less it could change where it ended up.

Fortunately, the *Atlas* had far less momentum built up than the *Teutoburg*. Unfortunately, the missiles had even less than that.

"Oh, no," Eileen and Joanna muttered in unison. It was becoming obvious that there was no way the *Atlas* would be able to avoid the missiles. They were too fast and too many. The open question was if the *Atlas* would be able to endure them. And if it couldn't, well. Maybe the ship's pieces would work just as well.

Joanna's voice broke Eileen's intense focus on the scope and remote control screens. "What will you do when this is over?"

"What?"

"Whether we succeed or fail, we'll need to go somewhere after all this. Or were you planning to stay on Jupiter?" Joanna's voice was even, but there was still a vague sense of concern.

"We'll deal with that later," Eileen said, turning her attention to the scope screen. "More important things to do, now."

"I think I don't want to go back to Earth. Not yet," Joanna said, thoughtfully. Eileen wished she'd just be quiet. "I don't want to stay on Jupiter, that's for sure. I just want to be a long way from all of this, just until things calm down."

"Sure," Eileen said, not really listening.

"If I went to Titania, would you come with me?"

"Um," Eileen jerked her attention away from the screen with some annoyance. "I don't know. Can't this wait?"

Joanna lowered her eyes. "Sure, Eileen. Just do your thing."

A few more drops of guilt should hardly even be noticeable at this point, Eileen told herself. She focused back on the screen. The first missile was about to hit the *Atlas*.

It hit. The explosion wasn't visible from their cockpit; the only indication it had occurred was one less missile on the scope screen, and damage reports scrolling across the remote control screens. It might've shredded a ship like the *Mary Ellen*, but the *Atlas* was made of tougher stuff. It had cracked the meteor shield, no more.

Second impact. The missile tore its way into the crew section. Modules shattered as the missile detonated, spraying heavy shrapnel through the *Atlas*' delicate innards. The reactor and engine were too far back, though. The rest of the ship was just a shield now; as long as the reactor was intact, and the computer didn't take too much damage...

A third impact. More of the same. The ship was getting hard to steer as its mass distribution changed in ways it had never been designed for. Twenty minutes until the deadline. Eighteen until the *Atlas* hit. The *Teutoburg* was trying to break orbit, but it wouldn't work, not while Eileen still had control. She tapped in a few corrections, wincing as the ship sluggishly moved to the new course.

A missile raced past the *Atlas*, too far away to do any damage. A second exploded nearby, riddling the ship's central strut. She was losing the ability to steer. Twelve minutes. The *Teutoburg* was running at full emergency power. She was pouring out hard radiation, heedless of any affect on her crew, as she tried with desperate speed to outrun the implacable mass bearing down on her.

"No!" Eileen bit off a yelp as her screens went blank. Outside the viewport, she could see a tiny flash against the dark side of Europa as a missile got through. It must've breached reactor containment: The *Atlas* had vanished from the scopes, leaving nothing but an expanding cloud of debris.

But an object in motion stays in motion, and the debris cloud wasn't expanding by much. The *Teutoburg* had turned a rifle round into a shotgun blast. Five minutes. Too late for them.

"Holy heaven," Joanna breathed. A second flash, brief and star-bright against the blackness of Europa's dark side. The *Teutoburg* had vanished from the scope screen. It had been destroyed. Foundation Home was safe. Stephen had, at long last, been avenged.

The iron gate in her mind, the bastion that had long held back the pillaging horde of grief, guilt, rage, and sadness, cracked, bent, and buckled. She just didn't have the will to reinforce it.

It broke, and Eileen sobbed.

Chapter 26

Rosetta realized she was gripping the podium so hard her hands were turning white. There were cameras here, lots of cameras, so she forced herself to relax. Hoping her knees didn't give out, she faced the capacity audience crammed into Belt Group's main conference room, and cleared her throat.

"I'm sure you've all heard the rumors, so I'll just confirm them right off the bat," she said, keeping her voice steady through sheer force of will. Much of the company's future rested on the outcome of this press conference. "The Belt Group's prototype refinery ship *Atlas* has been missing for almost two years." There was a slight hum of agitation from the crowd, but it wasn't a surprise to most of them. "We endeavored at the behest of UNASCA to keep this information isolated so as not to negatively impact the reputation of space travel." A slight exaggeration, but given UNASCA's unpopularity at the moment, why not?

"Recently, we discovered that Constance Kelley, the

Atlas' captain, had defected to the Free Jovians at the behest of Solomon Gracelove, and that he had held the ship in secret as insurance against any imagined Belt Group duplicity. In the process of recovering the ship, outlaws from the Free Jovian faction defeated our recovery team and, as you have already seen," Rosetta couldn't help sighing, "took possession of the *Atlas* and rammed it into the UNASCA warship *Teutoburg*, destroying both vessels in the process."

This time, the agitated buzz was louder, but Rosetta held out a hand to calm them. "Belt Group wishes to issue a formal apology for submitting to UNASCA's wishes for secrecy. The right thing to do would've been to come forward immediately, and we recognize that. By way of apology, Belt Group will be establishing a philanthropic fund to provide money to interplanetary search-and-rescue." They would've donated it to the UNASCA Lifeboat Service, but given the fluctuating nature of that group, it seemed prudent to be less than precise.

"I will now take questions from the audience."

The first question, asked by the *Portland Tribune*'s staff reporter in the front row, was exactly the one that Rosetta had been hoping for.

"Now that the *Atlas* has been lost, what'll become of the program? I presume it'll be canceled in favor of re-establishing your helium-3 operations on Jupiter."

Sometimes, when one was behind and in desperate straits, retrenching and consolidating were the best options to allow for a better resurgence in the future. Other times, the best option—or the one with both highest reward and highest risk—was to make a hard move and strike. This was the path that Rosetta had suggested to Chen, and it was the path that he'd agreed to.

"The *Atlas* program will not be canceled." The crowd murmured, and Rosetta took a deep breath. "We've been in talks with the Vanport Orbital shipyard to proceed on construction with *Atlas*' sister ship, *Hyperion*. We remain faithful that a long-duration mining operation in the belt will be profitable, and certainly the *Atlas*' initial results were promising. We're learning the lessons of the past, but we're forging ahead."

The crowd erupted. They were demanding to know why Belt Group was taking hard risks, demanding to know what would be different this time. Could Belt Group even afford to build another ship like the *Atlas*?

Rosetta didn't know the answers to these questions. She hated it like poison, but Belt Group needed to support the traitorous Gracelove and his Jupiter Cooperative. They needed men to work their extractors, to provide services to their container ships and their crews. They didn't have a choice.

The reporter from the *Eye on Space* blog shouted so loudly he drowned out the rest of the room. "What about the traitors that destroyed the *Atlas*? What's become of them? Will Gracelove turn them over?"

Rosetta had hoped to ignore the question, but the rest of the room quieted down just as the reporter asked. The faces that Rosetta could see through the spotlights were all staring at her in breathless anticipation.

"We have reason to believe," she said slowly, "that they were a suicide team. They did not survive the attack." The crowd roared again, but Rosetta shook her head. "No further questions," she said, and backed away from the podium. She had to resist the urge to flee backstage as the crowd noise surged.

Chen was waiting there, wearing the same dire frown that seemed to have been cast in iron since the bad news had come in. "It could've been worse," he shrugged.

"I think the *Hyperion* story is going to get a lot of press. Time will tell what kind. The suicide team thing..." She sighed. "It'll get found out."

"No luck tracking the *Mary Ellen* from Jupiter?"

"Not in the mess of ships swarming the planet. We'll find it, don't worry, but my analysis section is kind of in ruins. Forrester will be a tough man to replace." She shook her head. "I think I need a vacation."

"Request denied," he said, only half joking. "We have tough times ahead, and it's going to get worse before it gets better." *If* it gets better, he didn't say.

"Yeah."

"Your first priority is to manage publicity on the *Hyperion* project, but a close second is to find Forrester's replacement. I have a solid lead for you that I'm looking into; I'll get back to you on that."

"If you say so." Rosetta rubbed her forehead. It was going to be a long couple of months. "Do you need anything else today?"

"A million things," he said, but one corner of his mouth tipped upward just slightly. "But they'll wait. I can't give you a vacation, but I can give you a long night's sleep."

"Thanks." Rosetta nodded, and fled before Chen could change his mind.

The city lights of Portland lit up the low rainclouds

into permanent twilight. The company aerodyne set a course for her apartment in the Beaverton district, and Rosetta sat back, staring out the windows. The Solar System had changed so much in the past few months, and who knew how it would keep changing? The UNASCA building was still running swarming with traffic, as if nothing were different, but who knew if that would change?

There were so many unknowns. Too many. Rosetta had to back away from the window, closing her eyes. There was one certainty, at least. She was going to take a hot bath, she was going to go to bed, and she was going to sleep a long, long time.

Eileen didn't remember her flight back to the *Mary Ellen*. She couldn't remember docking. She had a brief impression of Piet Magnus congratulating her, and Eileen brushing him off. She remembered Joanna, though, gently guiding her along toward the hab ring, toward her quarters. She remembered, with slight shame, Joanna pulling off her shipsuit and helping her under the covers. Sleep had seemed impossible; her mind was too ravaged by too many long-repressed feelings.

Oh, Stephen. I love you so much.

But sleep had come, nonetheless. And when she had awoken, a dozen hours had passed. Eileen still felt exhausted, but it was time to get up. Time to move on.

She threw on a new shipsuit and washed her face before heading down the ladder to the microgravity operations section. Piet Magnus was there, in his now-accustomed place, and Joanna beside him in the co-pilot's seat. There weren't many status displays in evidence, just news reports.

"Oh, hey!" Joanna grinned wide and threw herself at Eileen. Eileen didn't have time to brace herself before she was engulfed in a rib-crushing hug. "Feeling better?" Joanna whispered into her ear.

"A bit," she whispered back.

"Good," Joanna nodded, pulling away. "Get a load of the news? Belt Group wants to make a new ship like the *Atlas*: the *Hyperion*."

"Good for them," Eileen muttered, pulling herself into the engineer's seat. "I plan to have nothing to do with it."

"You're a hero, Eileen Cromwell!" Piet roared, reaching back to slap her on the knee. "We all owe you a great deal!"

"I don't deserve it."

"Not to hear Belt Group or UNASCA talk about it! You're wanted as a traitor to the state. Of course, that doesn't make you unique around these parts, so I wouldn't let it get to you." He laughed, a jolly sound. It had been so long since Eileen had felt anything close to jolly.

"I guess we're not going back to Earth after all, then," Eileen sighed. "So much the better." She turned to Joanna. "I'm sorry I wasn't listening before—it's all kind of a blur now anyway—but did you mention Titania?"

"I did," Joanna said, her grin fading a bit. "I know Uranus is a long ways away, but UNASCA has no influence there, and neither does Belt Group. The Titanian settlers are supposed to be welcoming of outsiders, people fleeing the law. It might be good to let things blow over. And," Joanna sighed wistfully, "at least we could be together, right?"

Joanna was all that Eileen had left. Stephen was dead—she didn't try to suppress the grief—and the rest of her crew captured, held who-knows-where. Wherever Joanna went, Eileen would be stupid not to follow.

"We'd need fuel and supplies. And a crew, not to mention." Eileen shrugged. "It's a long trip."

"Don't you worry on either account," Magnus said, shaking his head. "As far as Gracelove is concerned, you're heroes. You get whatever you want, you go wherever you want."

"I'm sure Gracelove doesn't *really* feel that way, but it's nice to know we can still influence public opinion," Eileen chuckled. More soberly, she asked, "Are you sure about this, Joanna?"

Joanna nodded. "More sure than I've been in a long time."

Eileen sighed. The grief was still here, and showed only the slightest signs of ebbing. But she could think beyond it, now. Think of the future. "I'm glad to hear it. Magnus, inform the crew: we shall dock with Europa Transfer Station to load supplies. We're moving on."

THE END

Brad Wheeler was born and raised in Portland, Oregon, and remains a proud resident. When he's not writing novels, he's doing IT support, playing a game of some sort, or enjoying the great outdoors. *Fugitives from Earth* is his first novel.

17323706R00254

Made in the USA
Charleston, SC
06 February 2013